Dear Reader:

Every Woman Needs a Wife! The title itself says it all; this is one hot book. How many people have dealt with a cheating spouse or mate? Just about everyone, I am sure, whether you admit it or not; whether you even know about it or not. People—both male and female—cheat for various reasons. Imagine if you could take that situation and turn it around in your favor. Imagine if the person your lover is cheating with has to become indebted to you. Would you whip their ass every single day? Would you make every moment a living hell? Would you make sure they never, ever even think about trying to break up another happy home? Or...

Would you become their best friend? Would you realize that it is not all their fault; possibly not their fault at all? Would you be able to understand that they are a victim just like you? The possibilities are endless.

What Naleighna Kai has done with this book—this storyline—is create a work of imaginary genius. She has a couple—both needy in many ways—who find themselves in the midst of a threesome to end all threesomes. I have no intention of giving away all the twists and turns in this book, but I will say this: Once you start reading, you will not stop until you reach the very last page. Yes, this novel is that good!

Thanks for purchasing this book and giving an awesome author a chance to impress you. Naleighna is talented, creative, and I dare to say brilliant. I am sure you will agree and will be anxious to read her next book: *She Touched My Soul.*

Thanks for supporting all the authors I publish under Strebor Books, an imprint of ATRIA Books/Simon & Schuster. You can find more information on all of them at www.streborbooks.com and you can always visit me at www.eroticanoir.com. To join the Strebor mailing list, please send a blank email to Strebor-subscribe@topica.com and to join my personal mailing list, please send a blank email to Eroticanoir-subscribe@topica.com. That way we can keep you informed about new books, appearances, and events. If you would like to become an independent sales rep for Strebor Books and/or sell my personal body products and other items, please send an email with "Opportunity" in the subject line to StreborBooks@aol.com.

Blessings,

Zane

Publisher
Strebor Books International
www.streborbooks.com

Praise for *Every Woman Needs a Wife* by Naleighna Kai

"Off the hook, wild, and a thoroughly awesome ride! After reading Naleighna Kai's *Every Woman Needs a Wife*, I *knew* I needed one, too!"

—L.A. Banks, National Bestselling Author of *The Hunted*, *The Bitten* and *The Forbidden*

"Simply marvelous! An original story which takes a different approach on a subject that strikes a chord with all women. Definitely a novel that book clubs will be talking about for years to come. I haven't laughed so hard in ages."

—Ella Houston, The Book Lovers Club, Chicago

"Kai has given an original twist to an age-old problem that shows the many dynamics of marriage and what one must do to get over the betrayal. It also shows that it is possible to heal from past wrongs."

—Nina Lewis, RAWSistaz Guest Reviewer

"*Every Woman Needs a Wife* is an ingenuously crafted novel from Naleighna Kai which is more than a catchy title with over-the-top drama; it is a plausible storyline with an inspiring and empowering message for all women who have ever felt they were less than a woman if they did not have a man in their life. Naleighna Kai has created a compelling read with unforgettable characters and sub-plots. If you are looking for a contemporary fiction relationship novel to enjoy with a cold glass of lemonade or sweet tea on a warm, summer day, then check out Kai's latest novel."

—Yasmin, APOOO Book Club

"*Every Woman Needs a Wife* had me forcing myself to keep reading even when my eyes were telling me to give up. I couldn't. I wanted all the juicy details Kai was serving up in her tantalizing novel. I needed some more popcorn for all this drama. Just when you think it's about to come to an end, another twist is thrown in to put you on edge again. Brandi and her new wife realize they have a lot in common even though they are of a different race. Experiences see no color, they just happen. In the midst of their revelations, too much gets revealed. Will there be a cat fight? Or, will Brandi finally realize her idea was a bad one?"

—Esther "Ess" Mays for Loose Leaves Book Review

"I want a Wife, too! I loved the original concept of the book. And it is true, every woman does need a wife. Someone at home who can do the cooking, cleaning, scheduling, laundry, whatever, leaving you to pursue your career or whatever you're into. I thought Naleighna did an excellent job telling this story...by the end of the book, I was flipping the pages, waiting with bated breath to see how it would all end. I loved it!!"

—Gayle Jackson Sloan, author of *Wednesday's Woes* and *Let the Necessary Occur*

ZANE PRESENTS

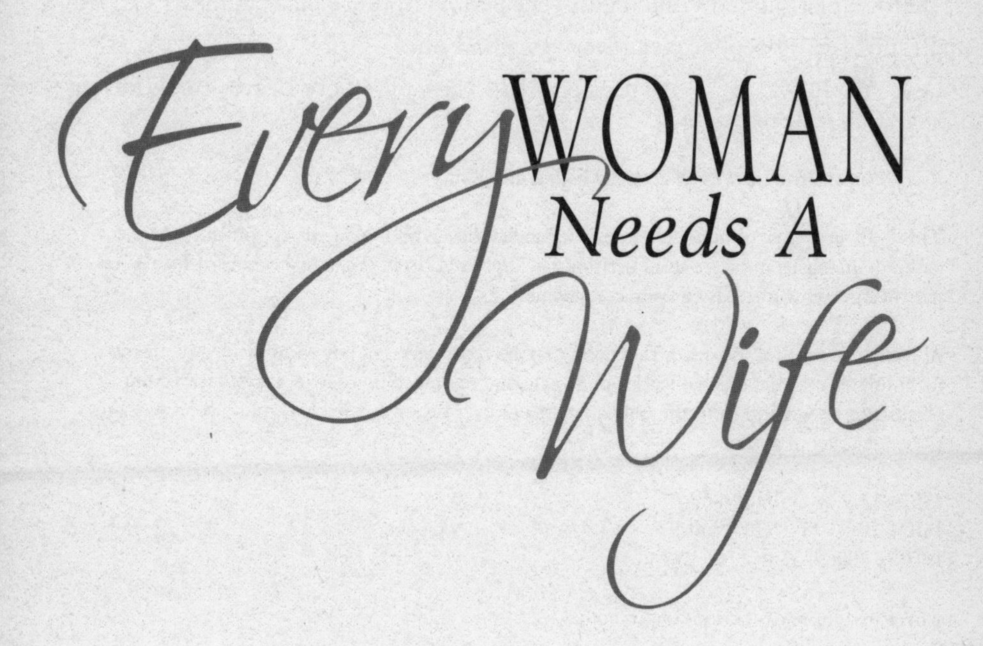

Naleighna Kai

SBI

STREBOR BOOKS
NEW YORK LONDON TORONTO SYDNEY

Strebor Books
P.O. Box 6505
Largo, MD 20792
http://www.streborbooks.com

This book is a work of fiction. Names, characters, places and incidents are products of the author's imagination or are used fictitiously. Any resemblance to actual events or locales or persons, living or dead, is entirely coincidental.

ISBN-13 978-1-59309-060-9
ISBN-10 1-59309-060-9
LCCN 2006923548

Cover design: www.mariondesigns.com

Distributed by Simon & Schuster, Inc.
1230 Avenue of the Americas
New York, NY 10020
1-800-223-2336

First Strebor Books trade paperback edition June 2006

10 9 8 7 6 5 4 3 2 1

Manufactured and Printed in the United States of America

For information regarding special discounts for bulk purchases, please contact Simon & Schuster Special Sales at 1-800-456-6798 or business@simonandschuster.com

DEDICATION

My mother, Jean Woodson
My grandmother, Mildred E. Williams
My brother, Eric Harold Spears
My aunts, Mabel Fosten and Ruth Scott
My sister and friend, Pamela Denise Franklin
and to Rev. J. B. Sims, Jr.

ACKNOWLEDGMENTS

All praise is due to the Creator. A special love and acknowledgment of my guardian angels, ancestors, teachers, and guides.

To my mother Jean Woodson, to my spiritual mothers: Bettye Mason Odom and Sandy Spears, thank you for your continuous inspiration. To my son, Jeremy, for his encouragement and for always reminding me that the Universe will always provide me with everything I need; my brother Donny and his wife, Diane, for their constant belief and support. To Rev. Renee "Sesvalah" Cobb-Dishman for your wonderful words of wisdom and for being such a healing force in my life, Mary B. Morrison, Vinah Collins, and Leslie Esdaile/L. A. Banks for always being there for me even at points when I was ready to throw in the towel; to Zane for having the faith when so many others didn't, to Charmaine and Carlita—the words "thank you" and "you are greatly appreciated" are not enough; Avalon Betts-Gaston, Esq., Marisa Murillo, Esq., and Jonathan Friedland for being the best lawyers and agents a woman could have.

To Aisha and Janice Lusk, Dr. Yosha Yvonne Tolbert (the woman who started the *Every Woman Needs a Wife* syndrome), Pat Arnold (the "No Drama" Queen), Cassandra Heining, Janet House, Earlee Hubbard, Lester Tehuti Dishman, Judy Clarke, Larry C. Tankson, Liz Thomas, Anna Moore, Lisa Brown, Wanda Muhammad, and Leslie Dishman for their kind words of encouragement; Tee C. Royal for coming through for me in a crunch (thanks also to the RAW4All family); Yasmin Coleman and the APOOO family, Gevell, Monica Sullivan, Esq., Michael Leonard, Esq., David Chizewer, Esq. and Debbie Chizewer, Esq., Frankie Payne and Alyse Payne (the Superior Office Services Team); to authors Gayle Jackson Sloan, Corlis Martin, Candice Dow, Tina Brooks McKinney, Karlyn LeBlanc, Brenda Hampton, Eric Pete, Darrin Lowery, Victoria Christopher Murray, Ehryck F. Gilmore, Cheryl Katherine Wash, and Nikki Woods.

Many thanks to Christine Meister, Marilyn Weishaar, Donna M. Rivera and Susan Mary Malone (my editors) for their expertise. Michael Slaughter & Barron Steward (the best cover designers and website designers in the world!); Pete Stenberg Photography; Althea Spellman of Simon & Schuster, and L. Peggy Hicks, my publicists, for much-needed advice. Much love to: the Slaughter family (Pam, thanks for adopting me!), Ella Houston, Deborah "the Miniature Queen" Mitchell, Elizabeth (Grannimouse) Hill, Tanisha Kwaaning, Audrey Johnson, Charlotte Manning, Geneva Arvinger, Allison Ferconio, Nancy Wheeler, Kimberly Morton Cuthrell and Eric Cuthrell; to the Aloha Documents Team: Tom and Ginger Peak; members of the MPG Book Club Collective, and to all the people who kept asking, "So when's the next one?"

I love and appreciate all of you.

Wishing you love and joy,

Naleighna Kai

"I could kill both of you," she said softly. "I'd probably go to jail, but I certainly won't feel guilty..."

Brandi Spencer turned the key in the ignition, still trying to come up with a good opening line as she braced herself to walk in on her husband and his mistress. Killing them would be too quick and painless. She wanted them to suffer.

Settling into the black leather seat, she tried something else. "Heifer, what the hell do you think you're doing with my husband?" No, too common and too weak. She'd have to use something a bit stronger than *heifer*.

"Vernon, do you think I'm stupid? Did you think I wouldn't find out?" That was lame and overused. She had let this thing ride for six months before deciding to confront him.

"Since I'm paying for half of this affair, what's in it for me?"

That might work!

Fingers of doubt sent a chill through her; she knew Vernon would have every excuse in the book.

The fading sunlight cast a subdued glow into the car. Leaning back in the cool seat, she realized that asking for a divorce while the woman he'd been sneaking around with for the past six months was looking on wouldn't leave him any breathing room. And she didn't mind one bit if he choked on what she was about to serve up. *If* she could find the courage. She reached into her purse, grabbed her equipment, and placed it in her bra, tucking it out of sight.

Brown and yellow leaves danced in the chilly October wind as Brandi left the security of her car and inched her way toward what could be a total liberation or her worst nightmare. Doing the unthinkable tugged at her mind, but common sense kicked in. How long would the pleasure from killing them last? She had to find a better way.

Walking up the cobblestone path, she gazed at the house her accountant said Vernon had paid for out of their business account. Taking a long, slow breath, she knocked on the wooden door.

Moments later, a tall, blonde with deep-set blue eyes and a curvaceous figure some women would give an ovary to have, appeared in the doorway. She was wearing a sheer red robe and not much else.

Gathering her strength, Brandi abandoned her rehearsed lines. "Good evening, Tanya. I'd like to speak with you and my husband," she said, breezing past the mistress into a spacious, tastefully furnished living room.

"Husband? Wait a minute," the woman shrieked, grabbing for Brandi, who shimmied just out of reach. "You must have the wrong house. Your husband's not here."

"Oh, yes he is," Brandi shot back, outrage fast replacing fear as she stood facing Vernon—a man whose charisma, handsome face, and tall, muscular build had put moisture in the driest panties. "That man right there on your sofa is actually married…to me." Brandi flashed her wedding ring in the woman's face before venturing further into the room. The table had been set with a candlelight dinner for two. The scent of grilled steak, mashed potatoes, and apple cobbler mingled with the fresh citrus smell of the house. Somehow, Brandi didn't think that the cozy little dinner would grace Tanya's lips—or Vernon's.

A quick glance at the mistress showed a flash of pink coloring the woman's high cheekbones before her sensuous red lips tightened into a hard line. She was strikingly pretty, with a heart-shaped face and classically pert nose. She looked as though she belonged on the pages of *Cosmo* or *Vogue* rather than hidden away in a bungalow on the south side of Chicago.

Vernon, dressed in a casual suit that complemented his warm brown skin, short-cropped hair, and piercing dark brown eyes, had been lounging comfortably on a plush maroon sofa in the living room when Brandi stormed in. He had one leg thrown over the arm, a glass of cognac in one hand and a remote control in the other. He quickly switched off the television, leaving only the faint sound of music drifting in from the dining room. His eyes widened to the size of saucers and his thin mustache twitched just before his jaw dropped. He jumped up, spilling the warm amber liquid onto the cream carpet. His mouth opened and closed, opened and closed, looking like a fish waiting for the first available hook. The action seemed to swallow every other sound in the room.

Unable to conceal a satisfied smile, Brandi used the calmest voice she could manage. "I want her to come live with us."

This time, Tanya's jaw dropped. Her face went from slightly tan to white as chalk in mere seconds. But the mistress recovered a lot faster than Vernon, whose mouth still hadn't closed. Brandi's lips lengthened into something between a sneer and a smirk.

"We're going to end the deception you've got going and save some money, too. As your wife, and the person who's footing the bill for this affair, I don't think this is an unreasonable request." Brandi leaned in close enough to catch a whiff of his earthy cologne. "The nerve of you to charge her upkeep to the business. You *wanted* to get caught."

"Baby, I'm just waiting on Jeremy and Craig, I—"

Brandi put up a single hand before whirling to face the woman who had entered her marriage like a bad odor on a windy day. Tanya stared back at her as though she had lost her mind. Brandi was beginning to question her own sanity, but watching her oh-so-handsome husband lose his cool had its own rewards.

Finally, Vernon backed slowly away, almost stumbling over the glass end table, putting some distance between him and his pissed-off wife. "You've got a lot of balls showing up here."

"That's right," Brandi shot back keeping in step with him. "I have my own pair, and right now I'm holding yours, too, my brother."

"Where are the girls?" he demanded, finally getting his bearings.

Tanya's shock finally gave way to anger as she folded her slender arms across her full breasts, glaring at Vernon. "Wife? You, you didn't say anything about a *living* wife! You said she died in childbirth and—"

The rush of words came to an abrupt halt as Brandi interrupted, with a bitter chuckle, "Yeah, right about now I think he wishes that was true."

The temperature in the room rose ten degrees. Brandi smiled sweetly, watching Vernon creep away and slump back onto the sofa. His eyes darted around the room as he grimaced, mumbling something she couldn't quite catch.

"Mr. Smooth himself, speechless? Definitely a first," Brandi taunted, following him, then leaning in, lowering her voice to a breathy whisper. "But what can you say, *Mr.* Spencer? The marriage license is burning a hole in my purse as we speak." She grinned. "I'd like to see you work a lie around this one." And the man could tell them, too. He could lie well enough to make a hooker pay premium price for what she got free every day. Brandi had fallen for a few lines in her lifetime, sweeping the smallest ones to the side to keep peace in her home. Those days were over.

Vernon slowly stood to his full height of six foot two and glared down at his wife. "I don't know what you're talking about. Check the record, Brandi. She's a client."

"Bullshit!" she snapped, head whipping around to the mistress. "A client? A *white* one at that?" Brandi lowered her gaze to the woman's groin. "Wearing a robe so sheer I can see blonde hairs covering the gateway to heaven. Or should I say the gateway to hell, if she doesn't know what to do with it."

Tanya wrapped the robe closer, averting her eyes.

"And since I've had to be awful friendly with Mr. Dildo these past six months, she apparently knows how to get you over here." Calm was returning slowly to Brandi. "If I have to use equipment to fulfill my basic needs, and I'm helping to run the business, taking care of the house, bringing home the bacon, frying it, and cleaning up right after, what the hell do I need you for?"

Vernon's gaze flicked between the two women before settling on Brandi. "She's *only* a client, Brandi," he said, trying to use a convincing tone—a tone that worked with their customers, but not with Brandi. Not anymore.

"You called me a client?" Tanya's words, almost a resigned whisper, had savage simplicity. "A client? You asshole!" She pushed him back onto the sofa with a single hand, strolled to the bar, and poured herself a drink. Brandi almost joined her; she needed a damn stiff drink herself.

All three silently held their ground, each waiting for the other to make the next move.

Tanya's statements only proved what Brandi thought—he'd spent so much time with the woman that she hadn't suspected a thing. Brandi decided she'd delivered her opening lines just right. Now all she had to do was wait for Vernon to tighten the noose around his own neck. Arrogance could always do that to a man, and Vernon had arrogance by the bucketful.

Faint light crept through the vertical blinds and splayed onto the carpet as the icy silence created a sliver of uneasiness that only heightened the tension.

Vernon stood, rubbing his temples. "We'll talk about this when we get home."

"No, we'll talk about this right now," Brandi shot back.

"Vernon," Tanya began, "I think she's right—"

"Shut up," he growled, casting an angry glance at Tanya, whose alabaster skin blushed once again as he snapped, "You stay out of this!"

"Don't tell me to shut up," she replied evenly, soft curls billowing out around her shoulders. "You brought this into my living room and you've lied to me. I have every right to speak my mind." The woman squared her shoulders, somehow growing her own pair of balls. The change was so subtle, it was neither movement nor sound.

The mistress was a startling contrast to Brandi's honey brown skin, light brown eyes, wide, fleshy hips, and full breasts that always used to make Vernon's mouth water every time he looked at them. Suddenly, Brandi felt a bit self-conscious about those extra fifty pounds. But then, her full-figured frame had never mattered to him—only her leading role in the business they started ten years ago had bothered him, causing more fights than she cared to count.

"Enough of this. This is not going to happen right now," Vernon said, with a swipe of his hand. "Brandi, go home!"

"Technically, I *am* home." Brandi dropped down on the sofa next to her husband, casually crossing one leg over the other. "Thanks to your stupidity, I own part of this one, too." Then a sudden thought came to her. "Hey! You want me and the girls to pack our stuff and move in?" she asked, lifting a single eyebrow as though warming up to the idea. "It'll be a little tight, but then again you're used to tight places." She glanced slyly at Tanya. "But then again, maybe not..."

Anger flashed in the woman's eyes as she cast a narrowed gaze at Brandi, but when she spoke, it was to Vernon. "Deal with this! I can't believe you pulled this crap on me!"

Glancing down, Brandi's anger came back faster than she could rein it in. Tanya had a block of ice on her left hand large enough for a whole village to skate on—with or without lessons.

Tanya edged away from the not-so-happy couple. "You could've gotten me killed. Suppose she came here with a gun?"

"Actually, I don't use those," Brandi said, plucking an imaginary piece of lint from her navy pants. "But I *did* bring a knife. I got it from my friendly neighborhood hoodlums. They say it works a hell of a lot better than a gun. Less chance of discovery. Notice, I haven't touched anything since I've been here."

Tanya's eyes widened as she swallowed hard. "Are you serious?"

Brandi shrugged. "The way I figure it, Biblically I have the right to kill both of you. You know, the adultery and casting the first stone thing and all." She sighed wearily, placing a single hand on her chest. "But stones can be a little messy..."

Tanya glared at her, countering with, "But there is that *do not kill* line in there, too. You do *know* the Ten Commandments, don't you?"

No this heifer didn't come back with that! Brandi leveled a stony gaze at Tanya, pissed that she had said anything at all, but then grinned anyway and answered, "Yes, Tanya, they're in Exodus. But two books later in Deuteronomy it says that stoning the adulterers is A-okay." She winked. "Now I'm down with that program. You first, babe."

Vernon's look was fierce, almost malicious. "You're out of your mind!"

"No, stud, you're out of yours," Brandi shot back. "How the hell did you think you were gonna keep giving me the short end of the stick?" She lowered her gaze to his waist. "Literally—and think I wouldn't figure it out?" She laughed. The outburst seemed to startle them both. "Normally, I can't get my panties off quick enough. Now I can't get a drive-by sniffing of dick. It doesn't take a master's to realize someone else is getting it, 'cause it certainly isn't me."

Vernon winced, glancing over his shoulder at the now-cold dinner, then into the corner, then slowly back at Brandi. Her gaze followed his, landing on the black briefcase she had given him for their last anniversary. He squinted, speaking through clenched teeth. "You've got things all wrong."

Brandi folded her arms across her breasts. "Oh, really? There's no problem here. I figure if you're gonna sleep with the woman, don't sneak around; just let me in on it." She grinned, hiding the pain that shot through her heart. "I should at least get something out of it. If she's reaping the fruits of my labor, she can come on home with me, help clean the house, wash your dirty drawers, and keep the kids."

Brandi glanced at Tanya, who stared ahead blankly, her bottom lip held prisoner by perfect white teeth. "She can even put some money on the bills, too. I don't have a problem with that. I'm all for *us* having a mistress as long as she does her share of the work. There has to be more to it than her just lying on her back to keep you happy. Hell, I wanna be happy, too. Clean my damn house, help a sister out—take some of the pressure off me."

Tanya flinched as Brandi's words chipped away at her dignity. She resembled a mannequin, staring at Vernon.

Brandi turned to gaze solidly into his face. Her fingertips smoothed over the soft material covering his muscular chest. She straightened the tie loosely draped around his neck. "If you're going to have a mistress—and this marriage is all about sharing, honey—then I should have a mistress, too. Every woman needs a wife."

Turning slowly to face a now-trembling mistress, whose eyes flashed with a glimmer of something that might have been pain, Brandi said, "Tanya, if you're going to sleep with him, you need to earn it just like I do." Then she rose, covering the distance between Tanya and her. A new, shocking idea forming with each step. "And you know what? Since I pay most of the bills, and I'm part of the reason he looks good enough to make you want to spread your legs," she said, swallowing her revulsion as she reached out to cup Tanya's buttocks strictly for effect, "then I'd like some ass, too."

CHAPTER *Two*

Tanya's face froze. Surely she hadn't heard right. Emphasizing the point, Brandi stroked Tanya's buttocks with one hand, relishing the woman's wide eyes and tense body with every move. Violated, Tanya's cheeks went from a bright red to white and back.

Brandi leaned in, whispering, "You should know that I'm the real source of the money. So I'm not above you doing me, either."

Tanya trembled, face darkening with anger as she jerked back. She glanced at Vernon and just as suddenly her expression changed. The startled look in her eyes slowly fading, Tanya tilted her head back and roared with laughter.

Interesting, Brandi thought, *and I was only joking*. The request was pure boldness, a way to shock them and frighten the hell out of Vernon. Judging from the third serving of cognac sloshing into his glass, she had managed—but then again, she had more up her sleeve. *If* she could make it home before he did.

Vernon stormed across the living room until the two of them stood eye to eye. "I think you're taking a little too much credit here." He took another long swig of cognac, nearly emptying the glass. "*I'm* the reason we're so successful. It was *my* money that started things. I'm the real reason we made it, so get off it, *Mrs. High and Mighty.*"

Brandi glowered at him. "You mean the money you got from your *daddy?* That was barely lunch money, just enough to buy a refrigerator and stove. And it may have helped to get things off the ground, but the ideas and drive to pull everything together came from me." Her gaze traveled the length of his well-toned body—one that hadn't been draped in anything less than designer suits for years. "The business, the Armani suits, the six-figure income were all a *joint* effort," she said, feeling a sudden rush of anger that he would belittle her efforts. "If I'd left things up to you, we'd still be stuck in that tiny storefront on Michigan Avenue, barely making ends meet. Seems like you forgot all that."

"Wait a minute—"

"Oh, shut up, Vernon!" Brandi dropped back down on the sofa, resting a hand on the arm. Tanya offered her a glass of vodka. Brandi gazed into the woman's eyes for a moment before accepting and taking a sip.

"Either we share Tanya and she helps me around the house, or we divorce right now. You'll keep the mistress," she said, holding up a single finger. "And I'll keep the house, the cars, and get alimony and child support. We'll split any profits from The Perfect Fit down the middle. I'm sure she," —Brandi nodded in Tanya's direction— "won't be happy with what you'll have left. And that will be…" Brandi rubbed her chin, gazing toward the ceiling as though checking an imaginary calculator. "Oh, let me see—about one-fourth of what you make now." She shrugged, grinning at Tanya. "Unless one-fourth will be all right with you?"

Scanning the woman's body, taking in the expensive La Perla dressing gown, remembering the burgundy Lexus sitting in the driveway, the Oriental artwork and Lalique figurines decorating the house, Brandi felt her anger springing forth like molten lava from a volcano. Hell, Brandi didn't drive a damn Lexus! And she'd never purchased anything from Lalique.

As her eyes continued their travel, the engagement ring made her pause—again. The damned thing was twice the size of the one he'd given her for their tenth anniversary, and four times the size of the one he'd given her on their wedding day.

Tanya followed Brandi's gaze to her slender fingers gripping the back of the loveseat. She looked into Brandi's eyes. "I'm truly sorry. I didn't know. Even the girls never mentioned you."

Vernon's eyes widened bigger than golf balls. He glared at Tanya as his lips formed a hard line.

There was no mistaking the sincerity behind the woman's words. Girls? The woman knew her children, too? Vernon would fry!

Tanya glanced at the ring; then at Vernon, whose dark, liquid eyes had filled with worry; and finally to Brandi once again. "He said he was a widower and waited so long to get married again because of his daughters. He wanted to build a business first. Then he told me he wanted his girls to be a little older." She grimaced as a tear fell from her bright eyes. "I wonder what excuse he would've given me next time."

Brandi wasn't a bit surprised; he'd taken this lying thing to a higher level. And now the children, this woman, and Brandi would all feel the crunch. Vernon, ever the man to land on his feet, wouldn't feel a damn thing. She would have to change all that.

Tanya loosened her grip on the soft cushions, pacing angrily, her eyes glazing over with unshed tears. "Amazing what they think they can get away with," she said. Eyes narrowing at him, she snatched off the ring and raised it above her head, aiming to hurl it across the room.

Then she paused, wincing as though struck by lightning, to roll the jewel between her fingers. The diamond was illuminated with a surreal glow, as though it was on display at Tiffany's. The woman's bright smile lit up the room as she faced Brandi, holding up the ring. "You don't mind if I keep this as his going-away present, do you?"

The woman was a lot smarter than she looked. Brandi shrugged, taking a small sip of vodka. "Go right ahead."

Vernon finally found the will to move. His gaze first fell on Tanya, then on Brandi, obviously trying to decide which was the better bargain. After several agonizing moments, he reached for Brandi's hand. "Baby, it's not what you think. She doesn't mean anything to me…"

Brandi's level gaze said she wasn't falling for the bullshit.

"We'll get counseling or something. You can't divorce me…"

Brandi watched the mistress back away, gripping her stomach as though she had been punched. For a split second, Brandi felt a tinge of compassion. She quickly brushed it aside the moment she lowered her eyes to her handsome husband, who had all but sunk to his knees as he put a vise grip around her waist.

He repulsed her, but she didn't pull away from him. She sank down on the sofa once again, listening to his sad speech, letting him say everything he wanted about staying together, that his little fling didn't mean anything—really. Brandi looked up at Tanya, who now stared at Vernon with a faint, bitter smile on her lips as her breasts heaved, a single hand resting on her chest. Tears streamed, pooling at her chin before dripping to the carpet in a steady rhythm. The woman was telling the truth. She hadn't known.

"I can't believe this," Tanya said, staring at the ring, then at Vernon.

Diamonds were truly a girl's best friend, and the size of the one on the woman's finger told Brandi that Tanya was more than just a fling. He was serious, but not serious enough to pull away from the business or his current life. Too late! Brandi would have that all wrapped up, as well as a few other things.

Brandi blinked to clear her vision as Tanya's pain triggered her own. How many nights had she longed for her husband? How long had she allowed the fear of losing him to cloud her judgment?

Tanya wiped her face with the back of a trembling hand, looking more like a child than the beautiful, confident woman who greeted Brandi at the door.

Brandi reached out, stroking Vernon's head gently as he pressed his face into the soft curve of her neck. "Brandi, I can make this up to you. I promise."

She touched him, knowing it would probably be her last time. Her world had changed. It had been easy to imagine the other woman, but seeing her husband in Tanya's house, settled in as though he didn't have a family somewhere else, brought forth emotions no amount of waiting could prepare her for.

While Vernon rattled on, Tanya scurried from the living room. She returned with suitcases, garment bags, all Vernon's things, which she piled directly outside the front door. Brandi watched every move, thinking, *Did she forget that technically this is not her house?* It didn't really matter—right now she was making a statement. Two women, both hurt—one man, the source of the pain. Vernon had lost both of them.

Brandi managed not to laugh as she pushed her husband away. She strolled toward the door, leaving a disgruntled Vernon struggling to get off the sofa to catch up with her. Tanya glanced at her as she touched the knob, their gazes locked in woman-to-woman understanding. If Brandi knew her husband as well as she thought, the rest of the night would prove to be very interesting. Very interesting indeed!

Especially when he found out what else awaited him when he got home.

CHAPTER 

The door hadn't closed when Tanya Kaufman pivoted to face a bewildered Vernon. In just twenty minutes, her life had gone from being on her way to happily married with two beautiful children, to practically homeless with nothing to show for her relationship with a man that the *Sun-Times* had touted as Chicago's Man of the Year. She felt lost, adrift in a lifeboat with no land in sight.

That smooth brown face, those luminous dark eyes and charming ways had made her fall for him. The day she entered the doors of The Perfect Fit looking for a job, Vernon had taken her out to lunch after the interview. More dates followed. He swept her off her feet, then gave her so much more. She had never considered having a relationship with a Black man before she met Vernon. But he swept aside any reservations, and she opened to him, loving him as much as she could any man, which wasn't saying much, since she had a low opinion of men in general.

The moment he called her a client, the second he said she meant nothing to him, the instant he dropped to his knees begging his wife's forgiveness, the love that had been growing slipped away like sand in an hourglass, replaced with a pain so indescribable she knew it would take years to recover. Like it had taken her years to get over what her father had done, and the fact that she could never return home under any circumstances.

When she didn't find employment with The Perfect Fit, she took a job as a waitress at Mitchell's and had been happy with it. Vernon was not pleased. He told her that he would take care of all her needs, if she'd take care of him. She refused. In another bid to get her to stop working, he said he would get her a private tutor to help her finish school. Now *that* had impact. But, somehow between his demands for dinner…sex, and her full attention, the private tutor never materialized.

Tanya strolled across the living room and switched off the music in the dining room. Turning to him, she demanded, "What the hell were you thinking?"

"Don't lecture me," he snapped, stretching out on the sofa again. "I was just trying to tie up loose ends. Then I would've told you everything. I needed some time."

Her lips twitched as she bit back a nasty retort. "You didn't have to lie to me."

"Would you have stayed?"

"No, but I would've had a choice."

Vernon's face darkened. "At least you had a roof over your head, clothes on your back, and—"

"A liar in my bedroom," she shot back. "How did you expect to keep this from me?"

He lifted a warm brown hand to pick up the remote and switched the television back on. "It worked all this time."

"Stupid me." She crossed the room, heading toward the bedroom. "It's over."

Vernon's hand snaked out, gripping her wrist so tightly that the color bled away. "You're not going anywhere until I sort this all out." She tried to yank away, but he held fast. "I see you've packed my stuff. Where did you think I was going? This is *my* house."

Tanya snatched her hand back, rubbing some color back into the painful flesh. "Well, as your wife so lovingly pointed out, it's hers, too," she said, trying to put a little distance between them. "You got busted and you still want to make demands? What planet do you live on?"

"Planet? Baby, this is a man's world, you have to learn the rules." Vernon lowered his voice to a whisper. "That world revolves around money. Money you don't have."

"And money you won't have either when your wife gets done." She stepped out of his reach, glancing warily at the front door. "I'd like to be a fly on the wall when you get home. If she's as smart as I think she is, you're going to have hell to pay. And you deserve to hurt as much as she's hurting right now, as much as I'm hurting now."

Only her father, the mayor of Social Circle, Georgia, had hurt her as much as Vernon had tonight. And when she tried to make him pay for what he had done, he used his power and took it out on the one person she would lay down her life for—her sister, Mindy. Men had been off-limits to her since she had left that small city. She had set sail at age fourteen, wandering through life trying to find roots, but had never quite managed—until Vernon. Now this home, too, had evaporated into nothingness.

As she turned away, he spun her back around. His cocky expression turned cruel. "You say it's over? Cool!" he said through clenched teeth. "Then pack *your* shit and hit the bricks. Because if you stay here, it'll be business as usual, babe."

Tanya pulled away and cleared the table, outwardly ignoring him, but inwardly cringing. *What happened to* I love you *and* I can't do without you*? What happened to* start planning the wedding for June*?*

He didn't move when she went into the office across the hall, pulling her personal papers from the drawers. He hovered nearby and she braced herself, expecting the worst. He had never hit her, but sometimes his quick temper could make him roar ferociously. Strangely enough, he had been meek as a lamb when his wife had pulled a fast one. Now *that* was a woman after Tanya's own heart. Boy, if she had the chutzpah Brandi had, Tanya would definitely be on the upside of life, instead of settling for being a kept woman.

"If it wasn't for me, you'd still be a poor little white-trash blonde looking for a job—a minimum wage job at that," he said harshly, following her upstairs to the bedroom. "So don't act like you didn't get something out of this."

She began packing, locking gazes with him as she said, "I've never been white trash. Strapped for cash, maybe—but never anyone's trash." She continued folding a gold blouse. "All I wanted was a man who loved me. An honest man. You couldn't even manage something as simple as that." Snapping the case shut, she yanked it off the bed and almost lost an arm because it was so heavy. "And you weren't the only one who got something out of the deal. How the hell else do you think I dealt with the fact that you're swinging two inches less than what I need for a *real* orgasm?"

Vernon reared back, his hand sailing through the air. Just as suddenly, it fell back to his side. "You bitch," he spat, his skin turning an even darker shade.

"Oh, come on, can't you do better than that?" she taunted, marching out of the bedroom. "Jeez, and I thought you were such a master of words." Then she grinned. "To be honest, my G-spot's been invisible to you since day one, although strangely enough *I* know how to find it so..."

Vernon appeared behind her. "I'm sorry for talking to you that way."

She didn't face him. "Save the apologies for your wife. You'll need them."

He reached for her, pulling her against him. "I'll take care of everything with Brandi. Just show me that you want to stay..."

"Which means I have to continue to sleep with you?"

"I know I lied," he said, glossing over that point. "But I can pull things together and it'll be all right. I just didn't know how to manage things between us and I didn't want to lose you. I still want you."

"Right now, I wouldn't screw you with somebody else's pussy." She jerked free of his hold. "And to tell you the truth, I've got a better offer on the table. I'll be seeing you around."

Vernon followed Tanya to the car. As she stuffed the last of her most important things into the backseat he asked, "Where the hell do you think you're going? You don't have any family. You don't have any friends. All you have...is me."

Something really ugly had come into his voice and she couldn't resist saying, "What I *have* is a Lexus. What I *have* is a diamond ring that can probably carry me for at least eight months. What I *have* is the common sense to leave while my ass is attached to my body. Thanks to your wife."

Tanya slammed the door, crossing to the driver's side. "You've lied to me and I don't mean a little white-collar lie, I'm talking a state prison kind of lie." She pulled the seat belt over her breasts. "It was different when I didn't know. Now that I do, it would be wrong for me to even *think* about staying with you. Really wrong." She cranked up the engine. "You dismissed me as if I were nothing but a pile of shit caught on the bottom of your wingtips. So screw you."

"I was good to you when it counted," Vernon said softly, gripping the edge of the window. "You didn't say anything then."

"True, but I would've appreciated a lot less attitude and dick, and a lot more honesty and love."

Vernon dipped his head, reached in and snatched the keys from the ignition. She grabbed his hand, which he yanked back, victoriously waving the keys. In the struggle his wallet had slipped out, lodged between the seat and the door.

He glared at her. "You can't take the car."

"It's in my name free and clear. Something I should've done with the house." She reached in her purse, scrambling the contents for a second before pulling out the spare keys. "The Lexus will probably get better mileage than this relationship," she said with a faint, bitter smile as she let the window up slowly. "And it certainly goes the distance, which is more than I can say for your bedroom techniques. And it hits corners much better. See you around."

She pulled away before he could reply, hitting the corner at Wabash before turning onto Eighty-Seventh Street. Then the tears came.

Growing up, her mother had read her all the fairy tales about Prince Charming—an ivory-skinned, handsome blond with blue eyes the color of the sky, six feet tall, and a smile that ushered in the sun. He'd come riding in on a unicorn—oh, how she had loved those magical creatures—and he'd sweep her off her feet and they'd live happily ever after.

In reality, Wilbur Jaunal, Tanya's father, the king of the castle, was a child molester who used his power and money to cover up his crimes. Margaret, "the queen," did whatever it took to keep him on the hill, even going so far as trying to kill Princess Tanya in the process.

Prince Charming Number One was the pimp who tried to rein her in the moment she got off the bus in New York. He soon learned that *country* was not synonymous with *dumb*.

Prince Charming Number Two was an East Indian man who needed her to marry him so he could stay in the country and continue his work as a restaurant chef. He had a wife back home whom he planned to bring over once his visa was in the clear. At least he was upfront about his sins. She declined this prince's offer because she didn't want to take three years out of her life trying to convince the Department of Naturalization that they were truly in love—especially not for the mere $15,000 he offered. Surely Princess Tanya deserved much more for three years of her life.

Prince Charming Number Three was the wonderful man she had married, who had loved her and treated her like a real princess. Unfortunately, he hadn't realized that not having a will leaving a portion of his business to his wife would lead to greedy partners swooping in like vultures, scooping everything up and leaving zilch for Tanya.

Prince Charming Number Four—Vernon—was a silver-tongued man who already had a castle filled with a queen and two little princesses in training. Somehow, the fairy tale had been one big lie. Could she sue the Brothers Grimm or Hans Christian Andersen?

She switched on the stereo and jazz filled the car. She glanced down at Vernon's wallet; it gave her a brilliant idea. She flipped it open and scoped out his driver's license, checking the address of Queen Brandi and King Vernon.

Tanya whipped into the nearest alley, pulled a U-turn, and aimed the car in the direction of the Jackson Park Highlands.

CHAPTER *Four*

Vernon stormed back into the house, grabbed his jacket and keys, locked up Tanya's place, and tore out of the driveway, racing to cover the distance from Chatham to South Shore. He had to catch Brandi before she got home and alerted the tribe *and* the troops. And he didn't want to discuss things in front of Sierra and Simone.

Slamming his hand on the SUV's steering wheel, the horn honked at no one in particular. Damn, he'd fucked up. He wasn't actually going to marry the woman, things were too perfect as they were. A Black woman who held down the home front and a submissive white woman in the wings to take care of his needs. And Tanya could put a shine on his dick better than Johnson's Wax.

Sure, Brandi was spectacular in the boardroom, but sometimes her demands for equal play in the bedroom were a bit too much—all that was missing were bullwhips and an occasional flogging with a side order of—"yes, Brandi, I've been a bad boy." Tanya was willing and soft-spoken. Just the way he wanted his women. Just the way Brandi had been in the beginning. Then she found her wings when they opened The Perfect Fit, a human resources and staffing agency, and she took off—sometimes without him, especially when he hesitated to take risks. She would leave him on the runway without checking to see if he was behind her. Most times he wasn't.

He made a quick swerve onto 87th Street and was soon in creep-and-crawl traffic. "Hell! I'm gonna make a career out of getting home."

His father had said that the two places a man needed to maintain control were the boardroom and the bedroom. With every deal she sealed, Brandi had the boardroom locked up better than a virgin's drawers. So a few months ago, he changed his strategy. When he stopped having sex with her, he expected a little more consideration all the way around.

It hadn't quite worked out that way.

His father had managed to keep a wife and three mistresses without anyone ever finding out. Well, at least not until two years ago when had Mama sent him packing, extracting a hefty divorce settlement in the process. That was not going to happen to Vernon. He could never please the man who had always said that his son would never top his accomplishments. He had to prove his father wrong.

Vernon had excelled in the business, and the League of 1,000 Professional Black Men accepted him just as it had his father. The men in the league were all about church, home, security, and business. Members frowned on infidelity, but as long as no one found out, it still happened. Now this little episode jeopardized everything he'd worked hard to maintain. *How the hell did Brandi find out? I made it home every day at a reasonable time. Who could have told her where Tanya lives?*

He had only given Tanya a ring to keep her with the program. She'd been edgy lately, but his promise to marry her had put her back on point. And when she was on point, *he* was on point. Both women had appetites that would make porn star Vanessa del Rio look like a saint.

That one time where Tanya had tied his wrists to the bedposts and had him whimpering like a child had taken every ounce of his energy to keep up. Then he went home that night and Brandi rolled over and wanted some, too. That night he'd almost been put into a coma. His dick had stayed hard hours beyond the act—and wouldn't come down. A trip to the hospital for a shot of muscle relaxant proved interesting. The chuckles of the emergency room staff only pissed him off.

And when had Brandi gotten a dildo? He'd never seen it around the house. If he found that little sucker, it would hit the garbage so hard it would bounce three times before settling. There would never be another dick in his house besides his—human *or* battery-powered. And especially not something that had the ability to bypass him even with a fifteen-year head start. No wonder denying her some nookie didn't get the results he wanted—she was still getting it on the regular.

"Move that piece of shit!" Vernon yelled at the driver who moved in front of him, into the fast lane, and dared to go the actual speed limit. *What's wrong with people*! Turning onto Stony Island, he punched the pedal to the floor and zoomed into traffic.

If he could get home, make sure the girls were in bed, square things with Brandi, and end it with a little tongue gymnastics followed up with some "below the waistline sunshine," he'd probably only feel her wrath for two weeks or so. Yeah, he'd get her back in line, too. Great sex had always won the worst arguments. All except one, and he still hadn't given up on Brandi letting him take over the business so she could stay home and tend to the girls.

Showing up at Tanya's? When had she become bold enough to do some shit like that? Brandi had always been the one to avoid confrontations in their marriage; he could recall only three or so. She would hold her ground silently until the situation or someone else proved her point. Passive, easy to maintain…when had she changed?

As his SUV lunged forward, a driver flipped him the finger. Vernon flipped one right back.

And how dare that white trash talk about him like that? She wasn't saying that shit when she wrapped her lips around his dick and sucked it as though gold had been layered on the opposite end. Damn, just the thought of those hot red lips on his—

"Get a grip, Vernon!"

His SUV swerved into the left lane, cutting off a grandma who didn't know the first thing about pushing that money-green Mustang to full capacity. Her horn blared as he barely missed swiping the front end of her car. "If you can't drive the damn thing, get off the road."

He jammed his foot on the gas to avoid danger, the engine roared, protesting every inch of the way. Moving between a beater held together by spit and shit and a contractor's van, he flowed into traffic, then swerved out again and thought he saw Tanya's Lexus. Heading toward his house!

The scream of sirens became louder with each second. Vernon glanced into the rearview mirror, straight into the glare of a windshield and the flashing blue-and-red lights of Chicago's finest.

"Damn!" Vernon banged the steering wheel. "Great. Just great!" He slowed, hoping the police wanted to zoom by on the way to a real emergency. But inwardly he knew the truth.

Unfortunately, Officer Friendly had kept pace with Vernon's SUV, obviously wanting to reel in a big one. End of the month was quota time—and without noticing, Vernon had just been reeled in right before 79th and Stony, the third longest speed trap in the city. Forty-five miles over the speed limit could not be easily explained. He'd never make it home in time to beat Brandi's call to her best friend…Avie Davidson. A lawyer who had never liked him all that much anyway. If she got started with divorce proceedings she would never let Brandi back down, no matter how much pressure he applied.

Vernon veered off to the right. The officer followed.

"Just what I need."

Vernon pulled over and parked on the shoulder, imagining Brandi whizzing through the house at that very moment, whipping up dinner and talking on the cordless, filling Avie in on everything. That meant it would all find its way to the League. Avie's husband, Carlton, was a member.

Officer Friendly, with a frame so wide he had to roll out of the car, moseyed over to the car. The dark-skinned man whipped out his nightstick and tapped on the glass.

Vernon lowered the window.

"License and registration, please."

Vernon searched his jacket with no success. Then he scrambled around in his pants pockets—no luck. Flipping open the glove compartment, his registration and insurance card fell out. He handed both to the officer, before continuing the search for his wallet.

"Do you realize you were going seventy-five in a thirty zone?"

Shit, was it that fast? Vernon cleared his throat, jamming his hand between the seat cushions as he said, "I was going with the flow of traffic, man. People were going faster than me."

The officer leaned in. "Yeah, but none of 'em were weaving in and out like an idiot."

Vernon grimaced as the man—Officer Holland, according to badge—continued, "What were you rushing off to? A fire?" He whipped out his ticket pad.

"Naw man, I'm trying to catch up with my wife. She just left my woman's house."

The pen froze. Officer Holland leaned in. "Come again?"

Vernon shrugged. "I was just busted, man. My wife showed up at my girl's house and raised holy hell."

The officer started chuckling. Seconds later he bent over letting out a loud guffaw.

"You think that's funny?" Vernon asked, bristling with anger. "She asked my girlfriend to come live with us."

This time the officer turned away from the car, holding his sides as the metal belt clanked against his keys.

"Then she demanded to get some ass, too."

Officer Holland roared with laughter, unable to say anything. When he regained a modicum of composure, he turned back to Vernon. "You know, I've heard some stories, but yours takes the cake." Putting away his ticket book, he said, "That's my laugh for today. You've got enough troubles. But slow it down, man. I don't see why you're rushing home. Your wife's gonna kill ya."

Checking the side mirror, Vernon watched the officer glance back at the SUV and start laughing again. Pulling into traffic, Vernon had a sudden sense of foreboding that his nightmare had not ended at Tanya's house.

❤❤❤

He'd seen exactly what Avie could do in a divorce. Vernon had come into his father's downtown office when the burly, baldheaded man was in an absolute rage. Though he was dressed in his trademark three-piece suit, which included the addition of a timepiece in left pocket—the man was far from professional at the moment. Luckily most of the employees were gone.

"She wants fifty thousand per month!" he roared in that booming voice that could start an earthquake. "She doesn't even spend that in a damn year."

"Well, Dad, you guys were married for forty years, she deserves something."

"She's living off my prestige, my image, my friends. She's trying to steal my life." William Spencer shook a pudgy fist in the air. "She wants the house. *My* house," he bellowed. "My money paid for that house, she didn't make a dime—just sat up on her ass and took everything I handed to her. Bettye Spencer and that money-grubbing family of hers have taken the last dime from me.

"I bet one of her relatives put her up to this." Then he glared and pointed at Vernon. "No, that wife of yours did this. She's getting back at me for that dinner."

"You were pretty mean to Brandi, but I don't think she told Mom about Avie on purpose."

"Hmph! A woman lawyer at that! Doesn't she have three kids?"

"Yes," Vernon said, cautiously. "But what's that have to do with anything?"

"She should have her tail at home raising her children. What kind of mother is she?"

Vernon shrugged, realizing he would have to choose his words carefully. "A modern Black woman, who works and raises a family."

"That's what's wrong with children today. Women gallivanting in places only men should be allowed."

Vernon took the glass of cognac his father offered. "So, you're saying women aren't competent enough to hold their ground in the boardroom? You haven't been watching the news."

"I'm saying men are having a harder time aspiring to success, now that women are pushing us out of our spots. Children are being raised by God knows who and are turning out to be God knows what."

Vernon remained silent for a moment as he watched his father pace. "And working women are the cause of that? I don't buy it, Dad. Brandi's good at what she does."

"Yes, in some ways she's better at running the business than you are," his dad said with a sly grin. "How will you ever know your full potential if she's around? I keep trying to tell you that but you won't listen. And where are my grandsons?"

"Brandi doesn't want any more children."

"*She* doesn't want? *She* doesn't want!" The man's voice got louder with every word. "Never have to wonder who's wearing the pants in your household."

"We share the responsibility in our house, Dad. That's how things are done these days."

"Pretty soon you'll be wearing an apron and doing dishes," he said with a bitter chuckle. "Have a few vacuuming tips you'd like to share?"

"Have a few *divorce* tips you'd like to share?"

That shut him up. Vernon slumped down in the sofa as worry lines furrowed his father's forehead. "She's not getting my house."

"Correction: Mom already has the house, and two of the cars, and a huge settlement. It's not like you can't afford it."

"That's not the point! It's the principle of the thing," he shot back. "Never in a million years would I believe that woman would leave me, then hire a big-boned, bitter bitch of a lawyer to try and take every penny."

By the time Avie Davidson was done, William and his lawyers were whimpering in defeat as the judge read the divorce decree and settlement. Bribes to the judge didn't matter. For every string puller Vernon knew, Avie knew another who could tie them together again. Her father was a judge; under no circumstance would he let his little girl go down without a fair fight.

When Vernon's dad didn't win on the financial front, he took things to an even uglier place. One day he told Vernon, "Either me or her."

Stunned, Vernon could only say, "Dad, I'm not choosing between my parents. I love you and I love Mom."

William, never one to be outdone, slowly found a way to dominate the majority of Vernon's time, then dangled the prospect of taking over the business in front of his son. Always one who could never seem to do enough to please the old man, Vernon took the bait and soon his relationship with his mother became more and more distant.

Inwardly, though, Vernon was proud of her. "Looks like Mom is a lot smarter than you gave her credit for," he told his father one day during another of the old man's rants.

"If she was so smart," William snapped, "she would've stayed married."

"*Three* mistresses, Dad? You expected her to hang around after that became public?"

"Don't fool yourself. She's known about Marlene Stewart for years. She only found out about the other two recently. And that's only because Mildred Roman's daughter met Crystal Chadwick at a sorority dinner and they became friends, and over a period of time the two compared notes. Then they talked with Marlene's youngest daughter, who knew Brandi. Brandi blabbed her suspicions to Avie, who then talked my wife into suing me for divorce. Damn gossipy women! The bane of every man's existence."

Vernon took it all in. "Well, it was bound to come out sooner or later."

"I would have preferred later."

"I would have preferred you weren't unfaithful to my mother at all,"

Vernon said, softly. "I still don't see how you managed to stay in the League after it all came out."

"Who, in their right mind, would even *try* to kick a founding member of the League of 1,000 Professional Black Men out of his own club? If you try to get away with it, you won't be so lucky."

As Vernon turned on Sixty-Seventh Street toward Jackson Park Highlands, he didn't see Brandi's car, but he had the distinct feeling that his father's words and Officer Holland's would come back to haunt him.

Chapter *Five*

Brandi scrambled out of the car with a bag of groceries in each arm, sprinting toward the house on Cregier Avenue. She passed several cars parked along the street—all leading to her packed driveway. Music grew louder with each step she took toward the split-level gray, white, and black brick home.

Brandi trotted across the grass like a trespasser, through a small grouping of shrubs, past the magnolia tree, and landed on the "Home Sweet Home" welcome mat. She had made it! And Vernon was nowhere to be seen. She just *might* pull this off!

As she entered the safety of her home and closed the door behind her, the blasting dance music made her ears throb. The scent of food reminded her she hadn't eaten all day. She placed the brown paper bags on the foyer's marble floor and turned toward the living room. The sound of screeching tires made her heart race and propelled her to the window. Peeking out through the sheer curtains, she saw Vernon sprinting across the lawn, black blazer flying out behind him.

She laughed. Evidently, he hadn't had much success convincing Tanya he would still make perfect husband material. Somehow, lies could always do that to a relationship.

Brandi clicked the lock to buy some time, then ran out of the foyer straight into the throng of waiting guests who had turned toward the front door, wearing a wide range of puzzled expressions. The music played on, even though the dancers had found something more interesting unfolding at the front of the house. Fireworks at Navy Pier would rate second to what would go down in just a few minutes.

Soon the music scratched to a halt. No one moved.

Several scrapes of a key against the metal tumbler signaled Vernon's struggle for access. The front door burst open. His nostrils flared. The fire in his eyes meant World War III was about to begin. Then again, with every one of their relatives looking on—maybe not.

He cast an angry glance around the room and slowed his pace toward Brandi.

She inched back into the safety of the crowd as Vernon blinked and froze, eyes widening in horror. Friends and family were scattered all over their house. A banner overhead said, "Happy Anniversary." Their anniversary—unlucky number thirteen. She fumbled in her pocket, trying to find the one thing that proved maybe thirteen wasn't so unlucky after all—at least for her. Vernon was a different story.

"Surprise...surprise!" everyone chanted, though not as enthusiastically as they had last year. People glanced curiously at each other, then at Vernon and Brandi, waiting for some type of explanation.

"Yes, surprise indeed," Brandi mumbled under her breath.

Vernon strolled past the glass curio cabinet, the rows of abstract paintings, and the fireplace in a daze. He scanned the living and dining room areas as though he didn't recognize the home he'd lived in for the past six years—a testament to the efforts they had put in to making The Perfect Fit a success. He stood absently in the middle of the floor, eyes darting around, landing on each person, reality dawning with each passing moment.

Brandi strolled over to the stereo, flipped in a tape, and punched "Play." Soon the sounds of his strong tenor voice filled the room—begging, pleading, and groveling. The micro recorder she had had hidden in her bra at Tanya's home had recorded much clearer than she thought possible.

Tori, her younger cousin, and Avie, her best friend since high school, reached up to the anniversary banner. Pulling it down, they revealed a "Bon Voyage" banner. Cousin Thomas, wearing a navy sheriff's uniform, strolled by Vernon, patting the shocked man on the back. Stuffing a jumbo shrimp in his mouth, he reached into his pocket and pulled out a document, which he handed to the stunned husband.

Vernon looked around, then down at the papers in his hand, growling, "What's this?"

Thomas struggled to speak around his mouthful of food. "It's called the new rules of the house. This is a contract Brandi wants you to sign, giving her the right to split the business and start her own company." Thomas grinned. "She thought you'd have a problem with this, but judging from all that begging you were doing, she doesn't need to worry, eh bud?"

People gaped, still listening to Vernon's voice on the tape; they stared, murmured, and pointed, trying to grasp the reality of the situation. Soon, the room filled with hearty chuckles. Everyone but their parents found the whole thing funny. Vernon's father and Brandi's mother glowered at both of them.

Uh-oh, Brandi was in a bit of trouble, too. She avoided eye contact with the woman who had helped her make every major decision of her life—including marrying Vernon instead of her first love. She hadn't bothered to ask her about this, knowing what her mother would say.

When the tape finally switched off, Brandi said, "All right, let's keep the party going," as though she hadn't destroyed thirteen years of her life with a flick of the wrist.

"DJ," she said to her brother Donny, "give me something I can move to."

Slowly, people hit the dance floor as a stepper's cut came on. Others gravitated back to the buffet and wine table, all abandoning the need for immediate answers. Good food and good wine can do that—a party is a party.

Brandi's gaze landed on the silver-haired woman with a wineglass in her hand in the middle of the dance floor. The woman's wide smile as she lifted the glass and winked gave Brandi a moment of relief. *Even my mother-in-law finds it hilarious,* she thought.

Bettye Spencer sauntered over; weaving through the dancing bodies, she managed to not spill a single drop. "Now, I don't appreciate the way you got me to this...divorce party." She took a sip of Verdi Spumanti. "But I sure appreciate your style."

For the first and only time that night, Brandi felt a stab of guilt. She stood toe-to-toe with Bettye wishing she had even an ounce of the grace and calm the older woman had shown when she found out about her own husband's infidelity. "I wanted to be sure Vernon couldn't lie to you and keep you on his side. Now everyone knows the truth. He can't spin the story in his favor."

"Vernon wouldn't be able to touch our relationship anyway," Bettye said, grasping Brandi's hands with golden brown, weathered ones. "We'll always remain close."

"I'm glad to hear that. Your wisdom has helped me in a lot of ways, and I love you," Brandi said, embracing the small, gracefully built woman, whose soft brown eyes and warm spirit had helped her in more ways than she could count.

"I know that, child." Bettye's gaze fell to her son. "Vernon hasn't been inclined to seek me out for any reason. His loyalty's been to his father since our divorce. Vernon followed the money—"

"When he should've followed his heart," Brandi replied. Knowing that Bettye wasn't a drinker, she removed the glass from the woman's delicate hand and took a small sip of the sweet, clear, bubbly liquid. "You knew about Tanya?"

"I'm not surprised. Like father, like son," she said, reclaiming her glass, then slinging back the last of her drink.

When Tori shimmied past with a tray of wine, Brandi's mother-in-law exchanged the empty glass for a full one, which Brandi swiped away from her. "Hey, how many of these have you had?"

Bettye grimaced, looking at Vernon's father and shaking her head. "Not enough to deal with being in the same room with my asshole of an ex-husband *and* his new woman."

Brandi had invited William Spencer; he had taken the liberty of bringing Julie, the new toy, twenty-five years his junior, to the anniversary party—probably knowing Bettye would be there. The balls of the Spencer men were big enough to substitute as doughnuts on a broken-down vehicle.

Bettye leaned over and said, "You know, William's going to direct Vernon on how to shaft you on this one. I'd let Avie get a head start if I were you. Mother's on the side of truth and justice."

Brandi lifted the glass saying, "Amen to that! I have no intention of being written off as some embittered, jealous, paranoid woman."

Avie appeared next to them, wearing a navy power suit, and powder blue blouse, which complemented her creamy, honey-colored skin. She wore her auburn hair pulled up into a love knot, accentuating her almond-shaped eyes and round face. "With your level of proof," Avie said grimly, "you'll get everything you want."

"I only want what I deserve," Brandi said softly, an uneasy feeling settling into the pit of her stomach as she took in the lawyer's hard glare.

Avie turned to Brandi. "And that's *everything*. And I'm going to make sure you get it."

Although her specialty was commercial real estate, Avie Davidson looked at marriage as a contract and, just like in corporate America, if someone didn't live up to their end—they had to pay. It was obvious that Avie was still angry at Vernon for trying to cut her out of doing work for The Perfect Fit. Brandi had fought hard to keep her friend as part of their new business venture, but Vernon had insisted on using a friend of his from college. Avie had checked over the "friend's" work a few times and caught several fatal flaws. When she checked the billing records and found the man had milked them better than a Wisconsin maid, Vernon had to relent. He was willing to let bygones be bygones, but Avie could hold a grudge so long it could become its own universe. Vernon would need more than a good lawyer to escape her clutches on this one—he'd need two extra pair of asses. Avie knew how to extract a pound of flesh from each cheek.

"Where are the girls?" Bettye asked, watching as all the men, except Donny and Thomas, gathered on the far side of the dining room with Vernon in the center, fielding questions like some rock star.

Brandi grinned over her glass. "They're sleeping at Avie's house with her three hellions."

Avie's eyebrows drew in. "Who are you calling hellions?"

"It wasn't *my* children who flooded the living room with the garden hose," Brandi shot back.

Her friend's lips curved into a sheepish grin. "Oh, well, that's different."

Brandi chuckled, saying, "I didn't want them here just in case things got ugly."

"With Donny here?" her friend said, eyeing the animated male crowd. "I wish Vernon would show his natural Black behind. I remember the last time those two got into it. Your brother locked his butt in the trunk for an hour."

Bettye looked over her glass of wine at her son. "Vernon will think twice before letting what's in his pants mess up his home life the next time he gets married."

Avie turned to the older woman, saying, "If he can afford a next time."

Brandi looked at Avie, seeing the hard glint in her hazel eyes. Knowing Avie, she had probably already started calculating how much they'd drag out of him in court. Brandi hated to disappoint her friend, but she didn't want a knock-down, drag-out fight. She just wanted justice—her way. And the truth be told, her spur-of-the-moment idea of moving the mistress here would really ram that lesson home. Too bad she hadn't been serious earlier. Seeing all the men getting on Vernon's case was better than anything she could do on her own.

Donny changed the record, then danced over to the solarium entrance where they stood watching everything. He pulled Brandi away from Bettye and Avie, and onto the dance floor filled with women. She danced freely to the blaring music as champagne flowed like the Nile. Vernon sat in the corner, nursing a drink while his friends stayed crowded around him like concert security, making Brandi's relatives move to another part of the house.

Brandi sang along with Peabo Bryson, moving smoothly in a side-by-side, stepping rhythm with her brother, singing, "*Imagine the bluest ocean. Imagine the stars at night…*""

The doorbell rang, barely audible over the music. Brandi checked her watch, and did a quick mental scan of the guest list. Everyone who was supposed to be at the party had already arrived.

Tori answered the door, and seconds later her thick frame came scurrying over to Brandi. "Hey, it's some chick for you."

The music kicked into high gear with everyone cheering the beginning of the Cha-Cha Slide.

Dancing her way to the door, Brandi flung it open and then froze.

Tanya stood on the doorstep. Her red lips curved into a soft smile as she leaned in and whispered in a sexy voice, "Honey, I'm home."

Chapter Six

Brandi's eyes narrowed as their gazes locked. Though she wore a leather jacket, the breeze lifted Tanya's sheer blouse, then pasted it to her body. She held Vernon's leather wallet in one hand. Brandi pulled the door closed as she stepped outside onto the concrete porch, folding her arms across her chest. "You've got a lot of nerve showing up here."

"No more nerve than you had showing up at my place," Tanya said with a haughty toss of her mane.

The woman had a point. But then again, Brandi had every right. *She* was the wife!

Brandi inhaled the scent of magnolias from the tree directly in front of her home. "So you came here expecting…what?"

Tanya held the wallet out to Brandi. "Actually, I figured that since you didn't have much success keeping your husband, and I didn't have much success landing one of my own, maybe being your wife might be a better idea all around."

Good point. And one that might bear some thought.

Brandi plucked the wallet from the woman's pale hand, opened it, removed the cash, and counted it. As an afterthought, she gave Tanya half. "Finders keepers." She tucked the cash in her bra and tossed the leather wallet, aiming for an obscure spot in the bushes.

Tanya snatched it from mid-air, took out his driver's license and the credit cards, and handed them to Brandi, saying, "Identity theft. You'll still need him to have good credit at some point."

"Good thinking," Brandi replied, tucking the gold American Express, the Diner's Club, Visa, and MasterCard in her bra next to the cash. "What happened with Vernon?"

Tanya let out a long, weary sigh. "He told me that I couldn't stay in the house unless I continued to sleep with him. And I told him that I had a better offer on the table anyway."

"Mine?"

Tanya grinned, shrugging as she said in a humored tone, "But of course." She leaned back on the bricks, resting a stiletto-clad foot against the concrete. "If he slept around on you, there's no telling what would happen when my turn came. What goes around comes around. I would've never wasted my time if I had known he was married. So my last words to him were, 'I'll be seeing you around.'"

Brandi grinned, feeling a sudden sense of elation as a dynamic plan came to mind. "He just didn't know that he'd be seeing you around at his house."

The door swung open. Donny poked his head out, scowling. "Hey, lil' sis, you all right?"

His gaze traveled the length of Tanya's miniskirt-wrapped body, long legs that didn't seem to end at her waist, then up to her breasts. *Real or plastic?* Brandi wondered. Only her cosmetic surgeon would know for sure.

"This is Tanya," Brandi said with a flourish.

Donny winced as thick lips turned into a frown. "He went *white?* What was he thinking?"

Tanya glared back at him.

Brandi grinned. "Same thing he was thinking with."

Laughter followed as he pulled his head back in just as the music kicked into "*Take it back now y'all. One hop this time…*" before fading once again when the door closed.

Things were shaping up to be a bit more complicated than Brandi had expected. She had wanted to humiliate Vernon, ending things in a way that would make him feel her pain. When she talked to Avie two months ago, she never thought things would turn out quite like this.

CHAPTER *Seven*

It had started with a simple, "Girl, he's been cheating on me."

Avie sighed, swiveling in the green leather office chair, asking, "What do you mean he's cheating? Who's cheating?"

"Vernon! I know the signs: late nights, last-minute travel plans, hanging up the cell phone when I enter a room." Brandi blinked back tears. "Then there's new clothes, as if he didn't already have enough to last him at least three lifetimes."

Avie leaned forward on the oak desk. "And new cologne?"

"Pheromone for Men." Brandi's eyes narrowed as she looked at her friend. "How did you know?"

"Classics, baby, classics. I think you should whip out the knife and go Lorena Bobbitt on his ass." Her thinly arched eyebrows lifted into half moons. "Try it the next time he wants some nookie."

"The only time we have sex is when I ask for it."

"You're kidding!" Avie leaned back in her chair. "The Black Stallion?"

Brandi laughed at her reference to Vernon's college nickname. "The Stallion hasn't been riding the range or grazing the pastures lately. And when he does, it's more like a 'you need to be grateful I'm still with your ass' kind of thing. God, I'm tired of that."

"No doubt."

"I'm going to stop asking, and start handling things the old-fashioned way," she said.

Avie laughed, a soft, silky sound. "Now, I feel you on that one."

"No, you don't!" Brandi shot back. "You're getting your fair share on the regular. When was the last time you masturbated?"

The lawyer blushed, dipping her head sheepishly before she stood. "Well, we're not going to get into that. I have to go to a closing," she said. "Why don't you come back to my office on Thursday and we'll discuss your options."

"What time?"

"About ten." She flipped open the calendar on her desk. "No, make it twelve, and I'll spring for lunch."

Brandi walked back into the law firm of Davidson, Royal, and Payne, slipped into the soft leather seat across from the desk, and kicked off her heels before propping her tired feet on the desk.

Avie Davidson reached out, swiping the feet away, forcing them back onto the carpet with a solid thud.

Brandi shifted in the seat, placing one leg up under her. "I don't do that when you come to my office."

"I haven't *been* to your new office."

"My point exactly," Brandi said, leveling her gaze on her friend.

"Hey, when you decided to move all the way out in Bumfuck, Egypt, you knew I wasn't coming out there that much. It's almost an hour out of the way and certainly nowhere near a courthouse."

"Yeah, yeah, yeah" Brandi waved off the excuse with a single hand. "And South Chicago isn't all that far."

"Add in parking-lot traffic coming from downtown and it is."

"You're just lazy, Heifer," Brandi said, giving her friend a wide grin.

"Call me what you want, but your tail can get down here in twenty; it takes an hour the other way around."

Brandi reached out, scooping up the blue glass paperweight globe in her hand. "Well, I haven't asked for any nookie, and now I'm sitting home brewing like a bitch in heat while that bastard's out giving it to some other woman. I'm the only one respecting our vows. How fair is that?"

"Girl, you need to follow him to her house and beat that ass," Avie said, propping her feet on the desk. "That woman knows he's married."

"You know, I'm not so sure about that," Brandi replied, tossing the globe back and forth in her hands, then casting a cursory glance at her friend's feet. "And why do you get to do that?"

"Because it's my damn office," Avie replied with a little shake of her shoulders. "I can drop my drawers and take a crap right on the wood and nobody can tell me different."

"Might lose a few clients, though."

Avie shrugged as she grinned. "Yeah, there is that." Her hazel eyes followed the trail of her favorite paperweight from one of Brandi's hands to the other and back.

"Since we've expanded and moved the business, he spends so much time away from home that he could probably pull off having more than one woman. The only proof he has that he's doing what he says is that new accounts are cropping up—and not just in Chicago."

Avie reached out, snatching the globe from mid-air and setting it safely back on its perch.

"So I'm not as angry with her—he probably lied to her, too. If there's any place my anger should be directed, it's at him for not being satisfied with what he has, or at myself for putting up with this far longer than necessary."

The door opened and Avie's teenage apprentice secretary brought in two Corner Bakery box lunches. She thanked the girl before passing one to Brandi. "I thought by now he'd change and get over his midlife crisis."

"Girl, he hasn't even made it to midlife yet." Brandi sighed, then looked down at the tan-and-black cardboard box in her hands. "And trust you to be cheap on lunch. Box lunches."

"You can complain or you can watch me eat yours, too."

Brandi snatched the box from Avie's fingers, knowing her friend would make good on the threat and wouldn't gain a single pound. God just wasn't fair with this metabolism crap. Brandi could sniff a piece of German chocolate cake through a closed refrigerator door and gain a pound.

She placed her lunch on the corner of the desk and began pacing the room. "I've been silent and it's been almost six months since he started with this woman." Brandi turned her back to Avie and gazed out on the foggy view of the Chicago River. "You know, I'm through acting like the content little wife. I've done everything a wife should, but Vernon's still dipping his stick somewhere else."

"Time to make some changes?"

"No lie," Brandi said with a nod. "I certainly don't want any more of his used dick."

Avie took a big bite out of her chicken pesto sandwich and scribbled a few notes. "You also shouldn't leave the marriage without some green-and-white tissue to wipe your tears on—"

"Yeah, the crisp kind that comes in several denominations," Brandi said, folding her fingers as though she held a stack of cash inside. "The *large* ones."

"Damn straight," Avie said, perking up. "How do you want to pull this off? You know I'm not in for playing Mrs. Nice."

Brandi sat back down in the chair, popping open the lunch box. "I'm not sure. I don't want the girls to suffer."

"You mean no more than they already have?"

She had a point. A really good one, too. When was the last time Vernon did something special with them? He had taken them to a client's house a couple of times—a Mrs. Kaulman or Kaufman or something like that. But that was about business, not about the girls at all. "You know, everything we've built together: the business, the house, the cars, the assets—half of it belongs to me."

"Actually, more, since you held up your end of the bargain," Avie said, scribbling more notes on the bright yellow pad while making headway on her sandwich. "Being faithful to him, making a good home for him and the girls counts for plenty. You can't take the soft road on this, baby girl."

Brandi's gaze focused on the wall behind the desk. Degrees hung between pictures of Avie with her husband, Carlton, and three children—Carlton II, Carrington, and Marilyn. The two friends had all but married Brandi's girls and Avie's boys off in the stroller. "Vernon practically insisted I have the children right away. I think he thought that it would make me put up with his crap—"

"And let's face it, you have. The children didn't have anything to do with that," Avie said in a grim tone. "I told you to watch out for him after that time he met with Mr. Adams and painted you right out of the picture. He played right into that man's male chauvinist attitude like a champ, acting as though the company didn't run without him."

"Oh, that was an ego thing," Brandi said, dismissing the memory of the painful episode with a simple gesture. "He can't admit that I'm just as important to the business as he is."

"Let Carlton try to pull that crap. I'd give him directions to his own ass-whipping so he wouldn't be late."

Brandi laughed, realizing that Avie always had a way of lightening up the heaviest mood. When they met at Fisk, they never realized that one day Avie would own a law firm, or that Brandi would marry Vernon, arrogance and all, and start a business with him. She also never thought that she would have two children to look after, when she swore up and down after her thirteenth birthday that she would never have them. God must've seen that as funny because he gave her two girls, and she worried every time they stepped out the door. Just like her mother had worried about her. And that worry was warranted. She was lucky she had even been able to have children after the surgery she'd had at thirteen to repair her damaged body.

Finally taking a tiny bite of her sandwich, she said, "Vernon's a good man, but it seems that the more successful we've become, the more he's changed." She rested her chin on the palm of her hand. "We're able to give our children anything and everything. My girls won't have to wait years to explore opportunities; they can create their own—like we swore on our wedding day."

"And I thought *that* would never happen," Avie said softly. "Remember how Vernon's dad almost cut him off completely because he had him all lined up to marry Veronica? Boy, did that girl have mud on her face." Avie laughed, a harsh sound that didn't mesh with an angelic face and model-perfect features.

"Don't be bitter 'cause she tried to get into Carlton's pants."

Avie's smile disappeared as her eyes narrowed to slits. "Wouldn't have been a problem if I wasn't already in them."

"What did you do to her that day?"

"I'm not telling on the grounds that it may serve to incriminate me."

Brandi roared with laughter, remembering how Veronica had stood up in the middle of Avie and Carlton's wedding, opening her wide mouth to object when the pastor said, "Speak now or forever hold your peace."

Avie had yanked off her veil, hiked up her white dress, and stormed down the aisle, train and all. "Can I see you outside, please," she demanded, yanking the wafer-thin woman by the hair, giving her no choice in the matter. All heads and eyes stayed glued to the mahogany doors, waiting for an outcome.

Avie, composed and all smiles, appeared five minutes later. Veronica wasn't heard from until three months later. By then she had packed up and moved to California.

Veronica had been a thorn in Avie's side since she and Carlton had gotten together. Brandi had had no such problems with another woman. Now she had a big one. "I've given my life to my family and to the business. There's never been time for me…"

"And whose fault is that?"

Brandi held Avie's wedding picture in her hands, trailing her finger across the happy smiles of the bride and groom. "And to think I turned down Michael Cobb, a Fisk man, for Vernon."

"And Michael was fine, too—and upstanding," Avie mused.

Brandi blinked to clear her vision, thinking of the one she let off the hook and tossed back into the water. "Vernon was a driven, intelligent, but compassionate man in the beginning—all the qualities of a Morehouse man. His only flaws were that famous Morehouse arrogance and being a little under his father's thumb. And I accepted that. Unfortunately, his 'flaws' have snowballed into something I can't bear."

Avie took a sip of Dr Pepper. "Time to pull the rug out from under the Black Stallion."

"Yes, it's time to stop playing at being married, stop giving so much, and start saving my money. My future, Sierra's, and Simone's depend heavily on the intelligence I went to Fisk to cultivate."

The fact that she had to think that way at all angered her beyond reason. The moment she got pregnant, Vernon had all but insisted she turn the business over to him and stay at home. They had a major argument, one that lasted the entire pregnancy. She worked up until a week before the due date, stopping then only because Sierra had decided to come a few days early. If Brandi had her wish, they would have wheeled her to the delivery room on the copy machine. Pregnancy was a bitch. She couldn't even keep water down for the first month and spent several days on intravenous feedings to get some nutrition. The smell of food had facilitated payments to the porcelain god so many times, she thought about just moving into the bathroom. She didn't know how Vernon talked her into doing it twice. He had pushed for a third and fourth. She told the doctor that if she got pregnant again, despite regular use of birth control, he could wake her up after the kid came out and she'd cut and tie the tubes her own damn self.

"Avie, it's time to get down to business."

"*Just* so you know, I'm gonna treat you like a real client."

Brandi grimaced. "So, after all I did when you bought this place—washing the windows, painting these walls, and scrubbing the floors—now I have to pay full price? What happened to the family discount?"

"Girl, please, when have you ever paid for me to represent you?"

Brandi's heart pained as she looked up at her friend. "I've never needed you this way before..."

Avie blinked twice before laying the legal pad on her desk. "I'm giving you a list of things to do. I want you to sleep on this tonight. Some of it's a little under the radar, but you'll have Vernon by the short and curlies."

Brandi turned to face her lawyer. "The who?"

"Pubic hairs. Trust me, it's better than putting a vise grip on his balls."

After what Avie had done to Vernon's father—the man didn't have any "short and curlies" left—Brandi knew her lawyer and friend was capable of bringing any man to his knees.

In some ways she already felt sorry for Vernon.

CHAPTER Eight

As Brandi slid a sly glance at Tanya, standing on the doorstep in all her glory, she saw more than a way to get back at Vernon. She now had an opportunity to strike a blow for every wife who had unwittingly shared time, space, and dick with the unknown and had walked away with a bruised ego, insecurities, and less than their fair share of the financial power they'd helped to build. This was one lesson she wouldn't fail to teach Vernon, and Tanya would be the main source of his pain.

Brandi and Vernon's family were still inside partying like tomorrow couldn't come fast enough. And probably for him, it couldn't. She stared at the "other" woman. Moments stretched between the two women before Brandi lifted her fingers to her temples, asking, "You said something earlier about my girls. How do know my daughters?"

In a somber tone, she answered, "He's brought them by a few times, but just recently. They call me Mrs. Kaufman instead of Tanya."

Realization slammed into Brandi like a crappy old car with a bad set of brakes. "So that's who they were talking about. He really did set you up in the database as a client. That mother—"

"That's putting it mildly," Tanya said softly. The breeze ruffled her hair, causing it to fly in her face. She moved it away with the soft sweep of her hand.

"You know, Tanya, I've heard women say all the time that they need a wife; now's my chance to pull it off" Brandi said, thoughtfully. "And if you're game, I'd love to teach Vernon a lesson he'll never forget."

"Count me in," Tanya said with a wide grin. "I'm good with the 'every-woman-needs-a-wife' syndrome. Do you know what you're in for?"

Tanya studied her hands for a moment. "I can cook, clean, organize, and I already know the girls." Then she looked up, locking her bright blue gaze on Brandi. "And I'm hoping that on some levels that you're a better *man* for anything that doesn't require a dick."

"Well, thanks to recent developments," Brandi said, dryly. "I've got one of those under the bed."

This might prove interesting. If Tanya became *her* wife instead of Vernon's, it would be the best form of revenge. He would never live it down—at least not until well after Brandi had rammed the point home. Bend over and oil up, baby! This was going to be a mofo!

Fueled by anger that hadn't really gone away, Brandi extended her hand to Tanya. "Wife it is. Go get your stuff."

Tanya shook the hand firmly, then turned, ran to her car, pulled out a few of her bags, and followed Brandi into the house. Brandi gestured toward the foyer closet, and her new "wife" parked her items inside.

Strolling across the room to the turntables, Brandi fumbled, trying to locate the volume. She picked up the microphone, waiting for the piercing whine to subside before saying, "May I have your attention, please."

All heads slowly turned in her direction. Tanya stood in the doorway, looking every bit the victorious woman instead of the spurned lover she had become during the confrontation at her house earlier.

Vernon sprang to life, jumping from the chair to stare at Tanya. The men followed his gaze, some admiring the new view, others with dropped jaws. The room went still as everyone stared at the only white woman in the room. Brandi gestured for her new "wife" to come stand beside her.

She grasped Tanya's hand, holding it up in triumph. "People, there's someone I'd like you to meet. My new 'wife.'"

Murmurs erupted from every corner of the house.

Vernon's father almost burst a stitch in his black suit as he yelled, "What!!!!"

But one voice carried over everyone else's. "See, I told you she was bisexual."

Avie whirled to face Vernon's friend Craig, who scooted back as the lawyer reared up like a racehorse ready to trample over him to the finish line. "What did you say, Negro."

"Nothing," he mumbled weakly.

She lowered the dinner plate. "That's what I *thought* you said."

Alanna, Craig's wife, crossed the room and punched her husband in the arm. The man's light skin turned a gray color that matched his outfit. He retreated from his wife's blow, patting his short-cropped hair back into place.

Brandi's gaze returned to her guests, who were obviously waiting to see what came next. She felt a little disconnected, somewhere between dreaming and waking. How much did she want to tell their family and friends?

"Brandi, I will kill you!" Vernon growled. Craig and Jeremy held him back, flailing arms and all. A fist connected with Jeremy's face. Jeremy, whose light brown skin was a perfect combination of his Black and Mexican heritages, ran a thick hand through his wavy hair as he cracked his neck to one side. Then he straightened his shirt, growling, "Chill out, man. 'Cause if you hit me one more time, I'm gonna whip your ass before Donny gets a chance."

Brandi stepped forward, pulling Tanya along with her. "My husband took the liberty of bringing this *wonderful* woman into our lives. And I can respect that. This is his mistress."

Tanya held her head high, shaking her curls out about her shoulders as more than sixty pairs of eyes bore into her.

Brandi's gaze rested briefly on each person, absorbing the shocked expressions with glee. "And, just like the Godfather, I've made her an offer she can't refuse." She patted the woman's hand gently, almost lovingly. "She's going to live here with us," she said, breaking into a satisfied smile, "as someone who keeps the home end of things together for me—sort of like a wife—*my* wife. That way I can get something out of the deal other than hard work on my part and a little slippery action between the sheets on his. Way to go, Vernon. I love you!"

Quiet settled around them as necks craned back and forth as though a tennis match had unfolded right there in the living room.

"I told you not to marry that crazy bitch," William bellowed, startling everyone with his pure angry baritone.

"Who are you calling a bitch?" Brandi's mother demanded, nearly dropping her plate as she whirled to face the heavyset, bearded, bald-headed man. "Call her that again and I'll beat the cow-walking bullshit out of your plump behind."

"Your daughter's the one who needs a beating," he shot back. Size-two Julie—the toy of the week—placed a hand on his upper arm. He shrugged her off, "Bringing this foolishness in my son's house."

"It's my daughter's house, too, you idiot!" Brandi's mother shrieked back. "And she has every right to invite who she wants. At least she's not sneaking around like your tired ass. I bet Bettye got the best of your tail on that one. Almost a quarter million per year. I bet you take hefty swigs of Pepto after writing those checks!"

William's face turned from a bright red to an angry green. "What? You *and* your crazy-ass daughter need to get the hell out of here before I—"

"Pop a button?" she asked, with her hands folded across her small breasts. "Don't see you trying to rein in that stud son of yours. Probably serving it up like Sunday brunch and can't appreciate a good thing when he has it—just like you."

Bettye choked trying to swallow her drink in one gulp. Without looking around, Avie patted the woman gently on the back, but didn't bother to shut her own mouth, which had fallen open and stayed there as she watched the circus.

Brandi slid in between her mother and Vernon's father. "Everyone, please. No need for alarm. Just treat Tanya with the respect and courtesy reserved for family." Then Brandi paused, her lips forming a faint, bitter smile, adding, "Come to think of it, y'all don't treat family too well. So, I'd better say it simply—be nice."

Vernon's father growled, "You've lost your damn mind."

"Not at all," she told him in her sweetest voice. "I think I've found it," she said, noticing that the light in Vernon's eyes had suddenly dimmed. She extended an arm to her wife. "Right this way, Tanya, you missed that wonderful dinner at your house. I'm sure you're starving by now."

Tanya looped her arm in Brandi's and strolled to the buffet table, gingerly picking up a plate before scanning the spread. She piled on the red beans and rice, macaroni and cheese, glazed turkey ham, corn bread and candied sweets, passed over the pasta salads, watercress sandwiches, beef Stroganoff, and scones, then scooped up a few spoonfuls of peach cobbler.

"You sure you're not Black?" Brandi asked, chuckling deeply as she noticed all the food landing on the woman's plate.

A wide grin lit up Tanya's face. "Shake anyone's family tree hard enough, there'll be a few dark leaves that fall out. Same goes the other way around."

Brandi watched her mother and William still going at it. "People are gonna trip. Are you gonna be okay with this?"

"Did you see the look on Vernon's face?"

Brandi shook her head. "I was too busy watching Daddy Dearest have a conniption."

"Yeah, he did seem overbearing when I met him last month."

Brandi's eyes narrowed at the man. "His father knew?"

Tanya nodded. "So did those two meatheads standing over there." Brandi followed her gaze to Craig and Jeremy. "The only people who weren't in on the full deal were me and you."

"Wait until I tell Lissette and Alanna. They're gonna kill them!"

Tanya took a hearty bite of corn bread. "If you had seen Vernon clamp down and bite his tongue, you'd realize that you're getting more mileage out of this than simply shock value." She held up her plate. "Hey, no turnips?"

Brandi shook her head absently, looking at the people gathered around a somewhat repentant Vernon, relishing her moment of victory. "I would never have expected to find you at my front door."

"And I would never have expected you to take him down like you did earlier." She grinned, making her even more beautiful. "A woman that can think on her feet like that is definitely the type of person I could learn from."

Brandi paused a minute to take that in. "Well, gotta make the rounds," she said with a weary sigh. "You hold up your end of the house and I'll hold up mine."

"Nice spread," Tanya called after her.

Brandi whirled back, saying, "Not as nice as yours."

"Touché," she said, balancing her overflowing plate to reach into her pocket. "Here's the key to my—his—um—your house."

Brandi looked at the little cold silver key that Tanya dropped in the palm of her hand and smiled. "On second thought… Tanya, I need you to make a phone call." Then she leaned over, whispering a set of instructions.

Tanya paused for a second or two, listening attentively, then laughed, plate still in hand, and headed to the phone to carry out the plan—given to her by her new "husband."

"Honey, you've had too much to drink."

Brandi turned, taking in the wonderfully warm and gentle face of her mother. "That's not it, Mama. I've only had one. Two, counting the one I had at Tanya's earlier. This is something that needed to be done."

"Baby, I know you're angry, but this isn't the way." In a warm flash, the normal expressive lines returned to Mama's oval-shaped face. The mocha skin had only a few wrinkles to show her age, her pink-and-brown pantsuit gave her the appearance of being younger than her sixty-five years. Her wide, bright smile and warm eyes were the things that most pulled people to her. "Having that white woman in your house with your husband and your kids is not the way."

Donny, with one headphone to his ear, eased the crowd into a moderate rhythm, but occasionally glanced over at his mother and sister.

"No, Mama, it's a new day and I'm making sure that the rules suit me," Brandi said, with a trace of a sad smile. "He didn't consult me about bringing her into our marriage, but it affects my life, my children, and my money. So why not do it this way?" Dancers had made their way back to the center floor. "Now he can't hide anymore and I get something out of the deal."

Donny eased up beside Brandi, whispering, "You want me to beat his ass?" The short, medium-built man eyed Vernon warily. "You know I'll beat his ass for ya."

Mama reached around Brandi and popped him upside the head as Brandi laughed, knowing he would do just that. "No, don't put your hands on him."

Her brother's face drooped with disappointment.

Brandi gave his hand a gentle pat, gracing him with a forced smile. "Maybe next time he screws up."

"Better not be a next time," he grumbled, squaring his shoulders as though preparing for a heavyweight bout.

Brandi reached out, pulling him into a warm hug. "I love you, big brother."

"Still think you're crazy," he said over his shoulder, then watched Tanya, who had leaned over on the counter to make the call. The powder blue miniskirt had ridden a little higher on her thighs, exposing the beginning of her ivory cheeks. The men near Vernon couldn't take their eyes off her. Even Vernon's dad kept giving her a few glances and received a glare from Julie.

Avie sidled up to Brandi. "Why didn't you talk to me before doing this?"

Brandi shrugged. "It just happened."

"How can bringing the mistress here serve a purpose?"

"I don't know yet. I'll get back to you on that." She turned to her friend. "And for the record, I didn't bring her here; she just showed up with his wallet and I had a bright idea and went with it."

"What happened to make her think she could come here in the first place?"

Brandi thought about that a moment. "I walked in on her and Vernon and laid my cards on the table. Vernon folded and went home. Tanya picked up her hand and played the big joker."

"No shit!"

Brandi laughed. "And that's what I call playing the game."

Craig and Jeremy gathered around Vernon like he was a wounded dog. Their wives glowered at them from across the room. Somehow, Brandi didn't think Vernon's friends would have a pleasant evening when they got home.

"And from the looks of things," Brandi said softly, "I still have the best hand."

Avie followed Brandi's gaze across the room. "Looks like the testosterone crew's rallying behind Chief Sperm-a-lot."

"Yeah, well, he really needed them at *her* house."

For some reason her friend didn't crack a smile. "Brandi, you know you're my girl and all," Avie said, eyeing the mistress warily. "But what the hell have you been smoking?"

"Forget you!"

"She looks like an Amazon warrior. She could've tackled your ass right there in her living room."

"She was too shocked to do anything." Brandi raised a hand to her temple, trying to rub away the beginnings of a headache. "Vernon lied to her, too. He'd even taken the girls over to her place a few times. Ain't that a bitch?"

The lawyer took a few seconds to absorb that piece of information, then turned back to watch the crowd. "Why didn't you tell me you were going to show up at her house?"

"For the same reason you're shitting a kitten right now."

Avie grimaced. "I would've talked some sense into your silly little head."

"I didn't need sense, I needed justice."

The elder Spencer loomed over Vernon's sulking form, arms flailing about like a choir director. "Look at the way my husband's getting reamed. I got mine, baby." Brandi gestured sharply to Tanya, who waved to Brandi from across the room. Brandi gave her a small Miss America wave. "Look at her, soaking it up like she came up with the idea. I couldn't have done this better if I had planned it from the beginning."

"So now what?" Avie's tone was dry.

"What do you mean?"

Avie's thinly arched eyebrows shot up. "She's leaving when the party's over, right?"

"No, dear, she stays," Brandi said, shaking her head. "He had her all to himself for six months. I deserve *at least* that." Brandi winked as Tanya twirled the phone in her thin fingers, carrying out her first duty as a wife. "No, Avie, the woman makes it up to me. She took time away from my children, she took time away from me. She's going to redeem herself for those six months. 'Cause somewhere in the back of her mind she knew he was lying just like I did. For every time I had to settle for less than Vernon's best, she owes me."

Tanya gave her a thumbs-up as she hung up the phone.

Brandi smiled back, returning the gesture, saying, "So as Polaroid says, let's see what develops."

CHAPTER *Nine*

Vernon dashed over the moment Avie vacated the spot next to Brandi. "Can I see you upstairs in the bedroom?"

Brandi turned, facing him. His shirt was unbuttoned, jacket ruffled, and his hair could use a comb. He looked annoyed, probably more with himself than anyone. "Why? Nothing's been going on out here that can't stay down here."

Yanking her by the arm, he dragged her backward up the first six stairs, growling, "Woman, get your ass in this room."

She shrugged him off, leveling a steely gaze on him. "Put your hands on me again and Donny locking you in the trunk will look like child's play. He already asked to give you a half-order of butt whipping tonight, I'll tell him you want a full one. He does deliver..." She followed him into the bedroom.

Vernon ignored her warning, growling, "What the hell are you doing, bringing that bitch in our house?"

Brandi pulled herself up to meet his gaze, snapping, "Oh, so *noooooow* she's a bitch? She wasn't a bitch three hours ago when you were lounging on her couch with a drink in your hand. She wasn't a bitch when she was giving your dick a hallelujah handshake. She wasn't a bitch when you paid her mortgage, her bills, and for that damn car." Brandi glowered at him, poking a finger in his massive chest. "I don't even drive a damn Lexus! So don't ask me what I'm doing! I'm picking up where you left off—"

"My family's out there," he said, pointing to the door. "*Your* family's out there. You bring this stranger into our home and—"

"*You* brought her in," she shot back, maneuvering toward the bed. "I'm just making sure she's all the way in. Every time you slept with her, I slept with her. Every moment you spent away from your family to be with her, she was cutting into *my* time. Time I bought and paid for when I married your tired ass." Brandi plopped down on the edge of the bed. "Now, I'm saving you the trouble of having to maintain two households. And I'm putting everything out in the open." She stretched out languidly on the cream down comforter. "You've had a mistress and now I'll have a wife. Hopefully, a better wife than you were a husband."

"I won't have her staying here—"

One eyebrow shot up. "*You* don't have a choice."

Vernon rocked on the balls of his feet. "So if I don't go along with this asinine plan, what's next?"

"That's on you," she said, shrugging. "If you're not willing to share your mistress, we can split everything down the middle fifty-fifty." She sat up, rubbing her sweaty palms across her thighs. "I'll take my clients and you'll keep yours. It's what I've wanted since Simone was born."

"I'm not giving up what I've busted my ass to build."

"You should've thought about that before Mr. Slippery took a swim in Mistress Lake," she replied. "Now I'm rowing the boat and it's nothing but upstream for you, *Mister Spencer.*" Crossing the few feet between them, she planted a single hand on his chest, whispering, "There's not a judge on this planet who won't give me exactly what I deserve after listening to that tape. Avie's ready to take a bite out of you so deep, she'll hit bone before she lets go. Can you say…ouch!"

That thought alone was enough to make any man wet his pants. Avie had just been awarded the Black Legal Eagle plaque—only a lawyer who had won a certain number of county, civil, and appellate cases could achieve that honor. The woman had brought his father to his knees, a man who'd had a team of lawyers and she still won. So Vernon had to go another direction. "Think of the kids."

"I am. They already know her as your—client? And somehow you've managed to keep them quiet about it." Then her light brown eyes narrowed. "It must've cost you a pretty penny in DVDs and video games."

Vernon grimaced. "iPods and laptops."

"Ahhhh," Brandi said, beaming and blinking, "I knew that was more than just fatherly love."

"She's not staying!" he roared.

Brandi relished the rippling vein near his temple. "Oh, yes she is, stud. She's part of the family now. They love her out there. Didn't you see your mother warm up to her?" Brandi winked, gushing as she gripped his shirt. "She's a beauty and a keeper. You did us proud, honey!"

"This is not going to happen in my house!" he shrieked. "Either I go or she goes."

"Oh no, my brother, that's not a threat anymore," she said in a normal tone while pointing to the exit. "The door's that way. So get your stroll on and mosey on down to the no-tell motel or heartbreak hotel, whichever one will take your tired behind in."

"Look, I—"

She held up a hand, cutting him off. "End of discussion! My...*wife*, the woman you've been *doing* on the sneak tip, is about to earn her keep the honest way—on her feet taking care of me, instead of on her back fucking you."

Brandi sailed past him and out to the party, closing the door behind her.

When had his wife become such a hard-core bitch? She'd been feisty when he'd first met her on Fisk campus, but it was the sadness in her eyes that told him something lay underneath, something deep and disturbing, though she tried to hide it with a cold brush-off for anyone who tried to get close. The only other man who had a chance was Michael Cobb, and sources told Vernon that the man was taking things slow. Too slow, because Vernon was able to inch in after Michael had laid at least two years of groundwork and was all set to close in for the kill. And he would never have thought Vernon would be competition. Especially since Brandi and Vernon went at it every time he showed up on the Fisk campus...

Brandi strolled down Seventeenth Street trying to keep up with Avie, who was on her way to chew Veronica Chapman out for trying to steal her boyfriend. Crowds had gathered on the left, spreading out over the campus lawn like weeds. As they passed the library, they ran smack-dab into the Morehouse Seven as Vernon and his friends, visiting from Atlanta, were called. She tried to avoid them at all costs, especially since the leader of the group always had words with her. None of them kind.

Vernon's smooth voice carried across the lawn. "Maybe if you'd loosen up and get a little dick, you wouldn't be so mean all the time."

Brandi whirled to face him, books in hand, as students who were engaged in conversation slowly turned their attention to the two squared off near the wire gate.

"Maybe if you had one that was longer than three inches, you might have a chance."

"Oooooooh no she didn't," someone said in the midst of the howls of laughter.

Vernon wasn't going to let that ride. "How can you even know what that is, since you haven't had dick since dick had you."

Brandi flinched. How dare he say that she hadn't seen a dick or had any since she'd been conceived. He wanted to play dirty? So be it. "Don't have to have any of yours to know that you're the reason masturbation was created."

The women in the crowd clapped and cheered as Brandi strutted past the men. And that was how it went almost every weekend. They fought like debtor and collection agency.

Michael continued to be the wonderful, charming man she had come to consider a constant in her life. He was quietly aggressive, but nowhere near as fiery as Vernon. Michael sat back thinking Brandi was a sure thing.

Vernon would show him that nothing was a sure thing when it came to women.

Now, it seemed, Brandi was going to use Tanya to teach him something he would never forget.

CHAPTER *Ten*

Tanya perched on a chair in the corner of Brandi's living room—the perfect angle to watch the dynamics of the family—trying to make sense of her new situation. Vernon's mother came over and talked with her a while, feeling her out, then offered encouragement when she realized exactly what her son had done.

As little groups converged trying to make heads or tails of Tanya, memories of Michelle Pitchford's family swam in and out of her mind, making her homesick for the family that had taken her in after a tumultuous time in her life. As she bit into a slice of sweet potato pie, Christmas at the Pitchfords brought a smile to her face...

❤❤❤

"Hey, what's this white girl doing here in Diane's kitchen?" Grandpa James bellowed as he came through the wooden door leading to the large kitchen. He locked his gaze on Tanya, who was helping Mama Diane fold the butter, vanilla, sugar, and eggnog into the mushy sweet potatoes in a metal bowl. Eight pie pans layered with homemade crusts sat on the counter. Scents of nutmeg and sage vied with the savory scents simmering on the stove to dominate the kitchen.

Michelle had warned that the old man would come in way after everyone else and inspect what had been done. His piercing brown eyes swept across the room—the largest in the wood-frame house—taking in the women singing, talking, and laughing as they worked in unison, each for a special purpose. Mama Diane had told Tanya that he wasn't too fond of white folks, so she had to be especially careful around him. He still bore a grudge for what those Jersey whites did to members of his family: The lynching of two couples on a road between Monroe and Jersey in July 1946 was still lodged in the memories of those who had loved them.

"She's family. Now behave yourself." Mama Diane's round mocha face broke into a soft smile as she kissed the man's weathered cheek. "She'll be living with us from now on."

Grandpa's plaid shirt tightened with every move, as his gaze swung toward the window and out to where his son, James Jr., stood yakking it up with the fellas on the front lawn. "Uh…something I need to know? They say Papa's a rolling stone, but didn't know he tried to hit a few rocks now and then."

"No, she's a friend of Michelle's," Mama Diane said with a hearty chuckle.

"Humph, better not be somethin' else goin' on 'round here," he said, running his hands under the water flowing into the sink. Then his gaze swung from Diane back to Tanya. "Did you make some Brummistew?"

Tanya frowned, thinking that maybe he meant the pinkish-red mixture that was sitting in a big silver pot on the back burner of the old stove. Mama Diane said they would serve it with light bread, crackers, or cornbread, but she had never heard it called Brummistew. "Do you mean *Brunswick* stew?" Tanya asked, looking up at him.

"Humph. *Y'all* might call it that, but 'round here, we call it Brummistew."

"Oh," Tanya said, throwing her head back so the long blonde braid fell down her back. "I only know it by the *proper* name."

"Proper my Black ass," he snapped, narrowing his eyes to peer at her. "Slaves invented that dish, and only our kind have the right to give it a name."

"Everyone eats the stew," Tanya said, beating the orange mixture with heavy strokes the way she'd seen Mama Diane do earlier. "How could slaves have invented that?"

"Boy I tell ya, youngsters just don't know nothing important these days." He took a deep breath and looked down at Tanya. "After the meals were prepared for the master and his family, the leftover pork was ground up with chicken and a few spices…" He picked up a group of small glass bottles. "Like these right here. And there ya have a Southern delicacy—Brummistew."

"Brunswick stew," she said with a wide grin.

"Little girl." He waggled a long finger at her. "Me and you ain't gonna get along so well."

Mama Diane turned from the stove and winked at her.

Tanya sighed and said, "Brummistew."

"Now that's better." He peered into the next pot on the stove, steam billowing out on the sides. "Y'all got any turnips mixed in with those collards?"

His eyebrows arched into half moons as he looked at Tanya.

"Mrs. Pitchford said that Mr. Pitchford didn't put them out this year."

"Didn't put them out?" he said, his voice filled with wonder. "Girl, you sounding mighty Black 'round here."

"Mama Diane's teaching me a whole lot. She said that turnips are a delicacy and since everyone doesn't plant them, it's hard to get her hands on them if they're not grown right here in Social Circle."

He lifted the glass cover of the cake dish to inspect the contents. "Who made the Red Velvet cake?"

"I did," Tanya said proudly. "And topped it with pecans."

"Hmmmmm," he murmured, giving it a once-over before replacing the lid. Mama Diane gave her a thumbs-up. Evidently Grandpa James approved.

Michelle had warned Tanya that Grandpa James would be a tough customer. Looking at his wrinkled skin the color of roasted pecans, the way his eyes missed nothing, and the little ways he joked and chided the rest of the women, she could believe it. No one got off easy. But Grandma Belle had his number, patting him lovingly on the rump every time he strolled past. Tanya didn't miss his satisfied grin, or the fact that he went past Grandma Belle on purpose, on out-of-the way trips to other parts of the kitchen—often more than once.

Most of Michelle's family had arrived late last night. The women, with their own seasonings in tow, brought the items to make their specialties. Tanya soon learned that Christmas and all other family gatherings always took place at the Pitchford home. Children stretched out upstairs on cotton pallets next to older aunts and uncles, resting up for all the fun that would happen the next day. This Christmas, with a small, decorated tree in the living room, and presents stacked up on all sides, was a warm contrast from the formal parties complete with tuxes, ball gowns, and stuffy attitudes at the Jaunal mansion, where Tanya had spent the first twelve years of her life.

Tanya had never stayed up all night, but managed to keep her eyes open as the symphony of so many women—with skin ranging from midnight black to as ivory as her own—orchestrated a spectacular Christmas dinner. She and Michelle were put to work peeling and dicing potatoes and celery for iced potato salad, stirring the pots of black-eyed peas and butter beans, or cleaning the greens in a porcelain sink—an endless job. Grandma Belle, along with Aunt Lily and Ruby Pearl, directed cooking traffic from an old wooden chair pulled up to the oak table in the center of the kitchen. The women took turns singing old hymns or even breaking into one or two secular songs and the time moved swiftly.

A peace had settled into Tanya's soul. She knew that she was now home.

Though they didn't appear to be as busy as the women, the men weren't exactly loafing. After they slaughtered a pig, they were up all night cooking it over a wide pit right off the front lawn. Once they got the pig over the fire, they tossed a few horseshoes while downing cans of Old Milwaukee and Country Club, and passing around bottles of Boone's Farm and Canadian Mist.

Uncle Jeff gave Michelle and Tanya a lucky swig of both along with some homemade plum wine, but made them promise not to tell Mama Diane. Of course they wouldn't tell. It was the first time Tanya had a taste of anything so strong. The girls brought the pig skin back into the house and passed the tray to Aunt Martha, who would season it and fry it up to crisp little kernels that would go into the crackling corn bread. Later, some would mix it with buttermilk and make a meal out of it.

Grandpa James dropped his horn-rimmed glasses and the lens rolled out, slanting downward toward the living room and coming to a stop under the sofa. "Hey, I told you about these damn floors! When are you gonna fix 'em?"

"Daddy, this house has been rebuilt for the last time," Mama Diane said from her place near the back door. "This floor is going to stay exactly how *you* laid it—crooked."

"I didn't do the floors, now. I did the frame. My brother Otis laid these crooked floors."

"And I measured them right!" Otis yelled across the yard. "Ain't my fault it's crooked. You laid the floors."

"Oh, Lord, don't get those fools started," Ruby Pearl said with a weary shake of her head. "We go through this every time they get together. A house that's been rebuilt as many times as this one is bound to have something wrong with it; at least the plumbing works. By now the old outhouse would've been full of shit, same as you, James."

His gaze leveled on the heavyset woman. "You're not too old for me to put over my knee."

She grinned and said, "You'd have to catch me first."

He jerked suddenly in her direction and she sprinted to the door and made a hasty exit toward her husband as the women broke up laughing.

Tanya looked up at Grandpa James. "How many times has this house been rebuilt?"

Then she stood over the waste can, peeling the shells off the hard-boiled eggs, listening to him tell how the parts of the Pitchford house had been moved from several different pieces of property before coming to stay put on the south end of Cherokee Road. The first time they moved the house from Monroe to a sharecropper's land in Covington so their family could work the fields. Then, when they were hired to work someone else's land, the house had been dismantled, the pieces hauled through the woods and back trails only to be rebuilt in Monroe again. Finally, on another stint, it landed on the current spot in Social Circle.

"Why not just leave the house and build another one?"

"Honey, where we come from, we just don't have that kind of money," Grandma Belle said, her skin peppered with perspiration, and her smile warm enough to sweep away the cold in any heart.

The first time the woman laid eyes on Tanya, she lifted her chin so that they were eye level. It was as though she could see into Tanya's very soul.

"This child's gonna need some serious looking after, Diane. You see these eyes? These are the eyes of a child who's seen too much pain, too early. You're in the right place, little one."

The woman had hugged Tanya to her massive breasts and for the first time Tanya could remember she cried long and hard. Cried until she was too dry to do anything else but sleep. And the Pitchford women had looked after her all through the night.

The heat in the kitchen was unbearable, but Tanya wouldn't trade it for the world. "When we move, the house moves, too," Grandma Belle said proudly. "Our people are natural carpenters. The whole family helps to build a house."

"And sometimes the floors aren't level because *someone* doesn't have the proper tools or doesn't know how to measure," James Jr. said through the back-door screen.

"I'm telling ya, it wasn't me!"

Everyone laughed.

That Christmas was one of the best Tanya had ever experienced. The Pitchfords didn't have the kind of money that her folks had, but they had something more—love and appreciation for small things and blessings that Tanya had always taken for granted. They accepted her without question, and after a while even Grandpa James softened up.

She could only wish she actually was a true part of the family. Then she wouldn't harbor so much pain in her heart. Pain caused by a father who believed that since he was mayor, he was above the law. And a mother who turned the other cheek and allowed the man to do anything he pleased—even if that anything was raping his own daughter.

"You want something to drink?"

Tanya jerked back to the present as she turned, looking up into the almond-shaped eyes of Brandi's brother. His slender frame, redbone coloring, wide mouth, and short, cropped hair combined to make a handsome man. The dry tone and scowl on his face didn't make him seem so friendly. In a flash, he reminded her a great deal of Grandpa James.

"A Scotch would be nice."

Donny stared at her. "Woman, where do you think you are?" he snapped. "Black folks don't do Scotch, we do cognac or a little Erk and Jerk—y'all might call it E&J."

Brandi gripped her brother's collar, comically snatching him away and patting him on the rear end. "The Cutty Sark is right next to the VSOP and Remy. Quit acting like we don't know what Scotch is. As a matter of fact, break out the bottle of Gold Label Johnny Walker."

Donny beamed as though someone had awarded him the Nobel Prize. "But that's Vernon's private stock," he whispered, grinning widely.

"Nothing's private anymore." Brandi winked at Tanya. "And half of it belongs to me anyway."

He threw a quick, wary glance at Vernon.

"Okay, so we'll just drink my fifty percent and put the rest back," Brandi said. "Go on, scoot. Get it!" She aimed him in the direction of the liquor cabinet, then called after him, "Hey! And serve Vernon up first."

William appeared next to Brandi, growling just loud enough for the three people nearby to hear, "This is nonsense. My son wouldn't need a mistress if you'd lose some damn weight. You're probably holding half a village under your armpits alone."

Tanya gasped, feeling a stab of pain for Brandi.

"Why do I need to change who I am for anyone?" Brandi asked with a proud lift of her chin. "There isn't a Black man on the planet who doesn't appreciate a woman with curves. And for your information, we don't smell, we don't tell, we're grateful as hell, and fuck real well." Brandi reached out, patting William's gut. "Handle that, Grandpa."

"Watch your mouth, baby," Brandi's mother said, wrapping an arm around her daughter's waist. "But tell the truth and shame the devil. Ain't nothing wrong with a little jiggle in the middle."

"What's gotten into you?" The heavyset man's bald head reflected nearly everything in the room. Not a pretty sight, given the canvas.

Brandi replied, "All these years, nothing I've done to make you like me has made a damn bit of difference. So I'm done trying." Then she lowered her gaze to a potbelly the size of an English kettle. "And you've got a lot of nerve talking about somebody needing to lose weight. That isn't a kangaroo pouch, is it? Or are you giving birth to twins?"

The man sputtered, trying to come up with a retort. Brandi's mother didn't give him a chance. "And the back side looks like two grocery bags fighting for space on a car seat."

"A woman should always maintain a *decent* size," he snapped. "That's what keeps a man's interest."

Vernon's mother came and stood next to Brandi, glaring up at her ex-husband. "And a man can spread out to the size of a football field and that's okay?"

"I'm not *that* big," he grumbled, instantly humbled by the woman's mere presence.

"Well, your stomach turns corners before the rest of you. I'd say it's getting close to the goal line." She jabbed him in the side. "Let the jewelry and cash stop, you'll see exactly how much the latest toy enjoys your love handles. Or are they just there so she can heave you out of the window, kill you, and then collect the cash?"

He glowered angrily at her, pulling up to his full height. "You're just jealous because I've found someone younger and more useful."

Bettye grinned. "I could never be jealous of someone whose only real qualities end and begin in the bedroom. Shows how *useful* she really is and how desperate you really are."

His eyes, dark and menacing, narrowed to slits. "I wouldn't need anyone else if you'd given me more children."

The twinkle in the woman's dark brown eyes signaled trouble as Bettye gave him her sweetest smile. "Well, if you stayed hard longer than three seconds that might've helped things out."

Murmurs went up from the nearby crowd, followed by laughter as the music lowered and a few inched their way closer.

Julie, the girlfriend of the week, finally broke away from the wine table and gripped William's arm. "Come on, honey, you don't have to take that."

"Yes, dear, go on and put Papa to bed," Bettye said, laughing and shooing them away. "Make sure you tuck him in real good, you hear?" Then she called out to her ex over the crowd. "Oh by the way, did Mary, Ella, or Cleopha give you children, too? No? Says something about the power down below." Then she lifted her arm, curling her hand into a fist—saying screw you and stay hard in one gesture.

William's flat lips curled into a sneer before he spat, "Good night, mother of one."

"Good night, father of..." She shrugged, lifting her hands in a helpless gesture. Then her gaze flickered to Vernon and back to William before giving William a suspicious wink.

Oh shit! No she didn't! Tanya braced herself for the fallout.

William pulled up short, almost tossing Julie to the ground, eyes flashing with anger. "What the hell?" he said looking over at his son as though seeing him for the very first time. "Vernon?"

Bettye held up her glass. "Cheers."

Tanya shook her head, eyes widening with wonder as she asked, "Is it always like this?"

"Aww honey, *this* is mild." Brandi gave the woman's hand a gentle pat, obviously enjoying the new developments. "You ain't seen nothing yet."

CHAPTER Eleven

As Julie steered Vernon's angry father toward the door, Brandi—with a glass of his special stash sloshing in a brandy snifter—breezed past Vernon. He followed, hot on her tail, maneuvered around her, and cut her off. "That woman is *not* staying here."

"Why not? It'll save money," she said, squeezing by him. She sped up, trying to get to her lawyer and her brother who were chatting with Tanya as they stood near the solarium entrance. "You brought her into our marriage, now she's a central part of it. Deal with it."

Again, Vernon blocked her path. This time she gave in and dropped down onto a wingback chair, crossing one leg over the other. "You felt that somehow I wasn't doing my job as a wife, taking care of the family, plus taking care of the house, I agree, I can't do it all. We *both* need a wife. Good looking out."

Avie and Donny appeared next to Brandi as Vernon began to speak. He stopped short, noticing the lawyer's angry glare and Donny's matching scowl. Where were Craig and Jeremy when he needed them? And why hadn't Avie's husband come tonight—he could've helped keep that pit bull in check.

Then he saw his friends trying to have discreet conversations with their wives, and realized he couldn't go back to them, either. They had all snapped at him about how this mess affected them, too. The women had powwowed and it seemed now that Vernon was in the doghouse, he had a bit of company, making it a full dog pound—complete with tags and leashes. And they blamed him. Losing his wife, his home, a mistress, and his friends? Not bad for one night's work. And the night wasn't even over.

Vernon pivoted, turning away from the fearsome threesome. His gaze landed on the palest woman in the room, her hair fanning out around her face, legs crossed under her in a sexy way that would normally bring a rise to his big fry. In high school and college, when the women were giving up pussy out of both panty legs, he was on either side making sure to stay on the receiving end. That all ended when he fell in love with Brandi.

Right now, the little stallion was resting at the gate, realizing, just like his buddies, that where pussy was concerned, he would find more famine than feast over the next few weeks.

Vernon strolled over to Tanya, who had perched on the paisley love seat as though she were a family heirloom instead of a stranger who should have never graced their doorstep. And she certainly should never have given his wife a stupid idea like this. "After all I did for you, making sure you didn't want for anything, how can you betray me like this?"

"Betray you?" she yelled, her skin flushing an angry pink. "Betray *you!* You're the one who *lied* about being married. You're the one who said your wife died giving birth to Sierra." Then she folded her arms across her breasts. "Or is there another wife hidden in the trenches who happens to be the mother of the two girls you brought to my house last week?"

Tanya? Angry? Talking back to him in public? What was wrong with his women today?

"If you stay with Brandi, I want all my shit back—everything," he said. "You walk away with what you came with—one suitcase and—"

"*Au contraire, mon cheri,*" Brandi purred in a fake French accent as she inched up to the not-so-happy duo. She placed a condescending arm around Vernon's shoulders. "She has every right to keep the jewelry, clothes, the figurines, and the artwork. They were gifts. If this was Texas, she could sue you for breach of promise to marry. I think there's a woman who wrote a novel about that..."

"It's called *Divorcing Your Husband,*" Tanya supplied quickly, taking a tiny sip of Scotch while keeping a keen eye on Vernon. "I think it's by P. M. Carroll or somebody like that."

Brandi nodded as she continued, "I suggest you pull it together, scoop your ego off the floor, and come to terms with the new order of the house. I now have something to show for *your* efforts." Brandi leaned in, whispering, "And I'm going to enjoy every minute."

Vernon reached out, pushing Brandi back toward the bedroom and yanking Tanya off the love seat so they could have it out in private.

Donny scrambled from behind the turntable, making a beeline for his brother-in-law.

Tanya whirled out of Vernon's grasp.

Craig and Jeremy reached Vernon before Donny did, and yanked their friend backward, dragging him to the front door. Vernon shrugged them off, shaking an angry fist in the air. "There wouldn't be a business, this house, or any of this if it wasn't for me. For *me!* Where do you get off making stupid rules like this?"

"Like I said before, the money was minor," Brandi said in a calm tone. "But I kept it going and growing…" Her lips spread into a near-evil smile as she winked. "Unlike *some things* these days."

Howls of laughter erupted all around them.

Vernon froze, glowering at the women now congregated on Brandi's side of the room. "I'll be back in the morning."

"Fine," Brandi said, shrugging. "I'm not going anywhere."

Vernon nodded toward Tanya. "And she'd better be gone."

The newest member of the family turned to Brandi, saying loudly enough for everyone to hear, "What time shall I serve breakfast?"

Brandi grinned without taking her eyes off her husband. "Seven-thirty's good for me."

Vernon took a tentative step toward Tanya. Jeremy and Craig reined him in, lifting him off the floor and, carried him—ranting, kicking, and yelling—toward the door.

As the three men reached the foyer, Brandi called out, "DJ, turn the music up. The party's just beginning, folks."

Vernon's gaze connected with his wife as she swiveled her shoulders to the rhythm of *You can't hit and run, I've got to be number one…*with a smirk on her generous lips.

Vernon's mind raced like a V-8 engine with the throttle wide open. Brandi and Tanya might think they had the upper hand, but they wouldn't be so happy when he returned tomorrow.

There would be no family or friends around to save them then.

CHAPTER Twelve

The grandfather clock in the foyer struck three. The house on Cregier was finally empty. Brandi Spencer had all but slipped into a coma. Tanya put the last of the plates in the dishwasher and turned it on. Sighing wearily, she rested her hips against the sink, wondering what the hell she had gotten herself into.

Walking the length of both levels of the house, she relished the quiet calm as she took in Brandi's eclectic taste. Evidently the woman was a minimalist, as only the necessary furniture held ground over the bedrooms, living room, solarium, dining room, den, library, and two offices—his and hers. Not one thing extra, making it somewhere between sparse and elegant. Paintings of Egypt and the honey-brown luster of the Egyptian Cleopatra and Nefertiti shared space with blue, lavender, and silver abstracts.

Strangely enough, Tanya had a likeness of a Macedonian Greek Cleopatra alongside the same brown-skinned Egyptian rendition Brandi had. Most people didn't realize that there were seven Cleopatras, and that by the time the Greeks had invaded the area, the last in their line was nowhere near the same hue as the others, though her life was no less challenging.

At one point, to protect herself from her family, the last Cleopatra had to be rolled up in a carpet and whisked to safety. Almost like Tanya, who had to be under police security in the hospital, then whisked away to live with the Pitchfords.

And also just like Cleopatra's sister, Tanya's sister Mindy had been killed because of something Tanya had done. As Tanya stared up at the creamy brown skin and the regal bearing of the Cleopatra on Brandi's wall, she wondered how Vernon's wife would equate to the queen.

Tanya had whipped the place into shape in record time—even for her. No one would be able to tell that just hours ago, the place had been spilling over with people who had more questions when they left than when they arrived. She pulled her bags from the foyer closet and settled them into a closet near the master bedroom. Thoughts of leaving had certainly crossed her mind, but she quickly pushed them away. She had to see how things played out.

She peered out the window and saw the Lexus still parked in the driveway. Earlier when she saw Vernon's car tearing down the street, she'd doubled back to the house on Wabash Avenue, searched the drawers, cabinets, and closets for any important items she may have missed, then packed the last of her things—including her pictures of the two Cleopatras—and put them outside in the shed where she could retrieve them later.

She thought of her sudden urge to return Vernon's wallet to Brandi just to see her reaction. And boy did she react!

The woman had directed a full-blown symphony last night, with strings, percussion, brass, and woodwinds. Tanya had never seen things done in such a way that no one could gossip—it was all done right there in the open. The woman even had nerve enough to ask, "Hey, are there any questions?"

Despite what Tanya expected, family and friends followed Brandi's example and treated her nicely. Vernon, on the other hand, caught the pure hell he deserved.

❤❤❤

Yesterday as she drove through the traffic-filled streets of Stony Island on her way to Brandi's house, she wondered, where would she go? What would she do? Vernon had been right about one thing—she had nothing and no family. Her father had made sure there was no one in the world who would lift a hand to help her, but that paled in comparison to what he had done to her. It ranked a distant third to what he'd done to the person she'd loved the most—the person he had killed to keep Tanya from talking.

She had driven through the winding streets, passing the house in the Jackson Park Highlands five times before stopping. As she strolled past the shrubs and up the black concrete pathway, at first thoughts of *what the hell do you think you're doing* swirled through her mind. Then a smidgen of worry came and went like the flickering light from a candle sitting in a gentle breeze. A simple idea had made life a bit complicated—once again. What was Brandi up to—really?

The slosh of the dishwasher pulled her back to the present as a sudden sense of loss washed over her. She missed Michelle's family more than she missed her own. Her father had the "Midas touch," but his real magic making to make sure his oldest daughter kept his dirty secrets. Even darker magic had made his youngest daughter disappear and turn up dead during his trial.

What he actually had was a sly charisma that reeled people in. What he had was the foresight to scope out the young women who were heirs to fortunes that would make even the Kennedy clan raise an eyebrow. What he had was the smarts to take Margaret Van Oy's virginity in the backseat of an old Chevy.

The pregnancy came after weeks of daily romps out in the fields, in the car—or behind the McCumbers' barn. When Margaret said she was getting an abortion, Wilbur demanded that she keep the child. When she refused, he told her that if she got rid of his child, he would tell the world how much of a whore she really was. He would describe exactly what he'd made her do to him—sick, perverse things—which would force her family to disown her. Tanya, growing just under her mother's hardening heart, was well past the "planning" stages and Margaret had no choice but to comply with his wishes. She gave in and they eloped, sealing her fate with him for better or worse.

The family demanded an annulment, but Margaret, fearing the worst from her quick-tempered husband, held fast. To Wilbur's dismay, the family disowned her anyway, leaving her at the mercy of a cold, calculating man.

One who had no time for the wife or child who were supposed to have been his link to a fortune. So Wilbur figured out another way.

A dropout from Social Circle High School, Wilbur vowed that the Van Oy family would rue the day they shunned him. And he would strike back by taking the thing they loved most—money.

The Van Oys owned all the factories in and around Social Circle. Many Southern towns were established around such businesses, since people moved to be near their jobs. One by one, Wilbur Jaunal shrewdly scouted out and purchased the railroad right-of-ways that connected one Van Oy factory to the next. Then he expanded to those that connected the surrounding towns.

While Margaret's family members still had their heads up their butts trying to figure out what was happening, Wilbur ended up owning all the ways to bring supplies into and out of Social Circle. Now the Van Oys had to pay premiums in order for their railcars to cross his land.

Then one day during peak production time he shut them down completely by denying access across his land, effectively putting them out of business.

A year later, Jaunal purchased the factories from his in-laws and enemies for pennies on the dollar. He put all of the people who were loyal to the former employers out on their collective asses, and hired Blacks from Social Circle and Monroe to take their place. That move almost caused a race riot that made Watts look like child's play.

In an even more clever move, Jaunal Industries directed the white population toward the factories it owned in the surrounding counties—meaning the people left in town were Blacks he counted on to be loyal to their employer: Wilbur Jaunal.

As whites moved closer to the other factories to avoid long drives to and from work, the Social Circle voting base became more and more Black. The remaining whites were rich and scattered. Wilbur's bid to become mayor was a lock. A power structure tied to a crafty but greedy hand that ruled by fear, intimidation and violence, if necessary, began as soon as he took office.

By the time Tanya turned twelve that fear had become part of her everyday reality. Sometimes going to school took the same effort it would take a mouse to move a mountain. Each day weighed on her like a dark cape covering a white blossom.

She carried a deep, dark secret so shameful she couldn't tell her mother… her best friend…anyone. Every morning, and sometimes in the middle of the night, she woke drenched in sweat, hurting and afraid, sure that no one could help. At any given moment throughout the day, she would burst into tears. She didn't know how long she could keep her secret, but telling would only make things worse. Her father—the richest man in town—had sworn that if she said anything, he'd make her sorry.

Even after she had gone to live with Michelle's family for her own safety, he still made good on that threat.

Tanya's life had moved in much the same way as the broad strokes she used to clear away the last of the debris from Brandi's rich blue-tile kitchen floor. Margaret Jaunal had turned her back on her oldest daughter. Tanya didn't regret the trouble that it caused her father, but she would take it all back if the one person she loved above all others had survived—the innocent one.

CHAPTER 

Strolling through the dimly lit hallway of Brandi's home, Tanya felt a disconnection from reality that she couldn't explain. She was in Vernon's house. No—his wife's house—and the woman had actually invited her to stay to teach the man who had hurt them a lesson. How real was that?

She thought about the past several hours and remembered the terrified look on Vernon's face and how she enjoyed the way Brandi handled the situation, calmly and with a matter-of-factness that she could never imagine any woman pulling off realistically.

She had a feeling that Brandi was a woman who had weathered a storm or two and now tried to keep the storms in her life to a minimum. Where did that kind of strength come from? Why did Black women seem to sail through life as though none of the things white women couldn't live without really mattered? And why had she ended up with a man like her father— overbearing, manipulative, lying?

Vernon's temper and his eerie silences were among the reasons Tanya's demands from him had been few. After asking the second time, she realized that going back to school wasn't going to happen, in spite of his promises. A few uninspired sexual romps had brought her jewelry, clothes, and that Lexus, but never what she really wanted—his full attention and for him to keep his promise. Now she understood why. He didn't want another woman as educated and as assertive as his wife.

Tanya passed the row of photographs displaying the Spencer family in various stages of happiness. A happiness Tanya never remembered in the mansion where she grew up. During the two years she spent with Michelle's family, she had healed and begun to smile again. Then fate intervened one more time and Tanya had to flee Social Circle under the cover of darkness. It had been nighttime in her life ever since.

None of the sofas in the Spencer house pulled out into a bed. Tanya refused to sleep in either of the children's rooms. Despite the size of the house, there was no guest bedroom. So where did that leave her?

Tomorrow would be a new day. She still wasn't sure what Brandi expected. Maybe she'd go back on her word like Vernon did.

Once again, she couldn't predict what her life was going to be like. Somehow her fate had constantly been decided by men, first her father, then the frog-princes in between, then Vernon, and now this. Didn't they realize that all a woman wanted was to be loved, cherished, protected, and respected? Respected more than anything.

As Tanya entered the master bedroom, she hesitated at the door a few moments before getting into Vernon's side of the bed. She draped the cream damask comforter over her body and closed her eyes. Tears welled up as a mountain of pain pierced her soul. She was so far away from the people who loved her, but she couldn't return. Contacting them would put their family in jeopardy again. And she couldn't bear it if one of them were killed. No one in Chicago cared about her. No one would miss Tanya Melaine Kaufman if her life ended. No one would come and claim her body. She might as well struggle forward, hoping that one day she'd have a chance to live on her terms.

What would life be like, being a wife to a woman who wielded more confidence in her little pinky than most women Tanya had ever met? What made Brandi strong enough to face her pain? And she *was* in pain; that was one thing the strong woman couldn't hide. Vernon had hurt her, but she had rallied, taking charge of the situation as though catching her husband with another woman was an everyday occurrence. Although it probably stuck in her craw that Tanya happened to be white, Brandi had focused more on dynamics than color.

Tanya, for some reason, had always felt, deep in her heart, that her time at the house on Wabash Avenue would be cut short abruptly. It had always felt temporary. She'd kept an overnight bag packed out of pure habit. And that habit had come in handy the moment Brandi Spencer had stepped through the door.

Sure, accepting Brandi's offer was a bold move, but Tanya really wanted to see how things panned out. And she did need a place to live. If nothing else, Tanya had been good at playing the "wife" role. She was organized, focused, and appreciated beauty. She only had a tenth-grade education and that had kept her from getting good jobs. She needed to regroup and ground herself somewhere. Why not in the same life that Vernon had promised her?

It didn't matter that Brandi would be pulling the train. Tanya was more than willing to clean the caboose and punch tickets to keep the woman of the house focused on making the money. As long as Tanya's needs were met, things would work out just fine.

Tanya reached up, wiping away another stray tear, weariness settling into her soul. The only things she had were her sanity and her morals. She had tried to hold onto them, but Vernon had taken even that by pulling her into this painful triangle. She should have known. Vernon was so... distant at times, but oh the man was wonderful in so many other ways.

Now she had no one.

CHAPTER *Fourteen*

The moon loomed in the midnight-blue Chicago sky. A chilly breeze whipped through the trees, shaking them to a loud crescendo before all fell silent again.

Vernon trailed his father and Julie into the library of the massive home in Reichert Lakes. Mahogany shelves lined with books covered most of the walls. A globe-shaped liquor cabinet sat off to the side of a desk with a leather map top. The oversized dark brown chair could easily seat the Jolly Green Giant, it was perfectly suited for his father's huge frame.

Julie, with Cupid's bow lips that made a man wonder how good she was at giving head, strolled over to William in a black dress that curved over her frame with gracious triumph. She kissed him on the top of his shiny bald head, then sashayed from the library, leaving a trail of Donna Karan Cashmere perfume behind.

The door to the library hadn't closed all the way before Vernon's father was out his chair and bearing down on him. "Son, what the hell were you thinking?"

Vernon shrugged, not even thinking of making eye contact with his father. The man's bellowing voice, portly frame, and overbearing attitude had always put the fear of God into Vernon. That immeasurable strength and unyielding power had made corporations shake; several Fortune 500 companies respected him. But somehow, the women in his life—and the women in Vernon's life—couldn't care less about all that.

Piercing brown eyes leveled on Vernon, making his balls shrink to the size of raisins. Damn! His confidence seeped out of his pores into the sofa cushions faster than a woman runs through child support.

"Haven't I taught you anything?" William paced the floor as though walking back and forth across the deep green carpet would bring answers. "You never bring that shit to your front door. Never!" He banged his fist on the desk. Vernon winced as though he'd been struck. "Keep the wife and the mistress as far away from each other as possible."

"I did," Vernon said, his throat parched from the effort it took to speak.

His dad pivoted, creating a breeze of Grey Flannel in the library. "The hell you did. Would we be having this conversation if—"

"Tanya lives in the city in Chatham, we live in South Shore, at least six miles apart."

"I'm not talking about location, you fool!" William said through clenched teeth. "That's only part of it."

He gestured sharply toward the phone. "You called her from your home. You charged some of the expenses to the same business you share with your wife—the same wife I told you should be at home raising children, not out running the business like she's a man. How stupid could you be?"

"Since we just moved the business and remodeled the warehouse into offices, cash was tight."

The worry lines on the older man's forehead furrowed. "Then you shouldn't spring for extra ass until you can afford it."

"So what am I gonna do? I can't go home with Tanya living there."

"Divorce Brandi!"

"Divorce her?" Vernon swallowed. Ending his marriage was a sign of failure. At least in his book. "I don't want a divorce. I want my wife back."

"Trade that fat cow in for a younger model," William said, slipping into his chair, grabbing up the newspaper.

"I don't want a younger model. And Brandi's not fat, she's curvaceous." And he loved every inch. He also loved the way her breasts jiggled as she walked. Those fleshy hips could make his mouth water just watching her walk away. And good Lord the woman could work that ass on his dick like a blender on high speed. Suddenly he felt the warm pressure of arousal and had to shift on the sofa to keep from getting hard.

"If she's so perfect, then why did you need a mistress?"

"Same reason you did," Vernon shot back. "And you had three!"

The old man flipped open the *Wall Street Journal*. "And I maintained all three women without the madness you had with just one," he said, giving Vernon a forced smile. "If you ask me, she put your nuts in a vise grip and gave them a nice little squeeze. You should leave her while you have the chance. I told you about picking women from the low end of the spectrum. A girl from Jeffrey Manor? Definitely not in our league."

"You married Mom and she wasn't rich."

"I could afford to marry beneath me. And she turned out just fine until your cold-hearted wife stepped in. Needed to leave her ass the day after you married her."

"I'm not leaving my wife."

The amused expression on his dad's face went somber. "If you're not leaving her, you'd better get that mistress out of your house. I can't believe she pulled some shit like that. That woman's got more balls than a brass monkey." Flipping to another page, his eyes scanned the sheet before folding the corner down to look at Vernon. "You'll be the laughing stock of this side of Chicago. If the League gets wind of this, you'll never hear the end of it and you'll be out on your ass."

"I'll try, Dad."

"Trying is lying," William snapped, folding the paper to put it away.

"She'll come around," Vernon said. "Brandi's just trying to make a statement."

"Well, everyone tonight heard her loud and clear," his father said. "She played the opening number and headliner like a professional. Let's see you top that, *young* Mr. Spencer."

CHAPTER Fifteen

Brandi turned over in her bed. The comforter slipped down around her waist. The sweet, nutty aroma of hazelnut coffee filled the air. Brandi opened one eye, then the other. She curled up in the king-size bed, relishing the feel of silk sheets reaching under her chin.

Stretching languidly, she noticed the fresh scent of citrus. Citrus? Where did that come from? Her hand landed on a soft, pliable form next to her. She froze as a shiver of uneasiness passed through her.

Brandi jerked upward, peering at the body on the opposite side of her bed.

Memories of last night flooded her mind. What had she done?

Glancing down, she sighed with relief. She still had her clothes on.

Lifting the sheet brought another moment of clarity. Tanya still had her clothes on, too.

The other woman stretched, rolling over to her left side, blonde hair flowing over the pillow like a waterfall.

Brandi's eyebrow shot up as she locked gazes with her…wife? Then she asked, "We didn't?"

Tanya's lips spread into a slow, easy smile. "No."

"So we haven't?"

"No," she answered with humor twinkling in her eyes. "Mmmmm, and that's one part of your offer I'd like to bow out of."

"Nooooo problem," Brandi replied, shifting her weight on the bed. "I'm not ready to settle for backup."

This time Tanya laughed. "Yeah, um, speaking of backup…you might want to put that some place other than the bathroom cabinet. The girls might find it."

"How did you—"

"I cleaned the house last night. Everything's all squared away."

The roar of a lawn mower kicked in. Mr. Lewis would probably receive another citation from the police by the end of the week. And he'd also get an earful from Mrs. Washington, who swore up and down that if he interrupted her beauty sleep early Saturday morning one more time, she'd set fire to his lawn. Mr. Lewis politely replied that if she needed beauty sleep after all these years, she should have started sometime before birth.

Personally, Brandi believed that the real problem between those two was from another lawn that needing mowing or grazing. Mr. Lewis wanted Mrs. Washington and she wanted him. If they'd stop the preliminaries and get to the real deal, the whole world could breathe a collective sigh of relief. And maybe the lawn mower wouldn't wake the whole planet on Saturdays.

"I smell coffee. Is someone still here?"

Tanya shook her head. "I was up a little earlier and set the coffeemaker for a quarter to seven so I'd get up in time to fix breakfast."

"I never could get that thing to work," Brandi said, amazed at the woman's resourcefulness.

Tanya slipped out of bed, glancing slyly over her shoulder. "You passed out before telling me where I'm supposed to sleep. I figured as long as I stayed on **his** side of the bed and didn't get any bright ideas…"

"Yeah, don't get any dark ones, either," Brandi quipped, eliciting a chuckle from Tanya.

"Breakfast will be ready in a little while."

Brandi felt a sense of impending doom as Tanya left the room. Even her mother had given her an earful before Donny swept the protesting woman out the door.

She had always listened to her elders, especially her mother. But, in this instance, most of them were saying just get over it and let it go. She'd done too much of that in her marriage. Too much of that in her life. This was the first time Brandi had ever defied her mother since the day the woman arrived at Forty-Seventh Street and Michigan Avenue, too late to snatch her only daughter from the jaws of danger.

❤❤❤

Brandi had just turned thirteen. She woke up that Friday morning, scooped her ice blue portable cassette player off the bed, and shoved it into her book bag before pounding down the stairway. She sprinted across the room toward the door. "Mom, I'll catch you later," she yelled, picking up the pace so she wouldn't be late.

"No!" her mother yelled back in a cold, hard voice that Brandi knew there was no escaping. "You'll catch me right now."

Did her mother know? Had she been found out? She hugged her book bag close, hoping her mom wouldn't ask to see inside. Brandi groaned as she made a quick U-turn toward the kitchen and the trouble zone. Man! She couldn't be late. Not today.

"Yes, Mama?"

Her mother's piercing hazel eyes scrutinized Brandi from the top of her head to the bottom of her shoes without so much as a flicker. Brandi was dressed in loose-fitting jeans, a navy turtleneck and Converse sneakers—all definitely in style. The colors complemented her skin and her five-foot-six, size fourteen frame. Her shoulder-length hair had been styled into a bob. Every outfit had to meet with her mother's approval—which meant covering every square inch of skin.

The makeup case, miniskirt, tight tank top, and high heels stashed beneath Brandi's science and English books told a different story. She just wanted to have fun. She was two grades ahead, had been a freshman at age twelve with good grades and all, but she still couldn't *do* anything. Today would be different. *If* she got out of the house.

"Who was that boy calling my house at ten twenty-seven last night?"

She knew the *exact* time? He must have woken her up. "Hollywood."

"I'm sure his mama didn't name him that," she snapped, one eyebrow raised.

Brandi cringed at the caustic tone. "His name's Derek Coles, but he likes to be called 'Hollywood.'"

Leaning forward so close that Brandi could smell that first cup of coffee, her mother said, "I don't care what he likes to be called. He'd better not call here again past nine. Do you hear me?"

"Okay." Brandi had warned Hollywood about her mother's rules. He didn't care much for rules. Or parents for that matter.

"And who is he anyway?" her mother asked, tapping her foot on the paisley carpet.

"A guy that goes to my school." Not just a guy. *The* guy. Brandi had had a crush on Hollywood since grammar school. At eighteen, his creamy complexion, slanted hazel eyes, and dark, curly hair—along with the muscles rippling down his body like Lake Michigan's waves—made him every girl's dream. Now he was *her* dream. He'd finally noticed her. It only took a whole year, but who was counting? Oh, that's right—she was, every single one of those days!

"I don't know what you kids..."

Bag weighing heavily on her shoulders, Brandi sighed, tuning out her mother's words—the same lecture, every other day. Blah, blah, blah. "When I was your age..."

Brandi hated those sermons. Her mother should have passed the plate when finished. Brandi glanced at the clock on the kitchen wall next to the pantry. Her mother didn't get the hint.

In a bolder move, Brandi twisted her arm and openly stared at her watch for a few seconds. Only a few minutes before Hollywood—

"Girl, are you trying to be smart with me?"

"No. No, Mama...I...I just don't want to be late for...school." Brandi swallowed hard. Ooops. Maybe she'd been a little too bold.

Mama's eyes bored into Brandi like a metal drill through rotten wood. Brandi's hand snaked out and brushed aside the hair, which suddenly had started to stick to her now-moist face. Not a good sign.

"Go on then," her mother told her with a dismissing swipe of her hand. "But put your friend in check."

"I'll talk to him, Mama." Brandi turned and raced toward the door.

"And I'd like to meet him."

Brandi almost dropped her book bag on the floor. She didn't turn around. Her face crinkled, mirroring the terror she felt. "Sure, Mama. You'll get to meet him," she said, thinking, *It'll never happen*. Hollywood was every girl's dream, but every mother's nightmare—bad boy to the core. He smoked, hung out all night, and did whatever he wanted. She never understood how he kept up with his schoolwork or even showed up for class.

Brandi clutched her bag as she broke out the front door. She hoped the letter she gave the attendance office at Chicago Vocational High School would avert a call to the house. If the school called, she'd be back in time to erase the message. But then she remembered the rollers in her mother's head. She got the feeling her mom wasn't going to work. Now *that* would be a major problem.

Brandi crossed the street and sped toward the meeting place, using the breathing techniques she'd learned in track. She passed the ranch-style homes and duplexes built on an area that had been for dumping waste and slag for years. The entire area was called Jeffrey Manor, but she actually lived in the northeast section called Merrionette Manor—a small place in the heart of the area built on a suburban street structure. The Manor had started the residential construction boom, as people from Irondale needed housing closer to the Wisconsin Steel Works.

She remembered her father sharing that tidbit as he took her on a late-night tour about a month before he died. Lord, she missed him! And she missed her brother, too, but he had found Champaign, Illinois, and the rest of their relatives more to his liking.

As she waited on the corner of One Hundredth Street and Paxton Avenue for a black Chevy Caprice, she perked up every time she heard an engine. Had she missed him? Hollywood didn't like his girls to be late. If he said eight in the morning, she'd better be there at seven fifty-eight just to be sure. "Oh, God, I couldn't have missed him..."

Thundering bass interrupted the warm, peaceful surroundings. One minute she heard birds chirping and the light breeze rustling the long strands of leaves on the willow trees, the next she heard a raspy, rugged voice coming blasting through speakers, making it impossible to understand the words. Her eyes scanned left. Her heart lifted, almost tearing through her chest. She hugged herself to keep from skipping.

The shiny black car crawled down the street as if it had no particular place to go.

Hollywood had promised her a day out on the town. She had planned for it all month. All week the hours seemed to creep like a snail across wet sand. She thought this day would never come.

The blaring music vibrated through the neighborhood and set off a few car alarms. Brandi's slender frame could feel the bass roll through her body like a personal massage. The car pulled to the curb only six inches away from Brandi's trembling body. Nervous wasn't even the word.

He nodded. "'Sup, chick?"

"Nothing much."

She waited near the passenger side for him to get out and open the door.

He stared back at her. "We ain't got all day."

Her heart felt a little twinge of disappointment, but she ignored it and climbed onto the black leather seat. Her father had always said men were supposed to open the door for their girls. Maybe someone forgot to tell Hollywood. The smell of Cool Water cologne drove her wild. She'd bought it for him three weeks ago for his birthday. He hadn't said thank you but that was minor, right?

She sat demurely, watching the soft curve of his lips, the strong jut of his nose, and the bushy eyebrows that hovered above smoldering eyes that made her melt anytime he looked her way.

As he turned down Torrence Avenue, the music made conversation impossible. She didn't even try. She beamed like a girl who'd won the prize trophy in a dance contest. They passed the airplane wing of their school. C.V.S. would be missing at least two students—a senior and a freshman—that day. With more than five thousand students, no one would notice.

Several minutes later, the town homes and duplexes gave way to newly constructed houses. Further on they passed empty, abandoned houses and even more vacant lots with grass that hadn't seen a lawn mower since they'd been invented. He slowed down on a block where paint hadn't touched the houses for years. She had been so happy just to be with him, she didn't even know where he was taking her.

Hollywood pulled to the curb in front of a ranch home. She felt another stab of disappointment. The gutter was barely attached to the house. Dirt filled places where grass should've been and the concrete steps were chipped, exposing the round rocks underneath. The silver chain-link fence had missing panels and a broken gate. Down the street boys and men sat on their porches, blasting music, drinking, smoking cigarettes and, if her nose told her correctly, probably something else.

A shiver sliced through her body as Hollywood switched off the ignition. She glanced at him nervously. "What's this place?"

He smirked. "My crib."

"I'll...um, wait here for you."

"No, you're coming in," he said in a short, snappy tone that didn't leave room for an argument.

She hesitated and finally said, "Okay, I have to change clothes anyway."

Hollywood smiled slyly, eyes scanning her body as though he just noticed her for the first time. "Whatever."

The door slammed, making Brandi wince. Strolling in front of the car, hands deep in his pockets, he headed for the crumbling steps.

She waited. Hoping.

He turned to face her and shrugged. "Come on."

Brandi grimaced before joining him. His baggy jeans and light blue Fat Albert T-shirt draped his medium-built body just right.

"You could've opened the door for me," she said in a voice so small she didn't recognize it as hers.

"What's wrong with your hands?"

She shrugged, lowering her eyes. "Nothing."

"That's what I thought."

Bad boy to the core. Nice guys didn't usually appeal to her, but right now a nice one would do her just fine.

He used a small silver key to open the door.

She swallowed hard, gathering courage to ask, "Why are we here? I thought we were going out to eat and go downtown."

His lips broke into something that wasn't quite a smile. "Later. There's something we need to do first."

Brandi clutched her bag as though the canvas covering her textbooks would keep her safe. Would he keep his promise? Why did she already feel he wouldn't?

She stepped through the old wooden door that barely hung on its hinges. The smell of burnt popcorn, greasy fried chicken, cigarettes, and liquor assaulted her nose like a defensive end tackling a quarterback at the goal line. Hollywood's long legs kicked dirty clothes, broken toys, and food wrappings out of the way. The ragged tan carpet had seen better days. Moving into the house, she tried to hold her breath. Someone had forgotten to take the garbage out—years ago. How could people live like this?

Dried food on the wall near the living room entrance made Brandi's stomach sink. A wave of nausea threatened to dislodge her breakfast. They passed an old tattered sofa with a man sprawled out on the right side snoring, television remote dangling from his hands. This house needed more than a housekeeper; it needed to be blown off the map.

There was a wide-screen television and plenty of records, but no one could pick up a broom, vacuum, or mop? Or spray some Lysol in this camp? Man!

When she reached the hallway, she stood as unmoving as a DuSable Museum statue. To her left was a bedroom. Eight people—two boys and six girls, all naked—sprawled across a mattress on the floor as though someone had pitched them in and left them. She could only imagine what had happened the night before. Even more people slept on a mattress on the floor of another bedroom to her right. Some of the girls looked about her age. Didn't they go to school?

Whoa! Didn't she have a lot of nerve? She wasn't where she was supposed to be, either. Now she wished her behind was firmly planted in Mr. Fisher's history class soaking up information on the Civil Rights Movement instead of walking through a battle zone, following Hollywood to nowhere.

"Hey, get your butt over here."

Hollywood's voice snapped her back to cold, nasty reality.

She entered the dark, gray bedroom at the very end of the hall. Cleaner, but not much. At least she wouldn't have to sit on the floor.

Inching toward the queen-size bed, she watched Hollywood pick up his clothes and throw them in the corner where a small pile instantly became a mountain of cotton, polyester, and rayon pieces she didn't recognize.

A single window opened to a view of the backyard. Old tires, garbage, and clothes decorated a lawn—again more dirt than grass.

Hollywood switched on the stereo sitting on a wooden dresser, peeled off his shirt, then sank down on the bed, pulling her next to him. He gripped her like a homeless man protecting a bag of groceries.

She shrugged him off. "I thought you said we were going out."

"Later."

She stood. "I want to go *now!*"

Hollywood glared at her so long, she got the feeling that he wanted to hit her. She shriveled under his icy stare. He shrugged, leaning back on the bed. "I thought you was down."

"I am down. I just want you to keep your promise."

"Girl, it ain't about what you want." His eyes scanned her up and down. "I knew I shoulda stuck wit' Alicia. I knew you were still a stupid little girl."

His words hurt her more than she ever thought they could. "I'm not stupid."

"Yeah right," he growled, rubbing a hand over his groin. "What did you think I wanted? To play on the swings, baby doll?" He shook his head. "You knew when you stepped to me what I'd want. You know better than playing games with me. Now get them clothes off and quit actin' like a baby."

Brandi froze. Hollywood's tone had gone from irritated to angry. If she didn't do what he asked he'd dump her or something…worse.

She liked being with him because it made her popular, made other girls—even her friends—jealous. What would they say if she showed up at school and Hollywood treated her like a bald-headed stepchild?

If she gave in, he'd like her, but what about all his other girlfriends?

They'd given it up, too—and he'd dumped them. He was no longer with Jackie, Jennifer, Shakira, Alicia...What made her different?

Even though she'd bought him the cologne for his birthday, he didn't say a word about her birthday today even though she'd reminded him several times. She thought he loved her. But now that she thought about it, he didn't seem to know what love was. Hollywood's bedroom in the heart of the hood was the last place she should be on a school day.

He grabbed at her blouse. A button popped off.

"Don't touch me," she snapped, backing away from the bed, struggling to fix her shirt. He had no intention of treating her right. He might be the cutest boy in school, but she didn't really know him. She didn't *want* to know him. When she looked up at him again, she gasped. He was fully undressed—butt naked, his penis reaching for the ceiling. Oh, God! She was in trouble now. She didn't want to have sex with him. Come to think of it, she didn't want to have sex at all. As much as she thought she was, she really wasn't ready.

"I'm not doing this."

"Then what you come here for?" he asked through clenched teeth.

"You brought me here!"

"Because you wanted some of this good stuff," he said, grabbing his groin again as if he had just found out he had one. "Stop playing games, girl, and show me that you love me."

"You don't know what love is," she said, jumping back to put three feet between them. "Take me home."

"Girl, you're crazy."

"Take me home *now!*"

Unmoved, he smirked. "Not 'til I get what I want. And I'm gonna get what I want. Trust me."

He didn't move.

Suddenly she began to tremble as though standing in the coldest Chicago weather.

He placed his hands behind his head, lay back, and grinned. Moments later, he leaned over on the bed, yelling at the top of his lungs, "Yo, Vince and Juan! Come help me train this bi—"

She didn't stick around for the rest. One of those sleeping zombies could awaken and come out of a nearby bedroom. Then she wouldn't have a choice.

Sprinting down the hallway, she fumbled with the lock and threw the front door open. Her heart slammed against her chest as a pair of hard, large hands grazed her shoulders.

Brandi slipped under them and ran out the door. She had to get away fast. *Where can I go? Who can I call? Will any of the people sitting on their porches help me?* she wondered as ran blindly down the street in a strange neighborhood.

"Hey, catch her! Train time! I've got first!" Hollywood yelled in between gasps. "Catch her and you'll get some, too..."

The sound of thundering feet and loud voices told her Hollywood was no longer the only one after her.

She didn't know where to turn. All she knew how to do was run and... pray.

❤❤❤

Brandi stepped out the shower, patted dry, ran a comb through her shoulder-length hair, then threw on a pair of jeans and a red shirt. Seconds later she strolled into the bright blue and white kitchen. "Tanya, we need to talk."

The woman turned from the stove. "I figure we'd have to do that sooner or later. I was hoping for later."

The softness of her voice hid a trace of a southern accent. "Where are you from?" Brandi asked.

"Social Circle, Georgia."

"Where's that?"

"About fifty miles from Atlanta."

Brandi took a moment to think. "If I hadn't extended that offer, where would you be right now?"

"A hotel or something." She gestured to the pictures of the children and Vernon on the wall near the sunroom. "I don't really have any family, so..."

"Okay, let me—um—get my head on straight and we'll sort everything out."

Tanya rested her butt against the edge of the counter that separated the solarium from the kitchen, leveling a piercing blue-eyed gaze at Brandi as she sipped her coffee. "Kinda put your foot in it last night, huh?"

"It was worth it just to see him lose his mind."

"Like MasterCard."

Brandi grinned, lifting her steaming cup of coffee. "Priceless."

Moments later, Brandi slipped into a clear vinyl seat at the breakfast table, pulling up to a plate of scrambled eggs, biscuits, turkey bacon, grits, and a glass of freshly squeezed orange juice. A sudden sense of triumph shot through her. "Shoot, I'm liking this already."

Tanya smiled, standing off to the side. The sun breaking through the clouds beamed into the glass-encased room, showering it with a ray of warm yellow light.

"You can sit down, you know. You're not the maid." After an uncomfortable pause, Brandi gestured to her food. "Aren't you going to eat?"

"I—I—sure." Tanya turned on her heel, returning moments later with an identically filled plate, and sat down across from Brandi.

Even without make-up, the woman was beautiful. Her round, smooth face blended her patrician features in perfect symmetry. Her soft voice and the way she held her coffee cup spoke of Southern gentility. She was a bit submissive and weak, vulnerable and lost, but spoke in a quiet, carefully controlled manner that signaled an upper-class upbringing. *How the hell did she accept living on the Black side of the city?* Brandi thought. *What happened that made her bounce from place to place like a hobo?*

"So…where did you meet Vernon?

"The Perfect Fit," Tanya said, between bites.

"You were looking for a job in Chicago?"

Tanya inhaled, stood, and crossed to the counter switching the radio on to some light jazz. "I wanted to see the Windy City for a while."

"What job did you apply for?"

"Receptionist."

Brandi froze mid-bite. "You moved all the way to Chicago for a job answering phones?"

"They said free training," Tanya replied. "Plus it pays double what I made on my last job."

Damn, the woman really did have it bad. "What college did you graduate from?"

Tanya hesitated, blushing a little before responding, "I didn't go to college." Her eyes radiated a sadness Brandi could almost touch. "I didn't even finish high school."

"That explains everything."

Tanya's face darkened with anger. "And what's that supposed to mean?"

"No aspirations."

Tanya placed her cup gently on the saucer. "I know what you're thinking."

Brandi lifted her fork. "You couldn't *possibly* know what I'm thinking."

Tanya pushed her plate away. "I'm a lot smarter than you think. I'm going to find a job, then a husband—"

"Why are you constantly trying to stay under the radar?"

"It takes money to go to college. Money I don't have."

"It takes drive and initiative," Brandi shot back, light brown eyes flashing.

"Spoken by a woman who went to Fisk on a full scholarship."

The sun shining through the blinds highlighted Brandi's beautiful features.

"Who told you that?" Brandi asked softly, suddenly thinking that Vernon had shared more with Tanya than she cared for her to know.

"It's on the wall right next to the fireplace. Presidential scholarship?"

"Well, I still had to earn that, it wasn't just handed to me."

Tanya concentrated on her meal, projecting shame and defeat. The grim set of her lips told Brandi that she had insulted the woman. "I apologize," Brandi said, "*if* I've judged you unfairly."

Tanya slowly exhaled. "It's all right, I'm sure this is new for you, too."

"Well, I have a plan."

Brandi waited until Tanya looked up again. "My husband had you free and clear for six months..." She hesitated, blinked, then picked up the glass of orange juice, and took a small sip. "So I think it's only fair that I get six months of service."

Tanya's head whipped up. "No ass."

"You seem a little disappointed about that," Brandi said, grinning. "Are you asking me to reconsider?"

"Don't even go there."

"Now you're *really* sounding black."

This time Tanya's eyes twinkled with mischief. "Y'all don't have a monopoly on that term. Six months, huh?"

Brandi nodded.

Tanya's gaze darted around the room before leveling on Brandi. "That's fair."

"And I have a contract for you to sign."

Tanya's hand halted halfway to her mouth. "A contract?"

"That's right. I want it in writing."

"You…when?"

"I slipped out and did my thing right after Vernon's boys carted him off. My lawyer hasn't seen it yet, but after you sign it, we'll have it notarized and it'll stand up in court."

"Why are you doing this?"

"To prove a point," Brandi said softly.

"You'd trust me in your house?"

"Honey, you've already *been* in my house. Every time he made love to you, then came home and rolled me over and did me, we became intimate by indirect contact, with no choice in the matter." Then her gaze narrowed. "Did he *always* use a condom with you?"

Tanya failed in an effort to smile. "After he asked me to marry him, he stopped."

"I rest my case."

"So this is all about revenge?"

"Not just that. This is about justice and fairness." Brandi slid the single sheet of paper across the table, then picked up one of her own and read Tanya the terms of the contract.

❤❤❤

Brandi knew she'd never have a marriage like her parents. She chuckled, remembering how they still made eyes at each other after twenty-five years of marriage. They acted more like kids than Brandi and Donny, who were nine years apart. Heaven forbid if Papa had made a date in the middle of the day and Mama, going about her business, would suddenly remember it when she was driving on the expressway. Jean Caldwell would cause a major five-car pileup just to get to the nearest off-ramp, and tear off to meet Papa at a restaurant or a nearby hotel. Their cryptic way of talking wasn't lost on Brandi, who soon knew that "four hours" meant one of those four-hour-nap motels on Stony Island. "Victuals" was short for vittles, meaning a quick bite to eat without the children. "Louis Vega" meant a quick, on-the-spot trip to Vegas.

But one night in particular showed her that a man could love a woman more than life itself...

Mama had passed out in the kitchen right in front of the stove. Papa called the ambulance, keeping his hand on the woman stretched out on the floor, hair spread out around her like an angel's halo. Brandi stood frozen at the door. Mama couldn't die. Mama was supposed to live forever. Papa, a tall, slender, caramel-colored man with thick lips and bushy eyebrows and a calm manner, gently scooped his wife from the floor and cradled her lovingly in his arms. His eyes glistened with tears as his lips moved in a silent prayer.

The ambulance came and whisked her out of the house, with Papa trailing close behind. "Stay here until your brother calls."

For a moment she stood on the porch. Then fear guided her footsteps.

Unwilling to stay in the house alone, Brandi ran behind her father, climbed onto the steep ramp leading into the ambulance, and gripped his waist. The paramedic gave her a quick glance before pulling the doors shut. With a jerk, the ambulance tore down Ninety-Fifth Street, sirens going full blast.

The gray-eyed paramedic's fingers trailed over the moist skin of her mother's chest only to begin compressions a moment later.

The monitor registered a faint, almost non-existent heartbeat.

Brandi could only pray as she gripped her father's trembling hand as though his massive fist contained a ray of hope.

The driver called in the condition: "Black female about three hundred pounds, Five feet, six inches…you should have an OR ready, she's probably gonna need surgery."

"Surgery, Papa?" Brandi yanked her father's arm. "Why does she need surgery?"

In a sad tone, with a faraway look in his eyes, he said, "Her heart, it's not doing so good, baby."

"She's gonna be all right. You wait and see," Brandi said, ignoring the seriousness of the situation.

When they got to the hospital, Papa ran behind the gurney, struggling to drag Brandi along, finally picking the twelve-year-old up in his arms without breaking stride.

A nurse whirled around to face him, stopping them on the outside of the silver doors. "Sir, you'll have to wait in the family room…"

They weren't a full family—the biggest part of their lives was about to be split open because the little muscle that kept life flowing to every part of her body was in distress.

Brandi sat on the brown plaid sofa in the soft blue room with vending machines along one wall and a desk along another. Her father cradled her in his strong arms. They were alone.

Suddenly her father stood up as a tall white man with reddish-brown hair entered, peeling off a mask. "Sir, we're trying to get her heart to return to a regular rhythm."

Papa just stared at him.

"Heartbeats normally go like this." The man opened and closed his fist again and again. "Your wife's heart is going like this." He shook his hand from side to side as though he had received an electric shock. "We can't do surgery when it's like this, but the moment it's stable we'll be able to go in and—"

"Do what's best, but I want my wife to live." Papa gripped the doctor's surgical scrubs. "Don't look at her as just another Black woman with no insurance. That's not just my *wife* on the table—that's my *life* on the table!"

With that, Papa—the one who could move mountains with a powerful baritone voice that could belt out a hymn in church, to stir even the most hardened sinner, the man who worked two jobs just so Mama didn't have to work if she didn't want to—did the most unsettling thing Brandi would ever see. He cried. That big, strong man who had shown her the world and taught her how to run, fish, and survive a grueling summer at camp, broke down in sobs so intense it scared her.

Brandi reached up, wrapping her arms around her papa's waist.

"It's okay, Papa. Mama's gonna be fine, remember?"

Brandi was right. Mama pulled through, but had a little pacemaker in place to help things along.

As they stood next to Mama's bed, Brandi's dad kissed the recovering woman's hand. "I don't ever want to live without you."

"You don't have to worry about that." She smiled up at him, eyes moist and alive.

The grin that split his face was a minor miracle. Brandi could feel the love between them. If she ever got married, that was the kind of love she wanted. Not that dreamy, running through the daisies, fairy-tale kind of love with eighteen bridesmaids, enough flowers to start their own shop and ride in a stretch limo. But maybe in this day and age it might be too much to ask.

Her parents were right about one thing—Papa never had to live without Jean Ellis Caldwell.

He died two months after his wife left the hospital.

CHAPTER *Sixteen*

After William's sermon in the library, which in no way resembled Christ's famous Sermon on the Mount, Vernon had stretched out on the sofa, mulling over the events of the evening. How the hell could Brandi and Tanya get along well enough to pull this type of stunt? They should be at each other's throats by now. Not teaming up like high school chums. Women!

Footsteps shuffled across the carpet, ending just a few feet in front of him. Vernon's eyes flew open. His father, clad in green silk pajamas that stretched to cover his huge frame, stood over him like a menacing shadow.

"You can't stay here tonight."

"Why not?" Vernon lifted his head from the sofa's comfortable pillow. "It's just until Brandi gets a grip."

"Well, since you've never been in control of your wife, there's no telling when she'll 'get a grip.' You can't stay here."

"Dad, I lost my wallet. I have no ID, my credit cards were in there, and I can't get to any cash right now. What's the big deal?"

"I...I, um..."

Julie walked past, offering both men a drink. She wore a sheer blue negligee and killer stilettos. Her gaze rested a little too long on Vernon's groin, then traveled the length of his body to his face. She smiled. Without thinking, he smiled back as she sauntered out of the library.

William moved to block his son's view. "I just don't want you here, that's all."

"Oh, I understand," he said, taking in the scowl on his father's not-so-friendly face. "You don't want me near Julie. Like I'd want that skinny woman."

His dad's lips curled into a sneer. "Well, your mistress is sort of skinny, so maybe your taste has changed from fat and out-of-shape to the more man-pleasing type."

"Brandi's not fat," Vernon shot back. "She's...pleasingly curvy. And I like curvy. And Tanya's not skinny. I can see Julie's rib cage when she breathes hard. That's not sexy, that's sick."

"Call it whatever you want," his father said angrily, "but you're not staying here."

❤❤❤

Vernon jolted awake in the backseat of his car. A scratchy blanket from his trunk had served as a covering from the chilly night air. Anger raged inside him as he remembered how he'd spent hours trying to get into the house he had bought for Tanya. Only Brandi could have gotten the locks changed and temporary bars on the windows that fast!

He shook himself, trying to get a strange dream out of his head. He had been on a cruise ship going to Nassau, Bahamas, and somehow had lost his wallet and identification. They wouldn't let him back on the ship without it. Instead, they put him on a yacht with a sandy-haired captain with a mustache that curled at the ends at the wheel. As the crew from the cruise ship dropped Vernon onto the deck, he glanced around and noticed the group of men chained to various places on the yacht. Not slaves, but businessmen—all looking like duplicates of Vernon, briefcases on the ground right next to them. Each had on an engagement ring like Tanya's, all gleaming brightly in the morning Caribbean sun.

The ship pulled away from port, speeding away from the Bahamian shore. Vernon looked up again and saw Brandi at the wheel, grinning down at him like a woman who had hit the lottery on the first try. She turned the yacht out to sea, and a school of mermaids swam past, all with blonde hair, blue eyes, and faces just like Tanya's. Struggling against his restraints, Vernon broke free, jumped into the aquamarine water, and stroked through the cool waves like the very devil was on his heels. The mermaids opened their mouths, baring three rows of sharp teeth. They each took a bite out of him. As he tried to swim back to the safety of the ship, Brandi wheeled away, leaving him to the vicious attention of the Tanya-like mermaids. One even took a single bite of his dick and snatched it straight off. He was sinking...sinking...sinking...

When he got to shore, Antonio Banderas and Melanie Griffith were there to pull him in. He begged the actors, "Please help me get back to Chicago, back to my life, back to my wife..."

❤❤❤

"Jesus, it's cold out here," Vernon said, turning the SUV on for heat. October wasn't supposed to be this cold. But then again, Chicago's weather was unpredictable—one of the main reasons he kept a trench coat, umbrella, Windbreaker, boots, and a winter coat stashed in back of the vehicle.

A light came on in the house off to his right.

Yes! Finally somebody was up.

Vernon scrambled out of the car, ran up the bricked path leading to a newly constructed town house. He scanned the area, noticing how empty the block of Ridgeland was at seven in the morning, then rang the bell.

Jeremy Shipp stepped outside, wearing a dark green robe and plaid boxers, his wavy hair mussed from sleep. He looked the same as the first day Vernon met him on the lawn in front of Morehouse—like a man who should be on the silver screen instead of owner of a national chain of restaurants that specialized in mesquite-grilled beef ribs and beef hot links, instead of the normal pork. The man had made a killing in the industry.

Dark, piercing eyes zeroed in on Vernon, who stood on the doorstep rocking from foot to foot, shivering in the crisp Chicago air. "Hey, man, what's up?"

Vernon blew warm air into his hands. "I need a place to hole up for a minute."

"Oooookay," Jeremy said in a singsong voice as he scratched his head. "Barbara Ann's Motel is still on Cottage Grove, right?"

Been there. Done that. Actually, he had checked into a "four-hour nap" motel on Stony Island—the only kind he could afford at the moment. At first he thought his only worry would be that his truck, packed to the roof, would be stolen from the parking lot—which did not bode well for a good night's sleep. But he had only been in the dank, musty room for ten minutes when he realized that the insect life—roaches and carpenter ants—already had the place on lock-down. He bowed out gracefully, realizing that he couldn't win against things he couldn't outrun. Trying to get a refund provided the motel manager with the best laugh of the night. Now Vernon was totally broke. Well not totally, if he could count the two quarters and a dime he found in the seat cushion.

Vernon swallowed his anger. "I don't want to stay in no damn motel!"

"Well, you can't stay here."

Wrapping the blanket tighter around him, Vernon demanded, "Why not? You're my boy!"

"And I feel that, but ahhh..." Jeremy glanced quickly into the house, then to his friend shivering on the front porch. "You're not one of Lissette's favorite people right now—"

"What did I ever do to her?" Vernon asked, as disappointment moved anger aside.

Jeremy pulled the door closed a little more, whispering, "You cheated on Brandi. She doesn't want me to get any ideas that I can do that shit, too."

"I thought you were the man of the house."

"Same as you, my man," Jeremy said, eyes narrowing just a little. "But I don't want to be outside holding my dick in one hand and a raggedy-ass blanket in the other, either."

"Oh, that's low, even for you," Vernon snapped. "Why don't you at least ask?"

"Do you see what I have on?" Jeremy said, pointing to his old pajamas.

Vernon allowed his gaze to pass over his friend. "Some shit I wouldn't wear on my worst day?"

Jeremy's gaze narrowed to slits.

"All right, clothes, man, clothes."

"Yeah, and I wanna keep it that way." Jeremy peered back into the house. "Lissette drilled me from the time we left that surprise anniversary—coming-out—divorce—or whatever the hell that was last night 'til the time she finally went to sleep. She thinks because you're sneaking around that I am, too—just because I kept quiet about you." His iron gaze almost bored into Vernon's soul. "Now I'm on the hot seat and there's only so much sex that'll smooth things over." Then he grinned as he cracked his neck left, then right. "But I'm working on it." His grin disappeared as he poked Vernon's chest. "And I don't need anyone messing that up. Especially the man who started this shit."

Vernon took a second to absorb that. "So I can't stay?"

"Sorry, man, I've gotta keep my marriage together. Having you here would put a serious damper on things. She's taken sides with your wife, so—"

"I can't believe this. You'll let me stay out in the cold?" Vernon shook his head, mumbling, "With your punk ass."

Jeremy's light skin darkened to an angry brown. "Call me what you want, man. I still have a working furnace to keep me warm and a place to lay my head." He leaned in, grinning. "And my wife isn't playing house with my mistress. So you really need to think about things or you'll be back here next week, still looking for a place to live." Just as suddenly as it appeared, Jeremy's anger vanished. "Why don't you stay at Tanya's house?"

"Brandi changed the locks."

Jeremy coughed a few times, obviously holding in a laugh. "Damn, she moves fast."

"You don't know the half of it," Vernon said, bristling at the fact that his friend found things so funny. "I can't find my wallet. All my credit cards and cash were in there."

"So you're strapped for cash?"

Vernon shrugged. "Yeah, something like that."

"Hold on a minute."

Jeremy went back into the house. Reappearing moments later with a maroon leather wallet, he pulled out a few bills.

Vernon fanned the money between his fingers. "Eighty dollars? That's all you have, man?"

"Do I look like a damn ATM machine to you?" Jeremy growled, favoring Vernon with an angry glare. "That's my part of our weekly allowance. We're saving for the baby."

"Allowance? Man, stand up and take charge of that shit."

"Like you've done?" Jeremy snapped back. "If my wife and I handle our finances together, there's nothing wrong with that. That's what marriage is about—honesty and sharing." He whipped out a long index finger and waggled it at his friend. "So if you want to consider me weak, then that's your issue. What I have is a warm bed and a gorgeous woman next to me. Can you say the same?"

Vernon parted his lips to speak, but Jeremy didn't give him a chance.

"I told you to end it with Tanya when you first met her two years ago, but nooooooo, Mr. Spencer said he had everything under control. Now I'm paying for your mistake. If it costs me our friendship because I won't try my wife's patience, then so be it. I love my wife and I plan on rolling over at ninety, dentures and all, and still having the woman I married lying next to me. So fuck you!" Jeremy stepped inside and slammed the door.

Vernon drove to The Perfect Fit on South Chicago, thinking he'd crash on the couch in his office. Unfortunately, the key card he needed to get in was not-so-safely tucked away in his wallet—a wallet he hadn't seen since he'd left Tanya's place. His life was in that wallet!

Vernon trailed back to the house on Wabash Avenue, testing the bars first to see if he could find a way in. No such luck. He reached in his pockets and pulled out the chump change his "best friend" had given him. Flipping the bills within his fingers, he came up with a brilliant way to show Brandi and Tanya he meant business.

CHAPTER *Seventeen*

Tanya leaned back in the vinyl chair in the solarium, scanning the contract a third time.

Brandi slowly read the terms, her voice polite, almost questioning. "Breakfast at seven, eleven on weekends, a packed lunch for the kids every day and one for myself when I request it. Dinner at seven every evening, whether I'm here or not. By the way, we don't eat pork or catfish."

"That's half of the good stuff. Are you guys Muslim or something?"

"No, but my good parents were." Brandi lowered her gaze back to the document. "Laundry, dusting, grocery shopping, the beds made. Kids' doctors' appointments, track, volleyball."

"Gardening?"

Brandi's liquid brown eyes twinkled with mischief. "No, we have a guy that comes in once a week."

"Windows?"

Brandi shrugged before taking a long, slow breath. "Schedule a service for the windows. As many as this house has, I wouldn't wish them on my worst enemy." Silence extended between them for several seconds before she shrugged. "No pun intended."

"This seems so…strange," Tanya said, taking a long sip of juice. "Why would you help me this way? You don't even know me."

Brandi was silent for a moment. "Because despite outer appearances, you're me with the same broken heart, you're me with the same broken dreams and no direction. And I truly believe we're both victims here—

not enemies. I just think that we'll both come out ahead on this one—and Vernon will get a lesson he'll never forget."

Tanya sighed. "I guess I'll just have to look at it as a new job—one with benefits."

Taken aback at Tanya's summary of the situation, Brandi asked, "What kind of benefits?"

"I can't have children. My mother forced me to have an abortion when I was about twelve."

A sudden welling of compassion flooded her soul. "She forced you? Your own mother? And you were pregnant at twelve?"

Tanya's expression crumbled as a flash of pain leapt into her eyes. "It's a long story. But it's one of the reasons I had to finally leave Georgia when I was fourteen. Why I was so happy that Vernon had children, and now..."

Reaching a hand across the table, Brandi grazed Tanya's arm with a soft, gentle touch. "You can always adopt."

"I didn't want to raise a child by myself."

"Remember, you're not alone now. You have a...*husband* for anything that doesn't require a dick," Brandi said. They both laughed.

The morning sun splayed brightly onto the linoleum floor. Tanya looked up from the contract. "You know, speaking of dick, people are going to think we're lesbians."

"I don't care what people think anymore," Brandi replied evenly. "I've always followed the rules—now I'm making them."

Tanya took a few minutes to absorb that. "What about the kids?"

"Wait a minute," Brandi said, bristling with uneasiness. "What's with all the sudden backpedaling? Whose side are you on here?"

Tanya, who never liked to be yelled at, blinked back tears. "Theirs. They could be hurt by this."

Brandi became suddenly still.

"I came here last night because I was angry and pissed off at how everything had changed so quickly," Tanya said hoarsely. "Never in a million years would I have thought you were serious."

"I wasn't."

Tanya's lips pursed as she wiped away a single tear.

Brandi lowered her gaze, grinning. "Well, at least not at *first.* Now I've put my mouth out there and I'm not taking 'I told you so' from anyone. We're going to make this work even if it kills us. Unless you're having second thoughts?"

"Third and fourth," Tanya said, searching Brandi's eyes for some sign of malice. "For every practical reason, you should hate me."

"I don't hate you. And between you and me, I don't hate him, either," she said, sipping from her second cup of coffee. "I'd still like to give him a swift kick in the rubber parts, though."

Tanya let out a peal of laughter, breaking the tension.

"I have an application I need you to fill out, too." Brandi reached into the folder and pulled out another sheet.

"A contract *and* an application?"

"So you can get health and life insurance from The Perfect Fit. I'm taking you out of the database as a client and putting you on the payroll. That way his money's paying part of your keep. When I get court-ordered maintenance it'll pay the rest." Then Brandi's eyes narrowed. "And another thing..."

Tanya sighed wearily before lifting two fingers to rub her temple.

"During the next six months you're here, take your ass back to school and get a GED or something."

Tanya relaxed slowly. "This is too much."

Brandi became quiet, looking down into her cup. "Did you love him?" She looked up into Tanya's eyes, waiting.

"Vernon made it very hard to love him. I appreciated the security. He was safe, or at least I thought he was. Truthfully, there's never been a time in my life that I could open myself up and trust anyone," Tanya said, her voice just above a whisper. She picked up the application. "Now I'm trusting the one woman on this planet that has no earthly reason to keep me nearby."

"Proving a point is a powerful motivator."

"Yes, but it can also hurt more than just Vernon. Did you think about that?"

Brandi took a sip of coffee. "I'm too numb to think, I can only react."

Those words didn't sit too well with Tanya. What would happen when the numbness went away and the pain truly kicked in?

After enduring a nosy old woman's questions at the currency exchange, the contract was official, with two signatures and a notary. They stopped by Avie's house to pick up the girls.

Avie's keen gaze narrowed on Tanya, who stared right back. The lawyer leaned on the driver's side door, saying, "Brandi, let me talk to you for a minute. Having her in your house will mess up my court case. You're supposed to be the victim here, not trying to make lemonade out of a sour situation. That's my job."

"She stays and that's final."

Minutes later, the girls sat on the couch across from the two women in the solarium of their home. Brandi said, "Mommy needs to talk with you about what's going on, okay?"

Sierra, the younger at ten, looked from Tanya to her mother, then to Simone. The older daughter was dressed in a miniskirt so short even Tanya would think twice about wearing it.

"Tanya's going to live with us for about…six months or so." Brandi looked at Tanya for confirmation. "She's going to take care of things, like keeping the house and getting you girls back and forth to track, gymnastics, and volleyball."

"We help around here. What do we need her for?" Simone demanded. "You're always saying you have three dishwashers: Kenmore, Sierra, and Simone."

"That's true, pumpkin," Brandi said, running a hand over Simone's hair. "But Mommy's been working a lot and there's more to it than just loading the dishwasher. You know what I mean?"

Simone eyed Tanya warily. "What about Daddy?"

"Well, um, Daddy's a little upset about things right now—"

"Why?" Sierra piped in, her soft voice so much like Brandi's.

"I think he wanted Tanya to live somewhere else, but right now I need the help, okay?"

Simone pulled a pillow from next to her and placed it on her lap. "Are you and Daddy getting a divorce?"

Brandi shook her head. "No, not that. We still love each other. It's just a little grown-up misunderstanding."

"A misunderstanding that has to do with his client?" Simone asked, glaring openly at Tanya. *Did the little girl know more than they thought?* Brandi thought. All she said was, "We're just working some things out. Don't you worry about a thing."

Sierra piped up. "Is Tanya still going to teach us how to bake Red Velvet cake?"

"I'm sure she will. Why don't you two get your room together and lay out your clothes for school next week."

When the girls were gone, Tanya let out a long sigh of relief.

Brandi laughed, giving her hand a gentle pat. "Let it go. I'm not going to blast you every time someone makes mention of Vernon. And I'm not blaming you for anything. Unless there's something you're not telling me..." Her gaze leveled on Tanya as she waited a few moments. "No? Then it's a done deal. Our contract will stand no matter what the outcome of my marriage or what happens in your life. If no one else stays true to their word, we, as women should. Deal?"

"Okay, okay," Tanya said, shaking Brandi's outstretched hand. "No matter what, we'll fulfill the terms of the contract."

"And you can't keep turning red every time someone makes reference to your relationship with Vernon."

Brandi was very much at ease with being in control of things, just like Mama Diane, Tanya thought, who had run a household of four girls and three boys with a warmth that had never graced the halls of the Van Oy mansion. The fact that the wheels were still turning even after she had closed in for the kill reminded Tanya of her own mother.

Margaret Van Oy Jaunal, a woman once known for her warm nature and sunny disposition, had become cold and distant by the time Tanya turned ten. The woman wouldn't stand up for herself even if Gloria Steinem gave her personal instructions. She stayed home to take care of her husband, relishing the fact that a mistake she had made in her teenage years had turned out to be the best mistake of her life.

Wilbur Jaunal actually couldn't read and write, but he could fake it by talking a good game and keeping only a few people close to him. Margaret Van Oy had spent time in between their romps on the backseat to teach him how. So with the help of his wife, they formed a plan to break down the structure of Social Circle.

When Jaunal became mayor—which he managed by using the manpower of the Black population—he believed that they would be forever grateful that he had favored them with employment over their equally educated white counterparts. He thought he could easily lead and direct Blacks. This thinking almost cost him more than his political office; it almost cost him the main source of his cash flow.

On a dark July night in 1956, an unmasked lynch mob from Jersey killed George and May Murray and Dorsey and Dorothy Malcolm as they crossed the bridge to visit relatives in Social Circle. Several rallies—with walks from Mars Hill Baptist Church all the way to the bridge that spread out over the Apalachee River—had signaled that it was time the killers were brought to justice. Blacks also began to travel in armed groups—knives instead of guns being the weapon of choice. People were liable to give you a deadly ear-to-ear smile than draw a gun and shoot—either way got the same results. Jersey whites gained a different outlook on Blacks from the area, especially when a few of the most racist disappeared with not a fare-thee-well to family or friends.

Years later Wilbur Jaunal's manipulations tried to bring that rift back to Social Circle. After making sure that Black folk were the majority of the workforce inside Social Circle, he tried to pull a fast one, lowering the pay scale across the board to a few notches above minimum wage.

Michelle Pitchford, Tanya's best friend, told her that her father had a convenient "accident" on that same day. Because he drove the carpool that brought in four other managers, it shut down the whole business for two days. When the middle-level management walked, the ones under them walked, too. Blacks were not to be taken for granted.

Jaunal reinstated salaries faster than the Social Circle Bridge Club could down a few bottles of plum wine.

Tanya had learned to never underestimate people based on their color. Most of the teachers in Social Circle were Black, which meant the intelligence base in this one small city was all on equal footing, even though Blacks were taught in a church up until 1968 when laws were passed forcing integration. Afterward, Black principals ran all three schools in Social Circle. White children in the area learned early on to respect their intelligence. Well, at least Tanya did. And no one looked at her sideways because her best friend was Black and from the poorer side of town.

Vernon had underestimated Brandi's intelligence and her ability to change a bad situation into one that worked for her. Vernon had also underestimated Tanya's willingness to learn from the best.

CHAPTER Eighteen

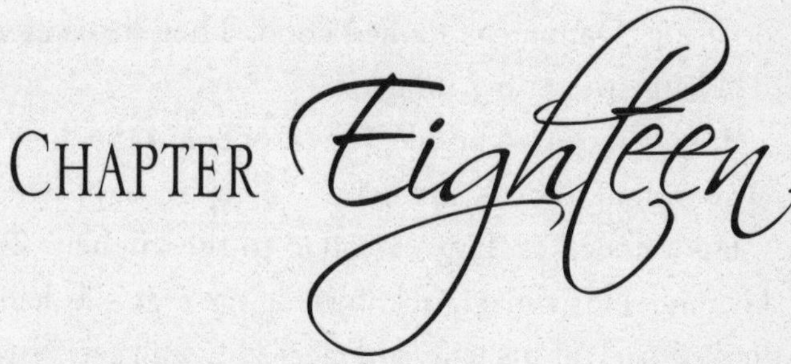

Vernon parked in front of Jeremy's house and sat for a moment. How had things come to this? He loved Brandi but wanted Tanya, too, though certainly not on her terms. If he let her dictate, the next thing she'd want was to run the whole damn show. Which was never gonna happen.

Afraid of getting another cold reception with Lissette looking on, he placed a call to Jeremy's cell, and practically twisted the man's arm to sneak out of the house to help with the U-Haul rental. Without a driver's license Venon couldn't do squat.

Later when they went back to Jeremy's house on Saturday afternoon to move his car, it was no longer in the driveway. Jeremy's neighbor was raking the leaves and looked up in time to tell him, "A flatbed came about an hour ago and lugged it away. Mrs. Shipp was standing outside when they did it."

Damn, Lissette had probably figured out what Jeremy was up to, called Brandi and they cooked that shit up, too!

Jeremy grimaced, taking in the sour expression on his wife's face. Then he popped Vernon upside the head before turning to walk away from him without a backwards glance.

Vernon pulled up in front of the house in Jackson Park Highlands in the U-Haul. He had waited all morning to get it and now it seemed pointless. He could only hope that his wife's plan had backfired.

Moments later he knocked. Tanya peeked out, then opened the door, looking better than he could remember. A halter top and a pair of chinos did nothing to hide her curves. The soft scent of Satsuma wafted over him with every shake of her head. His dick stirred and nearly rose to the occasion. Damn, she looked good. Then he came to his senses.

"I came to get my things."

Brandi appeared beside Tanya, opening the door wide, draping a single arm around Tanya's shoulders. "They're right where you left them."

He watched as Tanya strolled to the kitchen. Brandi's gaze locked on his, and she winked, acknowledging that she had seen everything. He looked back at his wife and cleared his throat. "I won't be long."

"Take all the time you want, dear heart. This is your house, too." Brandi's generous mouth stretched into a wide, sexy smile. God, what he wouldn't give to kiss her. Jesus! What was wrong with him? He could never live in a house with both of them. He'd be hard so often, people would think it was coat rack.

Tanya appeared in the kitchen doorway holding a steaming cup of coffee. The smell assaulted his nose like a criminal making a break for freedom. His empty stomach growled. Vernon hadn't eaten since Friday afternoon. He'd bounced around from place to place since then and still hadn't found a place to hole up. Judging by the solid stare and arms folded across her breasts, he knew it would be a while before Brandi came around. He could tough it out. The game was on.

"Why did you lock me out of my house?"

Brandi answered in a perky, cheerleader tone. "Because I want us to be one big happy family." Then her tone came back to normal. "We can't do that if you're living somewhere else, honey."

Tanya bit her bottom lip and swallowed hard, shoulders shaking slightly. Her eyes, with a twinkle of mischief flashing in them, never left Vernon's face. Slowly she twisted her wrist, checking her watch before giving it a little tap.

Bitch! Vernon turned to his wife. "You're lying and I know it."

Unmoved, Brandi sank down in the wingback chair near the foyer. "Takes one to know one. And I thought you had scooped up the Oscar for that category."

There was no way in hell to win an argument when she was like this.

An hour later, he'd packed his things in the U-Haul. He turned to face the women now sitting on opposite ends of the sofa. They were watching Lifetime on television. Just what they needed, female rights reinforcement.

As much as he hated to do it, he had to ask, "Have either of you seen my wallet?"

There was a slight hesitation as the women looked at each other and shrugged. "It should still be in your pants." Brandi grinned and winked. "Unless you're still having trouble keeping them on."

"You wiseass."

She blew him a fake kiss. "Ahhhh, you have such a way with words. See why I married him, Tanya?"

One of them knew where his wallet was. Monday the bank would sort things out, but until then he was strapped.

He turned to Brandi, whose smile had become a smirk. He knew she would refuse his request for cash or one of her cards.

"I'll cancel the cards on Monday. You might not have access to our accounts then."

"Oh, no, sweetheart," she said, blinking innocently, "we have two different numbers on our cards now. I changed them recently. Only yours will be affected." She winked and grinned so slyly, he wanted to jump across the room and wring her damn neck.

A sudden burst of alarm shot through him. Somehow he knew, just knew, that she had more going on than she let on. Had she already wiped out their accounts? Fuck!

Sierra and Simone filed into the living room. "Daddy!"

His heart melted at the sight of his little darlings. Bending down, he stretched out his arms to hug them. Simone was tall and slender with a ponytail draped down her back, Sierra, smaller and more round, had hair that barely touched her shoulders. Both had smiles that could make the sun rise and his heart dance with joy. Each was a perfect combination of Brandi's creamy light brown beauty and Vernon's chiseled features. At least that was something that was purely a natural thing. Because even something as simple as naming them had been an issue.

❤❤❤

Two months before Simone was born Brandi had said, "I want her to have my last name, too."

Startled out of good sleep, he had turned over and replied, "Children should take on the last name of their father."

"Why—because it's tradition?" she snapped. "Well, I'm not going for it. They'll have both of our names or just mine alone."

Fully awake, Vernon sat up in bed. "No way in hell is that going to happen."

"And why can't I have some say?" she asked, rubbing a hand over her huge stomach.

"Because I'm head of the household."

"Yes, but you're not the one who's enduring the morning sickness, going to the bathroom every ten minutes, backaches that last for days," she shot back. "Then I'm the one who has to squeeze a couple of heads of lettuce through an opening meant for a carrot. Unless you're doing more than just getting your rocks off on this one, stud, I suggest you get used to either a hyphen between our names or enjoy the extra space between us in bed. You pick."

The children had both their names. And it was only when they put Simone in school that he finally understood Brandi's logic. Caldwell was a lot further up the alphabet than Spencer. Having been called nearly last for the majority of everything in his life, Vernon could see the wisdom in the girls having his wife's last name. Still, it would have been nice if Brandi had voiced it that way instead of making it a major two-month fight. But then again, maybe he wouldn't have seen it that way if she had.

He had tried to get Brandi to at least try once more for a son, but she refused, saying she hadn't wanted children in the first place. At times he realized the mistake of convincing her to have children since it didn't get the desired result—a wife that would be so devoted to her kids she would stay at home and leave the business end of things to him. That had been wishful thinking on his part, and consistent pressure from his dad. Pressure that created more problems than Vernon could count.

"Daddy, we missed you."

"You did, sweetheart?" he said, hugging Simone.

"Yes!" Sierra said, gazing adoringly into his eyes. "Where were you?"

Vernon looked up in time to see Brandi's smirk reappear. "Oooooh, here and there," he said, glaring at his wife. "I'm going to be away for a little while, but I'll come and pick you up sometime, okay?"

"Daddy, please don't go." The soft, lilting sound of his younger daughter's voice pierced his heart.

"I have to, baby. I don't have a choice," he answered, looking back at a scowling Brandi.

Tanya being around every day wouldn't be good for them. Had Brandi thought beyond her own selfishness? Okay, he shouldn't have slept around on her and all that, but damn! He wasn't hurting anybody. And if someone hadn't clued her in, she still wouldn't have a problem. Neither would Tanya. An after careful thought, he knew who that someone was...

The girls held onto him, wanting to know why he had to leave. An instant of understanding coursed through him. If there was any way of pulling things back together, it was through the girls. The look on Brandi's face when the girls asked, for a fourth time, why he was leaving, had been worth millions.

His wife simply said in a stony voice, "Your daddy brought us a new family member who can help out around here. Then *he* changed his mind. I haven't."

Tanya leaned on the door frame, waiting for him to contradict the woman of the house. Now what could he say to that?

Things were getting real complicated, real fast.

Hours later, around sunset, after much soul-searching, he realized that he would have to do some tall talking, but maybe, just maybe Mama would let him stay. But after mentally preparing himself, especially after what he had done to her, then going to her house only to find her gone, Vernon ended up at Craig's house.

Craig opened the door and Vernon quickly made his request. Alanna, a dark-skinned beauty with killer curves and a luscious pair of lips, appeared beside her man, glowering angrily at Vernon. Seconds later, she yanked Craig inside and slammed the door. A stunned Vernon could hear their heated voices through the screen door.

"But that's my friend," Craig yelled. "You can't just leave him out there like that."

"You want to join him?"

Craig stammered, "I—I—I—No!"

"Then I suggest you keep your nose out of this business. This is *my* house and I won't have a lying, cheating asshole like him under my roof."

"I pay the bills around this place, too," Craig shot back. "We can't leave him out in the cold."

"Well, I'll give you a choice," Alanna shot back. "If Vernon comes in, I'm walking out—with the kids!"

Silence from the home team.

Game over, man. Game over!

Vernon strolled back to the truck and drove back to his mother's place, knocking on the door for what seemed an eternity, but there was still no answer.

A neighbor, Mrs. Morton, peeked over the waist-high bushes, saying, "You might as well give up until next week. She's in the Bahamas."

"Next week!" The whole world was against him. "What's she doing in the Bahamas?"

"On a literary cruise with someone named Zane or Strebor or something like that." Then the pug-nosed, silver-haired woman added in her raspy voice, "She went with that new fellow of hers. He's downright fantastic! She deserves him. More than I can say for that bigmouth father of yours."

Vernon resisted the urge to flip the woman the finger. His mother would never let him hear the end of it. New man? His mama had a new man?

When did that happen? And was the buzzard living with her? Where would that leave him? He turned to walk back to the car.

His mother's neighbor said, "They're going to Hedonism with the same group next month."

Vernon paused, and turned back to the old woman. "Isn't that the place folks walk around…naked?"

"Yep," she said, giving him a grin. "That's the spot."

His mother? Romping around naked on the beach with some man? Good Lord!

Having depleted the last of his cash, Vernon had little options. Parking the U-Haul in the lot at the office, hoping that the regular security guard would come on duty and let him in, Vernon yanked the blanket over his shoulders and curled up for another cold night.

CHAPTER *Nineteen*

Brandi stretched out on the solarium sun lounger, reading *When Somebody Loves You Back*, hoping the Mary B. Morrison novel would take her mind off her husband. Though it was an exceptional read, the steamy sex scenes only served to make her want to sprint to the nearest dildo. She missed her husband already. How arrogant for him to believe that showing up in a U-Haul would make her change her mind and take him back. If she made things that easy, he'd do it again. No, she and her little toys would continue to be best friends for a while until Vernon got the message. But then again, he'd always been arrogant, so she couldn't expect him to learn quickly. His arrogance almost caused her to overlook him in the first place.

❤❤❤

What was Morehouse doing to those men? Brandi thought as she and Avie cut in front of Fisk's administration building, trying to get to her dorm room at Crosswaite Hall. Confidence was one thing, but arrogance that boded on a superiority complex was a total waste of manhood—and every one of the Morehouse Seven had it. They came up every other weekend now, working with the spring line of pledges, and wreaked havoc with the female population the moment they stepped on campus. Fisk men had a southern gentleman edge laced with a Chicago cool that she found attractive. Michael Cobb was the man for her. Vernon had a touch of bad boy, reminding her a bit of Hollywood—a type she'd vowed to stay as far away from as possible. Vernon made that practically impossible. He and the Morehouse Seven showed up for all the parties in Jubilee Hall. Thanks to having a party animal for a roommate and best friend, Brandi showed up for the parties more than she wanted.

Vernon sprinted across the lawn, catching up with her and Avie before the girls reached Crosswaite. "So what's up, baby?"

"Nothing but education," Brandi said, giving him a cursory glance. He wore a Morehouse T-shirt over his muscular frame, and a pair of jeans that fit his butt in a way that said, "Touch at your own risk!" He was enough to make any woman spread 'em like Imperial margarine.

"So when are you going to let me take you to dinner?"

Brandi shrugged, but didn't break her stride. "Monday. Monday's good for me."

Avie let out a little chuckle.

Vernon's thick eyebrows drew in. "But I'll be back in Atlanta by then."

Brandi grinned and gave him a little wink.

"Oh, take the dagger out of my heart, woman," he said, jerking his fist away from his chest. "You're killing me!"

"You'll get over it."

He reached out and swiped the books from her hand. "Why do you think I keep coming up here?"

"Because you have nothing better to do with your time or money."

"No, I want you and I've never hidden that fact," he said softly. "Even that giant-sized Fiskite hasn't scared me off."

She stopped walking. "Michael?"

"Is that his real name? We call him monster. He told me if I hurt you, he'll slice off my balls and serve them up two days later for Sunday brunch."

"Ooooo." Brandi gleefully rubbed her hands together. "Now that sounds like a plan."

"Why are you so cold to me?"

"It has nothing to do with you and everything to do with your big head and the fact that you and your crew think that you're better than everyone else."

He grinned. "What's wrong with being confident?"

"That's not confidence! That's arrogance. You don't allow anyone else to admire what's good about you. I have a huge problem with that."

"Okay. So what *do* you admire about me?"

Avie looked over at him and shook her head. "You don't want her to tell the truth on that one."

"Try me."

Brandi shrugged and said. "I admire your gorgeous rear end."

He perked up with a cheesy smile.

"Because it means you're getting the hell away from me," she concluded.

"Woman, you're just plain mean," he said as she and Avie laughed. "Do you know what I like about you?"

"Oh, I'd hate to imagine."

Suddenly all humor left his handsome face as he said, "Your smile, when you grace the world with it, your laugh because it sounds like music, your quick wit because you always have a fast comeback. But mostly your eyes draw me." He lifted her chin with a single finger so their eyes met. "The sadness in them reminds me that there's so much wrong with the world."

She didn't have a fast comeback for that.

"If there was any way that I could make that sadness go away, I'd do it in a heartbeat."

At that moment, Brandi's heart opened and allowed Vernon partway in. He kissed her softly, gently—exploring the moist depths of her mouth with a tongue that teased just because it could. Damn, he tasted good. He ended with a gentle peck on her temple before walking away. His rear end, full and gorgeous, really did look wonderful.

Then the next weekend he brought her flowers.

"Cymbidium orchids?" she said, looking at the card. "Why can't you just bring roses like everybody else?"

"Roses? Too common, baby," he said with a little bow. "Roses say, 'George Jetson, you must've goofed up somewhere.'"

She laughed. "You're been watching too many cartoons. George Jetson goofed up most of the time and Jane had to get him out of it."

"I guess that's a matter of perception," he said softly. He spread his jacket out in the center of the open field which ran along all buildings of the campus. He lay down making himself comfortable before beckoning her to take the place next to him. Placing her books to the side, she sat down and watched him for a moment, marveling at how easy he could tune out the outside campus circling around them. Soon, he reached out, pulling her close and held her as they stared up at the Nashville sky, watching the clear blue coloring draped across the atmosphere as though it was an oil painting.

Her hands were laced in his, her heart raced at almost the speed of a locomotive, and perspiration peppered her forehead: Anxiety, curiosity, and fear trying to occupy the same space at the same time.

He turned his head, kissing her cheek.

Curiosity won, but only slowly. "I'm afraid."

"I know. That's why we're going to spend the whole summer getting you to a point where you don't pull away from even the simplest touch."

Their heads were touching at the hairline. She glanced down. "Uh, is that part of you going to be cool with that?"

"Hey, I got him under control."

"Famous last words!"

"Your eyes remind me of my mother," he said, stroking a finger across her cheek. "She's been hurt, too. Being married to my father is no picnic. I should've seen what was really going on with you at first, but I was too busy being your favorite asshole."

"Don't beat yourself up. You weren't being an asshole, you were being a *whole* ass."

He jerked his fist away from his chest, removing another imaginary dagger. "And she still manages to sneak one in."

"You asked for that."

He paused for a moment. "Brandi, I know this is short notice, but I was wondering, when you come home for spring break next week, will you come to my house and meet my parents?"

She rose up, resting on one elbow. "Really?"

"My mother's dying to get a look at you."

She was elated by the thought, but what he didn't say scared her a bit. "And your father?"

He tried to come up with the words. "Well, my father's a bit…he's um—"

"Indescribable. Sort of like you when I first met you."

"We're gonna have to do something about that sharp tongue of yours. Two teaspoons of honey every morning."

"I thought I'd get a call from you in the mornings."

"And so you shall."

Vernon was right about two things. She had his heart and William Spencer was indescribable. He hated Brandi on sight.

CHAPTER *Twenty*

Vernon strolled up to the front door of The Perfect Fit early Monday morning, still grumbling about his lost wallet. His key card was in there and the office sofa would have been a damn sight better than sleeping in the U-Haul all weekend. Today the regular guard was on duty and let him in, unlike that big bear of a bitch that had given him a hard time when he showed up on Saturday night. He would have her ass fired as soon as he got her name.

He walked through the slate-gray marble foyer, with its plush navy seats, and past the conference room. His gaze scanned the entire floor. A single light was on in an office at the end of the hallway.

Rage lit a fire inside him as he stormed down the hallway, past the file room and the cafeteria, realizing that the only person who could have started this whole thing had nerve enough to be in the office early. If things had gone as planned, he would have put back the money he used to purchase Tanya's house and ring before Brandi figured it out. Even if she had, he was ready with an explanation.

"Can I have a word with you?"

Michael Cobb, their accountant, looked up from the pink documents in his hands, staring expressionlessly at Vernon as he placed it to the side. "Sure."

"What in the hell possessed you to tell Brandi?"

Michael's skin turned a shade darker. His eyes flashed with anger although his full lips curved with a trace of a sad smile. "Because at the rate you were spending, it wouldn't just cost me the account with The Perfect Fit for keeping my mouth shut, it would also cost other people their jobs."

Michael's secretary, Jackie, wearing a fur that swallowed her small frame, stopped in the entrance. Her eyes swept briefly over Vernon, then took in Michael's angry glare.

Vernon kicked the door closed. He couldn't quite catch what she said next, but he sure heard her as she stormed to her desk.

"That was real *special*. A gentleman through and through," Michael snapped, eyeing Vernon angrily. "Let me tell you what raised a red flag for me. Ten thousand for an engagement ring? The money to cover that had to come from somewhere. Next thing you know the bills don't get paid around here, then pay cuts and layoffs follow." The tall, well-built man leaned back in his chair, leveling a steely gaze at Vernon. "I value my job, even if you didn't value your wife. She should've married me when she had the chance." He smiled, but it don't quite reach his light brown eyes. "But I believe in second chances. I've known since day one that you were going to mess up. All I had to do was wait. Thirteen years is nothing in the grand scheme of things."

"So that's what this is about," Vernon said, crossing the distance in long strides to lean over the man's glass desk. "You want my wife?"

"Correction, my man. I *will* have your…ex-wife." Michael stood, leaning into Vernon. "I've waited long enough and now that she's seen what an asshole you are—it's prime time, baby. The only reason's she stuck it out this far is because she hates failure. I'll make her see that divorcing you is not failure. You were just a starter husband, like the number zero—a placeholder until a *real* number comes along."

The man flipped his collar in a confident manner that irritated the hell out of Vernon, but he recognized the determination in Michael's voice. He had used it himself when trying to win Brandi over. "If you even *think* about touching my wife—"

"You'll do what?" Michael came around the desk, covering the short space between them with the agility of a panther. "Hit me? Negro, I'd like to see you try. I'll beat all the natural black off you, then go for the cowardly shit that's left behind. How dare you treat her this way!

"You know what?" Vernon said, as anger shot through him, "You don't have to worry about losing the account with us. You're fired! Get your shit and don't let the door hit ya where the good Lord split ya." The man was so close, Vernon could smell cinnamon on his breath. Silence expanded between them.

Then Michael said, "You're firing me? Good! Then I can go out in style—at *your* expense. You'll be hearing from my lawyer."

"You will never have Brandi. Not as long as I draw breath on this earth."

Michael perched on the edge of his desk. "Well, I can arrange for you to draw breath somewhere else." He shrugged as he walked back behind the desk and sank down into the chair. "Six feet under sounds good to me. Buried alive is something I can handle."

After a moment the words penetrated. Vernon turned to walk out.

"Mr. Spencer, there's a place that all divorced men go," Michael said in a somber tone.

Vernon yanked open the door, but turned back to face his self-proclaimed enemy.

"It's called Never, Never, Ever Again Land. I'll mail your tickets."

"Stay the hell away from my wife."

"*Ex*-wife." Michael pointed a single index finger at Vernon's chest. "*Ex* marks the spot." Then he grinned. "Come to think of it, maybe I should tell her the real truth about things before I make my exit. Your choice. Still want to fire me?"

Vernon stormed out of Michael's office, nearly trampling over a shrieking secretary who had the misfortune of stepping in his path. Minutes later he stood in front of Brandi's assistant. "Is my wife in?"

Renee gasped sharply, soft brown eyes scanning over him as she pinched her nose. "She...hasn't been in yet."

"I want to know the moment she steps in." Vernon turned. Every employee stared back at him, not a single movement among them. "What are you looking at?"

The group scattered, some turning back to their desks to begin working again. All left a wide berth for Vernon to go any direction he chose—as long as it wasn't too close to them.

Timothy, the marketing director, yanked Vernon's collar. The golden-skinned man with the shiny bald head glared openly at him. "Man, get yourself together. You look like hell. Your shirt's all wrinkled and your pants are unzipped. You look like someone dragged you out of the garbage, after they'd dunked you in a few times. Pull yourself together and quit snapping at people."

"When I want or need your advice, I'll pay you for it," Vernon snapped. Anger stemming from the weekend's events came to the forefront. Of course he wasn't in top shape. First his father kicking him out on suspicion of what he "thought" might happen with Julie, then Craig and Jeremy turning their backs on him; his mother being incogNegro, Tanya's house being locked up. And damn it, his health club card was in that wallet! Where the hell was it?

Timothy gripped his arm and ushered him toward the office at the opposite end of the hall. "I'll let that slide 'cause I know you're having a bad morning." His eyes shot daggers. "Here, let me walk you to your office."

Vernon pulled away. "I don't need you to—"

The man blocked his path like a football player protecting the goal line. "I can walk with you or carry you. Your choice," he said quietly. "I'd prefer you walk on your own." Vernon tried to walk around him, but Timothy's hand held him in place. "I'll lead. You smell a little ripe. I definitely don't want to be downwind."

At the door leading to his office, Vernon turned to his wide-eyed assistant. "Let me know the minute my wife gets in."

He barely saw her nod before Timothy closed the door behind them. "I know you're upset about what's going down, but taking it out on everybody's just not cool."

"Man, what the hell do you know?"

"More than I should," Timothy shot back. "And if you're going to be treating everyone like stepchildren around this camp, then take your grumpy ass home or wherever the hell you just came from."

Taken aback by the man's vicious tone, Vernon snapped, "I'm your boss! Don't tell me what to do."

"Then start acting like a boss instead of a man who's lost his damn manhood. You almost gave Charmaine whiplash. Quit acting like what's happening to you is the end of the world."

Vernon's gaze narrowed on the man in front of him. "How do you know what's going on?"

"There's three modes of communication in the world: telephone, telegraph and tell-a-woman. Fabian's a card-carrying member of the last club. She told the whole office about Brandi and your mistress. You didn't know the office gossip was sleeping with Brandi's cousin? Man, you're more out of touch than I thought."

Slumping down on the sofa, Vernon let out a long weary sigh. "So everybody knows."

"Thanks to that crap you just pulled, they will in a minute. Bad news travels faster than a check hits the bank before payday."

He settled into the sofa, a far cry better than the hard leather seats of the U-Haul, and the office was definitely a place he wouldn't have to fight little critters.

"Take a nap or something. Better yet, take some Midol. You have the worst case of PMS I've ever seen."

"Men don't get PMS."

"There's a first time for everything," Timothy said on his way out.

Vernon covered himself with a jacket. Amazingly, no one—not a single friend—would help him. The women of the world had bonded to make his life miserable. Damn! All he did was the same that most men do—have something going on the side. No harm, no foul. Even his father, three-timer that he was, the man Vernon expected to understand more than anyone else, had given Vernon an eye-opener.

No matter how many doors Brandi managed to close, he still wouldn't grace the doors of their home if Tanya were still there.

He should have returned the U-Haul by noon on Saturday. Instead, he'd been carting it around, still loaded with all of his things, for the past two days, still unable to find a home base. Asking an employee if he could stay with them was practically out of the question, but then again he did pay their salaries, right? He'd sleep on it for a bit.

Vernon stretched out on the black leather couch, pulling the throw up to his chin. His wife would have to show up to the office at some time. He'd just take a little nap until she did.

Brandi strolled into Avie's office just as her friend answered the phone.

"Avie Davidson, I'm here to help you."

Brandi plopped down in the chair, whispering, "Oooooh, I need about... two million dollars for starters."

Avie covered the phone and whispered, "Then you need to put on that tight black dress and hook it on the street right next to me. Rake in your own cash, heifer."

Brandi laughed, picked up a magazine, and leafed through the pages.

When Avie wrapped up the call, she dropped the phone into the cradle, and leveled a piercing hazel gaze on her friend.

"What?" Brandi said, laughing again. "You're not bringing in five grand per night anymore?"

"Taxes and cost of living, baby," she said with a wide smile. "What's up?"

"We need to get prepared for separation or divorce."

Avie said in a bitter, teasing tone, "But I thought you didn't want a divorce."

"Yeah, and I know that you were really upset about that, but I know him and I don't want to be blindsided either. If nothing else, I want to separate the company and our finances right away. I've wanted to do that for a while and he's been dead set against it."

The lawyer in her friend kicked in as she scribbled on her pad, then looked up. "All right. Now on to other things. You proved your point. It's time to get that heifer out of your house."

Brandi turned another page in the magazine. "Why?"

"How can you trust her?"

"How can I not?" Brandi looked up from the page. "It's been two weeks. She's been true to her word and the kids love her. She keeps the house immaculate and I start the day off with a hearty breakfast, come back at night to a home-cooked meal, and on a good day, I'll even have a packed lunch. She's organized my closets and she keeps my personal calendar."

Avie shook her head. "You could have a maid to do that."

"I don't think a maid would have a vested interest like Tanya does. She gets room and board, plus a salary and benefits—and she takes care of me." Brandi let her gaze pass over the new painting of the three founding lawyers in the corner. "This will send a message to him to never do this again. What more can I ask?"

Avie let her head drop, staring at the tan carpet. "It's just…so unnatural."

"Why? Because I put *his* behind on front street instead of being pissed off with *her*?" Brandi snapped. "Because I used the situation to meet my needs instead of taking it out on her?" She shook her head. "I turned my anger directly where it needs to be—on him and the situation." She pretended not to notice her friend's annoyance. "I've gotten the best end of the deal. His woman is now my wife."

Avie, ever the debater, remained strangely silent. She stared at Brandi as though she didn't recognize the woman who had been her matron of honor, the woman who had gone out of her way to help keep the relationship intact when Veronica Chapman had tried like hell to come between Avie and Carlton. When the wedding ceremony had been halted, and everyone started giving each other curious stares, Brandi had followed the two women and came up on them just as the argument had ended.

Avie returned to the church, and Veronica, persistent bitch that she was, tried to follow. Brandi's hand snaked out, pushing her down into the mud to keep her from coming back into the wedding to protest and spread the rumor that she was pregnant. Turns out it was a lie anyway—Carlton hadn't been with the woman since Moses held the rod.

"I think I enjoy being a husband. I'm tired of carrying the whole load." Brandi placed her feet on the edge of the desk, glaring at Avie, daring the woman to knock the heels away. "And I truly believe that if we bring home the bacon, just like a man, then we damn sure shouldn't have to fry it up and clean the damn skillet, too."

Avie shrugged hopelessly. "So that's your rationale for this bull?"

"You know, you're the last person I expected to object to this. Aren't you the one who said it's high time that we women flex our muscles? Well, I'm all for that. We can't always control what happens with the dick, but we sure can react a hell of a lot differently and make it damn inconvenient for men to pull stuff like this."

Avie took a moment to mull that over. "So this plan of yours means he can still sleep with her?"

"Oh no," Brandi said with a little laugh. "He won't come within twenty feet of the house while she's there. And she won't have anything to do with him."

"So they tell you."

Brandi winced at her friend's caustic tone. "If you heard her crying at night you'd understand. Every time she does something for me, she's learning more about who and what I am. She's realizing I was his partner, the one to whom he pledged his loyalty, through sickness and in health, until death do us part. I held to that. Right now, she's shedding the same kind of tears that I did when I felt insecure about myself, insecure about pleasing my husband. They're both learning something. And I'm not done yet."

❤❤❤

Strangely enough, it had been a conversation with Avie all those years ago that had convinced her that maybe she should give Vernon a chance.

"Arrogant Negro," Brandi muttered, trying to put some distance between herself and the crowd of boisterous boys hanging out near Jubilee Hall.

Luckily, they weren't allowed beyond the gold or blue rooms. As the tour guide told a group of parents and incoming freshman, "If your daughter was a slut in high school, she won't be a ho up in here."

That might have put parents at ease, but it only served to make the students more resourceful. When there's dick on one side of the campus and pussy on the other, they *will* meet somewhere in between.

"Homecoming's right around the corner, do you know where your date is?" Avie asked.

"I don't have a date. Michael's not speaking to me because he thinks I'm seeing Vernon—thanks to all that boy's bull." She grimaced as she looked at her friend. "I'm not as fortunate as *some* people to have my man lined up for the next hundred years."

"If you'd stop being so much of a bitch," Avie shot back, "then maybe someone would snatch your tail up. Someone like Vernon Spencer."

"Arrrrgggggh, don't mention his name to me," Brandi retorted. "You know what that asshole did? When I walked into the cafeteria, he had all the Alphas stand and look in my direction. Then they surrounded me as I walked to my spot."

Avie batted her eyes dreamily. "That's so sweet."

"Sweet my ass! You know people actually think we're together? I couldn't get a date if I prepaid for one."

"You can't get a date because of your stank-ass attitude, acting like you don't take a shit like the rest of us. Carlton said the fellas have named you Fudgsicle. Gorgeous and chocolate on the outside, colder than a witch's tit on the inside."

Brandi gasped. "No!"

Avie nodded. "Why don't you give the man a try? Just a date."

"Because he'll expect more than just 'thanks for dinner,' he'll want a side order of ass and I'm not giving it."

"So just give him a half-order—a kiss and a hand job worked for Carlton."

Janet Jackson's *Control* played in the background. One of Brandi's favorite albums.

"I've never even heard you talk about getting some," Avie said softly. "Are you going to stay a virgin the rest of your life?"

A sudden flash of that awful day came across her mind. "I'm not a virgin."

"Well, as your best friend, I sure haven't heard any juicy first-time stories."

"It's not open for discussion," Brandi said in a firm tone.

"It's like that, huh? I tell you about losing my virginity in installments and—"

Brandi's eyes widened. "You never said that—"

"I didn't tell you about that weeklong venture?"

"Nope. You told me your first time was with this boy named John and that's it."

"Okay, well, the real deal is that I didn't lose my virginity all in the same day. On the way to the store, I would sneak by John's house. I was curious about sex because my mother kept stressing that I should keep my legs closed. She took me to the doctor every week to confirm that I was still a virgin. I got tired of going and decided, what the hell! Let's see what's so important anyway and then the doctor visits will stop. People were beginning to think I had leukemia or something."

Brandi shook her head.

"Mama always gave me an hour to go to the store. If I ran, it really only took me ten minutes to get there, ten minutes to get what I was sent for, and ten minutes to get back home, which means I had a whole thirty minutes to play around." She lifted her eyebrows. "If you know what I mean."

Brandi shook her head. "You horny little heifer."

Avie nodded enthusiastically. "I would cut through Mrs. Nolan's backyard, hop the fence, and cut through Mrs. White's backyard to get to the next block. Then I crossed the street and two more yards and one fence later, I was at John's house. We didn't take a whole lot of time, either. We'd start with kissing," she sang the old Gladys Knight tune, "touching and hugging and…" Her voice returned to normal. "Well, you know the rest—all of this was trying to get me hot enough to do it. By the time we did all that and he put his penis at the tip, it was time for me to go. The first time it made it only to the opening. The next day it was about an inch in, but as he did, it was time to get dressed and go home. The day after that, he got it in two inches, then it was time to go."

"You're kidding, right?" Brandi said, laughing.

Avie shook her head. "The fourth day, he got it halfway in and then it was—"

"Time to go," Brandi supplied.

"The fifth day it was almost all in, but I made him stop because it hurt worse than all the other times—*and*—"

"It was time to go."

Avie grinned. "Then we had to wait, because I didn't do the store thing on Saturdays or Sundays. Sneaking in between while I was outside playing wouldn't work because John's father was home. So we didn't resume operation 'lose my virginity' until the following Monday."

"Girl, you're so crazy." Brandi stretched out on the bed and looked up at the ceiling.

"This time John's penis made it all the way in and he pulled out and gave me a couple of thrusts and then—it was—"

"Damn, time to go," Brandi said. "You're making me frustrated!"

"The next time—it was all out-screwing and that was the only time it felt all right. But then suddenly three of his boys appeared out of nowhere, dicks in hand, demanding a little piece of the action. No one was running a train on my ass, so I grabbed two of John's baseball trophies and swung out. I hit him first, then Jeffrey who was standing at the edge of the bed took one upside the head. Two of the boys backed away, but one said, 'She's only a girl.' Well this *girl* lifted the trophy to hit him as he came toward me, then surprised him by kicking him dead in the nuts. He hit the ground. I looked at the other two and said, 'You sure you want some of this?' Both shook their heads and took off."

"Girl, remind me not to piss you off." Then she leaned rolled onto her side. "So what happened on the next trip to the doctor?"

"I was looking forward to my mother finding out that I no longer was a virgin. Unfortunately, the patient-doctor privilege kept the doctor from telling about my escapades with John. He told me that he could never tell her, but at seventy-five dollars per visit, he was always glad to see us stop by."

Brandi let out a hearty laugh.

"He told me about different types of birth control and introduced me to condoms. Anything other than condoms would have required a consultation with my mother. So condoms became the weapon of choice."

Brandi laughed so hard she almost peed.

"Now see, that's a first-time story."

"Not every first time is like that," Brandi said, thinking back to her thirteenth birthday. "What happened to me was no laughing matter. I'll tell you about it, but just not right now, okay?"

CHAPTER Twenty-Two

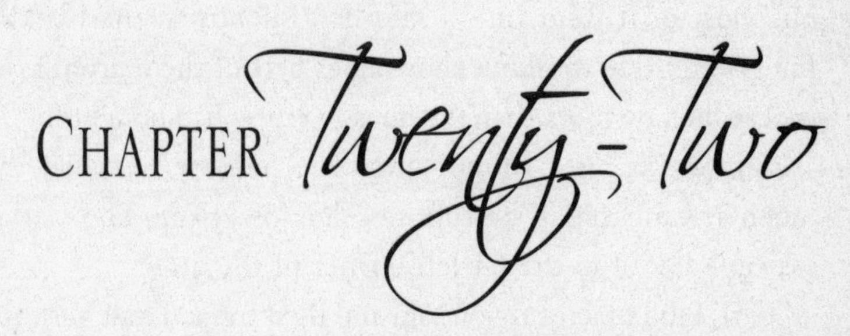

"Are you sure about this?" Avie asked Brandi, peering at her over their to-do list.

"Yes, very sure."

"Do you want the truth or the version that will let us remain friends?"

Brandi laughed heartily. "You know we'll always be friends," she said, grinning, "especially since you saved my tail that day in eighth grade."

"Yeah, Big D was about to spank that ass."

"Was she ever! All she had to do was sit on my skinny behind and it would've been all over." Brandi chuckled as Avie slapped the desk, shaking with mirth. "I think that chick was borderline butch even back then. But Big A had her covered."

"You bet your ass. Had to teach that zombie a thing or two. All right," Avie said, rubbing her hands together. "Now that we've got that out of the way, let me hear what you've done so far."

"Actually, I did what you instructed me to, and maybe a little more."

Two months earlier, Avie's lips had set into a grim line as she said, "I'm advising you as a friend, not as a lawyer. You feel me?"

Brandi had nodded, leaning in close.

"Here's what you do first..."

Brandi left Avie's office and went straight to a bank on LaSalle Street. Minutes later, she sat demurely in front of the private banker she hadn't used in decades and said, "I'd like to open a savings account, please."

The woman politely smiled, "Okay, Mrs. Spencer, we're going to—"

"No, I'm going to use my maiden name."

That was the first step. She sold some jewelry and cut corners on household expenses. Then Brandi slowly squirreled away what money she could without Vernon's knowledge. Some of the money went into her new account, but most of it went into a safe-deposit box in the bank's vaults. Those funds definitely wouldn't show up as part of the marital assets in a divorce proceeding, no more than the house Vernon had bought for Tanya Kaufman.

Four weeks later Brandi met Avie halfway between their offices for lunch at Café 200. They chose selections from The Carvery and took a seat in a booth in the far left corner of the diner.

"Girl, I did exactly as you said and then some. I had Vernon spring for two new charge accounts and replaced our furniture with less expensive pieces."

"So what happened to the other stuff?"

"I moved it into storage. I'm keeping those. I also added a few other pieces to take with me as—" she cleared her throat, "—the *consolation* prizes."

"Oh, come on," Avie said, between bites, "Vernon's not *that* dense. He has to notice something."

"All he ever did anyway was come in, eat, hit the library, the bathroom a couple of times, shower, then roll into the sack and possibly get some nookie. Now he's gone so much that when he does come home, he says something like, 'Oh, you're changing the furniture around—looks nice.'" Brandi laughed. "Yeah, all right. Changing the furniture? Suuuuure!"

"Okay, have the house appraised, then quitclaim—sign over—your interest in the house to Vernon and remove your name from the mortgage. Then start banking your portion of the mortgage payment, but leave Vernon's money in your joint banking account to handle the house and maintenance bills. Never take more than you'll actually need."

"At the rate things are going," Brandi said, lifting her glass in salute, "he'll need it more than I will."

Avie leveled hazel eyes on Brandi. "It's better than the other way around."

"While searching for a new place, I also checked out schools in the area for the girls. Next week, I'll put earnest money down on a sweet little piece of property in the Hyde Park area."

"You can't do that! That will have to come out in the divorce. You're killing me here."

"No, the paperwork says 'renting,' but the day after the divorce is final, the money I put in will be converted to an actual down payment."

Avie took a sip of Dr Pepper. "Why go through all that? Why not just wait?"

"'Cause the house might be sold by the time all this is done." Brandi gazed out at the heavy lunchtime crowd streaming in from the AON Center, where Avie had her office. "So the paperwork and earnest money means the house will stay off the market and I can move right in whenever I want."

"I can't believe you did all that in less than four weeks," Avie said, checking off a few things on her notepad. "It normally takes people six months to pull that off."

"Well, that's just your part of the plan. I might need your help on something else I need to do."

Avie tensed, shifting uncomfortably in her seat. "Uh-oh. Sounds like you're about to get me into some bull."

"No, actually, it's time to tie up the loose ends. Everything's set, except for one last piece of business." Brandi pushed away her half-eaten plate. "*Piece* being the operative word."

"I get it—the mistress."

"Riiiiiight," she said, eyeing the approaching figure of a gorgeous man whose dark brown skin, intense eyes, and muscular body reminded her of her husband.

"Vernon took the down payment for Tanya's house out of our business account, thinking our accountant, being a man, wouldn't drop the information to me. Fortunately, Michael values our business and pulled my coattail with not-so-subtle hints."

Avie grinned, scooping up a little mashed potato. "Doesn't hurt that he still has a thing for you."

"Old love dies hard." Brandi's fingertips glided over the coolness of the glass. "And I think I missed out by not being with him."

After Michael clued her in, time and research revealed everything she needed to know about the other woman. With all that Brandi had done to secure her finances and plan for a move to a new house in the heart of the city, she wasn't as angry anymore. Instead, she felt in control and ready for her new life. To hell with Vernon!

Then she had showed up at Tanya's house, handling both of them like a pro. Now one of her "problems" was God knows where, sulking like *he* was the victim. The other one had landed on her doorstep, with Vernon's wallet in hand and every bit of cash still intact, and was now pulling her house together. How cool was that?

Three hours later, she was still hanging around Avie's office, hesitant about putting her signature on their petition for legal separation. Instead, she grabbed a white notepad and began making notes for a new business plan. She knew she couldn't show up at The Perfect Fit because Vernon would create a scene if it would serve his purpose. As she had every half hour for the past three hours, she placed another call to her assistant. "Renee, is he still in?"

"I just checked with Jackie," her rushed voice came through the line. "He tore out of here driving a U-Haul about thirty minutes ago."

"A U-Haul? He's still in that thing?" Brandi held back a chuckle. Lissette had called to give her a heads-up. Then she and Jeremy's wife had put their heads together: Lissette called the towing company, but Brandi supplied directions to its final destination. Vernon hadn't guessed that the car was actually holding ground in their garage. But if he was home where he was supposed to be...

Brandi began packing her things. "So he's gone for the day?

"Looks that way."

"Great, *now* I'm on my way in."

Renee took a long, slow breath. "Are you sure? It's about two-thirty, the day's almost over."

"I might need you to work late so we can get some things in order."

"Uhhhh, I need to warn you that um...well, um...people are acting a little strange."

Brandi stuffed the last of Avie's documents in her briefcase, making a mental note to work up the energy to sign the damn things. "About what?"

"Uhhhhh..."

"Come on, woman, my temperature's set to 'wracked nerves' today. Spill it!"

Renee lowered her voice to a whisper. "Someone's standing in front of me. We'll talk when you get here." She hung up.

❤❤❤

Brandi pulled "her" new Lexus out onto I-94. Switching on the radio, B.B. King's "The Thrill is Gone" bellowed through the airwaves in his soul-filled voice.

Brandi let out a small bitter laugh. "Well, I knew that from the second verse and the chorus, romance was the first to pack its bags."

As the Lexus moved with traffic, she remembered how she thought that she could solve it with just one clever move. After the first month of several visits with her under-the-bed backup, her husband's trifling behind had yet to tickle her with what he called a little "below-the-waistline sunshine." Unfortunately, mentioning her frustrations had only made things worse. His attempts to close the gaps with phone sex only grazed the surface. Personally, she wished that grazing would take place in an area only God, her mother, and Vernon had seen more than once.

Vernon had promised to be more attentive. He'd promised to make their marriage the central part of his life—and with each failed promise, they settled more comfortably into a coexistence that was closer to friends than husband and wife.

Given the opportunity, she'd retire her Doc Johnson products just to have that delta between her thighs humming a precision tune all on its own. So she had hatched a plan. If he wouldn't give it up willingly, she'd have to smack him across the forehead and take it. A wife could do that, right?

With the children safely tucked away at Avie's, Brandi put her plan in motion. Wearing a sheer purple gown with lilac trim, dinner waiting lovingly on the table, she had greeted him one evening at the door and dropped to her knees. Soon screams and moans mingled with the liquid sound of heated activity as she worked him over with the technique of a professional.

That night she had sat in the emergency room trying to explain to the doctor why her husband lay on an examination table with an erection that wouldn't go down without a muscle relaxant and a day's rest, vowing that maybe next time she'd be a little gentler. *And then again*, she thought, *maybe not*. Problem solved.

Then the next day, Michael had called her into his office and filled her in on a few things. New problem. And a completely new set of challenges that had nothing to do with bedroom aerobics and everything to do with bringing back her insecurities full force. Was she too fat? Was she inadequate in the bedroom? Was she lacking in the mothering department?

Brandi strolled into the office thirty minutes later amid the curious stares of her employees. Renee, wearing a smart black suit and silver blouse, hair in a curly shag, swiveled in the desk chair, simply holding out the little pink messages without saying a word.

Brandi stared at the fleshy redhead for a moment. "And good afternoon to you, too."

Renee dipped her head, giving her a sheepish smile. Uncharacteristic for a secretary who was known for being a straight shooter. "Vernon was in rare form. Didn't know if you were going to tear off a few heads or not."

"And why would I do that?" Brandi asked, suddenly a bit nervous about all this secretiveness. "None of you have done anything to me." Turning slowly, she peered out at the other inquisitive employees staring right back at her.

"Well…you know how some women get when they're on the verge of… divorce," Renee said.

Brandi lapsed into an uncomfortable silence. "And just how did you know that?"

Renee swallowed hard, eyes darting around the room. "Uh…uh…Fabian told us."

"And how did *she* find out?"

Renee grimaced and hesitated.

"Renee…"

"Thomas told her," she mumbled.

"Thomas?"

"Your *cousin* Thomas. He was at your house last Friday and told Fabian that you invited your husband's mistress to live with you." Renee placed a single hand over her chest. "I told them it was bull. No wife in her right mind would bring a woman her husband was sleeping with into her home. No way!"

Murmurs swirled around them, blending with the smooth jazz playing overhead. Brandi pulled off her black blazer and loosened the tie at the neck of her floral blouse. She stared openly at Renee, weighing how much to tell her. She decided on a simple, "You're wrong." She cast a wary gaze over her shoulder, before facing her secretary again. "But everyone thinks I'm about to go off on them because of that?"

"Well, even you've said at one time or another that your temperature's been set to bitch lately. Why would today be different? *Especially* after Friday."

Brandi turned, eyes narrowing as she scanned the length of the office. Heads turned, dipped down, some whipped back to their computer screens; everyone averted their eyes, pretending to suddenly find work interesting. Brandi sensed that more gossip than work had taken place all day.

"Vernon tore through here this morning and almost killed some folks," Renee said in a low tone.

Placing her leather briefcase and the messages on Renee's neatly organized desk, Brandi strolled to the center of the office. "May I have your attention, please." Gee, she was saying a lot of that lately.

Like a symphony, everyone focused back on Brandi, necks craned. Employees in the back near the kitchenette stood to get a better view.

Brandi stared at the group for a moment, paying special attention to Fabian.

The skinny loudmouth ducked behind Ella Clark's wide frame, almost disappearing. Ella yanked the petite woman out of hiding and pushed her forward. "If you're woman enough to start it, then be woman enough to own up to it."

Brandi looked down at the weave-wearing woman—and a bad weave at that—and made a note to have a conversation with her later. Or was it even necessary? The damage was done. She did need to put her foot up Thomas's sixty-inch ass. Family business was family business.

"May I have your attention please. Just to dispel the rumors before they get out of hand, Vernon and I are experiencing a few personal challenges right now," she began in a loud, clear voice. "But it will not affect what's going on with The Perfect Fit. It's business as usual. I know that's a concern for you, with the holiday season just around the corner and all. Now... get your nosy little behinds back to work!"

Murmurs followed her all the way to her office as she whizzed past Renee, who handed her the messages again and turned back to her computer.

Brandi switched on the music in her office, settled into her black mesh chair, spread her notes out over the smoke-tinted glass desk that rested on two white Greek columns, and began jotting down what she would need to put in her new business plan.

Twenty minutes later she reached out. Punching the intercom, she said, "Renee, I need financial statements for the last two years, accounts payable and receivable to date, client histories, and client preferences."

"On everybody?"

Brandi said patiently, "Yes, ma'am. If you need to leave on time, go ahead. Just leave me a note showing where I can find things, but do the best you can."

"I called my husband," Renee replied; Brandi could hear papers shuffling in the background. "He'll pick up the kids and some dinner. I can stay as long as you need me."

"And I'll make sure we'll have dinner brought in and you'll take a cab home."

Renee's voice perked up. "Cool. Let me get started."

Eventually, Brandi and Vernon would need to split The Perfect Fit down the middle, whether she stayed with her husband or he decided that her new terms were too much for him to handle and went elsewhere. And she would hold her ground, too. Just having Tanya around was enough to make the man want to give birth to triplets.

Moments into the planning stages, she searched her briefcase and purse several times, but couldn't find a valuable piece of equipment that contained notes for the final projections. She placed a quick call to Avie and found her lawyer was in court and probably wouldn't return to the office. Grabbing her coat, she said, "Renee, I have to run downtown and get my handheld. Hold down the fort."

"No problem. Pulling these files should keep me busy until next week."

An hour later, just before she stepped into the elevator of the AON Center, Renee called on her cell. "Tanya was just on the other line. It's urgent. Something about your daughter."

CHAPTER *Twenty-Three*

Tanya, who had been relaxing on the sofa reading *Superwoman's Child: Son of a Single Mother,* looked up just in time to see Simone stroll through the front door. She slipped out of a neon green sweater, snatched the scrunchie out of her hair, shook the curls out like a runway model, dropped the book bag in the foyer, and sprinted toward the bathroom.

Tanya turned her attention back to the novel expecting Sierra to come bounding in the door any minute.

She didn't.

An alarm went off in Tanya's head as she quickly sat up, placed the book on the sofa, and called to Simone, "Where's Sierra?"

The tall, slender replica of Brandi shrugged as she come into the room and dropped onto the love seat with an iPod in hand. "Don't know. She wasn't on the bus."

"And you didn't think that was strange? You're supposed to come in together."

Simone draped a jean-clad leg over the arm of the love seat and didn't look up. "Well, I'm where I'm supposed to be," she said, voice laced with sarcasm. "Hey, she's got her life and I've got mine. She's ten years old and able to keep up with herself. I am *not* my sister's keeper."

Tanya snatched the iPod. "Technically, you are. Did you think about the fact that maybe something could've happened to her?"

"Like what?" Simone spat back. "She's too fat and stupid for anyone to want her for anything."

"That's real insensitive coming from her own sister," Tanya said, appalled at the girl's nasty tone. "I hope you don't say that where she can hear you."

Simone's angry brown eyes shot daggers. "She knows she's fat and her grades say she's stupid. What's it to you, Blondie?"

Tanya gasped at the blatant disrespect. She had never seen either girl act this way and was sure that Brandi didn't tolerate such behavior. "What you're not saying is that she's caring and kind, and she loves you," Tanya replied. "Now where is she?"

The feisty little girl looked up—eyes just like her mother's—staring at Tanya in silence.

"Your mother's gonna kill you."

Simone shrugged. "If she's ever home long enough to try."

Tanya ran to the phone, glancing out of the window just as a strange moving van pulled off.

Tanya glared at the defiant girl waiting impatiently for Brandi's assistant to answer. Finally! "Renee, is Brandi in her office?"

"She has asked not to be disturbed. May I ask who's calling?" Renee asked, almost spitting out the words.

"Tell her it's, um, her wi—" Tanya caught herself just in time. "Tell her it's Tanya, and it's urgent. Her daughter didn't show up after school today."

Suddenly Renee sounded as panicky as Tanya. "Oh, she had to make a run downtown. Do you have her cell number?'

"Yeah, I've got it. Thanks."

Seconds clicked by as Tanya dialed several times and it went to voicemail. Simone tried to get up from the sofa, but Tanya grabbed her before she got away, and pushed her back down.

Finally Brandi picked up. "What's going on?" she demanded.

"Sierra didn't come home from school today. Simone walked in but her sister wasn't with her."

Brandi gasped. "Did you call the school?"

"That was my next move, but I wanted to call you first."

"I'm on my way home. Call me back if anything happens."

Tanya quickly dialed the principal's office. She didn't bother with formalities. "Have you seen Sierra Caldwell-Spencer?"

"Her bus pulled off twenty minutes ago. She should be home by now."

"She didn't make it to the bus. Can you have someone check the grounds?"

"I'll call you back in a few minutes."

Simone propped her legs on the freshly dusted coffee table, a soft liquid smile on her thinly curved lips as she stared at Tanya. The girl's face was a blend of Brandi and Vernon, but that steely, stubborn determination in her eyes belonged solely to Brandi.

So would her ass if she didn't start talking.

Tanya took a long, slow breath. "I know this whole situation must be hard on you, being the oldest and all, but you can't take things out on Sierra." Tanya softened her tone. "Your mother says you've always looked out for your little sister. Sierra looks up to you. She even tries to buy clothes like you and do her hair like yours. You're her role model and don't even realize how important you are to her."

Simone's head whipped up, lips pursed in a thin, hard line. She folded her arms over developing little breasts.

"She loves you and you don't even speak to her sometimes."

The girl's eyes narrowed to slits. "What do you know about us? Daddy said you won't be here long no matter what Mommy says. You're on your way out." She picked up the iPod again. "So why do I have to answer to you?"

"You don't, but I'm sure your parents taught you to be respectful. I'm sure they taught you and your sister to look out for each other."

"Yeah, well, their stuff's messed up, too."

Tanya opened her mouth to speak and shut it just as quickly.

Damn, the girl *did* have a point.

CHAPTER *Twenty-Four*

"God, why is this happening now? Why now? Please, Lord, protect my little girl." If there was a God, how could He have let this happen? Brandi wondered, hoping the Creator would hear her even though she hadn't set foot in a church since she was thirteen.

Brandi grabbed the handheld from the receptionist and sprinted toward the elevator. She placed a quick call to Renee. "Go home Renee, we'll do this tomorrow."

"You want me to stick around just in case she calls here?"

"No, they'll call my cell if anything happens."

Brandi reached the marble-encased lobby, punched the silver button three times, as if that would make the elevator come faster. Where was her little girl?

She got on, flicking a quick glance at a man wearing a plaid shirt and corduroys, then to another tall, tattoo-riddled man with a long beard, and a bald head, and minus any type of deodorant. His menacing green eyes seemed to bore straight through her, sweeping aside her fear for a brief moment and making her uneasy.

Punching the button for the lobby, she turned to face the little display screen showing quick bites of today's news and stock quotes, and said a quick prayer. She had trusted a total stranger with her children and look what happened! The Polish woman who kept an eye on the kids for a couple of hours every day and cleaned the house had to quit because of her arthritis. She hadn't had time to replace Mariska, and she had become consumed with Vernon and Tanya. Actually, Tanya couldn't have come at a better time. But then again, maybe Brandi was paying for her role in this unfolding saga.

As the traffic and weather splashed across the screen, the elevator came to a screeching halt between floors eighty-two and eighty-three. All three occupants managed, with great effort, to keep their balance. The little screen went blank. The lights dimmed, died out, then flickered back on, all within a matter of seconds. The sudden whirr of the overhead mechanisms shrieked and whined momentarily. Then all was quiet. Trapped on an elevator? Exactly what she needed!

"Shit! I wish they'd get this fucking thing fixed. This is the fifth fucking time this fucking month," the man in the plaid shirt muttered.

Brandi turned to him. "You know, there are other words besides profanity."

She opened the gold door near the bottom of the elevator, yanked out the phone, keeping a wary eye on Mr. Plaid.

"Well, right now it fits the fucking situation."

"Yeah," the bearded one said, his raspy voice echoing in the elevator's tiny space. "I think hell and damnation would be a pretty good way of stating the obvious." He leveled a steely gaze on Brandi. "Especially since they haven't fixed the fucking phone in this thing."

Brandi, already filled with worry, barely hung on to her temper. She replaced the phone and frantically reached in her briefcase and tried her cell, but of course—no signal. Where was Sierra? The one who reminded her so much of herself—sure the girl was carrying around a few extra pounds, but her open smile and willingness to do anything to help people reminded Brandi of how she used to be before she was raped.

Her baby girl! She prayed that what had happened to her at thirteen would never happen to her little girls—ever. It was one of the reasons she had been so adamant about not having children. The world was not safe for little girls. Come to think of it, little boys didn't get off so easy, either.

A quick glance over the bearded man's body made her wince and clutch her case. Glaring back at her as though to taunt anyone's religious beliefs were tattoos on both arms stating *the devil rules*, a skull and bones on his upper chest, and a dirty shirt with the slogan: *There's enough Satan to go around, have you tried him on for size?* Suppose someone like him had gotten to her daughter. Oh God!

The combination of the man's odor, his disdain for positive reflection, worry for her daughter, stress, and a sleepless night worrying over the business were too much. She closed her eyes, sending up a fevered and heartfelt prayer. As her whispers grew louder with each plea to God to protect her child, and to shield her from the poor man and his love for Satan, the bearded smelly one roared with laughter. "Peddle it somewhere else, Nigger, we're not buying today."

"And I'm not selling," she snapped, ending her prayer. "I refuse to be locked up in this little silver cell with someone who thinks that Satan rules over the Creator and still thinks Black people can be *that* word." She flexed her fists. "And if you don't back up, I'm gonna ram this briefcase up your ass and follow it with my size elevens to make sure it stays put."

"Ouch!" Mr. Plaid Shirt said, coming to stand between them. When the Satanist moved back, the Plaid man slumped down to the thin carpet. "I don't think either one of you have a leg to stand on. I don't believe in God." Then he turned to the grinning bearded man. "Sorry, dude, I don't believe in Satan, either. And as for the N-word, only African-Americans are supposed to call each other that now," he said, giving Brandi a sly grin.

Brandi bristled with anger, but being outnumbered she wisely kept her mouth shut.

The tattooed man's smile vanished almost as fast as it appeared. He joined the other fellow on the floor, leaving Brandi standing in righteous annoyance as her reflection bounced off the silver walls, trying to ignore the two men, and keep a prayer line open to God, one that she hadn't tapped into since she'd been a little girl.

"Well, you have to believe in one or the other, man," he said. "It's not fair to straddle the fence."

"I don't and there's nothing that has happened in my life to make me feel otherwise."

"Only white people can afford not to believe in the Creator," Brandi said.

"We've had nothing but God on our side." This from a woman who hadn't offered up a prayer before today—maybe a quick grace and not much more—in years. *What a hypocrite!* Brandi thought.

"For all the help it did bringing your kind over here."

"Yeah? And I'm sure *your* kind had a lot to do with that. That wasn't about God, that was about greed in the guise of Christianity. Nowhere did Jesus condone slavery or the mistreatment of women. Nor did he state that men were supposed to rule over them. All were equal—male and female, Jew and Gentile. Those who bathe and those who don't know what soap and water are," she said, leveling a stony gaze at the bald one, whose armpits, with the increased heat in the elevator, had suddenly kicked in to Level II funk. She put her collar over her nose.

Mr. Plaid Shirt folded his scrawny arms over his chest, daring either one of them to say anything more. Right now God and her child were all Brandi could think about.

Mr. Tattoo glanced up at Brandi. "Let's see if we can persuade him to pick a side. I'm game if you are."

Brandi hated small spaces with a passion. With each passing moment, the air seemed to become heavier and more humid. Her heart had jumped into her throat, clogging any ability to speak. She shrugged absently, not caring one way or another, continuing to pray for Sierra inwardly, and gestured for him to continue. Anything to take her mind off the increasing heat and the smell that became stronger by the minute.

"Maybe you haven't been given a good argument," Mr. Tattoo said. "What I—"

At that moment, the elevator lurched downward, throwing Brandi to the floor. Her heart did a solid flip and skipped a few beats. Mr. Plaid Shirt took a quick succession of fearful breaths as his eyes darted around the elevator car. The bald one reached for the metal bars, bracing for the obvious. The trio had no time to recover as the elevator picked up speed, whizzing past seventy, then sixty-five, then sixty at a pace any race-car driver would envy.

Brandi bowed her head in another prayer for her child and added only a brief one for herself.

The bald, smelly one grunted, knuckles growing white as he gripped the silver railing.

Mr. Plaid Shirt clutched a tattered briefcase to his chest, glancing warily at Baldy, then to Brandi, as both men began, "Our Father, who art in Heaven..."

Chapter Twenty-Five

Vernon grinned as he hung up the phone. A frantic call from Tanya signaled trouble in paradise. She'd already failed at keeping the girls safe. A hushed call from his youngest daughter had set things in motion. Maybe he'd be able to go home sooner than he expected.

Vernon cased his mother's house like a hardened criminal all afternoon. Damn, this wasn't the time for her to take a vacation. He needed her! But he knew he would have to beg for help. He really hadn't stayed in touch as much as he should have after the divorce. If he had, his father would have stopped the cash flow faster than a hooker cleans up for the next customer. *A shame for her to have almost five thousand square feet to herself*, he thought as he looked at the house as though he'd never really seen it.

The house had five bedrooms, six bathrooms, and a solarium with an indoor pool leading out into the garden. His father had fought like hell in court for every square inch. However, Mama fought back in a vicious move fielded by Avie Davidson that laid his father on his back.

Bettye Spencer walked away with the house, two cars, a lump sum, the house in Florida, and a monthly stipend that made his father lose two years of his life every time he signed the check. Although Avie was Brandi's lawyer, too, Vernon would make sure that what happened to his parents never happened to him. Brandi would end this foolishness and he would tuck his tail and go home. He could wait her out. Everything would blow over. He was sure of it.

Vernon had had enough. His father, Jeremy, Craig, and a few other friends had rejected him. He'd spent the last of his cash on a seedy motel, and the U-Haul late fees were still mounting. Never in his life had he slept with tissue in his ears and nose, and his mouth turned into the pillow. He didn't even want to think about what could crawl into his mouth or what was growing in the mattress or that nasty carpet.

He cracked open a little used basement window, climbed into his mother's house, unlocked the basement door, and scurried to deactivate the alarm.

Within three hours, he'd moved his stuff into the basement, hung his clothes in his old room, and lay resting on the couch, showered and totally refreshed, finally feeling a sense of peace, and ready for a serious power nap.

Home, sweet home.

A shriek jerked him out of a sound sleep.

"What the hell are you doing in my house?"

"Mama, it's me!" he said, jumping up when he realized Mama was packing a twenty-two. Where the hell had she gotten that?

She lowered the gun just a little. "How did you get in here? You don't have a key."

"Well, I um—I—um, broke a windowpane downstairs, then climbed through. I'll have it fixed tomorrow."

She dropped her hand, then retrieved her bag from the doorway. "Doesn't explain why you did it."

Vernon sprinted across the living room to help with a suitcase that was large enough to hold a dead body or two.

Mama's golden brown complexion had turned a deeper shade of tan. Her eyebrows were arched in symmetric lines. Her thin lips had a bit of plum gloss—a color he had never known her to wear. Who *was* this new man? And what was Mama doing in the Bahamas with him?

He leaned over to kiss her. "You look great!" And in the next breath added, "I need a place to stay."

"Sounds like a personal problem to me," she snapped, waving him and his kiss away.

"But all my stuff's already inside."

She pursed her thin lips, cocked her neck, parted her lips, and told him, "You didn't ask."

Vernon stared at her.

The expression on her round face was unchanged and unreadable. She pointed, gesturing toward him, then to the door.

Out? Oh shit! Nooooo!!!! His muscles were already aching from moving stuff in! "Mama, you can't carry one of those," he said, eyeing the gun in her other hand.

"Try telling that to Mrs. Steele," she snapped.

"What happened to her?"

Bettye leaned back on the wall separating the foyer from the living room. "Burglar caught her off guard."

Vernon spread his hands in protest. "I'm not a burglar."

"Broke in, didn't you?"

An hour later, he had everything in the U-Haul *again*, then knocked on the front door.

The silver-haired, graceful woman with a fresh tan that a supermodel would envy opened the door and stood menacingly in the door frame.

"Mama, can I stay with you for a while?"

"Why didn't you go to your father?"

"I did, but—"

She cut him off with a raised hand. "He didn't want you hanging around Julie."

Vernon gaped. Was Dad that easy to figure out?

Mama laughed. "Wafer-thin heifer might like the younger player better than the washed-up, wrinkled version." She folded her arms over her small chest, hair glistening from the foyer light. "One month. Tops."

Vernon's mouth went dry, his heart sank. "One *month!*" Hell, it might take Brandi longer than that.

"*And* you'll have a midnight curfew."

"Mama, I'm a grown man," he protested.

Leaning forward, she whispered, "Then your grown ass can stay somewhere else. You've got a lot of nerve to ask me for a damn thing after taking your father's side in the divorce."

"Mama, he would've cut me off if I stayed here."

"Boy, he sure does know how to use that will, doesn't he?" she said bitterly. "And heaven forbid you don't see a dime even if the man outlives you. There comes a time when money doesn't mean a thing."

"Then why did you fight him so hard in the divorce?" he asked, his tone bitter and frustrated.

"Living with him, being married to him, was a full-time job and I deserved some compensation." She winked. "The same compensation Brandi deserves. I think Avie will make sure she gets it, too."

Vernon stood at the threshold, almost glaring at his mother, as nightfall and another night in the U-Haul or sharing a space with roaches and a few other insects loomed in his future. Or possibly a night stretched out on his office sofa. Neither was much of a welcome alternative to sleeping in a warm, soft bed in a clean house.

"Do you realize how much you hurt me when you turned your back on me? After everything I did to protect you from his overbearing ways and need to mold you into something that you clearly aren't? But now I'm seeing differently. All the crap I put up with for your sake crushed my spirit more than anything your father did to me."

"I know, Mama, and I'm sorry for that," he said, hoping to avoid the guilt trip she was about to send him on. She was packing his bag and printing airline tickets to send him away for a long time. He knew he was wrong in what he'd done, but he couldn't seem to balance both parents. And look at what it had gotten him. He had always feared being without money, especially on trips home to his mother's native Mississippi. He couldn't believe that she had come from such sparse beginnings. Judging by her bearing and the way she kept herself, the woman could easily have come from the richest of families. He still loved her and deep down he thought she would always be there for him. But in some ways he wasn't as sure as he'd been before.

"I don't think you're sorry about anything, but I think you will be," she said, pursing her lips like a principal looking down on a wayward student. "I think you're just saying that 'cause you're out on your ear right now.

And I still don't hear you agreeing to my terms, so..." A small smirk played across her lips as she pushed the door, closing him out.

"All right!"

She stepped back, opening the door just wide enough for him to walk in. "And I want it in writing," she said, turning her back to him as she walked into the living room.

"Jeez!"

"Don't take the Lord's name in vain," she snapped.

"I didn't say—"

Protests died instantly on his lips as she whirled to face him. "No back talk, either. Your father screwed up all those years of good home training. I plan to fix that while you're here."

Things were not supposed to turn out like this.

"You'll buy your own food," Bettye said, as he trailed her through the huge house to the kitchen. "And I will charge rent."

"Mama, what's gotten into you?"

"Common sense," she replied evenly. "Something you should've used before sleeping with that woman."

"I don't want to talk about that."

She pulled out a glass and sloshed sparkling grape juice into it. "*You* may not want to *talk*, but you damn well better listen." She held up the glass, winking. "And I've got plenty to say."

She sure did. Two hours' worth—every bit of it vicious.

CHAPTER Twenty-Six

The elevator came to a jerking halt at the tenth floor. Paramedics fished them out, but Brandi declined medical treatment though her back, legs, and thighs had aches in spots she didn't know existed. Where was her baby girl?

Thirty minutes later, Brandi rushed into the house, finishing a call to the mother of one of Sierra's friends as she dropped her briefcase near the door and ran into the living room. None of her friends or family knew where Sierra was.

Tanya stood hovering over Simone, who had a scowl on her normally pretty face that would make a sumo wrestler think she was a member of the club. The little minx knew something. Brandi could feel it.

All it took was one stern look from Brandi and her oldest daughter spilled her guts. "She's with Daddy."

Brandi counted to ten, but imagined her hands slowly wrapping around Simone's neck. "You knew that all along?"

Simone slumped further into the sofa. "Yes, ma'am."

"I could strangle you."

Simone averted her gaze, sulking. "Stand in line." Tanya had said the same thing.

Brandi dialed Vernon's cell.

His sleepy voice answered on the third ring. "What!"

She snapped, "Don't what me, Negro! You're sleeping?!"

"No, I'm lying here praying to the god of guaranteed hair growth! Hell yeah, I'm sleeping," he growled. "Especially after all the shit you've put me through."

"Where's my daughter?"

"Ask your wife," he shot back. "Isn't she supposed to keep up with the kids?"

"Don't fuck with me," Brandi retorted, lowering her tone as Tanya ushered Simone into the kitchen.

Brandi heard only his breathing.

"She's not here. I don't have her. Maybe your wife isn't as good as you thought. Are you sure you can trust her in our house?"

"You trusted sinking your—"

"You know what? I'm sick of hearing that," he growled. "How long are you gonna make me pay for that?"

"I'm not making you pay for anything. I'm serious about making this work."

"Get that woman out of my house!"

Brandi glanced at Tanya, who leaned on the entrance, eyes filled with worry. "No, she's part of the family now. You know, sort of like a sister or long-lost cousin."

"Brandi, get her out of there," he nearly shrieked. "I want to come home! I'm thirty-five years old and back at my Mama's."

"You can come home anytime you like, Vernon." She eased onto the sofa, slipping off her heels and giving her tired feet a much-needed rub. "I'm not stopping you. No one's stopping you."

"I'm not coming home as long as *she's* there."

"Then I suggest you get used to your mom's, my brother. 'Cause I'm enjoying my wife. Did you know she could make crème brûlée, cheese soufflé, and a mean pan of macaroni and cheese—with four cheeses? I may never pick up a skillet again." Then she grinned, allowing a sly tone into her voice. "I wonder what else she's good at?"

"You're crazy," he growled. "Get that woman away from around my children!"

"You didn't have a problem with it before, so don't have a problem with it now." Brandi signaled Tanya to pick up the extension. "Where's Sierra?"

Vernon took a long, slow breath before asking, "Where's my car?"

"I will climb through this phone and put an extra hole in your ass," Brandi warned.

"Send your *wife* out to find her," he said in a huff.

"I'm not playing with you, Vernon."

His tone became hard and mean. "Neither am I. Get Tanya out and I'll do what I can to bring Sierra home."

Brandi stood, wishing she could put a vise grip on his nose. "Negro, are you crazy? Holding my daughter hostage!"

"You're holding *me* hostage!" he shrieked. "I can't come home."

"No, you *won't* come home, there's a difference," she shot back. "Our children have nothing to do with that."

"Get her out and we'll talk."

Brandi slammed down the phone, glaring at Simone, was hiding behind Tanya. "I should whip your little tail."

Tanya reached a hand out to cover the girl. "Maybe I should leave."

"I wouldn't give him the satisfaction," Brandi answered on her way out

Brandi grabbed her old coat from the closet, slipped on some sneakers, and ran straight out the door.

She drove around scouting for her little girl, wondering if Vernon was telling the truth. She wondered if some maniac somewhere was hurting her child. The more she drove through the dark, empty streets, the more her chest tightened; her breathing became heavy and labored. She recognized the signs of what could be a panic attack coming on although she had never had one of those before, even on the day when she had every right.

Hollywood and his crew were hot on her heels. Each time Brandi's foot slammed against the pavement, more tears sprang from her eyes. If they caught her, they'd rape her, then they might kill her. That thought alone made her overlook the burning in her chest, the pain shooting up her spine. She had run for three blocks and could still hear them pounding the concrete right behind her. She didn't even remember dropping her book bag.

"Catch that bitch!"

As they ran past a group of apartment buildings some of the boys from Hollywood's block trickled away, but to her dismay even more boys from other blocks joined the chase. Tears blurred her vision, but she couldn't wipe them away. She needed her hands to propel her body forward; each pump of her arms increased her speed. "Lord, please let me make it to safety." Wherever safety happened to be.

She cut across a lawn, through the pathway of an old church, slipped between two brick houses, hopped the broken chain-link fence, landed in a mound of old tires, scrambled over a pile of garbage, picked herself up, and kept running. She glanced quickly over her shoulder. Only a few boys left. She had won the hundred-meter dash last month, but with her legs aching like someone had put a match to them and her lungs feeling like they would collapse any minute, she wondered—could she shake them?

She hopped another fence, ran between more houses, and cut through an alley, before coming out on a traffic-lined street. She stopped when the burning in her chest wouldn't let her run anymore. Her legs tingled as though they had fallen asleep. She plastered her body next to a building. The cold brown bricks were warmer than the fear chilling her heart. Her breathing came fast and furious. Why didn't she think? She should have listened to her mother.

Her mother had told her about keeping her virginity until she was married or at least until she was old enough to understand her body and emotions. Now, if she couldn't get out of God knew where she was now—she would pay for not listening.

Wet, salty tears streamed down Brandi's face. She'd give anything for her mother to be with her right now. She knew only her mother could get her out of this place. Would her mother love her anymore? Would her mother forgive her?

All thoughts ceased and her legs trembled as she heard Hollywood's car inching down the block. The music was almost as loud as the heartbeat slamming against her chest. The backseat was filled with boys; more were riding on the hood, others on top of the trunk. About twenty altogether—all looking for her.

Brandi couldn't move. She closed her eyes tight, held her breath, and hugged the brick wall like it was a friend. Her lips trembled. So did her legs. She had never been so scared in her life.

Several minutes later, she opened her eyes and saw that the car had passed. Brandi ran as fast as she could in the opposite direction. Sweat dripped from her forehead and onto her turtleneck. Her deodorant had long since given up its secret and wet spots formed under her arms. How could she have been so stupid? How could she think that he would love her and marry her one day like he promised? Very few boys married their high school sweethearts anyway. And Hollywood was far from being sweet or having a heart for that matter. Why didn't she see that before?

She scanned left, then right. Hollywood crept by, stopping at the corner. Another car filled with boys hovered at the end of the alley. She was trapped.

"Well, what do we have here?"

Brandi jumped, and then turned to see an old, wrinkled man, with dark, weathered skin and a big grin looking down at her.

Her throat was parched. She couldn't open her mouth to speak.

The man pointed toward Hollywood. "Your ride, gurlie?"

Brandi could only shake her head.

"How 'bout them fellas back there?" He gestured to the alley.

Brandi shook her head again.

"Hmmm." He watched both sets of boys for a minute. "Seems like you're in a bit of jam, missy"

Brandi nodded, gasping for air.

"Anybody you'd like to call to come get you?"

"My," she said in a breathy whisper, "mother."

"All right, follow me. You can use my phone."

Her heart almost leapt. Saved!

She followed him through the neat yard, past a bright green shed, and up the steps, but she hesitated at the door. His white shirt and green pants were neat and pressed. He seemed okay. The scent of cloves wafted outside.

The man smiled. "I don't have one of them fancy, um, cordless things. So it can't come to you. You'll have to come inside."

She glanced back at Hollywood's crew and then to the other boys on the opposite side of the clearing.

"Oh, you ain't got to worry 'bout them. They ain't coming in here. They knows not to mess wit' me."

The back door stayed open so she could leave at any time. That was some small comfort.

For a few seconds she stood calming herself and willing her fear to go away. Then she ran, snatched the dark gray handset and put it to her ear. The dial tone never sounded so good.

The man touched her hand, prying the phone away from her trembling fingers. "You can make your call, but there's something we need to talk about first..."

Every bit of hope vanished as she looked up into his face. A glint of something wicked flashed in his eyes. Had she just gone from one evil to another?

He gripped her shoulder, but she pulled away. A voice from a talk station filtered in from an old radio next to his chair.

"All I have to do is yell out dis here window and the boys'll be after ya again." He started breathing faster. "Daddy just needs a lil' attention and then you can go..."

Brandi sobbed, her shoulders heaving as he gave her hand a pat. Disappointment surged in her soul.

The man unzipped his pants, pulling out an old wrinkled penis, stroking it like a long-lost friend. "Just want you to suck it. Dat's all. Not like what dem boys want to do."

She stared at him. He was kidding, right? Brandi hesitated, fighting nausea. The man turned his head, yelling, "Hey!"

Brandi shrieked, "No! I'll do it."

She reached out to put her hand on such an ugly-looking thing. "No!" She jerked it back, then glanced up at the back door. Maybe if she ran, she could hop a few more fences and outdistance the boys. But could she take that chance? Her legs were so tired, so weary.

The man grinned as Brandi finally dropped to her knees, landing on the wooden floor with a solid thud. She barely hung on to breakfast. As she leaned in, the musky scent of his penis assaulted her nose. The hairs around it were gray and hard. She shivered with disgust.

"Come on, now, put your lips on Daddy..."

Brandi opened her mouth a little and nearly passed out from the smell. Tears welled up in her eyes, spilling over onto her turtleneck, some landing on the wooden floor. Suddenly, an image of her mother loomed in front of her, followed by feelings of shame and helplessness.

He turned his head glancing out the window. "And they're still out there, too." Then he grinned at Brandi. "But see, Daddy's keeping you safe, right?"

Safe? He called a mouthful of his nasty penis safe? Brandi stared ahead, her heart hammering against her chest, butterflies circling a morbid dance in her stomach. "Can I go now? I don't want to call nobody. I just wanna go." Was that her voice? That little pipsqueak of a sound? Jesus, she was scared.

Brandi whimpered as she turned her head, and threw up in the plant next to the chair. Most of it landed on the floor.

"Oh, you gonna pay for that, girl. You gonna pay." He yanked at her jeans. "Now pull dem panties down."

She didn't move.

"I said, pull 'em down, Gurl!"

Slowly, she pulled up from the floor, and trudged to the man. She glanced quickly out the window and saw Hollywood and his friends still waiting for her. God, what else would she have to do for this man, before he let her call her mother?

She turned back to the man. His face had suddenly darkened beyond recognition.

Slowly Brandi pulled down the little cotton coverings. The man didn't even wait until she finished. He reached out, grabbing at her vagina as though picking ripe fruit.

Her voice quivered. "Please don't do this."

He stopped and glowered at her. "Well, you gotta choice. All dem boys out there. Or lettin' me—just one man—touch it."

She didn't say a word.

"Now I wasn't gonna touch ya, but you done gone and messed up my clean floor. Took me three hours on my knees. It's gone take me some time to get it right. I figure you'll be gone by then so you gotta give me sumthin' for my troubles. I'm protectin' you, Gurl."

With that, he gripped her hips. She stared blankly ahead, closing her eyes against another wave of nausea. He guided her to his rigid member.

"See, dat's not so bad, now is it?"

Brandi couldn't utter a word even if she wanted.

He reached out, pulling her pants and panties all the way down to her ankles in one swipe. The cool air blowing from outside brushed against her bare buttocks.

"Just touch your pussy to the head. That's all. It's been a long time since Daddy had a little touch of sweet young pussy."

She pulled back. "I could get pregnant."

"I'm too old to get you pregnant! Now quit that shit."

Brandi cried as she peered over her shoulder. "You could give me some type of disease."

"I ain't got no diseases." His wrinkled face had taken on a murderous scowl. "Now quit makin' excuses and do what I tell you!"

Brandi sobbed, putting her hands up to her face.

The man lowered his voice. "I'm sorry for yelling. Just sit on Daddy's lap for a minute, and ride it on the outside, like a broomstick. That's all. I promise I won't try and put it in."

He pulled her down. His weathered old penis grazed her pubic hairs. Her body shook with anger and fear. Suddenly his hands gripped her shoulders, bringing her all the way down onto his lap.

"Now just move it back and forth on the outside, ridin' it like I told ya."

Brandi sobbed. "Please don't make me do this."

"Gurl, I ain't asking for much. It ain't gonna hurt you none. Just ride it a little, that's all. It ain't like the young boys ain't done it before."

She'd never allowed anyone to touch her, but could she tell him that? Would he believe her?

Brandi inched forward on the outside of his penis, it slipped back, then he pushed forward again—still outside of her body. She was grateful that he hadn't asked to put it in. She didn't want to give her virginity to Hollywood. She definitely didn't want her first time to be an ugly, nasty old man.

As he pumped forward and back, he whimpered like a wounded animal. He reached for the glass of water next to him; the cool water soon hit her vagina and his penis.

"That's right, gurlie. It's so good, gurlie. Ahhhh, yes, good Gurlie," he moaned

Brandi stared ahead and saw a picture of Jesus and the twelve disciples watching every move. She cried as the Savior swam in and out of focus. *Make this stop, Lord.* But this was one prayer. He wouldn't answer.

"Awww, gurlie." The man reached out with his clammy hands, and thrust them under her turtleneck to fondle her breasts. He pinched her nipples so hard she cried out. He continued pushing her body back and forth on him, moving her the way he wanted. His head buried into her back, gripping her, holding her close as though she were a newfound lover.

The she felt a sharp pain searing through her vagina. She bucked, trying to get away, he held her firmly in place. "I'm sorry, Gurlie, it's just so good."

Then he reached down and parted her thighs even wider. "It's just too good. Too good. I just wanna put the head in a little."

She shook her head vigorously, whimpering, "No! Noooo! Nooooooooo!"

With that he smacked her buttocks hard. Pain shot through her like nothing she'd felt before. Even her mother had never hit her.

"Please don't. I've never done this. That's why I'm running. I don't want to—"

"Well, them young niggers still waitin' on you. They gon' do worse, I promise ya. One man?" He shook his head, groaning. "Naw, this ain't so bad."

He placed his wrinkled old nasty penis to her vagina and pushed again. She screamed.

"Shut up!" he growled, shaking her like a rag doll. "Or I'll call 'em in here and let all of 'em have ya right here."

Brandi sniffled, clamping down on her lips, trying to keep any sound from coming out. Pain like she never knew enveloped her.

"Gotta teach you little young gurls a lesson. Do as your elders tell ya.

See, I bet you supposed to be in school right now, ain't ya? Didn't listen to ya mama, now, did ya? Now Daddy gon' teach you a good lil' lesson."

A sudden pain ripped through her insides like fire and ice fighting for the same space. He thrust forward—hard.

She let out a shrill scream.

He reached out and clamped his hands over her mouth as he pulled her back down on his lap—hard. Thrusting up like a galloping horse.

Pain became her entire world.

She struggled, trying to pull away—to get away from that tearing, searing pain. And they both landed on the floor. Her head hit the hardwood. But he kept galloping, gasping for breath as he seared her, hurting her, tearing into her. She hoped he would die.

He pulled her buttocks back to him, and thrust forward, moaning, "Good and tight, gurlie, good, good, good..." She reached for the floor lamp, missing as he pushed her forward, ripping her with every move. He spread her buttocks wide; she cried every time he slammed into her. Blood trickled down, spilling out on the floor, but he kept her within his strong grasp, moaning, "Gurlie feel good...gurlie feel so tight."

"Gurlie" had lost the ability to cry or speak. She lost the will to live as something in her mind crumbled and the world became black. The man didn't stop moving.

If she got out of this alive, she would never disobey her mother again. Not ever! If the pain would stop, she would do everything she was supposed to do.

The man pushed her away just as a stream of white stuff squirted into the air.

He fell back onto the floor. "Good gurlie. Good gurlie." He grinned, slowly stroking his groin, struggling for breath. Then he looked down, noticing the blood on the floor, the blood on his penis, and said. "A virgin? Must be my lucky day! We might havta do dat just one mo time. That's all, just one mo' time..."

CHAPTER *Twenty-Seven*

An hour later Tanya lay stretched out on the sofa, cordless resting on her chest, novel still in hand, television on. The Bachelor could have picked Godzilla for all she cared. The show raged on without one normally attentive viewer. She prayed that Vernon hadn't done anything stupid. She prayed that any moment Sierra would walk through the door and everything would be all right. Sierra, unlike Simone, was so innocent in her outlook on life. Tanya knew firsthand the dangers that awaited young girls out in the streets with no one nearby to look out for them.

❤❤❤

Tanya stepped off the bus at Penn Station in the heart of New York City. Immediately her eyes locked on the man leaning on the telephone booth. He must have been listening, because she didn't see his mouth move. Something about him said that it would be a good idea to avoid him.

She took the escalator up to ground level, walked through the glass doors, and out onto Eighth Avenue. She walked a few blocks over, and stood for a moment as the glaring lights, hurrying crowd, and noisy traffic flowed over and around her. Everyone in the world must be on this one street.

"Wow!"

"Yeah, it's something, ain't it?"

The man from the station appeared next to her. She hadn't even sensed him. He fit right in, wearing a white linen outfit that matched his pearly teeth, but was a perfect contrast to his dark skin. His hair was plastered to his skull in a succession of waves that ended in a thin goatee, which actually made him seem hard and unfriendly. Strange things happened to little girls in big places. She had to be more careful. Actually, she wished she didn't have to be here, despite the bright lights and the excitement the city offered.

Her parents had planned her life from day one, college at Yale, marriage to Peter Malcolm and the Malcolm fortune, two-point-five children, a house on Cherokee Road built from Social Circle's own resources.

She was supposed to have her father's charisma and her mother's gentility. She got neither. What she had was a meek spirit coupled with mild paranoia and a way of just moving along with life as if she expected everything to be handed to her. A dangerous way to exist, especially in a place as fast-paced as New York. Why had she chosen to come here, of all the places to learn by trial and terror?

She should have gone to Chicago. In the movies she saw, the Sears Tower reached for the stars as the Windy City landscape of tall buildings and overlapping expressways spread out for miles. And Chicago had a slower pace than New York. But the movies also showed Central Park in its glory, all beautiful lush green trees, and lawns that stretched for miles; or snow-covered paths and lovers in horse-drawn carriage rides. A winter wonderland.

"So where are you from?" the man asked, turning to stand in front of her.

Was he trying to block her way? "Georgia."

"Ooooooh, a Southern peach?"

"Something like that," she said, pivoting to get around him. "It was nice talking with you."

He grinned, but reached out and gripped her arm tightly enough to make her wince. "Hey, don't run off. Let me take you to lunch." His eyes traveled the length of her body. "You look like you could use a good meal."

Now that was a lie if she'd ever heard one. Her mother was always on her about her thick body, limiting her food intake constantly as though she were in some overseas spa.

And Michelle had said she looked like a white girl who had never missed a meal. God, she missed her best friend. She'd barely had time to toss a rose on Mindy's grave before stealing away from the Pitchford home under the cover of darkness.

"How old are you?" the man asked, still gripping her arm.

"Eighteen." Well, she was only four years off, right? She picked up her pace.

"Eighteen?" His lips spread into a sneer that unsettled her. He snatched her bag from her shoulder. "Okaaaaay, we're in business."

"In business?" she asked, jerking her arm away.

"You're going to need a job and I know about one that would be perfect for you."

"What kind?" she said, inching away. Two police officers were hanging near the Mediterranean restaurant about five storefronts away. They might as well have been miles from the corner as far as Tanya was concerned.

"Customer service," he said, gazing intently at her, before shifting to take in the officers down the street, "but we can talk about all that later," he added quickly. "Just let me get you something to eat."

Instinct told her to stay put. His sudden interest in her and the fact he had tracked her from the station shouted bad news. "We can talk about it now or we're not going to talk at all. Give me my bag. You'll go your way and I'll go mine."

"Look bitch!" he growled, flipping a knife to her midriff. The sharp edge caused an inkling of pain to shoot through her. "I'm trying to help your country ass out."

"You know," she said, looking him square in the eye, "normally someone holding a knife to me would scare the shit out of me. But after what my parents did, nothing scares me anymore." With the knife point still poking her side, she called out, "Officers! Officers! Help!"

The man's mouth dropped. "You stupid bitch." He pulled back his knife, eyes blazing as he turned to sprint away.

She waved as she said, "Bye-bye."

"What seems to be the trouble, lady?" the taller of the officers asked, as his partner went after the fleeing pimp.

"Gee, I don't know, Officer," she said in her most innocent voice. "He said he's lost but when I tried to tell him that I didn't know a single thing about New York, he pulled a knife on me and took my bag."

"A knife?" the officer asked, his radio suddenly crackled. He responded, then said to Tanya, "We got him—and your purse. The only place he's going is to the Midtown North Precinct."

After some other policemen in a squad car took her to the precinct, Tanya swore out a complaint and signed the necessary paperwork to get her bag back. Thank God! Everything she considered important was in that bag.

But the tall cop who rescued her wasn't going to let her back out on the streets before he said a thing or two. "You have to be more careful in a big place like this."

"I can't go home."

When he pressed her for a reason, she told him a few of the pertinent details about what had happened to her. The officer must have believed her because he took her to a shelter on Forty-Eighth Street. The elderly woman who ran the house was tough, but fair.

Tanya stuck with her four-year leap in age and soon found a waitressing job. Only when she began working at Class Is In and one of the restaurant's owners took her under his wing, did she begin to smile again.

Though she insisted she was eighteen, David pampered her and didn't touch her for three years—only showing her the wonderful things he loved about New York: music, art, architecture, history.

At Class Is In, David showed her things to do with food that had nothing to do with getting it to the plate and everything to do with tantalizing the senses. When she turned eighteen, he married her and she was slowly able to push away the shadows of Social Circle. David loved her—slowly, gently—and she came alive again. His gentle touch could make her wet every single time, and she opened to him, adored him as much as he loved her.

He was as round as the Pillsbury Dough Boy with dimpled cheeks to match, thinning hair, a bright wide smile, and a sense of humor, but he was as much of a social outcast as she felt.

David loved her—but unfortunately, not enough to leave a will ensuring her financial future. When he died of an aneurysm at forty, his partners paid off the restaurant's entire debt—as well as their own portion from his insurance policy, then bought out his shares. By the time she got a lawyer to sort it all out, he was only able to secure a small one-time payment for her, which she tucked away for safekeeping.

Then she saw the advertisement for The Perfect Fit in Chicago. With David gone, and his restaurant securely in the hands of his greedy partners, nothing kept her tied to New York. She learned one key lesson from her relationship with David: Finding a man who loved her more than she loved him was always on the menu—but she would never serve her heart up on a platter again.

❤❤❤

As Tanya lay on the sofa in Brandi's office, listening to the soothing sounds of the ocean coming from the stereo system behind the desk, the doorbell rang, jerking her out of a wonderful dream where David had reached out to her, loving her once again. She missed him so much. She jumped off the sofa, sprinted to the door, and opened it, but came to a crashing halt when she saw the visitor. "Where's Sierra?" she asked Vernon, her voice sounding much calmer than she felt inside.

Vernon pushed forward, trying to barge in. "I need to talk to you."

She pushed back. "Not without the woman of the house being home. I don't want her to think anything's going on with us."

He propped a foot in the small opening to keep it from shutting all the way. "I'm the man of this house! I can come in anytime I please," he snapped as he pushed his way into the house.

"Not the way Brandi tells it. And she who holds the gold, makes the rules. I'd rather hang my hat with the winning team any day." She glowered angrily at him. "Where's Sierra?"

Vernon stood just a few inches from her. "Why are you so worried? She's not your child."

"She doesn't have to be my child," Tanya snapped back. "It's really low of you to do this. I thought you loved your children. At least that's what you told me."

Vernon pulled back the curtain,and peeked out of the living room window before he turned to Tanya. "Listen, I have a proposition for you. One hundred thousand gets you out of my house and out of Chicago."

Boy, he really was losing it. She parted her lips to tell him off, but quickly closed them. Heck, with that kind of cash, she could buy her own house, pay for her own schooling. She wouldn't need either one of them.

She pushed the idea aside as reality set in. Even if she trusted Vernon enough to go along with it, she had a commitment to Brandi and to the children. She wouldn't leave until she'd done her time, fulfilling her contract, then her guilty conscience would be eased. Tanya didn't need the karma—she'd already lived down the worst of things. Because Brandi was right—deep down, she'd known that something was going on with Vernon. But she'd never pressed the point because she didn't want to rock the boat. If she stayed with Brandi, she would have opportunities instead of just a little extra wear and tear on her body.

Twirling a golden curl around her index finger, she met his gaze. "Can't do it."

Vernon gripped her shoulders and shook her. "What do you mean, you can't do it?"

"Okay, then…I *won't* do it." She shook him off. "I'm doing better now than when you lied to me."

"And she's working you like a dog or some glorified maid," he said, following her to the entrance of the dining room. "I'm talking money free and clear."

"Lower your voice, Simone's upstairs. She doesn't need to hear you talking like this."

"Come on, Tee. I want my family back," he said softly. "You know this is wrong."

She shrugged, switching off the television. "Brandi didn't say that you *couldn't* come home."

"I'm not coming home until you're gone," he said, eyes locked on hers. "This isn't right, you living here with my wife and kids."

"Then it looks like you're in for a nice long stay at the Rubber Room Hilton. My contract's up in six months."

Vernon winced, trailing her into the living room. "A contract? *What* contract?"

"A contract that makes up for lost time and love—to your wife."

"I knew she was crazy, but damn!" He rubbed a hand through his short-cropped hair as his eyes widened with shock.

Tanya grinned as she sat down on the sofa. "She's smarter than you are. She's also paying for me to go back to school."

"I would've done that," he said, lowering his voice.

"You were too busy keeping me active between the sheets to care about developing my mind."

"What do you need that for?" he asked, spreading his hands. "I gave you everything you wanted. Everything you needed."

"And look what I have now…not a damn thing!" Tanya stood, then perched on the sofa again and grinned. "At least I don't have to stroke her ego, kiss her ass, or deal with a shitty attitude or mood swings."

Vernon's face flushed an angry brown. "Damn it! I don't have mood swings!"

"Then with your bitching and moaning all the time, I should be more worried than I thought. They say those down-low brothers—"

Angry sparks flew from Vernon's eyes. "Woman, I know you didn't just imply that I'm gay."

She drummed her fingers on the end table. "What else would explain the way you act sometimes?"

"I was under a lot of stress!"

"Stress caused by lying all the time. I'd have mood swings, too," she said with a bitter laugh. "The major difference between you and your wife is that Brandi and I communicate regularly and she doesn't require me to put my feelings aside for hers."

"So now you're sleeping with her, too?" Vernon roared. "I can't believe this shit!"

Tanya shrugged, enjoying how much that prospect seemed to upset him. "Given how she handles everything else, she probably fucks better than you do, too. But I guess I'll find that out—later."

A peal of laughter flowed into the living room as Brandi strolled in, glaring at Vernon, Sierra hot on her heels covering her ears. "Go to your room, Sierra. We'll talk later."

The little girl cast an uneasy gaze at her father before scrambling up the stairs without even bothering to get her normal hug from him.

"I should kick your ass for scaring me shitless and sending me on a three-hour search for Sierra!" Brandi slipped off her sneakers and dropped down onto the love seat. "And now you're trying to steal my wife."

Vernon tore his gaze from Sierra's retreating form. "Will you stop with that crap?"

Tanya strolled to the bar, unlocked it, and poured a drink as Brandi said, "Oh, just 'cause I'm getting mine, it's crap?"

"You're embarrassing this family," he replied, going to stand near his wife.

"No, Vernon, I'm embarrassing *you.*" She accepted the drink from Tanya, nodding her thanks. "And that's the way it should be."

Vernon's gaze trailed Tanya's rear end before she perched on the edge of the sofa next to his wife.

Seeing the lust in his eyes, Brandi could only grin.

His gaze flickered from one woman to the other and back. "So you want the world to know you were so inadequate as a wife that I had to go elsewhere for good sex..."

Tanya felt a slash of pain in her heart for Brandi. God, Vernon reminded her so much of her father. She cringed at his smug expression as he took a seat.

Tanya left her spot and leaned over to fix his tie. "And if you're so damned good at what you do, what was *my* excuse for getting it elsewhere, *stud*?"

Vernon visibly paled, glowering at Tanya as she walked away and sat within arm's reach of Brandi.

Brandi nodded at Tanya, thanking her for the save. Then she turned back to Vernon. "What you did with your dick had nothing to do with what happened in our bedroom. You did it because you were greedy, just like your father. And selfish, too. What other reason do you have for picking Sierra up, then telling her she could go to Usher's concert when we agreed two weeks ago that she couldn't?" Brandi looked at him, a tear glistening in the corner of one eye. "Just to flex your muscle and cause us some grief? Grow up, Vernon! She used you, knowing she was wrong. And you used her, thinking what?" She shook her head. "I still can't call it. I had to have security roll with me into the Chicago Theater to yank her fast tail out of there."

Vernon looked back, defiance flickering in his eyes. "She was fine. Her friend's mother was taking them and picking them up. She wasn't in any danger."

"That's not the point. We agreed that until she started turning in her work on a regular basis, her privileges were gone."

"Do you know what people are saying about you?" Vernon tried to change the subject.

Brandi shrugged as Tanya walked toward the dining room. "Yeah, the women are saying, 'Damn, why didn't I think of that? I lost my husband'"—she flipped up the middle finger—"'my house'"—this time the index finger went up—"'and life as I know it over a piece of ass, when I could've kept him, his money, and had a bonus...my own wife.'"

"Dinner is served, madame," Tanya said, with a flourish as she pulled back a chair at the head of the dining room table for effect. She smiled at Brandi, hoping to end this painful conversation, especially since the girls were doing their best to stay out of sight at the top of the stairs. They didn't need to hear this, no matter how close to the truth it might be.

Brandi managed not to laugh as she crossed the room. "Thanks, Tanya. And what are we having tonight?"

"Well, I threw on my coat and broke out the grill," she said, imitating a Texas twang and winking at Vernon. "The cows saw me coming and it caused a stampede 'cause they were trying to get away. But I snagged us one."

Brandi let out a hearty laugh; all signs of her tears were gone.

"We're having beef barbecued ribs and beef hot links, burgers and turkey dogs for the girls; with iced potato salad, Southern baked beans, spaghetti, fresh squeezed lemonade, and apple pie àla mode ."

"Ahhhhh, summer in the fall," Brandi said with a little victory shimmy of her shoulders. Then she gave Tanya's hand a gentle pat. "My kind of woman."

Tanya glared at the girls peeking in on the argument from the stairs. She jerked her thumb toward the upstairs bathroom. The girls scrambled back upstairs and she could hear them in the bathroom, pretending that they had been nowhere in hearing distance as they washed their hands.

Tanya cupped a hand over her mouth, yelling, "Howwdeeeeeee. Come on, girls, chow's on!"

Brandi placed the fork on the edge of the plate and whispered to Tanya. "Did you really sleep with someone else?"

"No," Tanya whispered back with a grin. "I just said it to score one for our side."

"Thanks."

"No problem."

Vernon stormed toward the door, and then turned back to both of them. "You're gonna pay for this, I'll make sure of it."

"Like James Brown said—" Brandi lifted her fork and smacked her lips in unladylike fashion—"don't start none, won't be none."

Tanya's laughter followed him out the door.

Chapter Twenty-Eight

Vernon had managed to be civil in the office for the rest of the week, but the assistants had the added duty of messenger service between the two camps. Michael dropped by and Brandi reconfirmed his position as the company accountant, but brushed off the strong advances. He left saying that he was "there for her" if she needed anything.

As she sat in her home office, going over the business plan two more times, she thought, relationships that began on what "might have been" didn't always last. But Lord, Michael was a fine piece of work. If Vernon didn't get his act together soon, and that delta between her thighs started humming a precision tune, she might have to...

The phone rang. She checked the display. When William Spencer's cell number came up, she just let it ring. She didn't need any of his bull-shit so early on a Saturday morning. At least give her until noon. Yes, noon was a good time to deal with unsavory things. A person's had breakfast and dinner's a long way off.

Tanya had taken the girls to a track meet, giving Brandi uninterrupted time to pull everything together so splitting the company would have minor repercussions for the staff. The court date was only a month away, and Avie had said they needed to be prepared to prove to the judge that it was better for all involved.

The doorbell rang three times before she could push away from the desk. The impatient person on the other side had better not be a salesperson—he would definitely not be on the receiving end of "good morning."

She froze as her father-in-law's bald head, beady eyes, and thick mustache swam into focus. It was eight in the morning on a Saturday and William Spencer had nerve enough to have on a three-piece suit, complete with timepiece and chain.

She ran her fingers through her hair, bracing herself as she opened the door. She knew his presence on her doorstep so early in the morning wasn't good news.

He brushed past her into the foyer, quickly scanning the first level of the house. "Where are the girls?"

"They're with Tanya."

His jowls shook as he grimaced, obviously keeping his first thoughts to himself—the wisest thing she'd seen him do yet. "You've taken this thing a little too far, missy."

She closed the door, sighing wearily. "Nice of you to grace my home with your presence and unwanted opinion." She leaned against the entrance. "And what's too far? The fact that I've accepted my husband's mistress into our home?"

"It's absurd!"

Brandi grinned, enjoying the man's discomfort. "No more absurd than my husband having an affair. He took vows—vows that said he would keep to me and only me. I'm holding up my end. Why can't he?"

"It was meaningless," he said, waving her off with a dismissing swipe of a heavy hand.

"In other words, you knew about it, too," she said dryly. "All the men knew and not one of you wondered how I would feel. But then, there's not much I could expect. You probably gave him the rule book on playing the field."

His beady brown eyes narrowed to slits. "Mistresses are a common thing, little lady. Men have done it for centuries. There are more women than men, so something has to give. Having more than one woman has been a part of our culture for centuries."

Brandi smoothed out her sweat suit. "Then those men need to stay as far away from marriage as possible."

His thick lips curled into a sneer. "We would do that, if so many of you *desperate* women didn't push for marriage or demand to be kept. And this new crop of young women—these gold diggers—are all right with the way *we* like it. There's too many women out there for any man to stay with just one," he repeated.

"You really believe that bull?" she asked, watching him rock back and forth on his heels. "Okay, if that's the new program, then I can get with that. If I'm washing dishes, she'd better be on the back end drying some shit off. If I'm out making the money, she needs to be switchin' in the kitchen, baby. She'd better get with the program and help out; she's not getting no easy ride—literally."

"So give him a divorce," he said, glowering angrily at her.

"Hell no! She's not going to roll in and parlay up in my house after all my hard work. She'd better get used to me being all up in the program. I was here first and I'm here to stay!"

"For some reason he still...loves you." William sputtered over the words as though it hurt to say them. "If you will recall, I was against your marriage to begin with."

"I don't have to recall. You did everything but take out a billboard or hire the Good Year blimp." Then she pointed to his barrel-like form. "Maybe just a twenty-X shirt to fit around your middle would have done the trick."

"You—you—you—" he stuttered as he tried for a quick comeback. He would have to go the distance to top a Jeffrey Manor girl. The deadly scowl on his face was almost the same as the one he'd worn the first time she'd gone to dinner at the Spencer house.

❤❤❤

Spring Break, her junior year of college. Brandi walked into the Spencers' Kenwood mansion and looked up into the icy glare of Vernon's father. He looked like the Black, pudgy version of Mr. Clean—complete with a barrel-sized waistline— rather than a high-powered mergers and acquisitions man. He gripped the lapels of his three-piece gray suit, giving her a quick once-over and scowling. "A little *larger* than normal."

Vernon gasped and grimaced. "Dad, not everybody loves a bone. Even Mama's got a little size on her. And it looks good."

"That's right, baby. You tell him," Bettye Spencer said, making her way into the parlor. She wore a classic black A-line dress and a double strand of pearls. "Bones are for dogs and the only barking I've heard in this house is this old windbag right here." She poked at Spencer's middle. "Welcome to our home," she said, shaking Brandi's hand.

"Thank you, Mrs. Spencer."

"Oh, call me Bettye, dear, Mrs. Spencer is his mother," she said in a dry tone. "And she won't let me forget it."

Brandi trailed behind the graceful older woman, and was thankful that she had worn a simple black column dress, and matching classic pumps. Her father had given her the pearls and matching earrings for her twelfth birthday.

Vernon gave her a quick peck on the cheek as they moved past the Ming vase and strolled over the huge oriental carpet.

The house had intricately carved wooden inlays throughout the foyer, living room, and dining room. The butler's pantry off the pale green kitchen was as big as a master bedroom. A glass door led to a huge black-and-white solarium with a fourteen-piece wrought iron patio set to match, and a fireplace flickering with a warm glow. Another set of glass doors led to the gardens outside.

"Thank you for having me today," Brandi said, as Vernon held out her chair. "It's a pleasure meeting you, Mr. Spencer."

"I prefer to be called William. I'm sure that will be easier to remember."

There was an insult in that somewhere. Brandi hadn't picked up a fork before William asked, "And what college did your father attend?"

"My father didn't go to college," she said as Vernon passed a plate of mesquite-grilled chicken her way. Her appetite had taken a nosedive when Spencer's scowl became permanently etched on his light brown face.

He looked at her for a moment before pushing away his plate. "Hmph. Figures."

Brandi's fork didn't quite make it to her mouth. "Excuse me?"

"I said—"

"William, can I see you in the butler's pantry, please," Bettye said, giving him an angry glare.

As they left the room, Vernon reached for Brandi's hand and held it for a moment.

She pulled away and now felt more insecure than she could ever remember. "Where's the bathroom?"

"Here, I'll show you," he said.

When they reached the small room, angry voices rang out so loudly that Vernon tensed. He slipped into the bathroom with Brandi and closed the door. The door leading into the kitchen was slightly cracked, and his parents' conversation came through louder and clearer than they probably knew.

"Sit your behind down and quit insulting that young woman! She's the first one he's ever brought home," Bettye was saying.

Brandi smiled at Vernon as he leaned forward and kissed her lips.

"And if she's any indication of his taste," William snapped back. "We didn't need to see anyone else."

Brandi gasped, whispering, "Can we get out of here?"

Vernon shook his head and whispered, "They'll know we're in here if we move right now."

"She's from Jeffrey Manor—*working-class* people," William bellowed. "We don't *do* working class, we stay with our own kind. Why can't he settle down with Veronica Chapman? Now that's class."

"Veronica may come from money, but she's far from class, my dear," Bettye said, in a voice dripping with contempt. "Word on the street is that little hussy is serving it quicker than she can buy a new pair of drawers to cover it. And he doesn't love her. He loves this one."

Brandi laid her head on Vernon's chest. He kissed her forehead gently.

"Who said anything about love? People don't marry for love; they marry for lust or convenience."

"Well then, I guess I fall into a whole new category."

"Oh, do tell what that is!"

"I married you because I had nothing better to do at the time," Bettye snapped. "Lust had nothing to do with it. And this marriage hasn't been convenient since you spread out so far it's now a gymnastic sport just to get into your clothes. How dare you imply that *she's* overweight!"

Brandi's hand snaked out, covering Vernon's laugh.

"Woman, who the hell do you think you're talking to?" William said.

"A man who doesn't know how to let people live their lives and learn their lessons in their own way," Bettye shot back. "She's beautiful, absolutely beautiful and I applaud our son for choosing such a lovely young lady."

"He's a child!" William roared. "He doesn't know his asshole from an electric socket."

"No, he's a young man with goals of his own and if you keep trying to pressure him to fill your shoes, you're going to cause him to break."

"If I don't push him, who will? He's a weak-minded boy, thanks to you. Thinks with his heart instead of his head," William said gruffly. "He'll never gain half the success I have."

"He's a different person. Maybe he's not supposed to turn out like you. Maybe he'll be happy serving his community and with all that volunteer work he does. That's important, too."

"Volunteer work doesn't fill bank accounts".

"No, it serves a higher purpose. It gives people who wouldn't have a chance at a better life the opportunity to fulfill their dreams, too. Not just people who've had money dropped in their laps and can lay back and take it easy like you."

"Nothing in my life's been easy—especially since I married you."

"You know what to do. Don't let a little thing like a few trips to court and handing over half your money put you off. Bring it on, big boy."

Brandi absorbed every word, watching as tears welled up in Vernon's eyes—but he looked up at the ceiling and shook his head to keep them back.

She reached out, pulling him to her breasts, and he stayed there for a brief moment as she stroked his head. His father obviously didn't love him. In that moment, she knew they were kindred souls in more ways than one. Brandi trying to overcome the pain of the man who had hurt her, Vernon trying to live up to the expectations of a father he would never be able to please.

Maybe they could find peace with each other.

William Spencer—who had made her life hell, even going so far as to undermine their wedding plans up to the very point of "I do"—was still up to no good thirteen years later. His nostrils flared; at that moment, he looked like an oversized version of her husband. "You were too young to be married."

"That's not why you objected," Brandi shot back. "First, it was about my size. Well, I have news for you—just to please your tired behind I tried Weight Watchers and watched my weight go in the wrong direction. I signed up with Jenny Craig, then realized her tail is a little on the thick side and no one's complaining. I like who I am and I love my size. You're twice my size. It hasn't done you any harm, so get a grip."

William started to speak.

Brandi held up a hand. "And another one of your reasons—my father wasn't a Morehouse grad as you had the nerve to point out to your snobby friends," she said, anger shooting through her like an Apollo launch. "My father didn't go to college, but he was smart enough to stay with the same woman for thirty-seven years. Now that's a fidelity example for ya." She leaned forward. "Fifty-nine and single, sporting a new Barbie doll on your arm every two weeks, and for what, huh?" Lowering her gaze to his groin, she said, "Testing it out before it falls completely off?"

He flushed a deep tan. "Don't talk to me that way, young lady."

"Then don't come into my home trying to run things. Your laundry's a little dirty, too. Some of it's so foul that it's standing in the corner by itself funking up the whole basement." She turned, strolled to the door, and held it open. "There's no advice I want or need from you. You think people didn't know you were slipping it to Deborah Chadwick, Vanessa Stewart, and that other woman while you were married?" Brandi shook her head. "Think again, slick. You weren't *that* slick." She grinned as he stepped over the threshold. "With you sprinkling so much joy around the world, no wonder the former Mrs. Spencer's having so much fun with her new man."

William whirled to face Brandi so quickly he lost his balance and gripped the door to keep his meaty legs from buckling underneath him. "*What* new man?"

Brandi grinned, winked, and said, "Ooops." Then she slammed the door and went back to her office.

CHAPTER *Twenty-Nine*

The laughter soon died on Brandi's lips as she remembered admonishments from her own mother earlier that morning: "As long as Tanya is in your house we don't need to have a conversation." As stubborn as her mother was, Brandi knew she meant every word. But she had to do things this way. Their conversation led to a point where Brandi got angry and said, "Mama, Romans adopted people into their families when they were adults."

Mama looked at her, shaking her head. "That was only if they didn't have a son to carry on the family name, or their child got killed in combat, or if they didn't like the children they had given birth to—"

"But they adopted *an adult*," Brandi said, "And the new person took on the family name. I'm just sort of *adopting* a family member of Vernon's a little late in the game. She's already housebroken, and she cooks stuff I can't even pronounce. So what's the difference?"

No one but Donny and Tanya seemed to take Brandi's side in all this. But then again, Tanya really didn't *have* a choice. They had to stick together. If it were too easy for Vernon, he would believe he could do it again. Next time she just might go Lorena Bobbitt on his ass or like that other woman who whacked her husband's penis totally off, then fed it to the dog.

Her mother had been a stabilizing factor and the voice of wisdom for the majority of her life. Brandi hated to go against that, but she couldn't just roll over, forgive Vernon and let it ride, either. She had to hold her point no matter what changes came down the line, and even if Vernon got his act together she would keep her promise and see this lesson through to the end.

Mama had been so right about everything else in life, why hadn't she seen this coming? She had been adamant about Brandi marrying Vernon instead of Michael Cobb, the man Brandi had dated for two years at Fisk.

"There's something about that Michael I don't like. Reminds me of a cat—sneaky and quiet."

"You'll grow to love him, Mama," Brandi replied, rinsing an old china plate.

"Not if you paid me to," she said, brushing a hand over her blue paisley dress.

Brandi turned away from the sink to face her mother. "But he's asked me to marry him."

"So has Vernon."

How she wished her father were alive; she could really use his help right now dealing with her mother.

"But Michael's a gentleman, and patient and brilliant."

Her mother's chin lifted a little. "Vernon comes from an established family and a long line of money."

"But I'm not marrying for money. I'm going to make my own money," Brandi exclaimed.

"And you'll suffer for it, especially if you don't marry a man who can secure your future. He'll work himself into an early grave just like your daddy."

"No Mama, you're wrong. He died so he wouldn't ever have to face the pain of losing you." Instantly, Brandi regretted her words, especially when she saw the expression on her mother's face crumble into a mass of pain.

"Do you really think so?"

Brandi nodded. "How else do you explain a healthy man dropping dead of natural causes at the age of forty-seven, Mama? He knew you could handle his death better than he could handle yours. Why did he double the insurance policy a day after you recovered? He was ready to go even then."

Brandi told her mother how her father had reacted at the hospital.

Her mother could only manage to say, "He was a good man."

"Yes, he was, Mama," Brandi said, hugging her mother, "Yes he was."

❤❤❤

As Brandi swiveled around in her large office chair, she saw the signs of her accomplishments all around. She realized that although her mother had said marrying Vernon would bring about security, the opposite had happened.

Her life was just as far out of control as it had been on her thirteenth birthday.

❤❤❤

Brandi craned her neck out of the nasty old man's window. Hollywood was gone. Seconds later, so was she.

Heavy footsteps followed as he trailed after her. She pulled up her panties and pants as she ran. Every movement hurt, then a strange numbness settled over her that pushed aside fear and every other emotion.

"Come back. I won't touch ya again. I promise. I thought you had to make a phone call."

Fuck a phone call! She'd already paid enough for the first one she didn't make.

She ran through the yard, her vagina throbbing with every step, tears coming so fast and furious that she couldn't see more than four feet ahead.

She sprinted to the corner several blocks away, and there stood a tall blue, silver, and white box like her knight in shining armor. A telephone booth— just what she needed!

She snatched the blue handset and put it to her ear, fumbling in her pocket for the coins her mother insisted she keep with her for emergency purposes. This was definitely an emergency. Her fingers trembled as the coins finally made it into the slot and she punched the number.

Several seconds later a warm, comforting voice answered.

Brandi's breath came out in a rush. "Mama, I need you. Please...I'm so sorry. Please come and get me. He...he...this man...he...he..."

"Baby, where are you?"

"I'm on—," Brandi looked up, her eyes locked on the dark green sign with white letters. "—Forty-seventh Street and Michigan Avenue."

Brandi heard her mother's sharp intake of breath. Brandi knew what was next, but she didn't care. She would welcome any sermon right now. Anything, as long as her mother still loved her and would always be there for her. Especially now. "Mama, please..."

"I'll be right there, baby. Just get somewhere safe—inside a store or something, and stay out of sight. I'll find you. I love you."

Brandi couldn't hold back the tears as her voice cracked. "I love you, too, Mama. Mama, I'll be in..." She glanced around quickly. "A&B Liquor store."

She turned to the store's front glass window, which had a clear view of the street. She could watch her mother's car pull up. She went inside and huddled in a front corner. A group of men played cards next to the wine cooler.

"What you doin' there, girl?"

Brandi couldn't help shivering. "Please let me stay here. My mama's coming to get me."

"All right." The gruff voice bellowed across the room. "But you can't stay here all day. She'd better come soon."

While she waited, she thought about things her mother hadn't told her, like that nasty old man. She never told her that someone guised as a savior could also wear a cloak of evil.

Brandi slumped against the window, which reflected the inside aisles of the store and gave her an excellent view of herself as well. What it didn't show was the wounds burrowing a lifelong path in her mind. She would never be hurt again. She would always listen to her mother from now on.

An hour later, as she lay on the examination table in the emergency room, Brandi told her mother the truth. She told her mother everything, and then recounted the incident for the police, giving his description and the general location of the house, since she didn't know the address. She held onto her mother, welcoming the soft scent of gardenia. The doctor took evidence for a rape kit, explaining every step of the way, Brandi winced with every movement, especially when the cold steel went inside her already tender flesh.

Her mother quietly assured her that she would heal, and that some young man would love her and appreciate her. He would ask her to be his wife long before he asked to be her lover—and then that would happen on their wedding night. Her young man would stand before the Creator and the whole world to say he loved her, not sneak her off into some little hideaway that no one else could know about—like Hollywood.

"Mama..."

"It's all right, baby," she said, patting her gently. "It's all right. I never wanted this to happen. I always tried to be strict and it pushed you out there into..." Her voice trailed off as she tried to compose herself. "Sweet Jesus, my baby girl!" Mama's sobs pierced the air, ripping into her soul in a way that the man's attack never had.

Hollywood was arrested for attempted rape, and expelled from school. The man, Trevor Thompson, was arrested and convicted of rape. Across the courtroom, she could see the glint in his eyes and realized he wasn't the least bit sorry for what he had done to her. Jail time wouldn't give back her virginity, but at least he wouldn't hurt anyone else.

Now, twenty-two years later, she was picking up the pieces behind another painful incident, this one a broken heart. Instead of following her own mind, she had taken her mother's advice—advice that came from her mother's own fears. Now, just like her father, Vernon had hurt her beyond words: her father by abandoning her in death when she loved him and needed him so much; Vernon by not respecting their vows. Although he had been there in the flesh every single night, he, too, had abandoned her emotionally, spiritually, and intimately.

The soft, tinkling laughter of the children as they came in from the garage jarred her into the present. Tears escaped and landed on the financial projections as she willed away the painful memories.

Sierra and Simone burst through the office door and shot across the room, straight into her open arms. She held onto them—sobbing a little as she took in the soft scent of baby lotion, which soon filled the air around her. They had showered before coming in.

Brandi pulled away to look at the smaller versions of her and Vernon.

"I love you, Mommy," her youngest said, reaching up to take another hug.

"Me, too," Simone said. Not wanting to be left out, she reached out to wipe the tears from Brandi's face before burrowing her little face into the soft curve of her mother's neck. "I love you, Mom."

The one thing she knew the day she got married was that she *didn't* want children. She never wanted to put herself in a position like her mother, worrying about children.

Now she had two little girls; every day she prayed for their safety. Every day she held her heart in reserve, just waiting for bad news. No matter what she did to keep them safe, the thought that some man might be lying in wait to hurt them always lurked in the back of her mind.

Now she also could lay the prospects of a broken heart at their feet. And there would be nothing she could do to protect them against that, either.

CHAPTER *Thirty*

The November air was colder than expected. Normally snow would grace the ground this close to Thanksgiving, but it hadn't made an appearance yet. Working people were grateful. As soon as those little white flakes hit the air, people forgot everything they knew about winter driving, slipping and sliding into each other and adding to the already obnoxious Chicago traffic mess. And the judge had warned that if any party came late, he would rule for the other side.

Brandi sat next to Avie in courtroom 1900 and glanced over at Vernon and his attorney, Mason Myers—the attorney that Vernon had generally wanted as legal counsel for The Perfect Fit. Vernon, dressed in a dark business suit in contrast to Brandi's winter white dress, didn't look quite as confident as he had been before. *What happened to Craig?* Brandi thought. He was a lawyer. Evidently, Alanna didn't want him in the middle of the madness. See, women did stick together. Craig probably would have given Avie a little run for her money. But in the end she still would have mopped the floor with his ass. Brandi stole a quick glance at Vernon's attorney. Remembering Mason's incompetence in handling The Perfect Fit that first time out, Brandi smiled. This was going to be easy.

"All rise. The Honorable Judge Bowden presiding in the matter of Spencer versus Spencer."

Mason stood and addressed the court. "Your honor, we've filed for a legal separation."

"I can see that," the judge said, pushing gold-rimmed glasses up on a bulbous nose. "After reading the material from Mrs. Spencer's lawyer,

I'm surprised that she didn't file first." He looked in Brandi's direction.

"Oh, no Your Honor, I *love* my husband," Brandi gushed, laying a hand on her chest as she batted long, mascara-covered lashes. "I *wanted* my marriage to work. Ouch!"

Avie kicked her under the table, growling just under her breath, "You're laying it on too thick, Brandi. Cut it out!"

"She's lying about wanting to stay together," Vernon snapped as he brushed away Mason's hand. "She knows exactly what she needs to do if that was the real motive."

Judge Bowden peered over the edge of his glasses at Vernon. "And what's that?"

Mason leaned over, warning Vernon, "Let me do the talking, please."

Vernon ignored him. "She needs to get rid of that woman!"

"What woman?" The judge looked down, flipping through his papers. "Are you bringing charges of—?"

"No, I don't mean they're sleeping together," replied an embarrassed and somewhat subdued Vernon.

"Not yet," Brandi answered as she stared at her husband.

"Is there something going on here that I should know about?" the judge asked.

Brandi stood. "Well, yes—"

"Please excuse my client's outburst, Your Honor." Avie yanked Brandi down in her seat and hissed, "Hey, let me do the talking. That's what you're paying me for."

"I'm not paying you," Brandi shot back, grumpily.

"They don't have to know that!" Avie snapped with an angry shake of her head that sent her auburn hair tumbling across her face. "Leave me with some dignity."

"Oh, so you have that?"

"Don't make me whip your ass up in here," Avie whispered, hoping the others wouldn't hear.

Judge Bowden cleared his throat, hiding a chuckle behind his hand. "Actually, Counselor, I'd like to hear this in her words. It should be quite interesting." He reached out into a tiny glass bowl perched on the clerk's desk and pulled out a handful of pumpkin seeds and popped a couple in his mouth.

"Well, his mistress has moved into our house and—"

The court reporter blinked and her hands paused over the stenograph machine. The bailiff looked at the judge, then at Brandi. The clerk froze with a silver date stamp still in hand. The courtroom was eerily silent.

Judge Bowden nearly choked on a pumpkin seed. "Come again?"

"Tanya Kaufman is now a member of our big, happy family," Brandi said, with a wide grin and a perky California-sunshine attitude. "Isn't it just wonderful?"

The judge looked at his people before scratching his bald spot. "Okay, give me a second while I wrap my head around this one." He stared at Brandi, then at Vernon before he turned to the clerk and asked, "Are we well stocked with bubbly? I think we're *all* gonna need it."

The plump woman scrambled out of her chair and disappeared into the judge's chambers, returning with a bottle of sparkling grape juice and three glasses that she perched right in front of him.

Mason's and Vernon's jaws dropped.

The judge looked at both of them and said, "My courtroom, my rules."

Brandi managed not to laugh, but she decided this judge was her type of person.

The judge leveled a gaze at her. "You may proceed."

Avie covered her eyes with a single hand.

"Well, since Vernon felt it necessary to have a little outside…ahhhhh… *activity*—and we're supposed to share things—I thought we should share the mistress, too," Brandi explained.

The judge blinked at her, his lips crinkling in an effort not to laugh. He scratched his temple for a moment, then bolted from the bench and through the wooden door, leaving a cool breeze in his wake.

A sudden roar of hysterical laughter echoed from his chambers, bouncing off the high ceilings and tickling Brandi's ear.

Vernon's shoulders tensed as he gripped the wooden table. Oh, yes, this would be a piece of cake. Chocolate at that.

The portly bailiff glanced at the door, rocked on his heels, bit his bottom lip, and bolted for the judge's chambers. His hearty laughter joined that of the judge. Professionalism be damned.

Even Avie had lowered her head and let out an unladylike snort.

Several minutes later, composed, but still red-faced, the judge and bailiff returned to the courtroom. "Okay," the judge said, "we will proceed."

This time Avie spoke up. "Mrs. Spencer wants to separate the business right away."

Judge Bowden looked at Mason. "Can you at least agree on that to make it easy?"

Vernon hesitated, then turned to his attorney.

Brandi spoke up. "All I want are my clients and half the equipment—fifty percent. He can keep the house on Cregier—"

"The house?" Vernon looked over his attorney's shoulder to look at her.

"You don't want to just sell it and split the profits?" asked an astonished Judge Bowden.

"Nope," she said, with a quick shrug. "He can have the house."

Judge Bowden paused for a moment before asking, "And the children?"

"He's a good...father," she said with a sly glance in his direction. "Joint custody is fine. All I need is child support, and maintenance to help with the mistress's upkeep."

Judge Bowden shook his head. "I'm not sure I can rule on the mistress. She's an adult."

Avie lifted a single document from a redwell folder. "Your Honor, we have a contract signed by Tanya Kaufman putting her into service of the Spencer family for a six-month period."

She passed the notarized document to the bailiff.

When the judge got it, he scanned it as though he suddenly held the Holy Grail in his thick hands. "I've never had a case like this in all the time I've been on the bench."

Mason asked, "Is that a valid contract?" He looked from the judge, to Brandi and Avie, who both nodded.

"It's notarized and everything," Brandi said.

"Judge, can I, um—," Mason cleared his throat—"use your chambers for a moment?"

The judge studied Mason's face. "Sure."

The short man fled the room, followed by the clerk and the judge. Moments later peals of laughter again rent the air through the not-quite-closed door.

"This can't be happening. This is a nightmare!" snapped Vernon.

Composure somewhat restored Mason, the clerk, and the judge reentered the courtroom.

"I've had people fight over children, pets, and family heirlooms," the judge said. "This will be the first case in history that a couple fights for custody of the mistress." He rubbed his hands together as though preparing to dig into a good meal. "I'll finally get my name in the books without someone having to get killed.

"Since you guys really don't seem like you want a divorce, I'm ordering counseling with a court-appointed therapist. In the meantime, the wife keeps the house on Cregier Avenue. You will sell the house on Wabash and split the profits. You all will work out visitations with the kids, because either way I'm going to allow joint custody." Then he took a long, slow breath. "And the wife, as requested in this petition, keeps...the mistress. The contract is hereby entered into court. The husband is to have no intimate contact with Ms. Kaufman without his wife's express written permission."

Avie gasped and looked at Brandi. Mason's jaw dropped. A strange silence filled the courtroom—but at least no one laughed this time.

"I don't believe this—this—this—crap! You can't do this to me!" Vernon snapped, jumping to his feet. "What kind of judge are you?"

Judge Bowden turned and scowled at him. "One that sees the bigger picture here."

Mason yanked Vernon back into the wooden chair.

Brandi leaned back so she could see around Avie. "Hey, you've had her for six months. It's *my* turn."

The judge paused, gavel in mid-air. "Do you need time to reassess things?"

"What I want is my wife," Vernon said.

"What you've got is a problem," Brandi shot back as Avie tried, unsuccessfully, to pull her back.

"But she's living in *my* house," Vernon yelled at his wife.

"No, she's living in *mine*."

"You crazy Bi—" Mason quickly covered Vernon's mouth.

Avie pinched Brandi hard on the arm, trying to get her to keep quiet. "No, I think my woman meter's set to just plain PMS today. Try again."

Vernon growled, shaking off his lawyer, then stormed out.

Walking through the chilly weather, Vernon pulled his collar tight around his neck to avoid the Chicago Hawk. His father, his mother, his friends—the whole world was against him. He passed Marshall Fields on State Street, ignoring the elaborate display of a storybook Christmas in the large plate-glass windows. Tourists, somewhat oblivious to the weather that was cold enough to turn cornflakes to Frosted Flakes, had camped out in front watching the animated figures.

As he turned the corner, a scene of the woodsman from *Prince Charming and Snow White* came into view. A strange take on the childhood story, but as he looked closely at the woman caught between the two men, an idea came to him.

Whipping out his cell, he dialed the one man he knew who could put an end to Tanya's reign in his house. Snow White wouldn't know what hit her.

CHAPTER Thirty-One

Brandi signed a lease for space in Avie's downtown building. Avie was on the fifty-sixth floor of the AON Center and The Perfect Match would be on the fifty-fourth. "And I'd better not hear no crap about I'm too far away," she told Avie as they celebrated the new business downstairs in Café 200.

"Hey, I'll be there every day if you're buying lunch."

"I'd do better than your cheap ass," Brandi replied. "I bet you own stock in Corner Bakery by now."

"Actually, I do," Avie said with a brief chuckle.

The next week Brandi called her employees to the main conference room. "Vernon and I are dissolving our partnership of The Perfect Fit."

She waited for the murmurs to die down before continuing. "I'm taking all of the clients I brought in to start my own company—The Perfect Match. The others will stay here with Vernon. You have three choices: go with me as I build the new company, stay with Vernon and The Perfect Fit, or leave altogether and take a severance package."

Vernon sighed wearily, then grimaced before looking at his wife, who waited for him to speak. "You'll have a few days to think things over, talk with your spouses or significant others and—"

"I don't need time," Ella Clark said, craning her neck to glare in Vernon's direction. "I *know* what I want to do. All in favor of staying with a two-timing, lowlife of a man remain seated. All in favor of going with Brandi, come with me."

Brandi gasped. "Ella, this is not the way we—"

All but five people followed Ella out of the room as though she had suddenly become a full-figured Pied Piper, eighteen-hour girdle and all. Vernon stared after them, a flash of disappointment in his eyes. Brandi felt a small stab of guilt at the outward show of disdain for her husband, but said nothing as she turned her back to him and followed the last departing employee from the room.

She had thought they would both be left with something. Would clients treat him the same way? If so, things would be worse for her husband than she thought. However, given the way his father directed traffic, she would have been on the receiving end of unfair if she hadn't taken the initiative.

Falling in step with her, Michael Cobb leaned over and said in a voice as deep as Ossie Davis's, "Well, that went well."

She glanced at all dark brown, muscular, six feet of him. His deep-set light brown eyes sparkled with mischief, and a smirk played on a generous pair of lips that were made for kissing or—damn, she didn't need to think about that. Right now the delta was keeping track of lost time. She didn't answer that smile with one of her own, because she felt a slight sense of foreboding; somehow this was going to come back to haunt her. "It went a little differently than I expected."

He followed her to her office, closed the door behind him, took a seat across from her, and cleared his throat. "You're moving on and now maybe you can give a chance to the man you should've married in the first place."

Okay, how to handle this one? Smooth and easy, baby. Smooth and easy. "You know, Michael, this isn't a good time for me right now. I'm still married."

"And whose fault is that?" he shot back, his dry tone not at all characteristic of a man who never let much ruffle him.

Her lips twitched in an effort not to grin. "Behave, Michael."

"Behave?" he asked, winking. "Are you *cursing* at me?"

This time she laughed and a weight lifted from her shoulders.

"You filed for a divorce, right?"

"No, he filed for separation, but it made things look better to the judge for me to say that I wanted to work things out even though he cheated. So this may take a while."

Michael's massive hands trailed along the soft delicate curves of hers. "And I'll wait for you. I love you, Brandi. Always have. Always will."

"I'm sure you do, but it's just not enough," she said, breaking away before she fell for his touch, his seductive voice, and piercing eyes. The fact that she still wanted him after so many years didn't help matters. The fact that the delta was waking up and trying to join the conversation didn't help, either. "Vernon loved me, too. And look where that got me."

"Not as much as I love you." Michael reached for her, pulling her into a loving embrace. "Give him up, sweetie, and let me be good to you."

Just then Renee buzzed interrupting what could easily have been a serious mistake. She was so horny, she was ready to spread them right there on her glass desk and give him some just because he'd been waiting for it so long. Or because she hadn't had any in a while. Or because the sun came up that morning. Or—hell—just because!

"Brandi, your husband's at your door," Renee whispered.

"Tell him to wait!"

Renee lowered her voice even more. "He knows Michael is in there."

"Better yet, tell him I'm busy for a little while."

"Open this damn door!" Vernon yelled.

Brandi shook her head, ignoring her husband, relishing the long, slender fingers trailing a blaze of fire from her throat to her breasts. "First, I have to learn what it's like to be good to myself," she told Michael.

"Brandi, I'm gonna break this shit in!"

Brandi said, "Renee, please call security. And let Vernon hear you doing it."

Then something occurred to her as she looked up into Michael's eyes. "You knew about Tanya all that time."

Michael's handsome face went blank. His fingers froze on her lips.

"You didn't tell me because it was in *my* best interest, you told me because you wanted Vernon exposed." She pushed him away. "I can't trust you, either."

"That's not it. He could've taken this company under," Michael replied, impatience creeping into his voice as he reached for her again. "You married his lame, arrogant ass, when things could've been perfect for us."

Brandi softened her tone. "You wanted too much, too soon. I couldn't be the wife you wanted, the woman you needed."

"Yeah, well, it seems that Vernon couldn't be the husband you wanted. At least I would've been faithful."

"Given a chance you could mess up, too. So don't get cute," she said, inching further away from him. "He only messed up six months ago, just once."

Michael looked down at her, thick, bushy eyebrows drawn in as he blinked twice. "Wrong! Tanya's been around for nearly two years..."

Brandi gasped, a sinking feeling holding ground in the pit of her stomach. Two years? Vernon had been that damn good? Or had she been that damn stupid?

"The moment you landed that account with Avistar Manufacturing." His dark brown eyes held hers. "She came in looking for a job and evidently Vernon felt she deserved the *side benefits* first. She never did get the job she wanted. But then again maybe she got exactly what she wanted all along. A Black sugar daddy."

Rage shot through Brandi like a steel ball out of a cannon, but she calmly replied, "And it never once crossed your mind to say something."

"I only spoke up because he was spending more and more and your employees would all be on the unemployment line." He reached for her again. This time she didn't resist. "And I certainly didn't say anything before because I would rather have seen you with him and think you were happy, than to point out the reasons you shouldn't be."

Now that touched her more than anything else he had said since he'd been in her office.

"I knew he would mess up someday."

He kissed her gently, searching her lips with a warm intensity that flooded her with something she couldn't name and wouldn't try to, since her lips were now quivering with expectation, and the center of the pleasure zone had quivered a little bit, too. Jesus, she couldn't afford to get wet—she was wearing a thong today—the last time she'd do that shit. She'd spent more time readjusting the damn thing than enjoying having her cheeks roam free.

"Michael, we can't do this. If you really love me, you'll wait until I'm free."

"I've waited long enough to speak my mind," he said, holding her close. "I've never married. I knew our time would come, and I didn't want to be tangled up with someone when that time came. Drop this mess, and this Tanya person, and let's really make things happen. Let me show you that I've always been the man for you."

She paused, taking that in. "I don't want to be with anyone else right now. I need some time."

Michael's eyes held hers, a flash of disappointment within them. "Are you sleeping with her? Is that it?"

"Famous question," Brandi said with a small grin.

"Inquiring minds..."

"Will have to keep inquiring," she said, opening the door for him. Anger brewed underneath and she knew that the rest of her day was shot to hell. That white bitch had lied to her, too.

"Brandi—"

She pointed to the hallway. "Leave, Michael."

The sadness in his eyes sent a shiver of pain through her, but anger quickly swept it aside. A new love interest would definitely wait until she decided that her heart could expand and open to allow Michael in. Anything less would be unfair and he deserved more than that.

He leaned over to her, brushing his lips gently against her forehead before walking away.

Seconds later, she grabbed her purse and hit the door.

CHAPTER *Thirty-Two*

"You lying…heifer!" Brandi snapped with a quick glance at her girls. Tanya could tell that the word *bitch* was what the woman meant, but certainly couldn't understand why she would be angry with her.

Tanya paused when she saw the woman's nostrils doing a little dance of their own. Honey brown skin had turned two shades darker than normal. All the woman had to do was drag her feet on the ground, lower her horns like a Spanish bull and take off.

"You lying bitch!" Brandi growled, just loud enough for only Tanya to hear as she came closer.

Tanya looked over her shoulder. "Go upstairs."

They didn't move. Both heads craned to their mother, then to Tanya, and back to their mother. Homework definitely wasn't as exciting as this new development.

"*Now!!*"

Chairs scraped against the tile and the girls scrambled to the safety of the library overhead, as Tanya took a long, slow breath.

Brandi tossed her purse on the table and bore down on Tanya. "You were sleeping with him for *two years. Two years*! And didn't say a word when I said six months."

Tanya shrugged, digested the new problem, and came to a conclusion that made more sense than it should. "Six months or two years," she said softly. "Was it any less wrong?"

That took the wind out of Brandi's sails. Her lips quivered as she tried to find a quick comeback but couldn't quite put it together.

Tanya didn't move as Brandi stood in the middle of the solarium brewing like day-old coffee. "You had already come up with the plan. I didn't want you to be more upset than you already were."

Brandi leaned in close. "How could I have possibly been more upset than finding out my husband's fucking around with another woman? How could I possibly be more upset than finding out that while I've been busting my ass day in and day out trying to make a success of the company, and still take care of things at home, that it wasn't enough?" She paced an angry path on the tile. "Oh, I *couldn't* be pissed off about that. But for two whole years. Two entire years? And I didn't see a damn thing until six months ago? Oh, *noooooooooooooooo*, I couldn't be angry," she yelled, continuing her frantic pace. "No, never that!"

"Brandi—"

"Oh, shut up," she snapped, hands balling into fists. "There's no way in hell both of us could've been that stupid. You had to know he was married. All those nights he was away—"

"Same could be said for you *my sister*," Tanya shot back, pulling up to her full height—a few inches taller than Brandi. "He was *your* husband. Where the fuck did *you* think he was—golfing?"

Brandi inhaled, obviously closing her eyes against an internal storm. "Oh, now your ass got to go."

Tanya's arms folded against her chest. "You'll let me out of my contract?"

"Abso-fucking-lutely." She crossed the last three feet between them. "I could take this shit when I was sure you didn't know, but two years? Bullshit!"

"Is it me or yourself that you're angry with?" Tanya asked, leaving the room, breaking into a trot as she passed the dining room table on her way to Vernon's old office, which had become her bedroom.

Brandi ran after her and stopped short at the fully dressed dining room table. With one thrust of her arm, she swiped the dishes off the table. Honey-roasted chicken, mashed potatoes, and California vegetables all sailed across the room, crashing against the wall.

Her pent-up rage finally shot from her head to her toenails. Tears she hadn't allowed herself to cry finally poured down. She felt so…used. She had put herself on the back burner, trying to love this man, catering to his wishes because she loved him and she thought he loved her. What had Tanya done for him that she hadn't? Brandi had overcome her revulsion to many things to please him. And for what? For what!

She'd already lost so much. How could Vernon betray her like this?

She still had to pay the mortgage on this house, half the note on Tanya's place until it sold, and the *entire* rent on the house she had in the wings. Right now finances were tighter than a Playtex girdle struggling over sixty-inch hips. No one at the new business could work a single minute of overtime—and she needed them to pitch in more than ever. Rebuilding from scratch had been a bit more taxing than expected.

All that planning ahead for nothing.

Damn that judge! She'd never expected him to let her keep their house, especially after she insisted she didn't want it. If her feet could reach backward, she'd give herself a swift kick in the ass. But she didn't want Vernon to know that she regretted her decision. She could just see the smug look on his face if things fell through, especially since she hadn't given in to the one thing he wanted most. Now that she had the opportunity to run her own business, she was somehow on the path to failure...

❤❤❤

The night during the last month of her first pregnancy when he practically insisted that she stay home and raise the child, was one night she thought her marriage wouldn't make it.

"A real woman would stay at home and raise her children," he told her and then added insult to injury by asking, "What kind of mother are you?"

"A mother with a brain and the ability to do three things at once: raise a child, run a business, and keep her husband happy. What is it that you do?" she said. "Oh, yeah, right...um, help with the business? You don't lift a finger to do anything around here, and I'm sure diaper detail and housework is beyond your understanding."

"That's not my job," he shot back. "My mother managed to keep everything intact and was happy taking care of me and Dad."

"I'm not your mother."

His lips curled into a sneer. "Well *that's* a given!"

"You know what?" she said, waddling up to him, a hand splayed across her protruding stomach. "In a minute, I'm gonna put my foot so far up your ass, your intestines will thank me for cleaning you out."

He paused, as his jaw dropped. "I'm gonna let that slide, 'cause as big as you are right now, you can't make good on that threat."

"I'll try and manage it when you're sleep. You'll be too busy snoring and drooling to notice. You give a whole new definition to the words *full of shit*."

"How can you raise our children right if you're not here?" he asked, following her. "I don't want them raised by babysitters and day care centers."

"I didn't want children in the first place. *You* wanted them. You want to stay home and raise them? Fine with me! I don't see you volunteering to do shit else," Brandi snapped. "You want to be head of household? Let's see you do more than just talk a good game. Do what I do, which is practically every damn thing. So don't question me about how I want to do things!"

Vernon walked away and she followed, trying to finish her point. "Ever since the business moved up a level, you've been trying to run my life. I'm the same woman you married two years ago, with the same goals and everything. Now you want the reins because your father's pushing your buttons? Maybe you should stay with him and see what it's like. Fuck you and him," she said, looking an angry Vernon in the eye. "Don't make my life miserable because your balls are swinging a little low. I've had to do what you do and then some, so when you reach my level, then we can talk."

The argument, laced with vicious comparisons between her and his mother, would undermine the happy points of their marriages. But she had made a point before accepting his proposal to let him know that she had every intention of being a business woman. She had also let him know that she didn't want children—period. And surprisingly enough, he was cool with that—at the time.

The change began after his father started making hints about certain things: Brandi shouldn't have so much say in the business, Brandi should be at home with a family, Brandi this and Brandi that—all aimed at putting her where William thought every woman should be. Then when Vernon joined the League of 1,000 Professional Black Men, all that testosterone in one place only bolstered his arrogance. None of the men from the League had women who shared businesses with them. Slowly he began to pull away and the change in him became more pronounced. Oh, to have the Vernon she had met in college again.

He'd always been a bit arrogant, but underneath he'd been sweet, compassionate, and most of all patient. And his response to his father the day the man insulted her showed her that Vernon was willing to go the distance.

As Brandi held Vernon in the powder room, and the vicious words between the Spencers spiraled over them, she made a decision right there and then that she would marry him. She would prove Vernon's father wrong. She was not low class and Vernon was not average and uninspired.

Following the argument, Brandi followed Vernon back to the spacious dining room. He held out the chair for her before taking the space right next to her.

His father pursed his lips and glared at Brandi as he and Bettye reentered the room. "So, Martell. I mean, Champagne. Oh—I'm sorry, it's Brandi, right?"

Vernon stood, walked to his mother, and planted a gentle kiss on her forehead. Then he extended his hand to Brandi, who stood and placed the napkin on the table between the glasses and the shiny silverware.

"Where the hell do you think you're going?" William bellowed.

"Someplace where my future wife will be respected."

"You're—you're—you're not thinking of marrying this girl?"

Vernon looked his father square in the eye. "More serious than anything in my life."

Brandi saw the pain in Vernon's eyes. For the first time she understood his long spells of silence. She understood his drive to be better than everyone else. She also understood that Vernon would probably never accomplish the one thing he wanted most—gaining his father's approval.

He was the first man who had ever tried to burrow through the shell she'd erected. Even Michael had been too polite to do more than give a cursory inquiry into her past; almost as if he was following some rule book only he knew about. He didn't inspire her to give more of herself than required. Vernon, by his intensity, his patience, his gentleness, his aggressiveness—the very contradictions of him had pulled to her, forced her to love him.

That night, she opened up to him, giving Vernon a condensed version of the rape. That night, they only cuddled, and he held her as she cried. And she had cried more tears than a human body should produce. Cried for everything that had been done to her that day. She cried that her father had not been there to protect her and love her. She cried because she had finally found someone who loved her, truly loved her in a way that allowed Brandi to be Brandi. And lately, that first time was something she held onto during lonely nights.

She loved him then, despite his flaws. She loved him and always would. Even his involvement with Tanya wouldn't make that love go away. She was disappointed that somehow, despite everything, he would still let someone else dictate his definition of a man. The mistress thing had his father written all over it. How William managed to keep three with Bettye only finding out three years ago was a minor miracle. But Vernon was nothing like his father in some aspects, and alike in the places he shouldn't be.

No wonder he got caught the first time out.

CHAPTER Thirty-Three

Tanya swirled past Brandi, leaving a breeze of Satsuma behind. "I left the keys on the dinner table. The kids are at Avie's house." With a weary shrug of her shoulders, she strolled briskly, bags in hand, toward the front door.

"Wait."

Tanya froze, slowly turning back to face Brandi.

"I'm sorry, it's just been a rough day."

Tanya lifted her chin, lips quivering in an effort not to cry. "Then don't take it out on me!"

Her wavering voice sent a stab of guilt into Brandi's gut.

"You know, deep in my heart I knew that this was all about revenge for you." Tanya said. "And me? Well, it was because I was too afraid to go forward. Too afraid to try and make it on my own. I've learned a lot from you and I'm not afraid anymore."

Brandi just stared at the woman, mouth slightly parted to speak.

Tanya didn't give her the chance. "It's coming back to bite us in the ass. Every time something goes wrong with you and Vernon, you turn your anger my way. And I'm tired of that shit." Her chest rose and fell with indignation. "I may not hold a degree and I may not have a fancy business or anything like that, but I sure as hell don't deserve to be trampled on, either. I have feelings just like you, I have needs just like you, and though you swore up and down you'd do a better job, at least if you *had* a dick, you'd be understandable. I thought Vernon had you beat, but your mood swings are killing me."

"All right, I apologize." Brandi rubbed her temple, sure that another headache was trying to come through. "I want you to stay. Put your things away," she said with a dismissive wave of her hand.

"No!"

Brandi looked up, frowning. "No?"

"No." Then she had nerve enough to roll her neck better than any sister Brandi had seen. Oh shit!

Brandi leveled a steely dark gaze on the woman with a tear-lined face and pain-filled eyes. "I'm not begging your ass for anything."

"And I'm not asking you to," Tanya said softly, still holding ground in the middle of the floor. "But if you want me to stay, then there's going to be some changes around here."

"Like what?"

Tanya placed her bags down, and wiped her eyes with the back of her hand like a little child. "A new contract. This time I want *my* needs to be considered."

Brandi sank down on the sofa, mumbling, "Damn, the woman has been taking notes!"

It wasn't like Tanya was stupid in the first place. She was once an outgoing, popular student, who played the violin and flute, and was a member of the cheerleading squad and the debate team. At one time, there wasn't a party invitation or social event that didn't have her name written all over it.

By the time she turned twelve, though, Tanya had lost interest in everything that she once considered important. The beginning of the second semester of her freshman year, *party* didn't mean much to her anymore. People didn't, either.

Tanya's friends barely recognized her. She slapped her shoulder-length hair back into an untidy ponytail instead of wearing it in perfect spiral curls. Baggy jeans and sweatshirts that looked like she had raided the Goodwill store replaced the stylish clothes from Rich's, Macy's, and Belk's. She wore clothes much too large for her slender, shapely body—a body she tried to conceal at every possible turn.

Tanya usually wore a little lip gloss, eye shadow, and a light touch of blush on her cheekbones. Now her lips were cracked and almost bleeding. People walking past her on the street could easily mistake her for an unloved and abandoned little girl. No one would believe that Tanya had a mother who was part of the Social Circle elite and a father who owned most of the town. Her only comfort came from the one woman who had provided wisdom and a quiet calm for as many years as Tanya could remember. Mattie, their maid, kept a quiet watch over Tanya and her little sister, Mindy. Unfortunately, Daddy fired that wonderful woman at the end of seventh grade, about the same time Tanya had grown breasts. About the same time he began touching her whenever he walked past.

Even Michelle her best friend since first grade, didn't matter anymore. Though she was Black, people marveled at how much alike they were because their clothes, style, and attitude were close. Whenever Tanya purchased clothes, she always bought two—practically making them twins. No one could make that mistake these days.

One day in school, Tanya was ignoring everything as usual when she heard from behind her, "Tanya! Tanya, wake up!" She didn't have to turn to know it was Michelle.

"Girl, it's hard to catch up with your behind these days. What's up with you?"

"Nothing. I just want to be left alone," Tanya said, walking faster, hoping to outpace her friend.

Michelle sprinted forward, whirled around, and stopped squarely in front of Tanya, whose gaze landed on the short row of lockers leading to the bathroom, then on a few of the passing students. Finally, Tanya's eyes focused on the black and tan squares on the ground, but not before she'd gotten a look at Michelle's cute denim outfit and healthy golden skin. Tanya felt ashamed she'd even stepped out of the house. Michelle placed a hand on her shoulder, gracefully displaying a freshly done manicure. "Hey, it's me. Your girl from the east side of the tracks." Tanya couldn't even smile at the reference to her friend's home. "You've been brushing me off."

"No, I haven't—"

"Don't even try," Michelle snapped. "We don't do homework together. We don't do lunch anymore. You're always in the library or something. You even missed Alicia's birthday party, the one we talked about for weeks." The hand trailed over Tanya's shoulder. "What's going on?"

Tanya shrugged, slipped under Michelle's hand, and glanced briefly over her shoulder. "Nothing. Just leave me alone." The new glasses made Michelle's almond-shaped eyes even more beautiful, but Tanya didn't miss the sad look that flashed in them before her friend turned and trudged away.

Breathing a small sigh of relief as the last few students left their lockers, Tanya quickened her step, hoping to make it to her safe place—the library—before anyone else stopped her.

Mrs. Patton's slender ivory hand came out of nowhere, blocking Tanya's path as it landed on her shoulder. The sudden contact from her English teacher both stunned and frightened her. "I need to speak with you."

Tanya groaned. "What's with everyone today?" She shrugged off Mrs. Patton's hand as though it carried a lethal disease and tried to keep going. "I don't have time right now. Maybe later."

The loud, solid *splat* of a hand slamming on the wall right in front of Tanya made her wince, then stand still.

"We'll talk right now, young lady, or I'll have to call your parents."

Now *that* got Tanya's attention. Mama was the last person she wanted to see. And her dear old Daddy could be six feet under and that still wouldn't be a safe distance.

Tanya followed Mrs. Patton to the empty classroom across from the lunchroom, and plopped into the seat right next to the desk, a spot normally reserved for parent conferences, or students who needed a little extra help.

The gray metal desk was off to the left side of a dark green chalkboard. Yesterday's assignment displayed in bold white chalk was a frightening reminder that Tanya hadn't done her homework for the class. Actually, she hadn't done any other class work, either.

Soft gray eyes fixed on Tanya as Mrs. Patton opened her classroom schedule and grade book. "You've missed four assignments this week."

Tanya shrugged, staring absently at the chalkboard. "So."

"The work you've turned in," Mrs. Patton said, impatience creeping into her soft voice, "*when* you decide to do the work, has been poor. You're dangerously close to failing this class."

Tanya remained silent, wondering how long it would take the woman to get the message—*she didn't care.* The shrill ring of the final bell almost made Tanya jump from the chair. Her nerves were raw. She was angry with everyone and everything. That is, when she wasn't afraid, and there were a lot more of those times than she cared to count.

She pulled her black jacket tighter around her body, but the coldness she felt had nothing to do with the cool temperature in the room. The sun's rays pouring through the smoke-tinted glass windows were bright and warm enough to make Mrs. Patton's plants thrive, but not enough to sweep away the anger, pain, and fear that had become a regular part of Tanya's life.

Tanya took a long, slow breath. "Means I'll have to go to summer school. It ain't so bad."

"It *isn't* so bad," Mrs. Patton corrected, peering at her so intensely she wanted to shrivel up and disappear.

Tanya leaned back in the hard wood chair. "Whatever."

The teacher's gaze bored into Tanya until she felt naked and lost under the intensity. "What's with this attitude? You're the top student in my class and all your other classes. Well, at least you were. This attitude is so unlike you. Talk to me," she said, taking Tanya's hand.

Tanya snatched her hand away as though scorched by an open flame. "Don't touch me!"

Mrs. Patton's left eyebrow shot up as she stared at Tanya, who quickly regretted her action but couldn't help herself.

Several icy moments later, Mrs. Patton moved her chair, closing the gap until there were only a few inches separating teacher and student. "That's certainly new. Along with your snappy answers, lack of interest, the way you dress, and the way you don't make eye contact with anyone." Mrs. Patton closed the grade book, dropping a ballpoint pen on top. "If I didn't know any better, I'd say you were using drugs—"

Tanya's head snapped up. "I don't touch that stuff." This time, her eyes made contact with the teacher whose awards and plaques for an outstanding job were more a part of the classroom than pictures of her family.

"Good to hear, but something's going on and either you're going to allow me to get to the bottom of things, or I'm going to call your father; we'll see what *he* has to say."

Tanya sat still, trying to think of a way out.

Minutes later, Mrs. Patton's chair scraped the ground as she stood and said, "Fine. You leave me no choice."

Tanya gripped the teacher's white blouse so tightly it almost ripped. Wrinkles instantly appeared where her hand connected with soft cotton fabric. "Please leave Daddy out of this," Tanya whispered, trying to keep the few bites of sandwich she'd had for lunch from resurfacing. The classroom suddenly swam out of focus and she found it very hard to breathe.

"Come on, Tanya," Mrs. Patton said softly, patting her hand gently, eyes wide with alarm. "Let me take you to the nurse."

"No, I'm all right." Tanya said between breaths, willing the nausea to go away. "I just want to be…I'll turn in all of my work tomorrow. I promise. I won't give you any more trouble." Had someone turned the heat up in the room? Small beads of sweat peppered her forehead. Tanya couldn't break down. Not here. She had to get out of the room—and fast. "I'll be back."

Mrs. Patton spoke in a tone that painted a world of trust. "I'm not finished talking to you, Tanya. I want to help, but you've shut me out. I don't know what else to do."

Tanya's slender body trembled as she tried to breathe slowly, evenly. "Mrs. Patton," she whispered before turning away, facing the empty rows of chairs. She was used to the noisy comfort of her classmates, the spitballs being thrown when Mrs. Patton's back was turned, notes saying *I love you* being passed back and forth, or the sighs coming from the entire class when a pop quiz was announced. Tanya could deal with that, but her problems were now so much deeper. "I can't tell you. Even if I could, I don't know where to start." Tanya looked at the teacher who had always encouraged her to do more. Mrs. Patton was the reason Tanya had joined the debate team and cheerleading squad. She had told Tanya that with time management a girl could do whatever she wanted.

The woman cautiously reached for Tanya's hand. Tanya pulled away at first, then slowly, timidly, placed both hands in Mrs. Patton's. The warm hands cradled Tanya's cold ones. The move said, *trust me.* Tanya wanted to so badly, but...

"Talk to me. You can trust me. Let me help you. I'm here for you, just like I've always been." Mrs. Patton's thumb stroked gently across Tanya's hand. "Are you pregnant?"

"No." But Tanya had to think about it for a moment. "At least...I don't think so." Her voice broke and sobs poured forth no matter how much she tried to keep it together.

"It's all right," Mrs. Patton said, as Tanya reached out and held on to her.

She began rocking gently back and forth. A small cry of pain escaped her lips, followed by a low, whimpering sound.

"It's all right, Tanya. Take your time. Everything's going to be all right."

Tanya nodded as Mrs. Patton's reached for the tissues on her desk. Tanya's voice came out in a whisper. "He...hurt me." Tanya took in a breath and shifted uncomfortably on the chair. Her hands repeatedly rubbed her thighs as though wiping away imaginary dirt. "Daddy...hurt...me."

Mrs. Patton froze. Her small intake of breath sounded like a cannon blast in Tanya's ears. She felt the woman's body stiffen with anger, then she saw the teacher's face softened with compassion.

"At first it was just him...touching me," Tanya said softly. "It always made me uncomfortable, but I didn't know what to say. I didn't know what to do." Tanya sighed, then linked her fingers together, then loosened them, and began wringing her hands like a dishrag. "Then it started happening more and more. Then he started coming into my room late at night after Mama went to sleep or if she was out doing charity work. And he...hurt me. It...hurts. Every time." Tanya barely managed to say the words without breaking into sobs. "I used to love my daddy. Now I'm so afraid of him that I'm afraid to go to sleep. I'm afraid to go home." Tanya stood, almost knocking Mrs. Patton over, and rashed toward the door.

Mrs. Patton raced after her and attempted to console her as Tanya slumped to the floor.

"You can't tell anyone. My family is all I have," she whispered, fear penetrating every cell in her body as she realized what she'd done. "I want my mama, but I can't tell her this. She'll hate me." Tears blurred Tanya's vision. She felt so small. So invisible.

"Your mother could never hate you. She loves you so much." Mrs. Patton's warm, soothing voice echoed in the empty classroom. "She would never have wanted this to happen to you."

When Tanya glanced up, the wetness on Mrs. Patton's cheeks only made Tanya cry more. Mrs. Patton understood. She really did.

"I saw the signs, Tanya, but I wasn't sure. I hoped that you would come to me when the time was right. But I could see that you were sinking deeper and deeper in despair. I had to do something today."

"Maybe Mama won't believe me. Daddy owns this town. Mama might not want to see him go to jail."

Mrs. Patton shook head. "Your safety, your healing, your situation come *first*. Don't try to think or work out things for the adults who will be affected by your reporting the abuse. You have a right to be safe. Remember the incident happened to *you* and *you* are the person who needs protection and help." Mrs. Patton moved so that her face was only inches from Tanya's. "Do you think your mother would really care about money if she knew her little girl had been hurt? If anything, we'd probably have a hard time getting her to let the police handle things because she'd be so angry she'd want to go after your father herself."

Tanya wiped her tear-stained face with a baggy sleeve. "Mama will blame me. I mean, she's always telling me to wear those old conservative clothes."

Mrs. Patton shook her head sadly. "Grown women—grandmothers even—covered from head to toe or wearing business suits, have been raped. It doesn't have anything to do with what you're wearing. There are cases where boys have been sexually abused, and we know that they mostly wear jeans and T-shirts and don't have breasts or curves."

Tanya stared at Mrs. Patton as if her words alone would ensure safety.

The seconds ticked by as Mrs. Patton stayed silent. After a while she said, "I'll talk to your mother and tell her everything I know about sexual abuse and let her know about all the options available to both of you. I'm also a rape advocate for Walton Medical. I can be with you through this and help smooth things over with your mom so you can really deal with what happened to you. The choice is yours."

Tanya shrugged. "I still don't know. How can I tell her something like this? She really loves Daddy."

"Yes, but she loves you, too. Mothers have a special bond with their children. You've heard of mothers running back into a burning building to get their children out?"

Tanya nodded.

Mrs. Patton's soft smile warmed Tanya's heart. "Then know that same love applies to you now."

"You think so?"

"Yes, I really do. And you have your little sister to think about. This could happen to her, too. Your mother needs to protect both of you. In your mother's time, there weren't as many choices. Now there are. You trusted me, now give her a chance."

"All right." Tanya stood, brushed off her jeans, and helped Mrs. Patton from the floor. "I'm ready. Let's go home. She should be there."

About thirty minutes later, they sat across from Margaret Jaunal in the library and told her everything.

Mrs. Patton was wrong. Very wrong.

Tanya's life became a living hell.

CHAPTER *Thirty-Four*

Vernon opened the front door, frowning when he found Jeremy and Craig bundled in their warmest winter clothes as they stood on his mother's doorstep. Frost followed every breath.

"I don't want to talk with you Negroes. You weren't there for me when I needed you, so don't show your asses up now."

"Hey," Jeremy said, "I helped you rent a U-Haul."

"Yeah? And I couldn't sleep in that bitch, either."

Vernon slammed the door, turned on his heels, and headed for the couch.

Craig yelled loud enough to reach through the door. "Okay, but we'll miss you at Thighs High..."

Vernon froze mid-step, blinked as the name registered. *The strip club?* He whipped around in a complete 180 and ran back toward the door like a kid tumbling after the ice cream truck, grabbing his keys, coat and gloves, slipping on his boots just before he stepped onto the front porch.

Craig, wearing a black outfit underneath his wool coat, grinned as Jeremy folded his hands across his beefy chest.

Vernon grimaced. "Yeah, yeah, yeah, all's forgiven," he said with a dismissive wave, then fell in step behind them as they crunched through the snow toward Jeremy's navy BMW.

"Mmmmm, hmmmm," Jeremy said, giving him a once-over before getting into the driver's seat. "Mention a little tits and ass and his dick does all the thinking."

"Fuck you."

Craig roared with laughter as he snapped the seat belt in place. "See, too much time alone. Now he wants to play for the pink team."

"Yeah, I always wanted a pretty little house bitch like you."

"That's what I'm talking about," Jeremy said, before pulling out onto Forty-seventh Street. "We need to get your ass some therapy—quick."

"Thirty dollars to get into that strip joint is therapy enough."

Thighs High, named after an old Tom Brown funk-R&B tune, was exactly what the name implied. Gorgeous women in shades ranging from the darkest chocolate brown to the creamiest alabaster either took their place wrapping their sexy bodies around a gold pole that extended from the ceiling to the stage, worked the room with lap dances, or poured drinks. Everything from hoochies to high class all in one spot—one-stop pussy shopping. Vernon's mood lifted a little when he saw the women with smooth bare bikini lines and thighs, and a couple of them with hair poking out on the sides of their panties. The latter made him want to take a line from the old commercial: "Great Scott, what a lawn!"

"All this in one place is as good as an instant hard-on," Craig said, holding his beer midway to his mouth. "God's way of saying, 'Heaven belongs to us.'" His golden skin flushed as he rubbed his hands together, grinning like a kid who had just met the tooth fairy with a sack full of cash. "Ass to the left of us, ass to the right."

Vernon's gaze narrowed on his friend, who seemed a little too happy for the occasion. "Where does Alanna think you are?"

Craig didn't blink as he took a swig of Miller Genuine Draft. "Pool hall. There's one upstairs, right?"

Vernon turned to Jeremy, whose thin lips lifted into a sheepish grin. "Your mama's house, cheering you up."

"With y'all's lying asses."

Jeremy shrugged. "Hey, I did stop by!"

Vernon took a swig of Miller Lite. "And *I'm* the one in the doghouse."

"Hey, we also don't have a white mistress and we didn't get busted," Jeremy shot back.

Even in the midst of all the booty-shaking going on around him, Vernon missed Brandi, missed the comfort of his own bed and her luscious body curled up with his, the sounds of his daughters' voices as they squealed with delight when he entered the house. Some things a man couldn't buy, but others—like the tall, leggy blonde who started this trouble–were purchased in monthly installments. Something about Tanya had touched him, made him feel like protecting her, but he hadn't really loved her as much as Brandi. Tanya reminded him of how vulnerable Brandi had been in the beginning, but she had grown stronger each year of their marriage. The one night that would always stand out in his mind more than any other, was the first time he made love to his wife.

❤❤❤

Stretched out on a blanket in a secluded spot near a place called The Point, under the bright lights, towering skyscrapers, and liquid beauty of Lake Michigan reflecting Chicago in all its glory; Vernon reached out for her, kissing her long and hard, exploring the warm depths of her mouth with a searing moist heat. As moans spilled from her smooth, lovely throat, she ran a soft hand through his short-cropped hair. He peeled away her blouse, lifted her bra, exposed the soft mounds of flesh, and encircled her engorged nipples with his hot tongue. He took one into his mouth, sucking as though her creamy skin could provide nourishment. And for him it did. The fact that she allowed him to touch her in this way spoke volumes. The fact that she reached for him, drawing him closer to her breasts, said all he needed to know about her need to be intimate with him.

Brandi didn't tense when he lifted her skirt and slowly pulled the powder blue satin panties down and off, only to drape his tongue across the soft velvet of her thighs. Then he trailed a hot path to softly nestle in the curls at the delta. He parted her lips with his moist tongue, but teased along the outside, relishing each moan as he began a soft, gentle rhythm.

"Vernon," she gasped, not loosening the grip she had on his head.

He shook his head quickly, loosened her hold a bit, and placed his tongue directly in line with her pearl, which stood at Army attention, begging for his touch. Gently he flicked his tongue across the small pink membrane, grazing it with light strokes.

She rewarded him instantly with the slight buckling of her knees and the sway of her hips as she began to move with him, meeting the soft pressure of his lips. Nectar, hot and salty-sweet, poured forth and spilled out over his tongue.

He stayed within the moist heat, gently coaxing away painful memories he knew had become an integral part of her existence. He wanted her hot for his touch, unafraid to let him take her to a higher level of pleasure.

Maybe starting this way would be the right thing. He wanted her all to himself—no matter how much Michael Cobb stepped up his game.

As her body trembled almost violently in the throes of her first orgasm, he felt jubilant—almost elated.

She slowly allowed her thighs to part a little wider, giving him access to earthbound heaven. Tingling warmth spread from his loins, as a rush of blood gathered low in his body. Soon the heavy warmth of arousal growing beneath his stomach became too much, and he stood, hesitating only a moment to look in her eyes. All the months of waiting, of loving her, of holding her and bringing her out of that shell, could all go back to square one if she wasn't truly ready.

She reached down, unleashing his throbbing erection, running her delicate fingers across the veins. It throbbed in response and she smiled. She looked at him, taking in all of his face, slowly and honestly. "I'm sure, honey. I want you. I don't want to be afraid anymore." The gentle caress of her words cut through the sweet music of the Lake Michigan waves rolling behind them.

And they called this hot, writhing woman in his hands a Fudgsicle? How wrong they were!

With tortured intensity, he inched inside her moist heat as he locked his gaze on hers, checking for any sign that he should stop. The heat spilled around him like the steamy waters of an Arizona hot spring, as her walls gripped and welcomed him at the same time. Something like tiny pinpoints of light exploded in his mind as a river of blood pounded at his temples.

Her eyes fluttered and closed as he stayed within her—not moving, not breathing—just relishing the smooth velvety feel of her. Enjoying her arms wrapped securely around his neck, and her thighs locked around his waist in a loving embrace that every man dreamed of, but only few took time to appreciate.

She moaned again and he took that to be significant and moved more of himself inside her. He stayed there for what seemed an eternity, but was actually only a minute as he allowed her to adjust to his size and gave her the opportunity to pull away. She didn't move at first, until she favored him with a long, searing kiss—every moment she became more daring, more open to him.

Then he slid deeper into the moist depths of her and pulled away only to have Brandi welcome him back in once again.

"I want my wife back," he said, shaking his head, clearing the memories away and pulling his attention back to the heated activity at Thighs High. He shifted in his seat—his dick had started to reach for the sky with the thought of that wonderful time with his wife. He tried to clear his mind and focus on the stage. Watching the fleshy light brown woman quivering her cheeks on stage as though someone had put an electric prod to her did less for him than the memory of his first time with Brandi. The stripper looked like Brandi. And come to think of it, his wife had slowly overcome her apprehensions and could do a striptease that could put every woman in the place to shame. And he could make love to her all night, every night, or every day, all day, without having to worry about catching anything that could make his dick pack up and leave him. The thought of starting over was not appealing. "I'm getting my wife back!"

The atmosphere in Thighs High suddenly become more humid as a few extra bodies lined the stage. Vernon unbuttoned his shirt and struggled for air. He needed to get out. He wanted his life back. Right now!

"Just leave Brandi alone, man," Jeremy said, watching as another nearly naked angel dipped around the pole twice, undulating in a way that made every man in the place sit up and pant like rabid dogs, "before she puts a real hurtin' on your ass."

Strippers with the bodies of goddesses and the dexterity of trapeze artists quickly scooped up the money, which rained down on the stage from all directions. But to Vernon, none could compare to who he had at home. Normally, watching the show would uplift him (in more ways the one). Tonight all he could think about was his wife.

"You got busted, that's all there is to it," Craig said, interrupting his direct eye contact with a stripper the DJ said was named Sunshine. "Be happy you escaped with ass intact. If you'd been married to Avie, you wouldn't be so lucky."

All three men shivered at the thought.

"Let's go upstairs," Vernon said, loosening his shirt a little. "It's getting too tight around here."

Craig lifted his glass, touching it to Jeremy's. "Most men would consider it a blessing to have both of their ladies in one house, accepting—"

"And can you believe that shit!" Vernon snapped, reality settling in. "Both of them heifers laid up in *my* house, with *my* money. And part of it's going to Tanya's house and I still can't stay there. I'm sleeping at my Mama's house and I still have to pay maintenance *and* child support. Ain't that a bitch?"

"And they're probably sleeping together, too," Craig said, bellowing with laughter, as Jeremy joined him, falling in step as they reluctantly left their coveted seats near the stage and took the stairs leading to the pool hall and sports bar.

"Boy, I'll wrap this bottle around your head," Vernon snapped.

Craig held up his hand in mock surrender. "Hey, don't get mad at me 'cause you couldn't keep your women in check, player. Brandi knows how to play the game."

Jeremy draped an arm over Vernon's shoulder as they settled around a pool table. "Looks like Brandi made you a pawn in the game 'cause she's the master of the game."

Craig chimed in, "Not pawn—*peon*."

The two men busted up laughing. Vernon didn't find a damn thing funny.

In the left corner, a large television carried Fox News, which seemed to have ended the serious stories and started on the fluff. "And now for an interesting divorce case happening right here in Chicago," the strawberry-blond newscaster read. "In a surprise move, the wife asked for custody of…" He paused, read the sheet in front of him again, then looked up into the camera. "Get this! The *mistress*. And the judge granted her request!"

His female co-host chuckled. "Is that a true story, Bob?"

"Afraid so, Cheryl."

"Some unlucky soon-to-be ex-husband is probably out drinking his sorrows away."

"Boy, I'll say," Bob replied with a hearty laugh. "Hope there's not much more of this—um—wives pairing up with the mistresses or America will be in serious trouble."

Chuckles erupted from behind the three men.

A few heads turned to Vernon, as a sudden tension filled the air.

They were all laughing. At *him!*

Vernon slammed his drink down on the table. "Come on, fellas, let's blow this joint."

Jeremy gripped Vernon's arm, holding him in place. "With a thirty-dollar cover charge to get in here? You must be out of your cotton-pickin', chicken-pluckin', motherfuckin' mind." Then his light brown eyes narrowed. "Unless you can reimburse me for my loss."

Vernon stared at his angry friend.

Jeremy cocked his head. "No? Then we're in for the night, my brother."

Craig took a swig of his Miller. "Be a man, Vernon—you didn't have a problem enjoying the good parts of all this."

Jeremy took aim at the center of the racked balls. "It's colder than Brandi's plans out there. Suck it up and deal with it."

Vernon leaned against the wood-paneled wall. "Fuck y'all."

"If that's the way you want it," Craig said, laughing. "Might have to take that request seriously. Looks like that's the only ass you'll be getting for a while anyway."

Craig and Jeremy doubled over with laughter again.

"The judge granted her *custody* of the mistress. They had a contract and everything! Ain't that some unbelievable shit? And you fools are laughing." Vernon took a swig of beer. "Y'all just don't understand."

"Sure I do," Jeremy replied. "You miss your wife. You miss your mistress."

"I don't miss Tanya," Vernon shot back, realizing that sleeping with that woman had started his troubles. Troubles that didn't look like they would end anytime soon.

Craig had bent over the pool table to make a shot. Instead, he turned to Vernon. "Then what was the point? She's costing you a thirteen-year marriage and she's not even worth missing?"

Jeremy pushed Craig out of the way and hit a red-striped ball into the corner pocket. "If I was gonna pull the stunt that you did, I would never let my wife and my mistress meet."

Vernon took a swig of the cold brew. "You don't have a mistress."

"And that's the point." Jeremy set up to make another shot. "You get married, you're off the market. Bottom line."

"There's too many single women out there for that," Vernon shot back with a line his father considered a trademark.

Jeremy froze for a second, and didn't even try to make an obvious sure shot as he faced Vernon, glaring at him. "Then you've got a problem, Negro."

Vernon stepped back. Something ugly had come into his friend's voice just then.

"And it's gonna take more than what Brandi did to wake you up. Those vows mean something."

"Let me get this straight," Craig chimed in, standing at the opposite end of the table. "You still feel like you're entitled to a little piece on the side even though you just swore up and down you missed your wife?" He shook his head. "Something's wrong with that, man. And you're too stupid to see it."

Jeremy stood up straight, holding the pool cue in front of him. "So all that talk of trying to win her back is trophy time? Something that says to the world that you've won." He didn't take his gaze off the table. "Grow up, man. It's not about winning," Jeremy said scornfully, his voice dripping with contempt. "It's not about right or wrong. It's about fairness. I don't know how you could've changed so much from when you first married her. You were all into her to the point you stopped doing things with the frat. Do you realize we had to cover for your ass to keep you in?" Jeremy shrugged as a small grin slid on to his lips. "You're just pissed that Brandi got the upper hand."

Craig missed a shot and stood looking at the table. "And she's handling her business better than you ever have. You've gotta admire her for that. You didn't marry no punk bitch."

"That's for sure," Jeremy said, but his lips had lengthened into a long line.

Didn't his boys understand how the world was run? Vernon wondered. Didn't they know that men had the right to make the rules?

Jeremy was thoughtful for a moment, then said, "You know, if you were smart, Vernon, you'd quit being the victim and actually try to make things right with your wife. It's obvious you still love her. Especially since none of the ass onstage caught your attention tonight. I still don't know why we're up here playing pool."

"Making good on your lie." Vernon looked from Craig to Jeremy, asking, "Now about my wife, got any good ideas?"

Jeremy only winked and grinned.

"And I'm keeping your *ex*-wife as far away from my wife as the city allows," Craig said, finishing his shot. "I don't want her giving my old girl any ideas."

"She's not my ex!"

Jeremy ran a hand through his dark, wavy hair. "Too late," he said to his friends. "Mine already put in her request for a wife."

Craig craned his neck in Jeremy's direction. "You giving in?"

"Hell no! She can have a maid, but none of that other stuff. When that chick's finished the dishes and the laundry, her ass goes home," he said, pointing to the exit for effect.

"Mine tried to pull that shit, too," Craig said, with a wide grin. Jeremy and Vernon looked at him. "I told her that unless the new girl was giving up some ass, I'm not having it."

“What did Alanna say?” Vernon asked with a laugh.

He shrugged. “Fine, but she wants hers off the top.”

“Really?” Jeremy said. “And what did you say to that?”

“I don’t really remember—,” Craig scratched his head—“but I’ve been sleeping on the couch all week.”

This time Vernon and Jeremy laughed.

CHAPTER Thirty-Five

Vernon sat across from his wife at Banderas, a jazz diner in the heart of Chicago's Gold Coast. Black leather booths with dark wood tables lined the walls; barstools were made of cowhide; and a huge rotisserie oven roasted several dozen chickens at a time—right out in the open.

The restaurant was usually jammed with locals instead of the tourists who hit the area like swarms of locusts. The window tables had a great view of the Magnificent Mile's eclectic and upscale stores; but for a more intimate ambience, he requested a booth. When Brandi kept gazing toward the window, he asked, "Do you want to get a table by the window?"

She simply nodded.

He immediately signaled the hostess and requested a change.

The winter season had kicked in and the white Christmas lights draped along the trees lining the sidewalks were awesome. Six inches of snow bunched up around the concrete embankments that held flowers in the spring and summer. The city crews cleared the streets in the Mag area as soon as the frosty white stuff hit the ground.

Brandi wore a low-cut navy dress that glided over her full breasts and pulled in at her waist, then draped sexily over her wide hips. When she'd arrived, the appreciative glances thrown her way made Vernon cross the room and collect her before someone believed she was available. As far as he was concerned she was not! Michael could talk all day long, but there was no way in hell he would get Brandi. No fucking way.

The silver necklace he had given her for their fifth anniversary glistened on the smooth curve of her neck. This time she wore very little makeup, but the light brown beauty he had loved and married came shining through. He loved her. He just wanted her the right way. *His* way. Couldn't she understand that?

Vernon held out a chair for Brandi as she picked up the bouquet on the table. "Nice flowers."

Vernon shrugged. "Orchids are your favorites."

"Glad to see you remember *some* things."

Reaching for her hands, he brought her fingertips to his lips, saying, "There's a lot I remember."

A single arched eyebrow shot up.

"Like the time you tried to make dinner and didn't realize the pilot light was off. Served me raw chicken for dinner."

Brandi's lips broke into a sincere smile. "Oh, you would bring that up. I was nervous and it was my first time cooking for anyone. How was I supposed to know chicken shouldn't be pink after all that time? I followed your mother's directions."

Vernon laughed. "Or we could talk about the time you almost gave birth to Simone in the car because the cab driver wouldn't go over fifteen miles per hour."

Now that memory brought another grin. "I almost beat his ass, didn't I?"

"Let the police report tell it. You *did* beat his ass," Vernon said, taking a sip of his beer.

"One tap is not considered assault and battery."

"Brandi, you gripped the man's neck and said, and I quote, 'If you don't get me closer to the hospital and some drugs in the next five minutes, I'll stick the steering wheel up your ass and drive you instead.'"

She dipped her head sheepishly, grimacing. "I said all that?"

"Yep," Vernon replied. "Poor man probably has a complex about Black women to this day."

The waitress appeared and Vernon asked Brandi to order for both of them. She chose their favorites, something simple and wonderful—slow-roasted chicken so tender that the meat would fall off the bone, steamed vegetables, chive-studded mashed potatoes, and a house salad with garlic bread. An Oreo ice cream sandwich was a great way to finish, but if their record held true, they wouldn't have room.

"Nothing to drink?"

Her lips twitched as she looked at her glass of ginger ale, then back to him. "I'm pregnant," she said softly. "With twin boys."

Vernon choked, almost spraying her with beer. She reached out, trying to help him regain composure, before she added, "Just kidding. But your reaction's pretty good. I give it an eight." She looked up at their tall, spiky-haired waitress and said, "I'll take an Amaretto sour, please."

Straightening his tie he said, "Oh, that's cold. And you said that with a straight face and everything. God, you're so hard to figure out these days."

All humor died away as she looked across the table at him. "All right, Vernon. What's this all about?"

His fingers trailed a soft line over her hands. "I want to come home, baby."

"I didn't say you *couldn't* come home."

He searched her eyes for a moment. "I can't live there with Tanya in the house."

"But it was okay when you paid for her to live somewhere," she said, this time without a trace of sarcasm. As the days wore on, she was becoming more and more numb to the situation. "I don't see the problem."

"That was a mistake. A serious mistake."

She shrugged before taking a sip of her drink. "A mistake I'm trying to rectify in my favor."

"Brandi, I was wrong and I see that now. I want to get things back to the way they were *before* Tanya entered the picture."

"Things weren't all that great then. You were still trying to fit me into your mother's mold. Something you still haven't realized will never happen," she said, her soft weary tone making his heart pause for a beat or two. "And as far as I'm concerned everything's still the same—me, you, the kids, and the *mistress.* Nothing's changed except location, location, location." Brandi held up her glass and winked. "And maybe the fact that now I'm enjoying things, too." She nodded and smiled. "Yeah, that's changed. As Janet Jackson says, 'It's all right with me.'"

"I mean *before* that."

"You know, I kind of like things the way they are now." Then she leaned forward, whispering, "You have excellent taste in women, I'll give you that. Tanya makes the best omelets in town." Her lips lengthened into a grin. "*And* she likes to cuddle."

This time Vernon did spit out his beer.

She winked. "Just kidding, honey."

Vernon's heart sank as a sudden realization hit him that maybe, just maybe Brandi *wasn't* joking. "You'd actually sleep with her?"

"You know, I'd have every right to get some ass, too. Sharing things goes both ways. What's the difference in her sleeping with you or making love to me. I could always strap one on." She smiled as her voice took on a breathy tone. "And the sound of—," she gasped—"'yesssss, Mistress Brandi' has a nice ring to it."

Vernon choked, unable to recognize the woman he married. "You need help."

"And thanks to you I have exactly the type of help I need. At least she's doing her part to make amends. I don't see you trying. Although dinner is a nice touch, I'd like for you to finally realize that this marriage is about more than your needs. We set out to do things together, but you've been so busy trying to live up to your father's image, you've spent more time trying to show everyone that you're better than him, that you're good enough to follow in his footsteps that the togetherness got lost. You've been stuck on appearances while I've done the majority of the work, and you've reveled in my accomplishments. Be honest with yourself and maybe this marriage can be saved."

The jazz trio, which stood directly across from the large plate-glass windows, sprang into a smooth rendition of "Girl from Ipanema."

"Get her out of my house!"

"Not until her contract is up," she said, savoring a bite of her meal. "And since you can't seem to deal with things the way they are, why don't you contact me when it's all over? I give you my word—she's not leaving until she completes her time with our family. Quality time."

"I want to be home," he said, realizing Jeremy's suggestions were good, but wouldn't crack the hard outer core his wife now had. "I'll miss out on spending time with the girls."

"No you won't. You'll see more than you did when you were with Tanya—very little." She shrugged. "At least now you've been forced to do more one-on-one stuff with them. And they're enjoying it, too. So it's not a loss for them. Even Sierra, who you tried to turn against me on Halloween, has said that she hasn't seen you so much since whenever."

Vernon leaned back in the black leather seat.

"No, baby, when you went cat hunting, putting your energies elsewhere, leaving me to pick up the slack, things changed. This one's not going to be easy to fix. We started the journey with just the two of us and now there's more players—the children, Tanya, your father, and that Professional League. I'm not mad, I'm weary. And I still love you, but we're not the same. You saw to that."

Vernon reached for Brandi. "We could fix it if you get rid of Tanya."

"I'm enjoying having someone to look out for me for a change."

"So we *still* have to go to the counselor tomorrow?"

"Ah, so *that's* the real reason for the dinner," she said, slipping a bite of roasted chicken between glossed lips. "It's part of the court order. I'm going whether you do or not. Did you see his response to you? The judge will definitely watch this case very closely."

The soft approach hadn't worked. Vernon pushed away his meal. Damn, what could he do now? If he could ask his father for help, he would. But the man had been adamant about his stance on Brandi and would only rub it in. Vernon couldn't go to his mother, either; she was still mad because of the way he'd treated her after the divorce. And he was wrong then, too. Especially since she had always been in his corner.

❤❤❤

When he had gone to his mother about his plans to marry, she was elated for the couple. His father, on the other hand, didn't say a single word. He left all of his bellyaching for a late-night conversation that Vernon wasn't supposed to hear.

Unfortunately, the vents in the Kenwood house had been cleaned the week before. Equally unfortunate was the fact that Dad's voice could carry across international waters with just string and a Styrofoam cup.

"If he marries her, I'm cutting him out of my will."

"You do that and I'm leaving," Bettye Spencer snapped. "You will not use money to make our son give up on what he wants to do."

"Worked on you, didn't it?" William shot back. "So get off it."

"That was different," she said in a voice so weary. "I had a family to look out for."

Vernon had felt sadness in his heart, knowing how hard his mother had it growing up. Her family had been dirt-poor—living in thatched houses with dirt floors throughout; no indoor plumbing, only an outhouse. And his father never let Bettye forget.

"Yeah, I never knew when I asked for your hand in marriage there would be twenty others right behind it and they'd be out all the time."

Bettye Hancock landed a marriage with William Spencer in college, and not only was it a step up, but a step out of a life she'd never quite accepted. Attempts to help her family were met with some resistance, but finally they adjusted to the new large house she had built on the family property. Unfortunately, some had adjusted too well. And William never let anyone within hearing range forget it.

"I'm giving him my blessing whether you do or not," she said. "But know this: I won't stand for you trampling all over that girl's feelings or lording over Vernon's life. Let him be."

"So they can turn out like those lazy, good-for-nothing, waiting-on-a-government-check bums you're related to?"

Vernon bristled at against his father's vicious tone.

"I can't change where I come from and I'm not ashamed of growing up poor. You grew up with money and look at how you turned out," she growled.

"Successful, respected, and powerful," he said proudly.

"Selfish, inconsiderate, and a complete ass," she shot back.

Vernon rolled over, trying to tune them out. No luck.

"If I'm such a bother to be around, why are you still married to me?"

She let out a bitter laugh. "For the same reason I married you in the first place—comic relief."

Bettye Spencer held her ground and, along with Brandi's mother, planned and executed an elegant, but intimate lavender, white, and black wedding, complete with horse-drawn carriage and a candlelight ceremony.

For years afterward, Vernon watched his parents drift farther and farther apart. His relationship with his dad became nonexistent except for a few grunts in passing. Then his mother found out about the three little mistresses: one in a brick house in Lincoln Park; one in a condo in the Gold Coast; and the last in a townhouse in Englewood. And Humpty Dumpty had a great fall.

Avie Davidson, lawyer extraordinaire was on hand to pick up the pieces and put Mrs. Humpty back together again, leaving Mr. Dumpty with several cracks in the shell.

But right after the final divorce decree, something changed between Vernon and his father. All of a sudden, William began to pay attention to Vernon, offering bits and pieces of advice at first, then offering money to help expand the business. Vernon, believing that the success of The Perfect Fit had finally gained his father's approval, soaked up every piece of advice like an underused dish towel, regaling Brandi with details of business meetings and golf games (though Vernon hated golf—all walk and very little swing).

Under his father's tutelage, Vernon soon learned that the reason so many Black men and women missed major deals was because they didn't happen in the boardrooms of corporate America. The ones that mattered happened on lush green lawns of places whose names ended with "Social Club" or "Country Club"—and they were definitely on the side of town that didn't have many Black people as neighbors.

Billions of dollars changed hands every day—right there on the green. The same green of places that didn't allow Tiger Wood's father to crush the dew-laden grass underfoot, but had to change their stance when major televised events focused on that error and a star player who couldn't perform for America's public because of "hidden rules." William Spencer had also forced a few of those closed doors to swing wide open and caused others to open just a crack. When CEOs and presidents of major corporations made away with company cash or swindled unwitting employees of billions and needed a way to cover it up, William Spencer came to the rescue.

Those men, with sons in Harvard and daughters in Yale, had taken risks that put the family fortune in jeopardy. Only a discreet mergers-and-acquisitions man with no long-lasting ties to the elite society, which had been closed to anyone who didn't have a disposable income starting in the tens of millions, could set things right.

Selling a portion of their companies allowed those same men who wouldn't acknowledge they even knew William Spencer in public to keep their lies intact. William stood quietly behind every sale, gaining a power no one, Black or otherwise, had a right to command. He wanted his son to follow in his footsteps.

Unfortunately, Vernon didn't have the heart for shady deals or to help people hide money at the expense of working-class families. Somehow, he couldn't rejoice with each victory and found each celebration to be hollow and haunting. He just couldn't do it. But oh, did he try to learn all about it—just to please his father, the father who had made good on his threat to cut him off. And somehow as he drew closer to his father, Vernon had forgotten all about his wife—the woman who had steadily helped him build a company from the ground up—with practically no money at all.

CHAPTER *Thirty-Six*

Vernon pulled up in front of A Time to Heal, housed in a three-story, silver-and-blue building, with more glass than brick and mortar. The manicured lawns and knee-high shrubs blended easily with the smooth lines of the tiered structure.

Walking into the counselor's sleek office, the sweet smell of lavender, peaceful colors and abstract crystal sculptures that greeted him reminded him of Tanya's house. Paintings of angels of every culture adorned the light blue walls.

Brandi walked in a few moments later. The receptionist announced them, and from the opposite side of the lobby Sesvalah, a beautiful woman wearing a peach-and-aqua flowing garment, came out to greet them. She had light skin, thick, wavy hair, and a bright smile. Once they entered her counseling suite, each taking a seat across from each other on the matching sofas, her intense eyes sized Vernon up as she started their session. "So, the judge believes you need marriage counseling."

"We don't need no damn counseling, she needs to get the bi"—he glanced sheepishly at Brandi—"*witch* out of my house."

Sesvalah's head whipped to Brandi, one thickly arched eyebrow raised.

Brandi's lips lengthened into a soft smile. "His mistress is living with us."

"Living with *you*," he shot back, pointing a finger at his wife. "With you! I didn't have anything to do with it."

"Oh, get off it. You had everything to do with it. You slept with the woman for two years. Now that I've accepted it and formulated a plan to make things work for both of us, you're whining like a…a..." She glanced at the counselor. "You know."

Sesvalah blinked, looked over her paperwork, and glanced up. "Let me get this straight—the mistress is living with you, him, and your two children."

"That's almost right," Brandi said in a voice that rang with innocence. "He's playing a little hard to get. He's at his mother's for the moment."

Sesvalah pursed her lips to suppress a smile but the twinkle in her eyes gave her away. "I see."

Vernon pointed to Brandi. "See, she's crazy, isn't she?"

Sesvalah shrugged. "Actually, I think it's a brilliant concept. Everything's out in the open. A man couldn't ask for more than that, right?"

Brandi lifted her chin, grinning triumphantly at her husband.

Vernon's jaw dropped. "You're not going to tell her to make that woman leave?"

"That's not my call, Mr. Spencer."

"Then what the hell am I paying you for?"

Brandi chuckled, leaning over to pat one of his muscular thighs. "That's okay, stud, this one's on me."

"I don't get paid to tell you what you want to hear," Sesvalah said, leaning back in her high-backed chair. "Let's weigh all sides. What was going on with you two before Tanya came into the picture?"

"Everything was fine," Brandi said in a nonchalant tone. "You know: work, home, children—every now and then he'd grace the kitten with a little pickle tickle—but nothing out of the ordinary."

Sesvalah's lips twitched. "When did you notice a change?"

"I've never—"

Sesvalah cut Vernon off with a wave of her small, delicate hand. "Give her a chance to speak. You'll get your turn."

"When his father stepped in and had so much to say about us. When he joined the League of 1,000 Professional Black Men. But the biggest change came after I landed a deal with Avistar," Brandi replied.

"What was so different?"

Brandi looked at Vernon. "It was the first time in a long time that instead of having my husband, I had to make appointments with a rubber appliance that will probably outlast everyone on the planet."

Vernon groaned.

"So no sex?" Sesvalah asked, jotting down notes.

"Not even a half order."

Sesvalah turned to him. "Vernon, what happened to make you feel you needed to bring a third person into your marriage?"

"She was so busy making money she forgot about me." Then he paused, as though somehow he had made a point.

"Okay, let me get this straight," Brandi said, shifting in her seat so she faced only him. "You order up a side of ass, *white* ass at that, because I'm doing what I'm supposed to do? Taking care of kids I didn't want to have in the first place? Cleaning the house and raking in more cash? And you *fault me* for that? You mother—"

"Hey, watch it." Sesvalah's hand whipped out like an NBA referee. "We get the point."

"What about what *I* needed?" Vernon asked, facing Brandi. "All of a sudden I became more like an assistant than your partner."

"Well, if you'd take some initiative and do your share of the work instead of flexing and being the social butterfly, maybe I wouldn't have to work so damn hard on the back end."

"Ooooookay, time out." Sesvalah's shimmied into the three-foot space between them, handing them each a blank sheet of paper. "I want each of you to make a list of what you expected from marriage in the beginning, what you think you've accomplished so far, what issues you need to address now, and what you'd like to see happen in your marriage. The fact that the judge thought you might want to salvage the marriage says something."

Vernon glared at the counselor. "Can we do this later and bring it back in next time? I'm not paying you for sitting while you watch us write."

Brandi grimaced, biting back a smart retort. "*I'll* pay for it. We need this. I need to get some things off my chest. Things I've been holding in to keep peace—and it still hasn't made any difference." Against her wishes tears welled up in her eyes. The pain she had felt resurfaced, long after she thought she'd put those feelings to bed.

"The first session is free anyway." Sesvlah turned to him, eyebrows drawn in. "Did you read the court order?"

Vernon stood glowering angrily as his gaze traveled from one woman to the next.

Brandi snapped, "If you want to save our marriage, Vernon, make the list and quit acting like the world has done you wrong. You and your little wandering dick are the reason we're here, so you don't have a right to be pissed."

He turned to face the counselor. "All I want to know is if you're going to tell her it's wrong to have that woman in our house."

"I can't tell anyone that they're wrong," she replied softly. "I can only point you to answers that you have inside yourself."

"If I already have the answers, what the hell do I need you for?"

Brandi gasped. "Vernon, your manners are slipping."

Sesvalah looked up at him, and said calmly, "The way you tell the story, Mr. Spencer, you don't need anyone."

He lifted his head proudly. "That's right."

"Then why are you so adamant about going back to your wife?"

The silence in the office became overpowering.

Vernon glared at the counselor, then tore up the paper. "That's a cheap shot and you know it!"

Brandi looked up at him. "Sometimes the truth hurts."

Vernon tossed the pieces on the sofa next to Brandi, grabbed his coat, and left.

Sesvalah turned to Brandi. "Let's talk about the real reason you brought Tanya into your home."

Suddenly Brandi wasn't as comfortable as she had been a few moments ago. "She showed up."

"And?"

"We talked about it and I saw a way to make this work for me."

"You mean you saw a way to make Vernon angry."

Brandi shrugged. "That, too."

"Okay, let's look at the facts. You have a strange woman come into your household. She looks after your children, cooks your food, has access to all of your personal belongings." Sesvalah cast a solemn gaze on Brandi. "A woman, I might add, who may resent the fact that you've shattered her world. A woman who may hate the fact that your very existence has made her realize how trusting and naïve she's been."

"I don't think that's it," Brandi said after a short spell. "She had all of her belongings heaped up in the backseat of her car. She had no place to go."

Sesvalah remained silent.

Brandi took a long slow breath before explaining, "At first I enjoyed seeing how pissed Vernon was, and how smoothly Tanya played into something I'd said earlier. It seemed like justice."

"So how long is the justice phase going to last?"

"I don't know, but at least six months," Brandi replied, placing her sheet of paper to the side.

"Why that long?"

"That's how long I thought they'd been seeing each other."

Sesvalah crossed one leg over the other. "Do you think what you're doing is fair to the kids?"

"Maybe not. At the time I was only thinking of me," Brandi said, shifting uncomfortably on the sofa.

"You had every right to be angry. You had a right to be hurt," Sesvalah said softly. "But now you've brought a whole new dynamic to your marriage that may make it harder to put things in perspective or heal things for the long run."

Brandi's gaze shifted to the window. A pigeon pecked on it, then waddled off and pecked on another area. Evidently he couldn't find his way, either.

"Every time you see Tanya, do you see 'the other woman,' the woman who stole precious time and resources from you?"

Brandi thought about that a moment. "I see a young woman who was just as stupid and gullible as I was. She's an uneducated, visionless woman who's gonna be stuck in 'the other woman' role for the rest of her life if she doesn't do something now."

"Why do you care so much about her?"

Brandi looked up at Sesvalah, saying, "She's me, if my father hadn't pressed me so hard to get an education. She's me, if my mother didn't remind me that I promised him to go to college despite how much I was tired of school. She's every woman who's ever walked into The Perfect Fit looking for a job and had to settle for factory work because it was the only thing available for her. Tanya's not so different from my mother—an uneducated woman who settled for staying at home while my daddy worked like a dog to keep her happy."

"Education isn't everything, and not everyone can go to college, Brandi."

"Yes, but even a high school education or some trade training can make all the difference in the world to a woman. It means we have some power to make choices in our lives."

"And you abhorred the 'cook, clean, keep the kids, do the laundry, and balance the checkbook' life your mother had?"

"She could have been so much more..."

"Yet you've forced another woman into that same role?" Sesvalah pointed out. "And as Tanya's 'husband' what makes you any different? Your definition of a wife is no different than that of a sixties man. The only difference between you and Vernon is you're not sleeping with her. Controlling the situation the way you did meant neither one of you has taken her feelings into consideration."

"But I'm different! Vernon wants her out on the street groveling to come back to him."

"You want her in your house, serving penance for her sins."

"Having her close means I keep tabs on him, too."

She remembered the time she saw her grandmother place a wad of cash under her breasts, lifting up the huge mounds to put the money in place. Her grandmother had smiled and said, "These are the only suckers I trust with my money. And even they've run off with it sometimes. The only people you can trust is God and yourself."

Brandi had asked, "Well what about you, Grandma?"

"Child, I'm human, people are human, and they'll let you down the moment you need 'em most. Not because they want to, mind you, but because sometimes things are not within their control. Trust only God."

Brandi's eyes flickered across the room to Sesvalah as she asked, "So what do you think I should do?"

"My honest opinion would be that you might want to think about finding a fairer solution all the way around or let her go."

CHAPTER *Thirty-Seven*

Two days after her appointment with the counselor, Brandi thought she had come up with a solution. She pulled a sullen Tanya into her home office and said, "I've rewritten the contract." Brandi slipped into the chair across from Tanya. "Two years. And after you get your GED, I'll pay for your education at a community college. You'll get a smaller salary, but you will keep your benefits."

"Two whole years? And why a smaller salary? I like my salary!" Tanya protested.

"I'm cutting your salary and putting the difference into your education. You can't have it both ways, girlfriend." Then she noticed that Tanya still had a scowl on her round face. "You have any better offers on the table?"

She turned bright pink. "Well…no."

"Any trips around the world, Miss America?"

Tanya glowered.

Brandi leveled a strong gaze into the woman's blue eyes. "Then what's the problem?"

"I just feel…uneasy being here that long."

"My kind served your kind for four hundred years," Brandi snapped. "Two years is short in comparison."

"Oh, don't start with that slavery shit," Tanya shot back. "The white man didn't start slavery."

"Get a grip! They were the ones who brought us here."

"And who sold your people to them? Other African tribes! So much for brotherly love."

That shut Brandi up.

"Africans sold their enemies, neighboring tribes, and their own daughters off to the white men who had come to trade. So don't think it started with white people. It didn't just happen to Blacks. Slavery's a part of everyone's culture. Not just Blacks. And if you really dig deeper you'd find out that there were Blacks already here before anyone else 'discovered' American soil. So as much as you'd like to say your origins are across the waters, who's to say your ancestors weren't already here."

Silence hung like dense fog between the two women.

"How do you know all this?" Brandi finally asked, after realizing there might be some truth to that.

"Grandpa James taught me a lot when I stayed with the Pitchford family. Learning from Grandpa James was twenty times better than listening to that drivel they taught us in school.

"He showed me a two-dollar bill one day and pointed out that the only *Black man* sitting in the group was actually the first president on this continent. Calling you Black instead of African-American isn't an insult. You all were everywhere, but history dictates most came from a place called Kemet the 'Land of the Blacks' which may have started in a place in Northern African—but extended the more everyone spread out. There was even a Moor among the knights at King Author's Round Table—people didn't know it because knights were knights, ranked by character, not color. Same with Hebrews and their twelve different tribes. People weren't distinguished by color, that's why anyone who accepts the faith is accepted wholeheartedly and also why so many people have a hard time trying to picture those tribes being made up of different cultures we know today."

"Getting a history lesson from a white girl," Brandi said, with a little laugh. "I'll be damned."

"No, be better than that. Just be *Black*," Tanya said with a wink.

Brandi sighed deeply. "So, smart ass, why are you so upset about this new contact? Do you want to be stuck being a play toy for the next man that comes along?"

"I don't want to be *stuck* doing anything," she snapped back, shaking her hair away from her face.

"You will be if you don't get an education or some type of vocational training. There's a McDonald's on every corner and you'll be right there working fries until they get robots if you don't do something right now."

"Okay, I'll register for college," a reluctant Tanya said after a lengthy silence.

Brandi pushed the document out, Tanya scribbled her acceptance, and it was a done deal. "I'll have this notarized and Avie will file this new one in court."

Tanya huffed. "I know it might not be my place, but since we're being so open and honest about everything..."

Brandi's head whipped around. "The contract's solid and it works both ways. I hope you're not coming up with more excuses or more bullshit."

Tanya inched back, bristling at Brandi's caustic tone. "Maybe now isn't a good time."

"You brought it up, woman, speak your mind!"

"You're working too much," Tanya snapped back. "You're working too hard."

Brandi's expression darkened. "I'm providing for my children, running a business, and paying your salary and benefits, so I know *you're* not saying that to me."

"Your *children* are saying it," Tanya spat. "They've gotten so used to you not being here they don't even ask when you're coming home anymore!"

Brandi sighed, weariness filling every cell of her body. "If I don't pull this together there won't be a home to come home to."

"I understand all that, but—"

"But what?"

Tanya lifted her chin, anger flashing in her eyes. "I don't know what kind of day you've had, but I'd appreciate it if you didn't take it out on me...or the children."

Brandi took a slow, uneasy breath. "I apologize."

Tanya nodded. "The money will always come, your career will always be there, but your children are getting away from you."

"They're not getting away. I love them."

"Then stop putting them on the back burner," she said softly patting Brandi's hand gently. "It's not how much time you spend with them. It's the quality of that time. That means when you're here, you're here for them. No cell phone, no faxes, no www.com and no emails. It's all about *them*. And why don't you take them to church? You believe in God. What are they going to hold onto when they're in trouble? At least let me take them with me to Power Circle Congregation on Sundays."

Brandi leveled a stony gaze at Tanya. "You don't have child one. So who are you to tell me how to raise my kids?"

Tanya gasped, reeling from that blow. "I'm the woman who's here with them day in and day out. I'm the woman they tell their problems to. I dry their tears," she snapped, unable to keep the anger from her voice. "While I know you didn't want to have them, you don't have to make it so obvious!

"This competition thing with Vernon is making you bitter and angry and they can feel it. And not that it makes a difference to you—but so can I." Then she said, chest heaving a little as her voice broke, "And I may not have children...but I'm someone who knows what it's like to have her mother put someone else or—or—or *something* else ahead of her child. I would never have thought you to be that type of woman. But every day you're proving me wrong."

Brandi opened her mouth to speak.

Tanya silenced her by raising a hand. "I don't have to be a parent to understand that they love you and need you. I don't have to be anything but a compassionate person." A tear escaped her sad blue eyes as she said, "I'll go check on the girls."

Tanya made a quick exit, sobbing deeply.

CHAPTER *Thirty-Eight*

Gripping the porcelain sink in the master bathroom, Tanya stilled herself, fighting the wave of nausea as she remembered her mother's reaction when Mrs. Patton explained what had happened to her.

The coiffed woman with strawberry-blonde hair, cagey blue eyes, aquiline nose, and petite frame lifted her chin proudly "She's lying. Wilbur would never do that. He has me."

"And it doesn't matter if he's hurting her like she says he is?" Mrs. Patton's dark eyes leveled on Margaret. "Haven't you noticed the change in her?"

"I thought those clothes were some new style. She never dresses the way she should, trying to be like that Michelle person."

"Mrs. Jaunal, if you're not going to act, I'll be obligated to go to the authorities."

"You stay out of this," she hissed, momentarily losing her Southern Belle composure. "This is family business."

Tanya's teacher brushed her auburn hair back from her face. "Well, the only thing her family is doing is *hurting* her. Come on, Tanya."

Tanya took Mrs. Patton's extended hand.

Margaret Jaunal jumped to her feet, grabbing Tanya's other arm. "You leave with her and you can't come back. Ever. This teacher might buy into your lies, but no one else will."

She was right. After that initial police report, which they only filed because Mrs. Patton said that she would call the state police, then the FBI if they didn't do something—tongues wagged but soon hushed. Family members who once thought the sun rose and set with Tanya's smile became distant. The elite of Social Circle turned their noses up at her, the same ones who had practically begged Margaret Jaunal to match her up with their ugly but well-maintained sons. Now they wouldn't even say hello. Tanya lost everything. But truthfully, she'd had nothing of importance to begin with.

Mrs. Patton lost her job but when people protested, the school board reinstated her within a week. For the time being Tanya was safe from her father at Mrs. Patton's place.

Then one day she saw her sister at school. Limp blonde hair, pain in her blue eyes, and Tanya knew. Her father was hurting her baby sister. She had to get her out of that house.

She had Mrs. Patton bring her back to the mansion on the north end of Cherokee Road—on the pretense of needing some of her things—when she was certain her dad would be gone.

As she packed the last of her sister's things and waited for Mindy to come home, her heart rammed against her chest, hoping that her father wouldn't get there first.

Finally, Mindy inched into the room. Her golden hair had been pulled into a ponytail. Her Cupid's bow lips formed a smile as she thrust herself across the room. "Tanya! Please take me with you."

"That's why I'm here." She nodded to the door. "If there's something I missed, get it quick! I want to be out of here by the time Daddy comes home."

Then Mindy grabbed her hand and said something that confirmed what Tanya had suspected. "Daddy put his thing in me. My private hurts. I couldn't walk today."

Tanya froze, pain seared her heart as she hugged her little sister to her breasts and said, "I won't let anything else happen to you. Come on, he's supposed to be home in an hour..."

Tears blurred Tanya's vision as she watched her sister struggle to maintain her balance. Didn't anyone else notice? Any of her teachers?

All her life Tanya had been pampered and cared for—piano, tennis, ballet, and horseback riding lessons were things her mother insisted on for both girls. Her father had made sure she had the best of everything. Maybe he thought he had the right to hurt her. Deep down Tanya knew that no one had the right to touch her that way. And he certainly had no right to hurt Mindy.

She snapped the bright pink case shut.

"You lying, ungrateful bitch," her father spat from the doorway of the bedroom.

Fear stabbed her insides, churning them like a pot of stew as she suddenly found herself rooted to the floor. His wide frame blocked every inch of escape. Oh God!

He thrust Mindy out of the room and slammed the door behind him before crossing to Tanya, grabbing the case from her hands and tossing it on the floor. His sharp features twisted with anger as his fist slammed into her face. "Telling lies on me."

"You did hurt me, Daddy," she said, inching closer to the wall, holding a hand up to protect her face.

He reached down, grabbed her wrists, raised his hand in the air, and let it fly again. The pain that stung her face as her skull shifted from the blow was unlike any she had ever felt before.

Tanya opened her mouth. At first no sound came. Then an ear-piercing scream let loose.

"Scream all you want, missy. Your mama's entertaining your teacher friend in the library. She doesn't know I'm here—"

That meant that Mrs. Patton would never hear a thing. The library was in the west wing on the first floor. Her bedroom was on the second floor in the east wing. Miles apart. Worlds apart.

He pinned her to the bed with his full weight, but she finally freed her fist and connected with his head. He pressed her face down hard nearly cutting off her breath. She tasted the saltiness of her tears as he roughly shoved down her pants.

"You're going to pay for humiliating me in this town. Since I may have to serve time for this shit, I think I should make it worth my while."

This time his fist caused blood to pour from her nose and mouth.

"*Daddy, please,*" she shrieked, struggling to free herself.

He covered her mouth, leaning forward as he whispered, "Wouldn't want your little sister to come in and watch now, would you?"

Tanya felt the sudden painful pressure at the entrance of her vagina. Then he moved forward, crushing her face to the white lace pillows and the wooden canopy. The room swam out of focus as pain exploded in her pelvis—a familiar pain, but no less sharp and searing.

She thrashed beneath him, but that didn't stop him. Then her gaze fell to the table beside her bed. She reached, trying to ignore the overwhelming pain down below. Her father grunted like an animal with each move.

She lunged out, hand wrapping around the lamp. She swung it hard connecting with his head forcing him out of her body.

The lamp fell from her sweaty grasp as he lunged for her again. Tanya went for his eyes, trying to apply pressure to the bright blue pupils that were so much like her own.

Lifting his head, he bit down on her fingers, instantly drawing blood. This time he slammed her against the wall. The shock made her go weak with terror. Suddenly, he was inside her again, from behind. "If your mother won't take care of her wifely duties, you will. Hanging out with that bitch teacher of yours has given you some bad habits. And it won't make a difference. I can get to you anytime I want." His hands applied a painful pressure to her neck, cutting off all air. "I have my rights and I own you. I could kill you and no one would say a word to me."

With every word he lunged forward, pressing her further against the wall. He had never hurt her this badly. And it had never happened with the sun still shining. Always in the cover of darkness. Always with her mother out at one charity event or another—or even when she was home. Was that why Mindy and Tanya had been put in the east wing, so far away from their parents' room?

She gasped for air. Sobs wracked her body as blood continued to flow from her lips and nose.

"Wilbur!"

He froze mid-stroke. Tanya slumped forward as her mother's voice echoed in the bedroom. Lifting her head caused pain to shoot through her body.

Slowly, reluctantly, he pulled away. She welcomed his exit, but her body now throbbed with an unnaturally intense pain. Blood dripped from the end of his wrinkled pink penis. That, too, caused an alarm to go off for Tanya. She wasn't on her cycle. And he had taken her virginity over a year ago, just after her twelfth birthday. What more had he done to her?

Mindy ran into the room, a little pink suitcase clutched in her tiny hands, toys poking out of the sides. She looked from Tanya to her father to her mother. Distant blue eyes filled to the brim with tears as her gaze landed on her older sister.

Wilbur had all but pulled himself together. Tanya waited with anxious breaths for her mother, finally confronted with the truth, to do something, *anything* this time.

"I'm going with Tanya. I don't want Daddy to hurt me anymore." Mindy grimaced as she crossed the room to take her older sister's hand. She gripped the hand so hard it hurt—but Tanya didn't mind. This would be the last time either one of them would feel pain from their parents.

"Now you've got her lying, too," Margaret said.

Tanya gaped, not sure she heard correctly. Her father's sly grin infuriated her. Didn't the woman see his ugly penis hanging out? Hadn't she seen him raping her? Didn't she see the blood? What did she think he was doing—helping her pack?

Her mother stared absently ahead as Wilbur Jaunal zipped up his slacks. "Now you just go get cleaned up and everything will be just fine, dear," she continued.

Finally, Tanya found the strength to move. "Just fine?" The sudden reality made her want to die. "You've known all this time. You've *known!*"

Margaret dipped her head as she avoided eye contact with her daughter. "We'll just get him some help...that's all he needs is a little help. Everything will be fine."

"You're just as sick as he is," Tanya snapped, pulling Mindy even closer.

"It's not like you can't handle it," Margaret shot back. Her normally elegant, patrician features turned into a murderous scowl. "Hanging out with that—that—Michelle person. Those little Black boys sniffing around like some rabid dogs. You'll let one of them have at you sooner or later. It's better that it's one of our own. It's no difference."

"No difference!" Tanya shrieked, looking at her mother as though the woman was a total stranger. "He's my father. My *father!*"

"All the more reason why you should just—"

"To hell with you!" Tanya glanced out of the window, calculating the best way to jump if it became the only option.

"Margaret, go downstairs and tend to our guest," Wilbur said, with a bit of steel in his voice. "She must be wondering what's going on by now."

"Yes, Wilbur." Dutifully, almost blindly, her mother's face went blank as she turned and walked out of the room, leaving a stunned Tanya watching in her wake.

Then he turned on her little sister. "And just where do you think you're going, little missy?"

Mindy shrank behind Tanya for cover. He lunged forward; Tanya flexed her left leg and connected with his groin. He doubled over with pain, dropped to his knees on the floor.

Tanya grabbed Mindy's hand and ran for the stairs. Mindy couldn't keep up, but that didn't stop her from trying.

"Drop the suitcase," Tanya yelled, gasping with each step, pain exploding within her every time her feet touched the oriental runner that spread the length of all three hallways. The pink luggage bounced against Mindy's leg, causing her to pull Tanya to the side and slowing them down.

"But my teddy's in there."

"Drop it!" Tanya yelled, ignoring the pain as she picked up the pace. Wilbur's clunky footsteps echoed behind them.

As they turned the corner leading to the main corridor, the suitcase tumbled out onto the floor. All they had to do was make it to the west wing and Mrs. Patton. Just get to Mrs. Patton. Mrs. Patton...

Pain vibrated from every cell of her being. A wave of nausea followed right after.

They crossed the connecting corridor, doubled back up the stairs, and ran through the hidden corridor that linked the main areas of the house in a set of wooden pathways and stairways.

"My side hurts," Mindy whined.

"I know, but we…have to…keep moving," Tanya said, between gasps.

Tanya slowed a little so Mindy could catch her breath. A quick look left showed her sister's pale face had turned a bright, almost sickly color. But they had to keep going. Their father sounded close—too close.

"Almost there, Mindy. Keep moving."

As she opened the panel that would lead to a short hallway to her father's library, blood from her jeans dripped down to the floor. She threw open the heavy doors to the library.

Mrs. Patton jerked to her feet, rushing in their direction with an open mouth and wide eyes.

Tanya brushed past her mother, pushing Mindy forward into Mrs. Patton's waiting arms.

The words, "Daddy hurt Tanya again. Mama saw it," were the last things Tanya heard before her world turned black and she crumbled in a soft, bloody heap onto the Persian rug.

❤❤❤

Brandi Spencer touched Tanya's hand, jolting her out of the past.

Tanya took a deep breath, turned on the water and allowed it to spill over her hands. She splashed some onto her face, welcoming the cool jolt back to the present—back to safety.

"Are you all right?"

Tanya nodded, but she felt nothing close to all right.

Brandi gripped her shoulders, brought her into the living room, and made her sit on the sofa.

"We're doing things the same way that Vernon did it to us," Tanya said softly. "And you're right—I've just become so used to having men take care of me that challenging myself to take up where I left off in school seems too tough to handle. I wasn't bred to work hard, and that's all my life has been about—trying to have the life I was born to—being a woman kept by men."

Tanya shared her past abuse with Brandi, and Brandi slowly recounted her own rape the day she turned thirteen. By the time they were through, both women were in tears and had another chain in their unusual bond.

"I've never realized that we had so much in common," Tanya said, her eyes glued on pictures of the girls on the end table. "What happened to me should never happen to any woman or child, but the more I listen, the more I sense that it's already touched the lives of most women I know." She gazed out of the window. "I struggle hard not to blame outside sources for my pain, especially since the people closest to me hurt me the most. Me by my parents; you by that nasty old man who raped you, and a husband who gave us both a one-two punch. That's not a white or a Black thing."

Brandi looked out as the sun slipped out from behind the clouds. "Sometimes I believe what anyone else does to us outside of our own race doesn't quite match up. So while we're looking the other way, pointing the finger at everyone else, our own are slipping in and doing more damage than anyone. That hurts more because we don't expect them to hurt us. I'm tired of letting that time in my life keep me fearful and unwilling to move forward in life."

"So what do we do about that?" Tanya asked in a voice that was just above a whisper.

"We take control and move our lives forward." Brandi reached out for Tanya's hand. "I go to counseling on Wednesday. Sesvalah's also a sexual abuse counselor and family therapist. Do you want to come?"

Tanya cautiously placed her hand inside Brandi's. "Thanks. I'd like that."

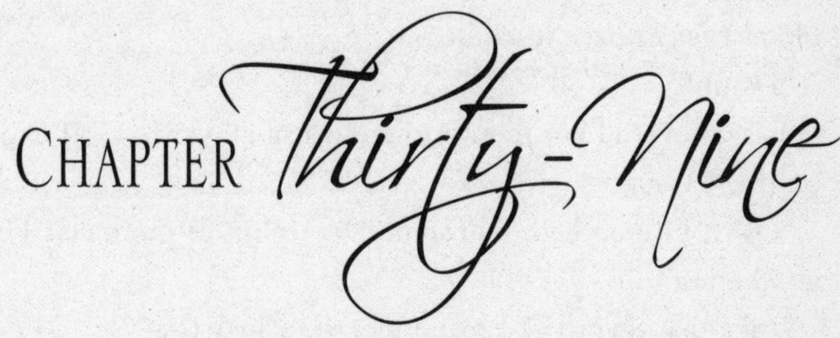

CHAPTER Thirty-Nine

Five weeks later, having completed their first series of separate counseling sessions, Tanya and Brandi were still working with two books: *Speak It Into Existence* and *Radical Forgiveness* while completing the worksheets that went with it. Sesvalah had them bring their work in for every session and so far the results were great. Both women had done at least two "forgiveness" sheets on their situations with Vernon.

Tanya dropped down on the love seat in the corner of Brandi's office. "We've got a problem."

Brandi tore her gaze away from the papers in front of her to look at Tanya. "Oh?"

Tanya crossed one leg over the other. "I'm horny."

Brandi paused a moment, blinking twice as she took that in. Then she leaned over, laughing her ass off. "Can't help you there, dear, I'm horny, too."

"Well something's gotta be done."

"Then order some," she said, still laughing. "And make it a large at medium charge." Suddenly her tone changed. "Wait a minute. I thought you were done with men."

Tanya shook her head. "I said I didn't want to take another man for a test-drive. Right now most of them are rentals instead of being for sale as advertised. I thought maybe a professional lover would put a different spin on things." She let out a small sigh. "Oh, for the days before AIDS."

Brandi laughed even harder. "Yeah, 'cause that stopped me from getting buck wild. That's why I wanted to get married. I wanted mine in-house and on standby. Or is that stand up?"

Tanya chuckled. "And I'm done with relationships, not sex. If I don't get some real soon, even your mood swings will look mild." Then her red lips spread out into a wide smile. "You don't want that one drop of Black blood I *might* have to come out."

"Damn!"

Tanya covered her mouth to stifle a small yawn. CNBC played silently on the TV screen.

"Okay, I'll purchase you some Doc Johnson products. They make real good ones."

"Like that Sword of Love under your mattress?"

Brandi nodded. "How do you keep finding that thing!"

"I clean this place, remember?" Tanya said with a laugh. "And for the life of me, I can't see why you keep it on your side of the mattress, must be a dreadful night's sleep." Then her gaze narrowed. "I don't suppose they come with a living, breathing human being on the other end?"

"No, that's the up side, it's all galvanized rubber and pure imagination," Brandi said, lifting her chin a little. "Works for me."

"Then you're a different breed of woman, 'cause just like every woman needs a wife, every wife needs some good sex."

Brandi leaned back in her leather chair watching Tanya from hooded eyes. "So what do you propose?"

"I don't know." Then she paused for a moment. "You know, speaking of dick, I met this guy at the grocery store, but something doesn't seem right about him. He's too persistent and it's almost like he's been coached or something—knows all the right things to say and do. It's weird."

"So how did you manage to spend time with him?" Brandi leaned forward.

"Well, after you and the girls are down for the night, I sneak off, but nothing's happened because it doesn't feel right."

"So that's where you've been," Brandi said, letting out a long sigh of relief. "I thought you were meeting Vernon. He's missing in action around the same time you are. A quick call to my mother-in-law gives me that info. I figured you'd slip up sooner or later and I could tack on a few more months to the contract," she said with a mischievous glint in her eyes. "Believe it or not, it's been…strange having you here, but it's also been…" Brandi shrugged, trying to come up with a term that seemed to escape her. "Kinda nice."

"Oh, you don't have to worry about me sleeping with Vernon again. I wouldn't screw him if it would get me off life support."

"Don't get drastic," Brandi said with a sly grin. "If sex could keep you alive, take him up on it. Doesn't make a difference to me."

"Yes it does," Tanya shot back. "I wouldn't be here if it didn't."

"You'd be here because it'd be in your best interest, so get off it."

Tanya blushed a little and dipped her head sheepishly. "The woman knows me too well. I don't want to bring a man into this house or anywhere around the children," she added softly.

"I appreciate it. Since my husband is still vying to return, I'm keeping the option open. Until our lives are decided—stay separated, divorce, or get back together. I'm not sure if I want to tackle anyone else."

Tanya grinned. "Even Michael?"

Brandi thought it over for a moment. "Even him. How did you know about him?"

"When you take your little catnaps on the couch, you call his name in your sleep. You must be having wet dreams, but you mess it up toward the end when you call out for Vernon. What a nightmare."

Brandi chuckled, propping her legs up on the edge of her glass desk, a duplicate to the one in her office at The Perfect Match. "I'm feeling something for Michael, but I'm not ready to move on to another man until this thing with Vernon is decided. I respect the vows I made. I can't do the things he has."

Tanya leaned forward, resting her elbows on her knees. "Well, I have a solution to my problem, but I'll need at least two weeks vacation. And that's one thing that's not in the contract."

"Two weeks? Woman, you haven't made it past the probation period and you're asking for a vacation already?" She sighed, but Tanya didn't miss the smirk on her lips. "Boy, good help sure is hard to find." Then her light brown eyes narrowed to slits. "And just where do you think you're going for two whole weeks?"

"Belize."

"Why there?"

"They love fleshy women with big breasts," Tanya said, giving her a sly grin.

"Really?" Brandi perked up. "Just like Jamaican men, huh?"

"No, they're just using the sex to get us to bring them here. Belize men aren't trying to leave their country, they love who we are—wide hips, full breasts…"

"Book two tickets."

"Sounds like a plan." Tanya practically skipped from the room.

Brandi would never admit to Tanya that she already had her backup lined up. Vernon had called and asked to see her at his mother's house. That could only mean one of two things: He was either gonna try for some toe-curling sex or another round of explanations.

Like Tanya, if she didn't get some live stuff soon, mood swings would be the least of everyone's worries.

"What's it like?" Tanya asked, coming back into the room with her gaze locked on the picture of the girls.

Brandi followed her gaze. "You mean having children?" She turned back as Tanya nodded. "It wasn't as painful as everyone makes it out to be," she said softly. "And motherhood—as Craig would put it—ain't no punk." Brandi folded her hands under her chin. "Simone was an easy delivery, but when it was Sierra's turn, it was cold enough to grow our own frozen vegetables.

"Vernon had been stalling about getting the car in the shop to have it worked on, but finally he had no choice. Wouldn't you know it—little Miss Sierra decided to make a half-ass entrance into the world. And I only say half because though I was in labor twenty-six hours, her little tail was asleep the entire time so they had to come in and shake my stomach every thirty minutes. And I wanted her out—out—out! The girl was interrupting my love affair with a good meal."

Tanya leaned forward soaking up every word.

"Anyway, we had to borrow the next door neighbor's car to get to the hospital in the first place—an old rusted-out Cutlass that had see-through spots on the back floors. We had a perfect view of the great outdoors."

Tanya perked up. "Mr. Dishman had a car like that? I can't see him driving anything less than a Mercedes."

"No, this was from our first house. We haven't always lived here. We used to live close to my mom's place in Jeffrey Manor."

Tanya frowned trying to take that in.

"When Vernon married me his father cut him off and we had to start from scratch—literally."

"Seems like something he would do."

"Girl, you don't know the half of it," Brandi replied in a dry tone. Then she perked up. "Okay, okay, back to the story. I had to ride all the way to the hospital with my legs hoisted up in the back seat and watching the snow scene on the floor. Then the car choked on the first five turnovers. I thought we were going to have to start the damn thing Fred Flintstone-style."

"You mean sticking your feet out of the bottom then peddling like crazy?"

"Exactly! And the fact that it was so slippery and the tires were more than bald—they needed rubber Rogaine just to grip the ground—"

Tanya bent over, giggling like a little girl.

"—we could only drive ten miles an hour. Then to top it off, I ended up in a teaching hospital, which meant a rotating group of interns and residents—doctors and would-be doctors—came around every half an hour to check under the hood. At one point I told them, 'I'm going to charge admission.' But then the main doctor grinned and said, 'But we're not going inside to watch the show.' And I said, 'Yeah, but you're hanging out in the lobby and it's all the same to me. Pay up, buster.' They didn't visit again until Sierra was ready to come into the world. But when she came looking like her sister, she was just as precious, a tiny thing with all of the same parts we had condensed into a tiny little bundle. I thought it was the most spectacular thing in the world."

"I could only wish that I could experience it," Tanya said in a small voice.

❤❤❤

Unfortunately, Tanya would never know the joys of motherhood. She had been rushed from the floor of her father's library straight to Walton Medical Center. For a few days they kept her under police watch.

Unfortunately, Margaret Jaunal had other ideas.

She waited in the stairwell for hours watching the flutter of activity and people going in and out of her daughter's room. In the middle of the night, as Officer Goodman nodded off at his post, she slipped by with a big burly man in tow. Tanya jolted awake only long enough to see the white cloth coming toward her.

She awoke later as the man placed her on what looked to be a kitchen table.

"We don't have time for anesthetics." Margaret Jaunal's cold voice snapped Tanya out of her stupor. "Just get it over with."

Tanya scanned her surroundings and realized she wasn't in the hospital. "You can't do this to me," she said, voice cracking with each word

"You're not having this child!"

The burly man gripped Tanya's arm. A hard sting on her face took a minute to register. Her mother had slapped her; she'd never done that before.

Then reality struck like lightening: they were supposed to take a sample of the amniotic fluid to confirm the baby's paternity, absolute proof of her father's crime. Unfortunately, the doctor wanted to stabilize Tanya before worrying about proving paternity. If this man performed an abortion there would be no proof and Wilbur Jaunal would be free.

Her mother and the quack tied her hands to the handmade stirrups and yanked her pants down. The moment she lashed out with her feet and connected with the "doctor's" face, she felt a hard blow to her own. Blood splattered across his already stained lab coat. "Girl, you do that shit again, and I'll kill ya," he growled.

The heavyset man's beady green eyes and cold stare showed he meant every word.

The butcher tied her feet to the cold metal stirrups. He didn't even clean the instrument before letting it hover over her face. Fear stabbed the center of her gut as a grin spread over his meaty face. In that moment she knew two things: This man would enjoy hurting her, and she would probably not live to tell about this.

She was right in one case.

Her screams rent the air as pain worse than anything her father had caused tore through her insides as though someone had split her in half—from the middle up. Her throat dried and constricted, but more hoarse screams still came through.

"Shut her up," he growled, wiggling a long silver instrument inside her, followed by a suctioning sound.

Margaret smacked her again—hard. "Is it done?"

"No! I just opened her up," he said, struggling to keep Tanya in place. "I have to scrape the kid out, then it's done."

"And scrape out everything else, too."

The man paused and looked up. "I'm not trained to do that!"

Margaret glared at him. "And you're not licensed to perform abortions, either. But you know something about the female body and where all the working parts are," she said through clenched teeth. "There can't be any evidence of DNA from this child left behind."

The man paused, staring open mouthed at the cold woman standing near Tanya's head. He said, "You owe me big-time."

"Just handle it."

"I know one way you can pay me," he said.

Margaret Jaunal leveled a steely ice-blue gaze on the man.

He nodded in Tanya's direction.

"When?"

He grinned, slick black hair falling into his face. "Right after I'm done."

"You sick bastard," she spat, inhaling sharply.

"Nothing like fresh clean pussy," he said with a leer. "And you can't talk much. You're covering up for that redneck you married. People in glass houses—"

"Get this shit over with!" Margaret snapped. "I'll settle up with you later."

The moment the cold steel touched her skin, Tanya flinched.

Moments later God did Tanya a favor by allowing her to pass out.

When Tanya regained consciousness Margaret's face loomed above her. "Hurry up," she said to the quack. "I want to be able to tell Wilbur it's all done."

"Finished." Then man rubbed his hands together as though he had just prepared a seven course meal.

"Come on," she said, glaring at Tanya.

"But what about—but I wanted—" the man sputtered, but instantly paused with an icy glare from Margaret.

"I said later!"

Tanya lowered her legs from the stirrups the moment the "doctor" untied her shaking feet. The world swam out of focus, and when it came back, she saw stars, stripes, and colors she never knew were in the rainbow.

The second her feet touched the ground, the pain was back—worse than before. Blood flooded the makeshift pad the man had stuffed between her thighs and would soon soak her jeans. If she didn't get some real help soon, she would die.

Margaret didn't bother taking Tanya home. She dropped her off at a rarely used Greyhound bus stop and didn't look back as the wheels of her silver Rolls Royce tore away from the curb.

But little did Margaret know that while she and the "doctor" were outside the room having another argument over his desire to have sex with Tanya, while Tanya was supposed to be getting dressed, the girl had stolen a portion of her baby from the little metal basin the "doctor" had carelessly left sitting there.

She was careful as she dipped the cotton balls into the bloody mess and then into a small bottle that had been sitting within her reach. As she tucked the little bottle into her waistband she vowed that her father would go to jail for what he'd done.

Through tears of pain and anger, she found a way to secure the jar so that it wouldn't move around, then covered it with her oversized sweatshirt.

The blood flow had slowed considerably, but she knew her next stop had to be the hospital. Unfortunately, Walton Medical Center was more than ten miles away. She would have to draw on every ounce of inner strength to walk that road. But that's exactly what she had to do in order to preserve any of the evidence her mother had damned near killed her to erase.

Slowly she raised her chin, looking at the rows of trees stretched out before her like an obstacle course.

She would make it, even if it took her very last breath.

CHAPTER 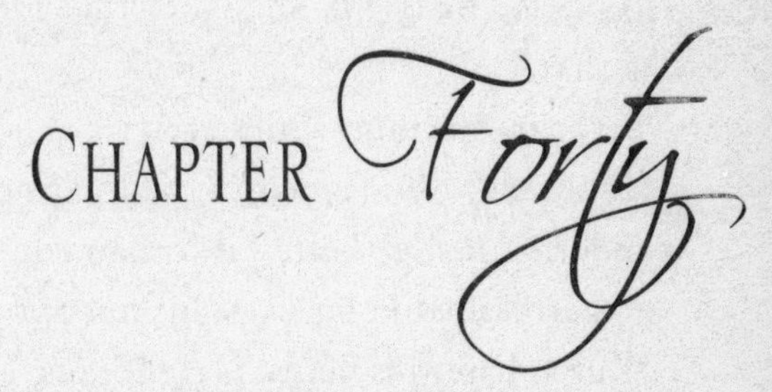

Dinner was lovely. Vernon had prepared honey-roasted chicken, rice pilaf, green beans almondine, tossed salad, and crescent rolls. She didn't even know he *could* cook. Hell, she didn't realize he even knew how to turn on the stove.

Vernon eyed her closely as she gathered her things. "Where are you going? We haven't even—"

"Home to my wife."

His face darkened. "When are you gonna stop with that bullshit?"

"Hey, you wanted to play the game. Don't get mad when I take all my toys and go home. I like things they way they are," she said. "If you have a problem with it, then put this separation into high gear, finalize the divorce, sign the papers, and let's get on with our lives."

"Let's just end this whole court thing; let me come back home. I don't want a divorce! "

"Neither do I," she replied. "But reality is reality. There's nothing you can do about Tanya right now. You've had her for two years, on my time and *my* money. Fairness says I deserve the same."

His eyes widened in shock. "So you're gonna keep her for the *whole* two years?"

"At least, maybe longer." Brandi winked. "She might like what I do for her." She leaned forward and kissed his cheek. "And she's doing quite well as my wife. I can't say it enough: You've got great taste."

Stunned, he lashed out, "You bitch!"

Brandi laughed as she tied the sash around her coat. "Not the nicest words you've ever spoken to me, but you've said worse."

Vernon stared at her.

"Let's get married," she said with a mild shrug. "Yeah, it was something like that."

"Are you sleeping with her?"

"Not yet." She leaned in, whispering, "But I'll keep you posted. I'm wondering if she's better at it than you are."

Anger flashed in his eyes; his nostrils flared just a little. He was pissed!

"But as happy as Tanya is right now, I don't think she'd have a problem overlooking the fact that I'm missing that vital piece of equipment." She reached down, stroking his dick through his trousers. "Good sex isn't about what you have dangling between your legs." She strolled toward the door, laughing. "But I'm sure you knew that already. But then again, maybe you don't."

Fury raged within him, followed by a feeling of helplessness. He thought he was close to getting his wife to see reason. Now he knew that nothing could be further from the truth.

CHAPTER 

CHAPTER Forty-One

"Judge, this ruling doesn't fit the law," Mason Myers said, standing to make his point.

Unmoved, Judge Bowden popped a sunflower seed in his mouth. "There's a legally signed and executed contract with the family, and a clinical assessment has been completed as to the children's take on things. They're actually loving the extra attention. To me, it's like Mrs. Kaufman is a live-in nanny, personal assistant, and helpmate all in one. There's no sexual involvement between the women." He lowered his piercing gray gaze to Brandi whose lips twitched trying to keep in a laugh. "Unless Mrs. Spencer has something to add—"

"Oh, no, Your Honor," she said waving her hand in a delicate flourish before placing it on her chest. "Live-in nanny, personal assistant and all that. Nothing more. She actually—ouch!" Brandi scowled at Avie, growling, "Woman, if you kick me again, you'll need your own lawyer."

"Then cut it out," Avie said through clenched teeth. She leaned forward, gripping Brandi's arm in her slender hands and addressed the court. "That's all, Judge. No sexual involvement."

"So my rulings *do* fit within the laws of community property," he said with eyes locked on Attorney Myers. "The contract belongs to the wife by execution, and to the husband by implied action. He had the woman's—ahem—*services* for two years, and the wife wants a little of the same. She keeps the two-year contract and the mistress, and will receive maintenance for her upkeep, plus child support. Her involvement with Tanya Kaufman will not be held against her."

Vernon stood. "So if I'm paying maintenance for Kaufman, then I should get something, too."

"What you already had is why we're here in the first place."

"And I paid for it then, too," Vernon shrieked. Then he scratched his head. "That didn't come out too good. I want custody and some time with the mistress, too, if I'm paying. I might as—"

"That's your wife's point, Mr. Spencer." Judge Bowden grinned. "Then let's even things up. Can your wife sleep with her?"

Brandi blinked and laid a hand on her breast, saying in a breathy whisper, "Well, if I must..."

"No! No—no," Vernon sputtered. "No!"

"Then you've got to keep it in your pants," the judge said with a small smile. "Maybe you'll learn something. No sexual contact with the mistress."

Mason's jaw dropped. He brushed off his maroon striped suit, then looked up at the judge. "Are you doing this because you're running for office?"

Judge Bowden craned his neck, looking behind him. Then he turned to Mason, one eyebrow raised. "The office is running away from me? When did that happen?"

"Sir?"

The portly bailiff laughed behind his hand.

"I don't run away from anything that's not running from me," the judge said, leveling cool gray eyes on the lawyer. "So I don't get your point."

Mason grimaced as Vernon glowered at him, saying, "Political office."

"Oh, that," Judge Bowden said with a shrug. "You think this is all because I'm playing up to the female population for a few votes?"

"Well, what else could it be?"

"The fact that the wife has done her homework and came prepared, and all your client has is accusations and hot air," he shot back. "And the infidelity issue is not helping him at all."

"You're too biased to hear this case," Mason said, rocking on his heels.

"You want to remove me from this case? This late in the game? Go right ahead and try it," the judge said with a sly grin on his paper-thin lips. "My fellow arbitrators only wish they had a case like this. And I guarantee they might not be so...nice."

Mason looked over at Vernon, who stared blankly ahead.

"Now as I was saying, before *someone* so rudely interrupted—" Judge Bowden flexed his pudgy fingers—"the house on Wabash Avenue will remain empty until it is sold. The proceeds will be split fifty-fifty."

Vernon jumped to his feet. "Why can't I live there?" Mason tried to yank him down, but Vernon shrugged him off. "I have to pay half the mortgage! So why can't I have a place to live?"

Judge Bowden peered over the top of his glasses at Vernon. "Because you're supposed to do counseling so you *can* go back home—*your* wish, mind you. The counselor said you walked out, when I've ordered you to be there."

"Your Honor—"

"Young man, you are trying my patience." Judge Bowden waved his wooden gavel. "If you all were crazy enough to bring this in front of me, then I'm crazy enough to rule."

"Your Honor, this is not acceptable!" Mason pushed his shoulder downward until Vernon ended up back in his seat.

"You're wasting my time," the judge said before pointing the gavel at Vernon. "Go home and work things out with your wife. This could all go away."

"Not with her there!" Vernon said with a quick glance across the room at Tanya.

"What's wrong with *her* all of a sudden?" the judge asked with a smile. "Did she turn purple and grow polka dots? She was fine three months ago. Or have you lost the...*holiday spirit?*"

Vernon remained silent, glowering angrily at the judge.

"Get outta my courtroom," Judge Bowden said, looking first at Mason, then at Vernon. "I've had enough of you two clowns today."

As Vernon left the building, the Channel 7 news crew and several other members of the media were ready for him with a barrage of questions. After five minutes of "No comment," he grew impatient and shouted, "Get that thing out of my face," then pushed through the crowd. He managed to get only three feet before finding himself face-to-face with the three women who were making his life a living hell.

Brandi, Tanya, and Avie strolled across the black marble and sand-colored pavement.

"Hey, I'm here to offer you a movie deal," shouted a bushy-haired man wearing an oversized Hawaiian shirt as he waved a business card in the air. "We'd like to shoot a film based on your story."

The man must've been from California, Brandi thought. Who else would wear a short-sleeve shirt in weather that was frigid enough to turn cold cream to ice cream.

"I'm not interested," Brandi replied, then pointed to Tanya. "But she might be."

Brandi's heels clattered down the stone tile as the man turned around and said, "How about it?"

"I don't know how to act."

The man grinned, closing in for the kill. "It isn't too hard. With your looks, you'd be a natural."

Tanya leveled an icy-blue gaze on Vernon, raised her voice, and asked, "Any harder than faking an orgasm?"

All mics swung in her direction.

Vernon visibly blanched, mumbling something the nearby newscasters struggled to catch.

Mr. California followed her gaze. "Maybe it's a lot less difficult than *that.*"

"Then I'm your woman. I've had two whole years of practice."

Brandi chuckled as the news teams tried to run Vernon down.

"Mr. Spencer, what's your take on all this? Your wife now has her own wife."

"It's not gonna last," he growled. "She's just doing this to get back at me."

A female reporter thrust a microphone in his face. "But you did sleep around on her, right?"

"No, I mean— Yes, I mean— Get outta my face!"

"And doesn't she deserve something, too?" The woman lifted her eyebrows twice. The implications weren't lost on anyone.

Vernon froze. "She's not sleeping with her. My wife's not gay!"

"And you know that for sure?" The woman leaned in wearing a sly smile on her thin pink lips. "Who knows? Maybe the mistress enjoys being her wife more than being your mistress."

The would-be movie director perked up. "Now that'd be a real story."

"Look," Vernon said, stopping to address the crowd, "this is just a phase she's going through. She wanted to prove a point." He said it loudly enough to be sure Brandi and Tanya heard him. "You mark my words: That woman will be out of my house real soon. I'll have my life back."

"Can we quote you on that?"

"You can quote anything you like. My wife, the woman I married, will come to her senses. And things will be back to normal."

The news crews in front of the Daley Center turned their collective attention to the women.

"Mrs. Spencer, are you—"

"No comment!" she growled, trying to pick up the pace.

"Aren't you setting a bad example for marriages?" asked a pushy young reporter from Channel 7 news. "Or was this a cover-up because you are bisexual?"

Brandi whirled around on one heel like a prima ballerina, leaving Avie stumbling to keep up. She drew in a deep breath and said, "Let me tell you something—"

Avie lunged forward, grabbing Brandi by the collar before she could get the rest out. "My client has no comment."

Tanya grabbed Brandi's other arm and they practically lifted Brandi off the ground.

Brandi looked over her shoulder, glaring at the mop-haired newscaster as she flipped the woman the bird before Avie could rein her in a second time.

Brandi nearly tripped into the glass doors, making a beeline for the safety of the parking garage. Tanya managed to keep up. Avie, high heels and all, was right behind her.

"How did the press know about this, Avie?"

Avie shrugged, pulling her synthetic fur coat around her thick frame, avoiding eye contact with her friend. Oh yeah, that heifer had something to do with it.

"Avie?"

"I don't really know for sure," she said softly. "I just know that I didn't have anything to do with it."

Brandi eyed her best friend, as they kept three steps ahead of Fox News. "Mrs. Spencer, tell us about the case."

"Yes, we want to hear your side of the story."

"Hey, can I get an exclusive?"

"Will you give me a moment to talk with my lawyer?" Brandi bellowed loudly enough to wake the residents in Oakwood Cemetery.

A sudden hush fell over the few newscasters and people trying to get around them, as everyone inched back. Tanya snatched up the keys and ran into the garage. "I'll bring the getaway car," she said over her shoulder.

Brandi turned to Avie. "Woman, if you don't start talking, I'm gonna tell Carlton who really scratched up his Barry White *Unlimited Love* album."

The lawyer gasped, holding the briefcase to her chest as her hazel eyes widened with horror. "You wouldn't!"

"Try me."

Avie lowered the leather briefcase to her side, saying, "Vernon's lawyer kind of...*mentioned* that he might, ah, *you know*."

Brandi leaned forward until they were almost nose to nose. "And you didn't think of mentioning *you know* to me?"

Avie swallowed hard. The first time Brandi had ever seen her at a loss for words. "I didn't think he'd really go through with it."

"What possible reason could he—"

"Vernon wants you back. He doesn't want a divorce," Avie said, pulling back some. "If he made things public, he hoped that pressure from outside sources would embarrass you enough to put the mistress out and let him come home. And I didn't see too much harm. You still love him and want him back in spite of every warning I could give."

"Traitor!" Brandi pushed Avie's shoulder. "How could you do this to me?"

"Because he has a point!" she shot back, before taking aim on the reporters who had inched closer to take notes. "If you motherfu—"

"Avie, cool out!"

The reporters got the message and filed out of the parking garage.

"You've taken things much too far. We've gone back and forth to court wasting resources and time for what? To prove a point! You don't want a divorce and neither does he."

"So now you're playing house with Mason."

"No, I'm looking out for my friend," Avie replied, throwing a quick glance over her shoulder. "A friend who's making an absolute fool of herself."

The sound of stick drummers on the corner of Randolph Avenue and State Street filled the air and drifted into the parking garage. The rhythm of their drums steadily vibrated up her spine.

Brandi turned to walk away, then stopped suddenly and faced her friend. "Did you think for one moment how all this publicity would affect the kids?"

"Did you think about how having that strange woman in your house affects the kids?"

"Tanya wouldn't hurt them!"

"You don't know that! She could be setting you up for failure—big-time. Don't forget this woman slept with your husband; she wants him, too."

"She wants no part of him in bed or out. She's just as prime for our arrangement as I am," Brandi replied. "He used both of us."

"This is sad, Brandi. You've taken this martyr bit to a whole new level."

"I'm not a martyr, I'm a survivor," Brandi said, poking a finger in Avie's fur. "Something that a whole lot of women aren't able to say."

"A survivor who's exposing her kids to her husband's infidelity."

"*He* already did that," Brandi said, glowering angrily at her best friend. "I'm just making it work for everybody."

"You're making it work for *you.*"

Brandi took a moment to absorb what she'd heard and said during the last few minutes. "If I ever find out that you've sold me out again, it'll be the last time we speak. You're supposed to be watching my back, not plotting my downfall. You pick now of all times to act like a lawyer."

"That's ripe, even for you, Brandi."

"So maybe this will help keep you focused," Brandi said, scribbling out a check, handing it to her friend.

"What is this?"

"For all the times we've gone *back and forth* to court. This is a thirty-five-hundred-dollar retainer. Maybe now you'll act in my best interest and stop sleeping with the enemy."

Avie tore up the check and tossed the little pieces in the air. "Screw you and your raunchy ass attitude!"

"If that's an offer, I refuse. *I've* already got some lined up. If you meant that as an insult, *you've* already got that covered." As Tanya pulled the Lexus in front of her, Brandi gestured back to the Daley Center. "Live at five, news at ten, right? Thanks a lot, *friend*!"

CHAPTER Forty-Two

Vernon sat in his father's office—a room big enough to sleep a family of eight—on the eighty-second floor of the Sears Tower. He had always hated the building, especially since they were so far up. Every time the wind blew, the building would move with it—almost like a ship sailing across choppy waters. Vernon avoided visiting his father whenever possible. Those times he couldn't avoid meeting with the old man, he parted ways with his appetite for the rest of the day.

William cracked his knuckles, then his neck. "So what happened to the guy you put on to Tanya?" he asked as he sipped his brandy. "I thought you said he was a sure thing with white women."

"Mark normally is, but he said he did all the right things and she became suspicious. Then she stopped taking his calls. Tanya was never a gold digger. So appealing to her that way will never work. She never asked for anything. She was satisfied with the things I gave her."

"Must be nice," William said, casting a wary glance at Julie's picture. "So," he said with a stifled yawn, "on to Plan B."

Vernon was afraid to ask, but he had to. "What's Plan B?"

"The League. If you can't get your wife to put that woman out of your house, you'll have to find a way to get her attention."

An uneasy feeling settled in the pit of Vernon's stomach. "What can they do for me?"

His father's sneer almost made Vernon sick to his stomach.

❤❤❤

An hour later in a banquet room at the Hyatt Regency McCormick Place, Vernon hung back near the door. Black men wearing business suits and ties mingled in the room. Vernon wasn't comfortable with his father's plan. It was downright mean and Vernon never played the game that way. A little dirty, maybe, but never mean.

His gaze swept across the room, taking in the men, who all had college degrees and either worked in high-level positions at Fortune 500 companies across the nation, or had their own businesses. The League had hit about twenty-five thousand members in forty-five chapters nationwide. The board did not allow a chapter to begin unless they had at least two hundred-fifty, half of the required number of businessmen to pull it off.

As the meeting moved on to new business—Vernon's category—William signaled him to the podium.

Vernon slowly took the microphone and turned to greet his brothers in business. "Good evening, League."

A sea of voices rang out, loud and hearty. "Good evening, Brother Spencer."

A quick glance at his father got an encouraging nod.

Vernon turned back to the men and began, "As you've probably heard on the news by now, I made a huge mistake and I'm paying for it. I need your help to get my life back..." He paused a moment before explaining. "My wife moved my mistress into our house and I moved out."

At first nothing. Then the expected laughter erupted from all sides of the large room.

Several minutes later Vernon managed to get their attention again. "The case has gone public and she's gaining ground, which means if this is allowed to happen—from now on women will all pull the same stunt when they get mad."

The laughter came to an abrupt halt. Vernon filled them in on a few coached details, then the questions came.

"The judge gave your wife custody of the mistress?"

"Yes sir," Vernon said to Andre Adams, president of Avistar Manufacturing—the most successful producers of tradeshow displays and promotional items in North America.

Turning to his lawyer, who sat two aisles over, the sharply dressed man asked, "Is that legal?"

Attorney Lloyd Howard shrugged. "I'd have to see the contract."

Vernon reached into the folder on the podium and slipped out the mistress contract, as Howard came forward.

The lawyer scanned it twice, and each time he choked, obviously holding in a major laugh. Then he looked up and out at everyone. "It's a valid family contract with his wife's signature on it. The judge accepted on that basis." Then he looked down again. "You're paying maintenance for your wife and your mistress, plus child support?" His thick lips broke into a grin. "We should give Brandi Spencer your membership. That was clever as hell."

Vernon shot him an angry glance. "Would you say that if Doreen brought your mistress home?"

"Why are you talking about *my* bedroom?" Howard asked with an angry gaze at the people nearby chuckling at his expense. "It's you whose drawers are hanging out."

"I'm just pointing out that you could be next, he could be next, anyone could be next," Vernon said, pointing around the room. "No one here is blameless. For all that pious posturing, at least seventy-five percent of y'all have mistresses. So don't point fingers my way. "I'm asking for your help, not your judgment. I know what I did was wrong, but how she's treating me has far bigger implications. It's all on the news and even talk show hosts are poking fun at it. If this sets a precedent and becomes a part of my divorce decree, the moment you mess up, you'll also be taking care of wives, mistresses, *and* the children as part of a court order." Vernon's gaze swept across the audience. "So think about that before you laugh at me and let's come up with a way we can put an end to this nonsense."

CHAPTER Forty-Three

Weeks passed without a word from Vernon except when he came to pick the girls up every weekend. His silence didn't sit too well with Brandi. The quieter he was, the more worried she became.

Winter break had come faster than Brandi could imagine, but Vernon had planned some things with the girls and that picked up the slack. He still bristled every time Tanya answered the front door, but he'd stopped barking at her and also had given up on the little dinners with Brandi.

Something was up. Brandi was certain that eventually they would find out exactly what. She only hoped she would be prepared.

As she sat across the kitchen table from her girls, Sierra reached out to get her attention, asking, "Mommy, what's a lesthian?"

Brandi dropped the fork in her hand. "A what?"

Sierra shrugged. "You know, a *lesthian.*"

Brandi blinked twice before realization dawned. "You mean a—lesbian?"

"Yeah, yeah," Sierra said, nodding. "One of those." She scooped a spoonful of Frosted Flakes into her mouth as she continued, "So what's that?"

Brandi frowned, glancing at Tanya, who gaped, then collected herself and instantly turned back to the stove. "Where did you get that word?"

"Penny's mother told her that you were a lesthian."

"What?"

The little girl continued chewing her cereal, the crunchy sound drowning out the light jazz playing in the background. "And don't tell me I'm not old enough, neither, 'cause Mrs. Williams told me the same thing."

"Jesus Christ!"

The little girl stopped eating for a second. "*He* was a lesthian?"

"Quit saying that word!" Brandi shrieked, trembling with anger.

Sierra slumped down in her chair. "Okay, okay, okay!"

Tanya moved forward, clearing the breakfast dishes in record time.

Brandi was, frozen, unable to come up with a single word. Lesbian? People were saying things like that to her child?

"That's okay," Sierra said, lifting her head in triumph. "I'll ask Daddy, he'll tell me."

Brandi didn't miss the mischievous glint in her youngest daughter's eyes. "The word is *lesbian*. And it's, um..." She looked at Tanya, who shrugged and leaned against the counter. "It's two women who love each other."

"So I'm a lesthian because I love you, Mommy."

Oh to be so innocent again.

Tanya let out a long slow breath, covering her mouth with a single hand, waiting for Brandi to make a comeback.

"Well, it's more like adult women who love each other."

"Oh," Sierra said, taking in that bit of information. Then she looked up, gaze locking with her mother. "So why did Penny's mother ask me if you slept in the same bed with Tanya?"

Brandi groaned inwardly, mumbling, "Oh, hell."

CHAPTER Forty-Four

Brandi strolled into her office, ignored her messages and Renee, closed the door, and blocked out the world as she laid her head on the desk.

Working eighteen-hour days was really catching up with her.

Thirty minutes later, her eyes flew open as the door cracked. Brandi looked up just in time to see Renee's flailing arms trying to signal for her to get herself together.

Andre Adams, president of Avistar Manufacturing, pushed past Renee, crossing the threshold into the office. "*Mrs.* Spencer, I hope you have a few minutes to see me."

Uh-oh. Her long-time client had called her by her formal name, rather than the normal Brandi. This wasn't a courtesy call. She took a deep breath and sat up. "Of course, I always have time for you."

He didn't take the chair she offered. Another bad sign. Instead he stood, towering over her in a gray suit and a short Afro that had seen better days.

"I regret to inform you that we've chosen to stay with The Perfect Fit."

Disappointment seared her soul and it took every ounce of control to remain calm. "Even though I'm the person who brought you in?"

"Well, um...," He cleared his throat. "For *stability's* sake, I'm sticking with Vernon. I'll expect our files to be returned to his office promptly."

Great! Just what she needed to hear a week before Christmas. She chose her words carefully. "But he's not even in a position to handle the business right now."

"I just gave him two-hundred-fifty thousand as an advance so I think he'll do just fine. You may want to rethink this Perfect Match thing, though, and go back to your husband. Some of my colleagues are not too happy with this personal vendetta you have against Vernon."

So, members of the League had banded together on Vernon's behalf. The good-old-boys network was alive and well. No surprise there.

"But he's the one who didn't keep his promise to me. Now I'm supposed to roll over like a pet dog and let him scratch my underside?"

"I talked with him," Andre said, pacing the floor. "He's learned his lesson. It was really nothing." The man actually had nerve enough to pat her hand. She wanted to take that same hand and smack him upside his football-sized head. "And if you were the woman I thought you were, you'd forgive him and move on."

How dare he give her advice on her personal life. "He didn't cheat on you."

Andre gave her a stony glare, but didn't say a word.

"The contract states that you're to give three months' notice, not one day."

"So sue me," he said, with a lopsided grin. "You can afford that, right?"

Actually, she couldn't. Avie was not a contract lawyer. She'd have to bring in another attorney. Avie aside, Brandi did not trust lawyers.

Andre's grin widened. "That's what I thought." He leaned over her desk so that he met her gaze head-on. "Play some silly little games and hold my files, and see if I don't destroy you. Hear? Vernon's got more friends than you know."

He sauntered out of the office knowing that those few words had destroyed her bottom line. Tanya's expenses, the children, payments on the house she couldn't move into, and payments on a house she didn't want were sucking up finances better and faster than a Hoover.

And that was just the beginning of her hellish day.

"Mrs. Spencer, I need to speak with you."

Brandi looked up into Marie Johnson's round face and deep-set eyes.

The woman was dressed down in a sweatsuit, since everyone was working on files and organization these days. Some boxes that were sitting in conference rooms hadn't even been touched.

Wringing her hands, Marie said in a wavering voice, "I'm giving notice that I'm quitting—today."

Music to any employer's ear. Brandi felt a sudden sense of foreboding that Andre's deflection and this new development were connected.

Brandi took a deep breath and tried to calm her nerves. "May I ask why you're leaving so suddenly?"

"I've got a better job offer and it starts tomorrow."

Brandi leveled a stony gaze on the woman who had been in charge of new hires for five years.

"Vernon offered four dollars more per hour," she said, then added, "To all of us."

Brandi couldn't say a word as anger raged inside.

Marie's thin hands spread out, in an earnest plea. "Mrs. Spencer, I've got two kids in college and no husband. I have to look out for us."

Game could recognize game, and Vernon had just upped the ante. All she could manage to get out was, "I understand, Marie. I wish you the best."

Marie was just the first of a stream of employees who suddenly became former employees with the same seven words followed by a host of excuses—or lies. By the time four o'clock rolled around there were only five left.

Renee poked her head in. "Are you okay?"

"If you want to leave, too—"

"No way! I'm sticking with the original. Copies tend to get dull and lifeless after a while."

Brandi managed a weak grin.

CHAPTER Forty-Five

Brandi paced the carpet of Sesvalah's office as she and Vernon looked on. His business suit draped his muscular frame in a way that would turn most heads. Given a chance, Brandi would love to turn Vernon's head—right off his body.

Sesvalah had traded in her characteristic loose-fitting gown for a cream-colored pantsuit that showed every curve to perfection.

"First things first. You stole my clients, then my employees," Brandi said angrily.

Vernon's sensuous lips lengthened into a wide grin. "And you expect me to apologize for that? It's business, Baby. Strictly business."

"Business? No, honey, that's just straight-up robbery." Brandi huffed. "Do you realize I'm going to have to cut back on things for the girls? Especially since everything you're supposed to pay comes a week late, if at all."

"I've got my girls covered." Then he shrugged. "Oh come on, Bee."

She whirled around, glaring at him. "Don't call me that!"

"I've *always* called you that," he said in a calm tone that irritated the hell out of her.

"Yeah? Well, lately you've been adding four other letters behind it. I don't want you to slip up—again. Then I'll have to stomp your ass."

"You know I didn't mean that," he said with a small shrug followed by an even weaker grin. "I was just angry."

"I don't know what you mean anymore."

"Well, you called me an asshole!"

She cocked her head, noting that their counselor had remained strangely silent. "And what part of that isn't the truth?"

A bouquet of orchids lay on the sofa next to her briefcase. Cymbidium orchids, ones he hadn't bought. "Where did you get those?"

"Michael," she said with a sly smile of her own.

"You've been dating Michael?" His nostrils flared.

Finally, something had gotten under his skin. "Yes, *that* Michael. So what if I am? I have to fulfill my needs somehow." She couldn't wipe the smile from her face. "My husband's too busy whining like a bitch in heat and stealing things to do the right thing."

"Is this funny to you?" he said, bearing down on her. "I'm here at counseling trying to make things right."

"No, you *think* you're trying," she retorted, slipping back down onto the sofa. "In no shape, form, or fashion could you have thought that anything less than my new demands would be acceptable."

Vernon faced her head-on. "I'm not coming home until she's gone."

"Somehow you haven't figured out that isn't the threat it used to be."

"Jesus! And why would you go to Michael instead of taking me up on my offer?" he said softly. "Maybe if you got laid you'd lose that crappy attitude."

"No thanks, masturbation is working out entirely too well," she said. "But you're speaking like a true lover." She shimmied and gave him a little wink. "I liiike it!"

"Okay, getting things out in the open does help a lot," Sesvalah said, taking a deep breath and shaking her head a little. "But let's move on to our lists."

"I've got a better idea," Vernon said with a cursory glance at the orchids.

Both women waited for him to continue.

"Let's not do this at all."

Sesvalah stared up at him with a sad glint in her dark brown eyes. "You do realize that not completing the counseling can work *against* your case."

"I don't need counseling," he said, eyeing her with disdain. "I want my life back."

"If you'd really try to put some effort into the counseling," she said gently, "this can be a step in the process."

"Not if you're not telling her to get rid of Tanya."

Sesvalah shook her head. "I can't tell anyone what to do. I can only point out obvious issues for you to discuss or suggest alternatives."

"Then *suggest* she get rid of her."

Sesvalah's thin lips parted in a patient smile. "I can't do that, either."

"Well, why not?" Vernon paced the floor, anger expanding with each step.

"That was Brandi's way of dealing with a disappointing and heartbreaking situation. When she's ready to let Tanya go, then she will. Your response to it is only making her dig in her heels." Sesvalah looked at him again, her small expressive face a mask of concern.

"So I should just follow her program and move in with her and Tanya," he said sourly. "Lady, are you crazy?"

Brandi laughed but quickly covered her mouth. "You're posing that question to a therapist?" Then all humor left her face as she said. "And I didn't say that when you were on the sneak tip."

Vernon finally turned to face his wife, eyeing her cautiously. "So if I move back in, I still get to sleep with Tanya, too?"

Brandi looked at Vernon with an openmouthed stare.

"If that's the only question you can come up with," Sesvalah said softly, "then you're not serious about returning to your wife."

"I'm leaving!"

"The court has ordered you to be here."

"It doesn't matter," he said, throwing his coat over one arm. "I've been ordered to pay child support, maintenance for my wife, and Tanya, half the rent on the Wabash house, half the rent on the Cregier house, and after all these years I'm back at my mother's. Don't worry, lady," he said, bitterness dripping from every word, "it seems like the court's already against me."

CHAPTER Forty-Six

Tanya slipped into a soft, pink sweatsuit, and pulled her hair back into a ponytail. She checked on the beef stew simmering on the stove. Fresh-baked bread cooled on a rack on the counter.

She waited outside of Brandi's office for a few moments before she cleared her throat and said, "I have an idea for a business."

"I'm all ears," Brandi snapped without looking up.

Tanya hesitated. "Do you want to discuss this when you're not having a PMS moment?"

Brandi sighed, took a long breath, and pushed the *Fortune* magazine away. She then pulled *Black Enterprise* to the top of the stack, and said calmly, "I'm all ears."

"What about a place that does background checks strictly for women who are just getting into a relationship?"

Brandi blinked and stared at her. A bit of Tanya's confidence slipped.

She explained a bit more. "If a woman wants to get involved with or wants to marry a guy, she can have him checked out and see what the references say. Just like a job. You do background checks on new applicants, right? Same thing."

"Vernon really hurt you, didn't he?"

Tanya inhaled sharply. "More than I can say."

Brandi flipped open the magazine, scanning the pages. "You've got to get over it."

One sandy brown eyebrow shot up. "Have you?"

"No, but then again, I signed up for the long program—thirteen years.

I still love him, but I have regrets. I should've married what was behind door number one. I can't spring for a new business right now. I can't split the focus. I'm struggling to make ends meet, and if there's no turnaround, and I mean real soon—we'll be meeting the end." The rush of words stopped for a moment as she thought things over. "Here, I'm gonna give you a template for a business plan. If you're so sure that it'll work—you do the research and fill it in."

Tanya gasped, eyes wide with shock. "I can't do that. I don't know anything about running a business."

"You know how to run this house, right? Balance a checkbook? Straight-up accounting. Groceries? Supply and inventory. Sierra and Simone? That's human resources," Brandi said, flicking a finger up with each point. "Coordinating three meals a day is time management, organization, and synchronization. Apply your life skills to what you know, then do the research. The rest is trial and terror."

When Brandi spoke again her tone was softer. "You passed your GED, and got pretty high scores on the ACT and SAT. And now you're taking English and calculus college courses. At some point, you've got to step up to the plate. You have an idea—develop it. See what you can do before you say the words *I can't*."

"Okay," Tanya said, in a resigned whisper. "I'll sell my engagement ring. Soon I'll be able to buy my own."

For the first time in a long time Brandi smiled. "Now that's the spirit!"

Yes, Tanya Kaufman had spirit by the droves. Though she may not have been born that way—the long walk to Walton Medical Center that cold night had served to bolster a strength rich girls didn't seem to gain until marriage number three.

Margaret Jaunal had been more concerned with her husband's status than with her daughter's well-being. What other reason could there be for that back-alley abortion? Tanya couldn't let them get away with it.

She walked down the side of the road, steeling herself against the pain with every step until it subsided some. Her footprints were visible in the mist-covered grass that the moon's reflection made into a white glow. Where was Mindy? If her mother had gone this far with her, what had her mother done to silence her little sister?

Tanya slowly made her way toward the Mars Hill Baptist Church, remembering the times she'd skipped the quiet and calm of Catholic mass to visit the fiery and soulful services of Michelle's church. Closing her eyes against the pain, she moved forward, but pictured the inside of the church. No organ, but an occasional guitar. Mr. Jefferson banged the life out of that old piano. The choir sang old hymns, and the men's choir sang a cappella. She could hear them now, their melodious voices draping over her, shielding her from her pain. She imagined the choir marching in their flowing white robes, taking their places in an area that only had twenty-five chairs and three step-up rows. But those powerful voices had reached her soul. And the memories were reaching her now as surely as if they had marched up the street beside her and had spread out in a circle of protection around her.

The oak pews in Mars Hill had red cushions that matched the carpet. The baptismal pool lay flush against the wall next to the kitchen area. Her parents didn't know that when was ten she had been baptized with Michelle one Sunday, accepting Christ as her savior and letting the Lord into her heart. Then she screwed up all that good salvation by telling her parents that the reason her hair was wet was because she went swimming. Well, it was called a "pool," right?

Tanya called on God to help her as she walked toward the well that signaled the beginning of Social Circle's life and history, a time when merchants were required to close their stores at ten. Any person found on the streets would have to give a satisfactory account of their presence or spend the night in the guardhouse. Luckily, times had changed or Tanya would have had to give an earful to the police officer who stopped her. She wondered if he would be someone who was in her father's pocket.

In the distance, she could see the small airport that only housed crop dusters and her father's private plane. If she could, she'd hop in that plane and fly as far away as its wings would carry her.

Then she braced herself to walk past the antebellum home, that had once belonged to a Dr. Brown. The house had a permanent guest who had made the place legendary. A strange calm spread over Tanya as she passed by what everyone called the Brown Plantation. Anyone who mentioned the place was sure to be asked, "Have you seen her?"

At the moment Tanya did see the fair-skinned woman, with a wide hoop skirt, dark hair pulled back into a bun, a small smile on her lips and a sad glint in her eyes that mirrored Tanya's own.

The woman glided across the grass, catching up with Tanya's slow pace and extended her hand. Aghast, Tanya placed a shaky hand inside the ghost's hand and followed her, as though in a dream.

Wild plums used to make wine and the small wild grapes that Tanya once ate by the handfuls littered the grounds making it difficult to walk, but Tanya kept her eyes on "The Lady," as everyone called her. She was known for watching over the children in the house and had never been sighted outside of the Brown Plantation. The Lady guided Tanya along the path, then turned her toward the east side of Social Circle.

Tanya couldn't believe she had walked the five miles; for the second time in her life, she collapsed. This time it was on the doorstep of Michelle Pitchford's house.

When she came to, members of the Pitchford family were scooping her off the cold ground. She reached down into her waistband, passed the jar, its gory contents surprisingly intact, to Diane and said, "Please get this to the hospital and tell them that it's my baby. Promise me you'll get it there."

Mama Diane did more than that. She yelled for the rest of the family to come help. Edward Pitchford placed Tanya next to his wife in the front cab of their pickup truck and turned it in the direction of Walton Medical Center.

Tanya laid her head on Mama Diane's soft shoulder. The woman stroked Tanya's matted hair.

Tanya looked out of the car just in time to see The Lady from the Brown Plantation wave and turn away.

CHAPTER *Forty-Seven*

As angry as she was at Vernon, Brandi finally gave in and agreed to see him and to get inside his head. Now she lay next to her husband at the elegant Fairmont Hotel. The suite's French décor was supposed to set the mood. It would take more than a suspense movie, dinner at Charlie Trotter's, and a suite overlooking the Chicago River. Vernon grazed her breasts with his soft tongue.

"Wow, dinner, a movie, and the possibility of some really great sex? We're really moving up in the world."

Vernon paused midway to her navel. His gaze locked on hers.

"It's amazing how different you've become."

"A husband sleeping around on you can do that." She looked down at his erection and said, "By the way, where's your condom?"

Vernon shifted on the huge bed. "Condom? I've never used a condom with you."

"Rumor has it that you didn't use one with Tanya either." She leaned back gracefully. "So like I said, *where's your condom*?"

"This is ridiculous," he said, never taking his gaze from the lower half of her body. "You're my wife! I don't have to use one with my wife. That's one of the main reasons I got married—"

"Then you should've made sure you did everything in your power to keep it that way," she said, grinning up at him, thighs swinging open and closed like a camera shutter.

Vernon let out a long, weary sigh. "How long are you gonna punish me for one indiscretion?"

"Not just one time, my love, *several* times with her over a two-year period. But who's counting. Oh, that's right—I am!"

He reached for Brandi. "It didn't mean that she meant more to me than you."

"Don't give me that bullshit!" she snapped, pushing him away. "You introduced our children to her. You were taking it to a whole new level."

"I was never gonna *leave* you for her."

She shrugged and looked him square in the eye. "Then that's a pity, because you were satisfied to use her and throw her away. Just like our marriage: add one mistress—," she snapped her fingers—"will dissolve like Alka-Seltzer."

"Aargh!"

The hard-on that had been swimming strongly out to sea was now floating back to shore, shriveling like a California raisin.

"Let Tanya tell it"—Brandi wagged a finger—"And she did give up all the dirty details, you naughty boy—your dick's got more mileage than the average used car. I would never trust you enough to let you ride bare-back again."

She gave his warm bare cheeks a solid pat. "You either saddle up, big boy, or you and your leeeeeeetle friend can mosey on down to the saloon and take your pick of local whores. I'm sure someone out there would appreciate second-hand dick." Then she beamed as her eyes widened with delight. "Hey," she said, perking up. "Tanya may even be up for a small touch up around the edges. And then again, maybe the old girl could use a full relaxer."

Vernon could only stare at the woman he'd been married to for thirteen years. "When did you become so cold?"

"The moment I found out that you didn't think I was good enough. The moment that I became Tanya's…husband."

The woman was actually serious! He could give in or kiss quality time with his wife good-bye. "I'll go get a condom."

She nodded. "You do that."

Then she turned her back to him, pulling the blanket over her luscious naked form.

Rain pelted the windshield as Vernon drove to the nearest Walgreen's. The elation that he felt when he first decided to seduce his wife had quickly dissipated. Purchasing a condom to have sex with a woman he loved and had been with for over thirteen years brought home the fact of just how much things had changed.

Underneath all the posturing, he loved his wife and missed the conversations about business, the kids, or sometimes nothing at all.

He wasn't her first choice for marriage and he understood that. So he spent the first part of their marriage trying to show her she'd made the right choice. He always felt that no matter what he did, he was never good enough. Then she took the business in a whole new direction, changing to an upscale décor and starting an aggressive campaign for new clients. So far, he'd spent the second half of their marriage competing with her, trying to excel in the same places she did.

She was steadily gaining the upper hand, something his father had told him should never happen.

He admired her. He loved her. And he was downright jealous and ashamed. She had become more like his father than he cared to admit. Her hard work had turned The Perfect Fit from a company breaking even to one with a quarter of a million dollar profit each year. Comfortable. Nice.

"Hey, I know you," the gray-haired cashier said with a wide grin. "Aren't you that guy with the wife and mistress living in the same house?"

Vernon didn't answer. Instead he slid a twenty-dollar bill onto the Formica counter.

"I'd love to be in your shoes," the slender man said with a hearty chuckle as he dropped the Trojans in a small plastic bag. "You must be on cloud nine."

Grimacing, Vernon reached in the bag, stuffed the condoms in his pocket, took his change, and walked away. He realized he was nowhere near cloud nine. He hadn't even left the ground.

Thirty minutes later he arrived back at the Fairmont a note on the empty bed:

Thank you for the flowers, dinner, and the movie.

With all the new developments in our marriage.
I think the timing's all wrong for anything else.
Despite everything, I still love you.
Brandi

Vernon swiped the wineglass from the nightstand. Glass shattered against the nearest wall, splintering into tiny lethal weapons. Slivers lodged in Vernon's arm and a piece wedged in his upper foot. As he slumped to the floor in the corner, he didn't feel any physical pain. The pain stabbing forcefully into his heart had taken a front seat and was driving his emotions to the nearest cliff.

Vernon realized that winning his wife back would take more than seduction and a little "below the waistline sunshine." The open trust he'd taken for granted had disappeared like the Chicago skyline in a thick layer of fog. And trust—that one element had done more for his marriage than he thought. She loved him, but trust was something that was possibly out of reach.

Yes he could play it her way. Yes he could start all over—new wife, more kids, new business—but he loved Brandi and his girls, and old habits die hard. He would do everything in his power to remove Tanya from his life. He would not stray again, no matter what his father said. A man deserved to be happy. And he had been happy with his wife. Now he'd have to do something that gained her respect. Something that showed her that he was the man she wanted all over again.

He reached for the phone. "Dad, I'll be in your office about eight tomorrow. I'm ready to go to Plan C."

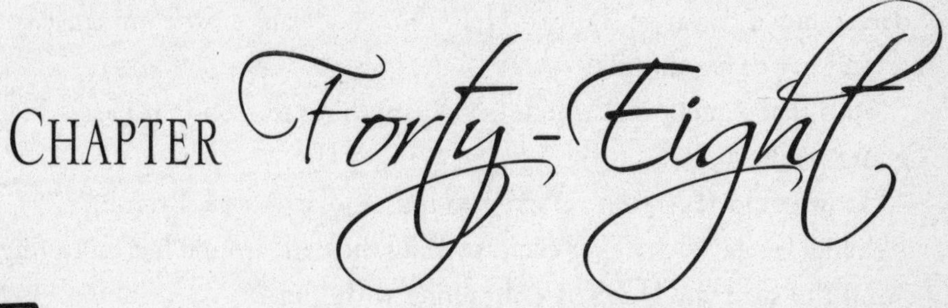

CHAPTER Forty-Eight

The phone rang, disturbing Brandi from the tedious tasks of trying to come up with enough money to make payroll. She answered on the third ring.

"Brandi, we need to talk. I—"

She politely replaced the receiver on the cradle and kept reading the latest accounts payable reports.

It rang again. She picked up.

"Look, heifer—"

Brandi hung up again.

Three minutes later Renee strolled in, golden skin flushed a deep red. "Avie said I should deliver this message word for word, and though I'm a good Christian woman and I don't curse—here it goes: 'If you hang up on her again she will come over here and beat your ass bitch-style and then throw in an old-fashioned ass whipping at no extra cost.' "

Brandi thought for a moment before saying, "I'll take the call."

Renee swallowed hard and backed away toward the door. "I was hoping you would."

The intercom buzzed twice before she picked it up, letting the handset hover over the cradle for a few seconds before finally putting it to her ear. "Yes."

"Don't yes me! What's wrong with you?"

"This line is reserved for family, friends, and clients. You qualify as none of the above."

"You know, I'll let that slide because you're angry."

"Damn right I'm still angry," Brandi said after an uncomfortable pause. "I shouldn't have to watch the people in my own camp. You might be wondering how I can trust Tanya—Hell, I'm wondering how I can trust you."

"I didn't *do* anything!"

"And that's my point! You didn't do anything to stop that bastard from going public."

"How could I? Mason referred to it as a joke. A *joke*, Brandi!"

Brandi leaned back in her chair, twirling the cord around her index finger. "And I'm sure you laughed right along with him."

Silence from the legal team.

"Hmmmm, like I thought."

"I didn't think he'd actually go out and do it. It hurt Vernon's case, too."

"But it hurts the girls more."

"Don't you think you should've taken how it would affect the girls into consideration before all of this?" Avie asked, not bothering to hide her sarcastic tone.

"Only our close family and friends were supposed to know."

"Well, thanks to your family—blabbermouth Thomas—and his little spare tire, Fabian, the office got hold to it."

"Yeah, I got on him about that." Then she lowered her voice. "I didn't know he was sleeping with Fabian."

"Please, I'm getting a mental picture here and it's not pleasant."

Brandi laughed and for a moment all anger was forgotten. "Do you think he can actually find the hole?"

"Honey, I think it's an aerobic experience just to wipe his own ass."

Brandi busted up with laughter. When they both settled down, Avie said, "I didn't mean to hurt you."

"I know, girl, it's just a lot going on right now."

"So how's business?"

"Both of them are slow as hell." Brandi scanned the documents detailing her cash flow—or lack thereof. "The Perfect Match is at a standstill. Tanya came up with a great concept to take it in another direction, and though we've been implementing it, she didn't count on the fact that getting the women to sign up would be easy, but that men aren't too willing to have a dossier compiled and shown to the women they're trying to get with."

"And you thought men would rather have it all out in the open, rather than feed it to them bit by bit, and squirm their way out of things like normal?"

Brandi grimaced, realizing her friend was close to the truth. "I didn't count on the fact that women could be pressured into putting off getting information they should have before taking that final step. Or, that women with children wouldn't try to find out the criminal histories of the guys they're letting into their homes." She picked up another file that almost brought her to tears every time she looked at it—the one that said closing The Perfect Match would be the best thing overall. "So far, at least eight out of the twenty applicants turned up felons, three of them child molesters. When we pointed this out, the women made one excuse after another and I'll bet you any type of money the men are still there."

"You know you'll have to report it, right?"

Brandi looked up from the reports and stared ahead. "I do?"

"Yes. The men aren't supposed to live with children under any circumstances."

"I'll get on it after I finish this call."

"So, what about us?"

"What do you mean?"

"Don't play dumb, woman."

Brandi thought about that a moment. Her best friend had betrayed her, but so had her husband. She had forgiven him in a way, so she could forgive Avie, too. "We're cool. Just don't let it happen again."

"No problem," she said, letting out a long sigh of relief.

"And you owe me lunch every day for the next month," Brandi said, realizing she could capitalize on this new development. "Something that costs more than Seven dollars and fifty-eight cents. *No* Corner Bakery."

"Ouch."

CHAPTER *Forty-Nine*

Vernon landed at Hartsfield-Jackson International Airport in Atlanta, rented a midsize car, and soon was on a happy journey to Social Circle, Georgia. Soon he'd have enough information on Tanya to get her out of his hair.

He whizzed along Cherokee Road going over his father's plan in his mind. Then he ran into traffic. The overhead banner read, "Cruise In." Classic cars lined both sides of the road. He couldn't inch forward if he paid someone. Inhaling a whiff of fresh country air, he choked as an unpleasant smell drifted in from the cows out to pasture in a field off to his right. He rolled up the window. Things were a little too fresh for his taste.

Chicago hadn't been warm, so he'd worn a heavier suit. He'd had to take off his jacket and unbutton his shirt the moment he touched ground.

Two hours later, he'd only made it as far as the Wiccams General Store. Just his luck that he'd come in during a major event.

He hoped he would get this finished and be back on the plane before the end of the afternoon. No one would know but him, his father, and the Good Lord.

Tanya had only told him two things: She was from Social Circle, Georgia, and her father was mayor. Hopefully, what he knew would be enough to get what he needed.

She'd mentioned her brief marriage, and living in New York, but was vague about everything else. It didn't matter to him at the time—what really mattered was what she did in bed. The more he racked his brain to remember other things about her, the more he wondered: Who was the woman he had spent two years of his life with? She had been tight-lipped about her life before Chicago. Suppose she was some type of criminal!

As he strolled the aisles of the Wiccams Store, he passed huge barrels of flour, sugar, grits, and rice. An old man with a long pinkish face, white shirt, suspenders, and plaid pants asked, "Can I help you, son?"

Vernon hesitated for a moment, then realized that the man seemed friendly enough. Almost like a traveling salesman. "Do you know anyone from the Kaufman family?"

"Kaufman?" The man rubbed his chin. "There's no one 'round these parts by that name." Then his friendly face broke into a warm smile. "Where you from?"

"Chicago." Damn, what was Tanya's maiden name? "You sure?"

"Son, the Wiccams family's been in Social Circle since John P. Blackmon first bought out his partner for thirteen cents an acre back in 1824." The man poured wine into a coffee cup, and handed it to Vernon. " 'Bout how long we're talkin' since they've been here?"

"Maybe thirteen years or so?"

"Hmmm," he said, taking off his baseball cap to scratch his head. "Don't reckon I can put my finger on who you're talkin' 'bout."

"Her father was mayor at one time."

"No, no mayor by the name of Kaufman." He studied Vernon closely, eyes glancing over his suit more than once. "Sorry I couldn't be more help."

"You think someone else might know around here?"

"Nobody but family's ever worked here and if I don't know 'em, they wouldn't know 'em either. Nothin' against your kind, mind ya, but only family's allowed to work in the store. Don't reckin' no African-Americans floatin' in the blood. At least none of 'em spoke up yet." Then he laughed at his clever joke. "Maybe you might want to talk with somebody on the east side of the tracks."

"Why there?"

"That's where the nig—Negroes—I mean; colored—sorry, Blacks—Shoot! African-Americans live," he stammered. "It's so hard to keep up these days."

Was he being funny? Vernon replied, "No, she's a cracker—um, redneck— I mean she's as white as they come: blonde hair, blue eyes."

The man peered at him for a long time, taking in the returned insult. A few kids walking around had scurried out of the store.

"White?" Mr. Wiccams finally asked, obviously realizing that Vernon wasn't one to be toyed with. "Why didn't you say so? Well now, that puts a different spin on things." He leaned over, resting his elbows on the wooden counter. "The mayor we've had for the past thirteen years is Nicholas Steward. Before that it was Wilbur Jaunal, but he's been in the slammer for thirteen years. Just got out. There was some family scandal about him and his daughters. One disappeared and the other turned up dead. Found her body over there on the east side of town. Least folks suspect it was her. Couldn't really identify that little girl. Teeth were smashed, fingers were sliced off..."

Vernon's stomach churned.

"Blonde hair and blue eyes? Father was mayor...I reckon you're talkin' 'bout Tanya Jaunal. That might be who you're lookin' for. Seems about the right age," He said, letting his gaze pass over Vernon again. "What you want with the Jaunals? That man's meaner than a junkyard dog."

"Oh, nothing really," Vernon said quickly. He was in over his head. "I don't think she's the one I'm looking for."

"You sure you ain't tryin' to collect that there hundred thousand dollar reward for knowledge of her whereabouts?" The man pointed to the powder blue sign tacked up on a board showing a teenage Tanya with a gorgeous smile.

"How long has this been here?"

"That wanted poster of her has been up for thirteen years. Seems like a whole lot of people are lookin' for that lil' girl. Think Jaunal's looking for some payback for all that time in prison. Her court case started a federal investigation that didn't stop until they put his butt in the slammer. Was as rich as the Rockefellers. Now he's poorer than a church house mouse."

At that moment, Vernon realized his visit to Social Circle should end— pronto. Even though one hundred thousand could help pay off what he'd borrowed from members of the League and put The Perfect Fit in the clear a lot sooner than the two years he projected, no way could he serve Tanya up to a man like that.

Tanya came from a rich family? Why did she make it seem like she didn't have a dime? A sinking feeling settled in the pit of his stomach. The more he learned, the more he knew he should turn tail and catch the first thing smokin' back to Chicago.

They thought she was dead like her sister and he had shown up to prove them wrong. How could he get out of this?

"Uh, I think you've told me everything I need to know about, uh... Tanya Jaunal. But I don't think she's my girl." Vernon slipped the man a hundred-dollar bill.

The man glanced down at the cash and grinned. "Oh, you don't have to do that. Information's always free," he said, sliding the money back across the counter. "Now order up another glass of that plum wine you're drinkin' right now, and that'll cost you plenty."

Vernon grinned at the man and raised his cup. "Thanks."

"My pleasure."

Vernon picked the pace as he left the store. If he had turned back, he would have seen good old Mr. Wiccams pick up the rotary dial phone. If he had stayed close to the entrance, he would've heard, "Cousin, I think I'm gonna be the one to get my hands on that money you're offering. How soon can you round up the boys and get over here?"

Vernon slammed the car door, started the car, and punched the pedal to the metal, feeling a strange sense that something bad was about to happen. He couldn't put a safe distance between himself and the beautiful country fast enough. What was he thinking, opening up that can of worms?

He returned the car to the rental husband, took the shuttle to his terminal, hoping to make it to the Delta Airlines counter. He was almost home free!

Then he pulled up short, making tracks as he came to a sudden halt. All sense of safety seeping out of his pores. A group of white men in dress ranging from business suits to overalls stood in front of the entrance. As though guided by some inner voice, all heads turned in his direction. Mr. Wiccams pointed a shaky finger and said, "That's him right there."

Vernon did a half turn and hauled ass, went through another set of entrance doors, pounding the pavement better than a Dallas Cowboy running with an open path to the goal line.

His heart slammed into his chest as he staggered through a group of flight attendants. He ducked past a newsstand but they were still hot on his heels. People turned to stare as he sprinted past heading toward the construction area, a Black man with a trail of white men on his tail—ranging from skinny, to overweight, to giant-sized. Damn, where was security? This big ass airport and no one's helping? For a moment, he felt a connection with his ancestors. Back then it was about lynching. Vernon had a feeling that if this group caught him he would suffer the same fate.

Vernon had the lead and was home-free to make it back outside and get into a cab. Then a little boy grinned up at him. Something about that smile was all wrong. At the very last second the boy stuck his leg out. Vernon didn't see it soon enough to avoid the headlong tumble that landed him on the ground with the boy pinned and yowling underneath. Served the little bastard right.

"Hey, watch it! You pervert," the mother shrieked, planting little kisses all over her evil seed's pudgy face.

A meaty hand jerked Vernon to an upright position as the men crowded around him and dragged him with them. As they trekked back to the construction area, Vernon tried to find a way to escape, knowing that if they pulled him away anything could happen and no one would find him until it was too late.

"Get his wallet, Bubba."

Vernon's gaze flickered to the speaker. A man with a wide frame, menacing scowl, and blue eyes just like Tanya's.

The giant-sized guy holding his neck jammed a hand in his back pocket and scrabbled to remove his black wallet as Vernon struggled against his restraints.

"Let me go!"

A man stepped forward wearing a blue-and-white-striped suit Vernon wouldn't be caught wearing to his own funeral. "Not until you tell us what we need to know."

"I don't know anything!" Vernon struggled to get out of Bubba's death grip. "Let me go!"

Wilbur Jaunal flipped opened the wallet and looked at the license inside. "A Yankee boy! Now just what are you doing 'round these parts?"

"Vacation," Vernon supplied quickly.

The man looked on either side of Vernon. "With no bags?"

"A short vacation."

"Hmph." The man's blue eyes scanned Vernon's face. "Maybe you should come on with us and we can settle on exactly what you know and what you don't."

"What's goin' on here?" A brown-skinned, silver-haired man with a sharp gaze, a slight scowl and a uniform stood a few feet from the crowd. His dark eyes swept across everyone in the group before landing on Jaunal.

"Mind your business, boy. He's got my girl in the family way—we just want to make sure he does the right thing by her. We're handling a little family business. Off with you," Jaunal said, shooing the janitor away.

Vernon yelled, "Help me! They're trying to kill me! Help—"

The sudden pressure of a gun in his side put an end to his pleas.

To Vernon's dismay, the man shifted off.

"Where's my daughter?" Jaunal growled, jamming a hand around Vernon's neck.

"I don't know who your daughter is."

"Tanya Jaunal," he said evenly.

"No, it's Kaufman now." Mr. Wiccams broke through the sinister-looking crowd. "He was lookin' for a Kaufman. She must've changed her name."

The men fanned out protecting the door as people tried to peer into the split in the tarp.

Mr. Wiccams leaned in. "Hey, you'd better not stiff me on the money, either," he said, poking a long finger at Jaunal's chest. "Or I'll just tell that D.A. person that Margaret paid my boy to get rid of that kid for you. Said that little girl was bleeding like a stuck pig when she got off his table. He said Margaret was doing it on your instructions. I'm sure."

Bubba jerked Vernon forward. "You want me to take care of him for you, Boss?"

"No, there's too much at stake," Janual said, scanning the crowd. "Can't trust you guys to do diddly-squat. She's still breathing, ain't she?"

Vernon knew he was not getting out of Social Circle alive.

Chapter Fifty

Brandi strolled through the empty cubicles of her company. The place was like a ghost town. The sound of copiers rolling, fax machines churning, chatter, and gossip was sorely missed. The sounds meant business, which meant cash flow, which lead to progress. The latest projections were horrible and she had to face facts.

She called another company meeting with the last remaining employees. A lump formed in her throat as she stood before them. "The Perfect Match isn't doing so well. And as much as I'd like to keep everyone on board, I suggest you take any offer TPF has extended..."

Short, bitter, and to the point. With solemn faces and very few questions they filed out of the room.

Ella, Renee, and Michael all stayed behind.

"I'm not leaving," Renee said with a pat to her red afro. The woman could never keep a style for long.

Though warmed by the gesture, Brandi knew there really wasn't a choice. "I'm tapped out. I can't pay your salaries right now."

"Then lay us off," Renee replied softly as she looked over at Ella Clark. "We can file for unemployment and still come to work. You can pay me a 'consultant fee' for the difference—in cash."

Brandi gasped, looking at the woman as though she had lost her mind. "But that's unethical."

"No, that's survival, honey," Ella said, giving Renee a thumbs-up. "Works for me."

Brandi hesitated, needing to think about the consequences for The Perfect Match. Avie would kill her. But then again, her lawyer was also the one who had helped orchestrate the little savings plan that had kept the business running for all this time. Now that green safe-deposit box was empty.

Then she thought about Renee's suggestions, knowing that things could turn around if The Perfect Match could survive the storm. "The work will be doubled up."

"When have we been afraid of a little hard work?" Ella shot back, lifting her chin.

"Okay," Renee said, rolling back her sleeves. "We can do this!"

Michael waited until the two women had filed out of the conference room. "You know you don't have to pay me a dime. I only came on as a freelance accountant to clean up the mess Vernon's friends had made. You insisted I have an office here, but my own business is doing quite well. So money isn't an issue."

Brandi knew Michael would always come through for her and she felt a little bit of relief that he still had her back. Then he messed it all up by asking, "Have you given any thought to my offer?"

Lord, she didn't need this right now! "Do you want the truth or a good lie?"

"I don't like the sound of that." His tone was dry and a tad bit angry.

"Then you definitely won't like my answer," she shot back. "I've got too many other things on my mind to deal with this right now."

A flash of anger lit and died out in his brown eyes. "You know, I would have supported you in anything you wanted to do. I would never have fought against you like this—ever."

"I know, Michael," she said softly, realizing that he would have done just that.

"So you still need more time?"

"Lots more, and you still might not get the answer you want," she said, as his eyes bore into hers. "I know I felt something for you back in college and I feel a little something for you now, but that doesn't mean when all is said and done that I'll feel more than that."

"Brandi, two years was a long time to wait for you. And then Vernon came through and whoosh—you were gone. And he wasn't all that patient, either."

"Very patient, loving; arrogant," she said softly, "but I could overlook that last part. And that's why I married him." She perched her hips on the table, swinging her legs back and forth like a child. "Michael, you're one of the sweetest men I've ever known, and I felt something for you, but it wasn't nearly as powerful as what I felt for Vernon. I adored you, but I loved him."

The crestfallen expression on his face made a slice of doubt sliver through her mind. Was she making the wrong decision again?

"I can't just chuck him over the side because of this, Michael. We've gone through so much. And I still love him. If I went to you right now, you'd be getting leftovers and that's just not right. If there's any chance that my marriage will work—I have to try."

The same decisions she had to make right after college were popping up all over again. This was her chance to right old wrongs and be in the clear. Michael had dated several women but never married, probably because he was still waiting for her. But sometimes his quiet, intense energy was frightening—even now. Yet, she was curious, too. Maybe it took being with Vernon all this time to prepare her for someone like Michael. And she couldn't just put all of her hopes in Vernon, either. So she said, "Okay, why don't we start with a date—just a date."

His lips spread into a beautiful smile and his eyes lit up with a love that was almost painful to see.

She wagged a finger at him. "And you keep your hands and lips to yourself."

"Damn, you sure know how to take the fun out of life," he said, still grinning as he moved and centered himself between her thighs.

She couldn't help but smile back. "And just what were you planning?"

His left eyebrow lifted twice, as a single finger traced a fiery path along her cheekbone. "Nothing I can say out loud."

"Behave, Michael."

"Woman," he began softly, brushing his lips against her temple. "Will you stop cursing at me?"

CHAPTER Fifty-One

Vernon sent up a silent prayer as the men escorted him toward the airport exit. The gun in his rib cage kept him on the straight and narrow, just in case he got any ideas about escaping. These men were crazy. How had he gotten into this mess?

The old janitor appeared again, this time blocking the path of the group.

"What do you want?" Jaunal growled.

"Since you called me a boy, implying that I'm not grown enough to ask what you folks is doin' on my own, I brought along my mama and my papa." He shifted to the left allowing full view of the male and female police officers standing directly behind him.

"Now like I said, what are you folks doing here?"

"They're trying to kill me! And they stole my wallet," Vernon said, glaring at Bubba who still had a death grip on his shoulders. He yanked forward out of the man's hold. The gun disappeared as the not-so-jolly man grunted and reached into the pocket of his blue overalls, producing the wallet. Vernon snatched it and turned to the janitor.

"Now, sir," the old man said with a grin. "I'm sure you've got a plane to catch. So if you'll follow me."

Vernon brushed off his suit, stepped around Bubba's massive form, through the rest of the group, and walked briskly away.

The policewoman stepped forward, scanning the crowd. "Now if y'all just follow me...we'll sort it all out."

Wilbur Jaunal tore his arm out of the officer's grasp, his cheeks flushed with color. "Do you know who I am? I own—"

"Well, I know one thing, you don't own airport security," the burly woman said, practically lifting the angry man from the ground. She scanned the crowd once, then said in a voice that meant business, "So let's get moving."

Vernon thanked the old man, whose gaze narrowed as he said, "You tell little Miss Tanya that Grandpa James is still waiting for another serving of Brummistew."

"You know Tanya?"

James nodded. "Stayed with my family for two years before that Jaunal tried to force us to send her home." He grunted, looking over his shoulder to see that more police had arrived and rounded up all of the Jaunal clan. "That man just ain't right. What he did to that girl was downright evil."

"How did you know they were talking about your Tanya?"

The man's pace slowed a little as he said, "I overheard them when they passed the skycaps. I'd recognize Jaunal's ornery behind anywhere," James said. "So what's he doing?"

"He's offered a hundred-thousand dollar reward for information about her."

"Yes, we've known about that for years, but none of us are talking. Haven't seen her since she slipped out that night." Then the man's expression darkened and became almost deadly. "He made a mistake when he touched my granddaughter. Sending her home with that note on her wrist. We made sure that he got some of what's comin' to him before they carted him off to jail. And jail time wasn't easy for that old boy. I'm sure right about now there's parts of him that'll remember the place far longer than his mind will."

"One hundred thousand is a lot of money."

"Some things in life are more important than money, son: the Good Lord, family, health and strength, and living life in a way that makes you proud. We loved that little girl. Tanya has an old soul and a good heart. She shared everything she learned from those highfalutin folks of hers; how to waltz, set a fancy table, how to play tennis and the piano. And we taught her how to hold her head up despite what her parents done to her." Then they passed the newsstand again, and the old man looked over to

Vernon. "Actually, she's the one that made me think different about white folks. Then it's men like her daddy that goes messin' it all up again. She left to protect us from that man. She didn't have to do that. We have our own way of dealing with the likes of Jaunal."

The overhead announcer called out the final boarding for the flight to New York City. Vernon wondered if a Chicago flight would happen anytime soon.

"So you're her fella?"

Now how could he answer that? Truthfully might be the way to go. "I was, but she's living with my wife right now."

The man stopped walking to stare at Vernon who realized that the truth didn't come out quite so good. "Long story."

"Y'all ain't got her involved in some of that kinky stuff now?"

"No, I got busted by both women and they joined up to kick my butt."

"Serves you right," Grandpa James replied with a hearty chuckle as he started walking again. "You look like a decent enough fella, but you can't treat womenfolk just any kinda way. If it wasn't for our women, we woulda never made it through slavery."

Vernon kept pace with the old man, but he looked over at him, waiting for a better explanation.

"They sucked the new masters at their breasts and sacrificed their bodies to the old masters which sometimes kept us alive. They've always had the master's ear—and it's happening today, too. Look at that Rice lady—president made sure to keep her around, didn't he?" The man kept a nice easy pace as they walked toward the ticket counters. "That old Southern boy knows exactly what he's doin'. You think about that the next time you get an itch you need to scratch. I've been married to my Belle for forty-five. Ain't never thought about being a back door man. 'Cause that's exactly what my woman would've shown me—the back door. And I was as randy as they come," he said with a grin. "Loved me some women, though. They're downright the most beautiful creatures God made. And He made 'em strong, too. He knew we was gonna mess up sometime."

"Mister..."

"Pitchford." The man extended his weathered hand. "James Lee Pitchford."

Vernon shook it heartily. "Thanks for the advice, man. I won't forget it."

"Now that them Jaunal boys are on your tail, you'd better watch out. They had your wallet, right?"

Damn, that's right! "Yes, sir."

"You be careful. And tell Tanya that the Pitchfords still live in the same place if she wants to come home."

"I'll do that."

He turned to walk away but James Lee grabbed his wrist. "Word is there's a lot of money tied up in that girl, money that Jaunal would kill to put his hands on. Her being alive is damn inconvenient right now. You take care of our little girl."

Vernon could only nod. "I'll do what I can to protect her."

"Jaunal has a private plane, but you've got a head start. Make the most of it."

CHAPTER Fifty-Two

A frantic banging on the door brought Tanya's head up from the novel in her hands. She placed *The Things I Could Tell You!* on its face and hurried to the door.

Vernon rushed in. "Pack your stuff and let's go!" He slammed the door behind him.

"Will you stop this?"

He peered out of the window. "I'm serious. I just got back from Social Circle and had an unfortunate run-in with your father. He has a hundred-thousand dollar reward out for you."

She let out a little laugh. "Vernon, you are so good! Your delivery is Oscar-worthy. Let go of my arms!"

"Tanya, I'm only going to say this once," he said, shaking her. "Pack your shit, the girls' things, and something for Brandi. We have to get the hell out of here. Jaunal, Bubba, and Mr. Wiccams were hot on my tail—"

Tanya's hand shot out and hit him square in the jaw. "What did you do? Oh God, Vernon! What did you do?" She sank to her knees.

"I'm sorry. Truly, truly sorry. I didn't know," he said, cradling a hand over the right side of his face.

She glowered angrily at him, chest heaving up and down, wishing she had the strength to totally punch out his lights, but she was too angry to move. Too frightened to really think about what he had done. He had put this family in more danger than he knew.

"You can hate me all you want," he said through clenched teeth. "But get the girls. We need to break camp like yesterday. I dodged them at the airport in Atlanta, but they have this address, and—"

Tanya stood slowly, anger shooting through her unlike any she had ever known. "That bastard killed my sister to cover up his lies. He'd think nothing of killing me, you, Brandi, *and* the girls. A reward out for me? This is about money and lots of it. He killed my sister and she was only trying to get away." She punched him hard in his chest. "You fucker! It's taken years for me to be safe and you destroyed it all in one day! I hope we all don't pay for your stupidity."

Guilt washed over him like a waterfall, but he quickly pushed it aside realizing there was more at stake. "Sierra! Simone! Come quick," he yelled upstairs. "We've gotta get going."

A rumble of activity indicated that the girls were on the move.

Vernon followed Tanya into Brandi's office. "What about clothes?"

"We can buy clothes anywhere. I only need passports and birth certificates."

The girls bounded down the stairs in jeans and bare feet Sierra, a few steps ahead of her sister, asked, "What's wrong?"

Vernon scattered the contents of the drawer behind Brandi's desk. "We're leaving."

Taking in the frantic activity, Simone asked. "Why?"

"I'll tell you when we get in the car."

The doorbell rang. Vernon paused in the center of the office, then looked at Tanya, "Oh my God. That must be them." He ran out of the office, Tanya right behind him and the girls right behind her.

Before he could get to the door, the glass window to the side shattered and sprayed out on the marble tile foyer. He covered his face just in time.

Moments later a beefy hand, covered by a denim shirt, beat out the rest of the glass. Vernon hightailed it past Tanya with the girls' hands in his. As Tanya ran toward the side entrance, trying to catch up with Vernon, moisture peppered her brow, then poured down her face.

She kicked off her heels in route, her arms pumped back and forth, propelling her even faster. She heard a crash, followed by a loud thunder of footsteps on the upper level of the house. Her heart pumped faster.

This couldn't be happening! If she got out of this alive, she would shoot Vernon!

Shadowy figures rushed toward her from the garage. The girls broke free and sprinted back into the house with Vernon right behind them. Tanya froze, then spun around quickly to find the others bearing down on her from the opposite direction. She turned again. Trapped!

Vernon quickly turned and kicked Bubba, who was nearest, in the knee.

Tanya kicked her father in the groin, then ran past his doubled-up form to get the girls to safety. With no prompting, they went upstairs. They found no safety there.

Men filed into the living room, some from the solarium. Some came through the open front door. Two men brought the girls and Tanya downstairs, pushing them forward into the living room.

Wilbur Jaunal reached out for Sierra then took her to the sofa.

"Don't touch her," Vernon growled. Bubba punched him in the gut.

Jaunal grinned, pulling the little girl onto his lap, patting her thighs possessively.

"You've grown up into a lovely young lady, Tanya," he said, leering at her. "Hate I missed out on so much growth."

Then he turned a frightened Sierra to face him and smiled. "Well, little girl, how 'bout dem Bulls?"

Vernon lunged forward. "Sierra, come here!" Sierra struggled to loosen Jaunal's grasp on her waist.

"No, she's fine right where she is," he said, gripping her even tighter. "I'll take good care of her. Like I took care of all my girls."

Tanya's insides boiled as she broke away from her uncle Hank's grasp and lunged for her father. The man shoved Sierra to the side; she let out a whimper as she ran to Vernon. Before anyone could stop her, Tanya went for her father's eyes, fingers going in one of them as he raised a fist to beat her away.

Tanya fought back, gouging his face with her sharp nails.

Uncle Hank yanked her back, but she managed to thrust one foot out and connect with Jaunal's face. A spray of blood poured out onto his starched white shirt.

"You bitch! First you cause me to lose everything." He blinked, trying to recover. "Now you're trying to blind me."

Tanya suddenly stopped struggling as her mother walked in, followed by a wide-eyed Aunt Nadine and a sulky-mouthed Aunt Peggy. Shock took her breath away.

Her mother gave her a scathing glance from head to toe. "Turned out all right, didn't ya?"

"Which is more than I can say for you," Tanya shot back.

Margaret leaned forward and said in a voice that was just above a whisper, "All you had to do was give us a son. Things would have been fine. But you messed it up by telling that teacher of yours. I would have raised it and no one would have known a thing—"

Tanya was sickened to learn that her mother had *wanted* her father to have sex with her. "Why would I want to have my father's child?" she choked out.

"That was the only way to get our hands on the rest of the Van Oy fortune, neither of my sisters produced sons and none of their daughters were of breeding age."

Tanya was too numb to feel anything. Her parents' greed knew no boundaries. "Did you realize how much he hurt me?"

The hard woman shrugged. "It always hurts that first time. You were a big, strong girl. You could get over it."

"So why didn't you just have one of your own?"

"Can't," she said in a hushed tone. "I was too old." Then she cast an angry glance at Wilbur. "And your father couldn't get it up for anyone but young girls. And the DNA had to show that it was my bloodline *and* his," her mother continued, oblivious to Tanya's disgust. "So you were the obvious choice. You would've been taken care of for the rest of your life. If you had just kept your mouth shut."

"So what was his reason for hurting Mindy?" Tanya said loudly enough for everyone to hear, pain and anger holding ground in her heart. "She wasn't of 'breeding' age."

Nursing his eye, Jaunal said, "I never touched her."

"You raped her just like you did me," Tanya said angrily. "Then you killed her to cover it up."

Her mother gripped her arm, forcing Tanya to face her. "We would've owned all of Monroe, Social Circle, Jersey, and Covington. Nothing would have stopped us. Then you and that Mrs. Patton started spreading lies. Your sister's death is on your hands. She wasn't home where she was supposed to be. It's your fault."

"She stood by and let it happen. She knew he was raping us, but she wanted her precious money!" Tanya cried.

"Enough!" Margaret said. "Enough! Just sign these papers and we'll be on our way."

"Oh, you'll be on your way sooner than that."

Heads turned to the Black woman standing in the doorway brandishing a metal pipe. The silver-haired Black woman standing next to her held a gun that would make Clint Eastwood jealous.

CHAPTER 

Brandi reached out, pulled Margaret in front of her, and put the gun to the woman's head. "By my calculations you all will be leaving within the next ten minutes. Your escorts are on the way."

Bubba grabbed for Tanya. "Come on! It's just two women. We can take them."

A shot rang out, causing Tanya to wince. Smoke curled from the end of Bettye's gun as she glared openly Bubba. He grabbed his foot and was too busy doing the pain dance to care.

"I was told to shoot the stupid ones first. Anybody else think two women can't hold their own? Try me!"

"Sierra, Simone—run down to Avie's," Brandi said. "Tell her we need Jeffrey Manor assistance. She'll know what I mean."

Sierra turned back. "Should I call Uncle Donny?"

"No!" Vernon said. "If he comes, the game will be over before the police get here."

"Avie's packing, too?" Tanya whispered to Brandi, relieved that the ugly situation was under control. "Who in their right mind, would give that woman a gun?"

"I thought the same thing." Then Brandi turned to the Jaunal crew and said, "Now, I hate to break up this little family gathering, but I didn't invite you. Tanya didn't, either. And we certainly don't want you to stay."

Tanya unplugged a lamp and wrapped the cord around her father's wrists; she looked across the room at Bubba. "If one drop of blood falls on the carpet, I'll give you something to be sorry about. I shampooed two days ago. You don't know how hard it is to get out bloodstains."

Uncle Hank whipped off his jacket and gave it to Bubba.

"Now what's all this about?" Brandi asked, trading weapons with her mother-in-law, but keeping it trained on Margaret. "Don't think about it, Jim Bob. I'll put a cap in your ass."

"You're right. They *are* my family," Tanya said eyeing Vernon with a glare that should have put him six feet under. He, along with Bettye, continued to tie up the rest of the family. "Vernon went down to Social Circle and they came pouring out of the woodwork and trailed him here."

Brandi threw an angry glance at Vernon.

"I'm sorry! I didn't know about all this."

With the Jaunal clan tied up waiting for the police to arrive, Tanya told Bettye, Brandi, and Vernon her story.

"After I moved in with Michelle's family, I was fine for a while. I learned how to cook, sew, take care of a home, and I learned about God. I was going to stay with the Pitchfords forever if they'd let me. And they would have, too." Then she looked at her father. "But a note left in my locker warned me if I testified I would be sorry."

And sorry she was.

As Tanya sat in the wooden chair of the Social Circle courthouse, being sworn in, the police still hadn't located her sister. Whoever snatched her didn't do it because they didn't want the littlest Jaunal to testify; her testimony had been recorded earlier. The kidnapping was a warning for Tanya. One she didn't heed, but should have.

As she lay in the bed next to Michelle that night, unable to sleep because she knew that something was wrong, she overheard Mama Diane and Mr. Edward talking in the kitchen…

"They threatened to fire me if I don't return Tanya to her family."

Mama Diane's soft, silky voice carried through the thin walls. "She needs our help—"

"Yeah, but if I lose this job, I won't be able to take care of you and the kids. We can't get involved with this mess. She'll be okay. White folks look out for each other all the time. Who's gonna look out for us?" Mr. Pitchford asked pointedly.

Mama Diane said in a voice filled with steel, "We're not going to let some redneck stop us from doing our Christian duty. That child's family now."

And they had made it through that crisis.

Then the youngest Pitchford child had come straggling in two days later, beaten, blood covering her small blue shirt and a note tied securely to her wrist.

Get that white bitch out of town
or your family will suffer

❤❤❤

That night Tanya slipped out of bed, as Michelle's soft brown eyes brimmed with tears, knowing exactly what was about to happen even though the two girls hadn't spoken about it. Tanya knew that the D.A., who had used Tanya's medical report as part of the defense, wouldn't stop until he had Jaunal on the ropes. The man had a hard-on for Jaunal since Tanya's father had forced the D.A.'s family to pack up their old family home and move to Covington. The case wasn't all about justice for Tanya, it was about payback for the white people Jaunal had mistreated.

Thanks to the media's involvement, Jaunal's crimes were known to everyone in the Social Circle area. He would stand trial for the aggravated sexual assault, but unfortunately he made bail. During the trial, the body of a little blonde girl turned up on the opposite side of the tracks near the trailer parks. Someone wanted to make it look like people from the east side of town had done it. But Tanya knew better.

They didn't have to tell her that Mindy had been raped before she was killed. They didn't have to tell her that they couldn't get prints from her sister's flesh, because someone had sliced her fingertips off. Tanya knew exactly the day her sister had been killed. The day she opened her mouth and told the world that her father was a beast and her mother allowed it to happen. People still whispered, but not too loudly, because their livelihood still depended on Jaunal Industries.

But when she found out that the small bright red spots inside the pink membrane surrounding Mindy's eyes meant someone had strangled, she knew with an absolute certainty that her father had killed Mindy personally instead of having one of his henchmen take care of things. Once when he came to her room, he'd wrapped his massive hands around her neck, cutting off her ability to breathe, as he raped her. Sick fucker!

Tanya had thought that after her testimony she and her sister would be free. Well, in the most morbid of ways they were. Her sister was free in death, walking with the angels. Tanya had been set adrift to make her way in life the best way she knew how. And she wasn't prepared.

If she had stayed within her own circle, she would have been protected and sheltered from the vicious realities of life. The only thing she would ever have had to worry about was what to wear and to what social function. Minor things. Stupid things. Being pushed out of Social Circle had taught her more, but mentally she had shut down. Because of the pain in her heart, stemming from the fact that she had had all the money in the world and no real love from her parents, she didn't think beyond her next meal or the next place to lay her head.

She had only held on to the thought that she would never be as selfish as her parents. And she could sleep well knowing that for all of his influence with the judges and local police, her father was in prison and would never hurt another human being.

But now he sat across from Tanya in her home in Chicago, looking every one of his advanced years. If she had the guts, she would take Brandi's gun and do the world a favor. But then, too, she had another idea.

"I have to make a phone call."

Moments later she came back to the living room and smiled. "The District Attorney said they'll send someone to get you from the police station. You're out on parole and being here is a violation.

"I think you're about to spend a few more years in a place where you don't want to be. And we're going to make sure this time they look into Mindy's death. I hope you fry for it." Tanya, filled with rage and indignation, shook a fist at him. "And if they'll let me, I'd like to pull the switch.

"And you," she said, turning to her mother. "I hope you get exactly what you deserve. Only a coldhearted witch could love money more than her children. You'll die old and alone, and if I have anything to do with it, you'll die broke. I'm calling Avie Davidson, the best lawyer in the world, and I'm pressing charges for what you did to me. Then I'm taking you to civil court. By the time I'm through you won't be able to afford a proper shoeshine."

Margaret lifted her chin defiantly and glared at her daughter.

After the police had carted the Jaunal tribe off to jail, Vernon turned to Tanya. "Grandpa James said to tell you that you still have a place to call home."

At the mere mention of the old man's name, tears brimmed in her eyes and spilled over. "He's doing okay?"

"The whole family's doing okay. They're a little upset that you slipped out on them that night. He said they would've taken care of your father in their way."

She shook her head. "I just didn't want anyone else hurt because of me."

"I know." Then he peered at her. "What's Brummistew?"

Tanya laughed as she wiped away her tears. "Brunswick stew! And it's a long story."

Brandi came to stand between Vernon and Tanya. "Don't worry. We've got nothing but time."

CHAPTER *Fifty-Four*

A week later Vernon lay on the floor in his mother's media room. Gladys Knight's sultry voice piped through the speakers, singing, "Overnight success..."

By all reports on his bank account, overnight success would be true. Tears sprang from his eyes unchecked as the pain in his heart expanded. His ego had finally checked itself at the front door and he'd been right there on the floor for hours, listening to music and searching his soul trying to figure out his life. He had put his family's life in jeopardy trying to follow the instructions of his father.

William's life and accomplishments had always been his guiding light. Vernon had just never realized how dim that light really was. Now he had to break loose and find his own way and come to the reality that life was more than just money and power.

The Perfect Fit was doing okay, not as good as it had when Brandi was around, but it was floating above the surface. He had a newfound respect for Brandi's talents—*they* were a perfect fit and truthfully he felt that way across the board. A deep shiver of unhappiness filled his soul. An emptiness that was sudden and unexplainable overcame him.

Who she had become was who he was falling in love with all over again. Tanya had made him feel special, like he'd done something great by saving her from poverty—it made him feel powerful and needed. Brandi had never really needed him. Not as much as he needed her.

"Vernon?"

"Yes, ma'am," he said, though he didn't tear his gaze from the ceiling.

"What's wrong, baby?" Her voice was soft, soothing.

Could he say everything? Yes, everything was closer to the truth. "Nothing, Mama, I'm just thinking."

The soft sweep of material sounded under the music. His mother kneeled next to him. A delicate hand reached out, brushing away the tears that kept falling.

Slowly she lifted his head, curling him into her arms. He held onto his mother welcoming the comfort—the only real comfort he'd had in months.

"I miss her. I mean, I really, really miss her."

"I know, sweetheart," she said, patting him gently.

"But I don't know how to get her back. I don't even think she wants me back anymore. I almost got them killed."

"Yes, that stunt you pulled was downright stupid and I hope you learned something from it."

Vernon pulled away to look at the glowing silver-haired woman. He had yet to meet the man who was putting such a light in her eyes. "What do I do about my wife?"

"It takes time for a woman to heal."

"But how much time? I'm dying over here."

"I talk to her everyday. She still loves you, too, but just like you're doing some soul-searching, so is she. The counseling sessions are doing some good and some of your points about what's going south in your marriage are valid, and I believe she's thinking things over. Trust me, she's missing you, too."

"I can't tell."

His mother's soft tinkle of laughter was like music to his ears. "Just because she's not hunting you down, or falling all over herself to get you in the sheets, doesn't mean she's forgotten you."

"Why is marriage so complicated? It just doesn't work anymore," Vernon said softly. "So many divorces. I mean I know I messed up and all, but..."

"People have stopped being friends," Bettye said softly. "Attraction might bring people together, and sex that's enough to have you climbing the walls might keep people smiling in the bedroom, but friendship—real, honest-to-goodness friendship—and companionship have been pushed to the back burner. People forget that they spend more time outside the sheets than between them. Something else has to fill that space, and it had better be about quality—not superficial things—like status and money."

"I understand that now."

She leveled her dark brown eyes to his. "Do you really?"

He nodded.

"Then why are you down here feeling sorry for yourself?"

"I saw Brandi today. I've never seen her so…tired, so worn down. And the fact that I had something to do with that…" He shrugged. "I mean, at first I was pissed that she brought Tanya into this, but I can understand her point now. Then the business thing, it was a game—you know, to show her that my contributions had some value, too. She didn't do it all by herself," he said softly as he reached over to turn Gladys down some. "Now the League's involved and people are really out to crush her—and they're succeeding. I don't know how to stop it. There are too many people involved and I don't know who they all are anymore."

"Come on," she said, patting his arm. "Get up. Let me put some food in you."

Vernon trailed her to the kitchen, silently reflecting on recent events and feeling every bit of guilt over what he'd done.

"If you love her," his mother said, pulling out the makings for a salad, "you'll find a way to make things right. She didn't set out to hurt you. She only wanted to show you how she felt. You took it to the extreme by bringing the League in."

"But Dad—"

"Vernon, you can't always live in your father's shadow," she said, slicing the tomatoes. "Sometimes you have to do what's right for *you*. Quit letting his life define who you are. The man is nowhere near perfect. Trust me on that. If you need an example of how to treat women, look at how Jesus did things."

"Yeah, He can't tell me much," Vernon said chuckling as he pulled up a stool. "Jesus didn't have marital problems, either."

She stopped and looked up at him. "Son, do we have a full Bible?"

"What do you mean?"

"There's more to His story than most people know. And there's more to that Adam and Eve story than most people know. When you get an opportunity, read up on Lilith—the woman who was supposedly created before Eve and was made to be equal to Adam. He screwed up and she screwed up. It's a part of Jewish folklore and scriptures and was used to show why there are two different types of women—strong and rebellious or submissive and weak."

Vernon racked his brain for a moment, then remembered something he read on the Internet when the Lilith Fair concerts had popped up all over the country. "But the story about a woman being equal to men was supposed to be a myth."

She smiled. "All stories are based on some truth, Vernon. Even the Bible, which was written to explain the unexplainable, is laced with history, stories, and parables to teach a lesson. There's so much to learn and all of it didn't make it into the Bible we have today. A whole lot's been taken out to accommodate the male-rules-over-the-woman story line—and the original sin piece, too." Bettye paused, then wiped her hands on the dry towel.

Vernon tried to say something, anything, but he soon realized he and his father had based their views of marriage on the Bible. "But it says men are to be head of household."

One eyebrow shot up. "If we don't have the full Bible as it was supposed to be given to us, do we actually know that God said that? Did Jesus say that? Or was it one of those knucklehead disciples who didn't believe in marriage in the first place? The ones who came from an area that believed women were strictly for breeding. Or was it the men who altered the Bible to retain power and status over women—making it their God-given right to 'rule' over a woman? Get a grip, Vernon," she said with a soft laugh. "Come on, let me show you something."

Moments later, he stared at the brand-new Apple computer on her desk. "When did you get this?"

"About a month ago."

He looked under the desk. "Where's the hard drive?"

"It's built right into the monitor." She clicked the mouse a couple of times.

Marveling at the colorful display and the ease at which his mother navigated through the software and the Internet, he asked, "And when did you learn to use it?"

"Same time," she said, taking in his wide eyes and shocked expression. "Whoever said you can't teach an old dog new tricks *wasn't* an old dog."

She typed a few swift strokes on the keyboard. "Check this out. Here is the Lord's Prayer as we know it, and this—" she clicked the mouse again—"is the original translation directly from Aramaic to English."

Vernon scanned the screen looking at both. "That's nothing like what we say."

"Exactly. It's worlds apart, not even the same meanings. Like I said, some things have been altered and some have been left out or put in. And if they took liberties such as this with the Lord's Prayer, what other drastic changes have been made?"

Vernon took a minute to absorb this, while his gaze remained glued on the correct translation of the prayer.

"We can learn the most from what they told us about the peaceful way that Jesus lived and what He said—there is neither bond nor free, Jew nor Gentile, male nor female—*all are one*." She turned to face him. "Nowhere in that statement did He say that women were secondary to men in God's eyesight."

"But God created man before woman—"

"So they say..." she replied with a smile. "God created everything in duality—light and dark, heaven and earth, water and land, male and female animals. Then when He got to man, he created a single entity, a woman a whole lot later? Common sense, my son. Use common sense. Listening to men like your father is gonna keep you on the opposite end of progress and that's certainly not a place you want to be."

Vernon thought about this for a moment. "Gotcha." Then he followed her back to the kitchen, his appetite returning slowly. "Mama, did you learn anything about mergers and acquisitions while you were with Dad?"

"I probably know as much about it as he does," she said, dicing a few pieces of grilled chicken.

"Do you think some of your friends who were married to the League members have that same amount of know-how?"

"Yes, all of the wives are college-educated. That's where we met our husbands." Bettye stopped chopping and peered at him. "What are you brewing in that thick skull of yours?"

Vernon could only smile.

CHAPTER *Fifty-Five*

Blinding rain made it nearly impossible to navigate Chicago traffic. It was coming down as though the very gates of Heaven had opened and spilled over. A few drops caused a meltdown. This kind of rain turned streets into instant parking lots and littered streets and highways with fender benders. He might have missed his time with the girls.

Vernon had left the office after calling a special meeting of the League. He was vague about the reason, just said that the League's reputation was at stake. Calls went out and the meeting would convene when the confirmations reached eighty percent. His father would probably disown him, but one person would be proud of him—his mother. That would mean more to him than anything in the world right now.

He pulled into the driveway of his mother's house, giving thanks for making it home safely when so many accidents on the way in signaled just how dangerous traveling had become. By the time he ran from the car to the house, his dark brown suit was plastered to his body. Chilled to the bone, he walked through the door, shook off the excess water and prepared to make a mad dash for his bedroom, a hot shower and some dry clothes. He glanced into the living room and froze at the doorway.

Brandi lay on the sofa, hair splayed across a pillow, bare feet propped up on the edge, a sliver of her breasts displayed in their luscious glory. Soft lamplight a few feet away illuminated her smooth skin, high cheekbones, and thinly arched eyebrows; the glow on her red lips begged for a kiss. The navy skirt had slipped high on her thigh, exposing a curvy bit of flesh that caused a familiar stirring in his groin. God, she was beautiful, more beautiful than he remembered.

The chill that ran through his body this time had nothing to do with the rain. It had everything to do with fear—fear of losing the best thing that had ever happened to him. What if he couldn't win her back? What if he turned ninety, was rocking in a chair somewhere, wondering "what if?" Or if, for some reason he had not found another woman quite like the one he had married? He had watched her grow from a college student who shut everyone out of her world, to a strong woman who had the strength to carry more weight on her shoulders than she had a right to endure. Could she forgive him for being blind to that fact? If she held even a seed of love within her heart for him, would she allow him to water it and help it grow?

He moved to the sofa as though pulled by a magnetic force, whipping off his jacket and tie along the way. He trailed his fingers softly across her face, expecting her to awaken. She didn't move. He dropped to his knees, brushing his lips against her temple.

Brandi stirred and turned toward him. The skirt made a hasty dive toward her hips—exposing a navy garter, flesh colored thigh-highs and lace panties underneath. He kissed her again, lingering as his tongue slithered out to trace a slow outline of her lips. This time her eyes fluttered open and her gaze locked on him, lips trembling with the sudden movement.

Encouraged by the fact that she didn't push him away, he leaned in, pressed his lips gently to hers, slid his tongue into the small inviting opening as she parted her lips. Slowly, as though for the first time, he explored the soft recesses of her mouth, delving deeper as a small moan escaped her lips.

Locking his gaze on hers, he increased the intensity of his tongue's movements, watching as her eyelashes fluttered, then covered her eyes with a final sweep, following another breathy moan. The kiss lasted mere minutes, but the torture of blood rushing to create a full, throbbing erection felt like hours.

Vernon pulled away just long enough to ask, "Where are the girls?"

Her eyelashes fluttered again, then she blinked twice before fully opening her eyes. "Huh? What? Who?"

He smiled at her obvious confusion. "The girls? Where are they?"

"Sleeping in the guest bedroom," she said, in a voice that was just above a whisper. "You know I don't like to drive in this kind of rain."

Leaning in, he unbuttoned her blouse. He cupped her breasts before his lips tasted their sweet softness. Taking the lace material in his teeth he pulled her bra away, exposing the hardened nipple. He watched her through hooded eyes, as her body lifted toward him. In one smooth motion he lay on top of her, burying his head in the soft swell of her breasts, as the warmth of her body swept away the cold of his. Her hands, delicate and trembling, reached for him, pulling him closer as he teased the nipple with his moist tongue.

As his erection throbbed, demanding to be inside her, he pulled away. "We can't do this."

Her hands gripped the back of his head in a lock. "What the hell do you mean we can't do this?"

A low chuckle escaped Vernon's lips. "Let me rephrase the statement. We can't do this—*here.*"

She released her death grip and shifted to a sitting position. A glint of disappointment flashed in her light brown eyes, giving him a sliver of hope. She wanted him, right?

"My mother could walk in on us."

Her lips lifted in a small smile. "And when has that stopped you?"

"Since the last time she saw more of my ass than she needed to. And a glimpse of this," he said, cupping the moist mound of flesh between her thighs. "Proving that you were indeed…a natural woman."

"We-ell, if you put it that way," she said with a sheepish grin.

His fingers laced into her silky hair as he said, "Then she made me start doing my own laundry."

Brandi laughed, the sound was sultry and warm. He looked into her eyes, seeing the weariness ease away—a weariness that he had caused. A stab of pain pierced his heart. He had promised never to hurt her—and he had done more than that. He had nearly destroyed her—and for what? To prove what to whom? Nothing to no one that mattered.

He pulled her toward him, held her close, and kissed her as he lifted her from the sofa and settled her in his arms.

"Now you know you need to put me down."

"Shhhhh, let me handle this." He maneuvered her through the long hallway past his mother's master bedroom, then toward the guest room where Sierra and Simone were sleeping. He peered in at his angels, making sure that they were indeed asleep. Simone ripped out a snore that could call every hog in the area. Sierra had kicked off the covers and lay so close to the edge of the bed, a single finger could tumble her onto the floor. But she always managed to stay in—no matter what.

Shifting his gaze to Brandi, he paused, realizing that she had lost weight—and that, too, was his fault. He would make up to her—he would make a mission of it.

"If you drop me, I'm suing," she said with a slight pout.

He laughed, put his back against his bedroom door, and swung it open. "I won't ever let you fall."

The moment he stepped inside he set her gently on the bed, then scurried back to lock the door. For a moment he watched as her gaze fell on the small desk, the baseball trophies, the posters of Vanity, Apollonia, and a few other '80s babes. In the center of the wall across from his bed—a picture of Brandi with a smile so wide it stopped his heart, eyes so vibrant it saddened him to realize he had extinguished the light in them.

"It's clean in here."

Miffed at her tone, he replied, "I *always* keep a clean room."

"No," she said with a grin. "I mean *military* clean."

"Mama."

She laughed softly. "I feel you."

Hands that had a mind of their own whipped through the rest of the buttons of her blouse and the bra's key hooks, and tossed both to the side. She leaned back on her elbows, allowing him a full view of her bare breasts. Cupping one in her hand, she offered it to his mouth. He took it willingly and hungrily, teasing her until her body trembled with pleasure. Savoring each of her moans, he moved as close as humanly possible, stroking her back with his hands, then lowering her to the bed in a smooth glide.

The skirt zipper gave way with a good tug, allowing it to slither over her fleshy hips with minimal movement from Brandi. Tiny silver latches connecting the navy lace garter to flesh-colored thigh-high stockings all caught his attention. Damn! When had she started wearing those?

She watched him with a smile playing about her lips as he stared at her thighs. He looked up at her, but didn't dare ask. For a moment he wondered...had someone else been with his woman? Though he had no right to claim her like that—he couldn't help it—she was still his. He would make her his all over again.

Gently rolling the silk stockings down her legs, then removing them from the tips of her red manicured toes, he soon held her bare flesh in his hands. But one part of her body called to him more than the rest. Leaning in, the sweet musky scent of her sex beckoned him, and the slight parting of her thighs was all the invitation he needed. Pulling her forward, he draped both thighs over his shoulders, giving him open access to a world of pleasure. He trailed his tongue alongside her left thigh causing a tremor through her body that resonated all the way to her toes. Oh, yes...she still belonged to him—he would show her—oh yes!

He placed his lips on her swollen clit, she lifted her hips to him, and he answered her call with swift nibbles on the soft, pink flesh.

She cried out and gripped him so hard he couldn't move even if he wanted.

At this moment, getting away from this little piece of heaven was as far from his thoughts as giving up on his wife, his marriage, or his life. He had to have her back. And he had to have her now! He encircled her center with his tongue.

Her thighs trembled, then clamped onto his head as if her very life depended on him remaining right there. He tasted the salty-sweetness of her, relishing the moans and tremors that ripped through her like a personal earthquake. He had to make her his—*now*!

Her voice, sultry and smooth, uttered his name in broken English.

His elation at being so close to his wife again propelled him forward as he buried his tongue inside her, swirling it around the sensitive points of her center.

"Oooooooooooooooooooooooh!!!" she nearly screamed, before he covered her mouth with his hand.

"Shhhhhhhh, baby. Shh. It's all right," he said before going back to work, wanting her to want him so badly that she wouldn't dare end this—not this time! Filling his senses with the very essence of her, he gripped her hips, beginning a slow rhythmic assault that made her throw her head back and mewl, the sweetest cry-moan-scream he had ever heard.

He unzipped and removed his pants and briefs in one fluid effort. She reached for him, wrapping a trembling hand around his erection, forcing him to adjust his body and hers on the bed. Poised to enter, a small stab of worry filled him as he realized one thing and pulled away—again. "Baby... I don't have a—"

She lifted her head, locked his gaze with a steely look, and said through clenched teeth, "If you stop one more time I will kill you and bury you where no one can find the body."

What a way to say, "Keep it coming!" Seconds later, he pressed at her core, savoring her moist, tight heat. She gripped his cheeks in both hands, pulled him forward with a strength he didn't know she had, and in one strong solid thrust, buried him to the hilt in a tight sheath of rippling flesh that welcomed him like a long-lost friend and gripped him like an unwilling prisoner.

Brandi tightened her thighs around his waist as she shimmied her hips until he hit the spot that caused a quivering that never seemed to end. Her moan gave way to a shaky scream, which forced him back to reality. He covered her mouth again, cooing soft, comforting words in her ears as tears pooled in the corner of her eyes, before traveling to her chin.

"Oh, Vernon..."

He moved within her slowly at first, answering each move of her hips with a thrust of his own, until her gyrations outdistanced him, driving him at a pace he never thought possible. Her heat drove him mad. The sounds escaping her lips forced his rhythm to a fevered, almost animalistic pitch. The feel of her skin next to his was enough for him to cry out his own pleasure. She didn't bother to cover *his* mouth.

She reached for him, pulled him in for a passionate kiss that started with swift explorations and ended with total abandon as his hips rose and fell to a rhythm she had started, but he had every intention of ending—but not soon. Lord, not soon!

"My woman," he whispered against her hair. "Still mine!" A smooth liquid thrust balanced each word. "God, I missed you…I missed this…"

She sobbed, pressing her cheek to his, whispering to him a single word of admission, "Yesssssss. Ooooooh, yesssss." Her voice broke and with it, her body shook with a force that threw him. "Yes!"

With that one word, he went over the edge, spilling his seed into her in short, hard bursts that made breathing impossible, thinking impossible. Saying anything except, "Brandi…" became impossible.

Spent and satiated, Vernon lay next to his wife, relishing the flush of color in her face, the satisfied look in her eyes, the small smile playing about the red lips that he couldn't resist kissing again.

"It has never been like this for me…"

Her smile widened broadly, letting him know she understood exactly what he meant, without saying a word. She pulled him to her breasts, offering comfort every cell in his body craved, but he had no right to enjoy. Could she forgive him? Really? Could she love him again? Or did loving her unconditionally mean letting her go? As much as it pained him to answer that last question, he knew the truth. He could push all he wanted, but Brandi would decide their future—and making love would not influence her one bit. It only fed their immediate needs—a need that was deeper than he imagined.

The rain had stopped pelting the window long enough for the moon to make an appearance. Moments later as she cradled him at her breasts and his lips sought solace in the warmth of the soft mounds, the world around him swirled into a sensual explosion of her taste, her scent, her feel, her sound. Reality and responsibility drifted away at the sight of her trying to catch her breath and for the first time since whenever, Vernon fell into a dreamless sleep.

He didn't need to dream. He had one right in his arms.

CHAPTER Fifty-Six

Tanya scouted out the Jaunal mansion on Cherokee Road. If anything had changed about the place she couldn't tell by the outside. But a lot of things had changed about Social Circle. Burger King and Papa's Pizza now graced Cherokee Road, along with the Blue Willow Inn. The Clegg Family's Farm & Home Supply was still around, not too far from Cotton Bale Antiques. Even O'Kelley's BBQ and Breakfast was the same as she remembered. The gas station on the O'Kelley's property had burned down at some point, but somehow they'd never seen fit to rebuild it.

She had been sitting in the rental car over an hour, confronting old memories and gathering strength. She would meet with the D.A. later that day.

Then she saw her, the old decrepit woman bent over the flower bed in the front of the place.

The woman's face had taken on a miserly look that in no way resembled the well-kept, well-coiffed woman Tanya remembered. Margaret had aged in just the few days since she'd seen her. And she hadn't looked too good then.

A knock on her car window made her heart jump. Tanya's gaze locked on another older woman with whisper-thin hair and gray eyes. Her wrinkled skin was the only thing that might have told her age.

"Hey, aren't you Tanya Jaunal?"

Tanya couldn't speak as she tried to put a name to the face.

The woman's eyes narrowed as she repeated, "Aren't you Tanya?"

Tanya still hesitated, but was inclined to shake her head.

"Oh, don't bother denying it," the woman said, brushing her off. "You look just like your mother."

Tanya finally found her voice. "And that's supposed to be a compliment?"

The woman's thin pink lips spread into a soft smile. "I'm Mrs. Rankin. You used to play with my kids. Actually gave my Nathan a bloody nose for putting his hands in places he shouldn't. Why don't you come in for some tea? I'll catch you up on your folks."

"I don't want to know about them," Tanya said bitterly, forcing herself not to look back at the place she grew up.

"Oh hush. You wouldn't be here if you didn't."

Tanya followed Mrs. Rankin into her elaborate, but warm, wood-frame house. Two acres of land spread out behind it, and horses grazed in the pasture out near the pond.

The woman placed a tray with the tea service and cookies in front of Tanya. Then she poured two steaming cups of orange tea. "Did you see all that commotion downtown?"

"Yes," Tanya replied. "There was a marching band and food vendors and everything."

"Ah yes," she said with a grin. "The Annual Social Circle Friendship Festival."

Tanya took a bite of a shortbread cookie. "When did they start that?"

"About eleven years ago." The woman sipped her tea gingerly. "Well, your daddy just got out of prison last month and he's already back in."

Tanya felt only a small sense of victory. If there was any way she could get them to look into the death of her sister, she'd make sure she did everything in her power to see to it that he got the maximum. Her mother, too.

"Yeah, they strung him up for what his sorry tail did to you and your sister. And your mother's family came in and snatched up everything he took from them."

Realization dawned on Tanya as the cup made it part of the way to her mouth. "So they're poor now?"

"The house is all she has and her health is failing." The woman peered at Tanya through narrowed eyes. "She has a thirty-million-dollar trust—in your name. My husband was your father's lawyer. He told me that no one can touch that money without your signature or proof of your death. Even your sister's trust reverted to you so that no one could come after Margaret or Wilbur for the money." The woman looked out of the window to the Jaunal mansion, grinning. "My husband said it was a darn shame your mother couldn't find you. I told him you'd come home when the time was right. He's not alive so I can't tell him I told you so."

Tanya took a moment to absorb that bit of news. "So that means I'm rich?"

"Yes, indeed."

Tanya's gaze went to the window across the room. A horse trotted across the pasture. "And they're penniless?

"Exactamundo."

"So how were they offering a hundred-thousand dollar reward for me?" Tanya asked, looking back at the woman.

"It was probably a scam. Or maybe they were banking on the money in that trust fund to pay the person off." Mrs. Rankin rose and went over to a desk in the living room. She pulled out a large white envelope. "Here's the paperwork that explains everything."

Tanya tore open the envelope and the documents slipped out into her hands. "You've held onto these all this time?"

"Watched for you every day." She smiled, displaying a youthfulness that was endearing. "My Jimmy called me just plain stupid."

"Thank you," Tanya said, scanning the sheets a second time. "Thank you so much."

"So now that you're a rich girl, what do you plan on doing?"

"I'm not sure yet." Tanya said, clutching the papers in her hands. "But there's one thing I definitely have to do."

She finished her tea, hugged the woman, and was shortly on her way.

Fifteen minutes later she pulled in front of a freshly painted wood-frame house. For the second time today she was hesitant to touch base with her past. Bracing herself, she took a few deep breaths and got out of the car.

Tanya lifted a trembling hand to knock on the wooden door. Instead it swung open wide before she could connect. A man with piercing dark brown eyes and short silver-gray hair and generous lips, which slowly lengthened into a warm, wide smile, greeted her. "Miss Tanya, did you bring me some Brummistew?"

"It's Brunswick stew!" she choked out as a knot formed in her throat.

"Little girl—" he waggled a long finger at her—"me and you ain't gonna get along so well." He stretched out his slender arms.

She threw herself at him and he soon enveloped her in a warm, loving embrace. Tears of joy filled her eyes and spilled over. She didn't bother to wipe them away.

Grandpa James pulled her away to look at her, then craned his neck toward the house. "Hey, come quick. Tanya's home!"

Chapter Fifty-Seven

Vernon had entered the Fairmont ignoring the curious glances aimed his way. He didn't wait to be called. Instead he took the podium and braced himself. "I stand before you today asking that you cease all activity with regard to my wife."

Murmurs of dissent flooded the air.

"I'm pulling back and reassessing things," he said, looking out at the sea of men. "I'm ready to try to win her back the right way—not by bringing her down, but by facing up to my shortcomings."

"You know your membership will be revoked," William growled, his eyes blazing.

Vernon turned to his father, meeting his angry glare. "I'm aware that that's the way things are normally done, but I don't think that will be the case with me."

"Your father can't protect you from this one," George Payne said, moving to William's side as the other nine board members looked on.

"And I wouldn't even try!" William replied. "How stupid can you be?"

"And the founding members can do no wrong?" Vernon shot back, looking at the eleven men stretched behind the podium. "All but one of you have a little honey on the side. So if there's any finger pointing or memberships being revoked, let's start from the top..."

William turned red. The board members turned to each other and whispered in hushed tones. "Boy, do you want to get lynched in here?"

"I'm doing what you taught me," Vernon shot back. "I'm playing the game."

"By putting people's business in the street like that? What's wrong with you!"

"Afraid of a little truth, Pops?"

William crossed the distance between them. "Afraid my only son's making an utter fool of himself!"

The audience was strangely silent as the mic amplified every word, no matter how low they spoke.

"Then there shouldn't be two sets of rules here." Vernon pointed to the exit. "Care to join me on the sidelines?"

"You're out of your fucking mind," William answered through clenched teeth. "I founded this organization."

"Then it would be no problem for you to practice what you preach."

The whine of the microphone caused everyone to flinch.

George took the mic from Vernon. "People, we'll continue this issue at the next meeting."

"Oh no, my brother!" Jeremy Shipp stood and yelled from the center of the room. "We'll do this right now." He and Craig Richmond had just become members a month ago, when they finally met the financial requirements.

Hearty applause followed murmurs of assent.

"Yeah! We're not sweeping this one under the table," Craig said, supporting his best friend.

"This meeting is adjourned," William Spencer bellowed at the top of his lungs.

"Wait a minute, let him speak." John Macon, one of the oldest members of the board of directors, turned to face William. "I've had to keep my boxers tight all these years and you Negroes have been getting busy out of both drawer legs? Hell no, we're not talking about this next time." He snatched the microphone from William. "Didn't you get busted with two—"

"Three," Vernon supplied, then looked out at his best friends and winked. They nodded back. They had followed the plan just right.

"Yeah, three," John said. "How can you all dismiss five hundred other men and y'all's shit ain't right? If the members who were dismissed for the very same reason—ethics reason don't get letters reinstating them, then there's going to be hell to pay."

"Oooooo-weeee," Jeremy said, rubbing his hands together, and grinning broadly. "There's gonna be some changes 'round here!"

Seeing that the meeting was getting out of hand, William said, "Look, no one's perfect, but—"

"Speaking from experience?" John asked, staring William down. Something that Vernon had never seen happen.

Without taking his icy gaze from John's face, William snatched the mic. "We'll take your request under consideration."

John snatched the microphone back. "False pretenses and fraudulent practices are against the charter's by-laws...we want our dues back. All with me, take a stand." Almost four hundred-fifty men—apparently the ones who hadn't been caught cheating on their wives— stood.

"If it's no infidelity among members, then that goes for everyone, not just for those who've gotten away with it."

"You—you can't call this now," William sputtered. "Majority rules."

"To hell with majority rules!" John scowled with indignation. "What about fairness?"

Craig and Jeremy settled down in their chairs, preparing for what would be a long night.

Vernon Spencer had single-handedly started the biggest debate in the history of the League.

As the argument raged back and forth, William Spencer grabbed his son's arm and forced him to make a hasty retreat into the lobby.

"You're destroying what I've taken years to build!" William growled, bearing down on his son in a way that made most men tremble with fear.

"No, Dad, I'm rebuilding an outdated forum. And the truth is out in the open. No more double standards."

William's hand fell away from Vernon's as he searched his son's eyes. "After everything I've done for you! How could you hate me so much?"

"I don't hate you," Vernon said simply. "Right now I don't have any feelings about you and that scares me. When I could hurt, it meant that I cared."

William's jaw dropped as he stared at his son.

"All my life I've tried to live up to you, Dad," Vernon said, in a weary tone, "and didn't realize that all it took was a step down to reach the goal."

"You're letting it slip away and you're trying to destroy me!"

"I'm not doing things your way anymore. Listening to you and following your lead instead of my heart and mind got me into this mess," Vernon told him.

"So you think you know it all now?"

"I'm not saying that. I know that it does not take tearing down the strong to build up the weak. I've wanted your love and approval for so long that I didn't realize it had become the most important thing in my life."

Jeremy and Craig peered out of the door leading into the conference area. Vernon waved them back in.

William glared at them and back at his son. "I let those two hooligans in as a favor to you and now they're starting trouble. If you do this, I'll cut you out of my will."

"You think that means something to me right now?" Vernon spat. "How can I be ruled by something that's no guarantee? Something I won't see for another fifty years if God is kind. Now if you had said you wouldn't love me anymore, that might hurt. But since you've never loved me at all..."

Something in William's expression crumbled. "Son, look—"

"I'm not your son, Mr. Spencer," Vernon snapped. "A son would be a duplicate of the original. All I've been is a pawn, something you've used to keep Mama in line. Did you ever think about the fact that the reason you're so successful is that Mama had something to do with it? All those parties and charities she hosted on your behalf? Our women have played a bigger part than you've ever given them credit for.

"Just like there are certain parts of The Perfect Fit that miss and need Brandi's touch, there's part of The Perfect Match that could benefit from my wisdom. We aren't doing this by ourselves. And neither are they." Vernon lifted his head proudly. "I'm getting back with my wife and this time I'm respecting her contributions to our marriage instead of beating her down because she's excelling in areas you feel are manly."

"You were nothing without me and would still be scraping the bottom if I hadn't stepped in!"

"Dad, it wasn't that much help." he said with a little laugh. "Right now being nothing without you is looking pretty good," Vernon felt his spirits lift with every word. "I'm living my life on my own terms and I'm feeling pretty good about me. I'm rebuilding my relationship with my wife—the wife that's perfectly fine as she is. If I can help turn things around for her, and she'll let me, I'd like to team up with The Perfect Match to get men more prepared for the workforce and to also help them become better mates and marriage material. They can learn from my mistakes—and yours."

"All this to please some low-class bitch," William spat, his skin turning a sickly red color. "That woman's got your nose wide open."

Vernon took a deep breath. "I don't see the difference in this and when I tried to please another…bitch," he said, leveling a cool gaze on his father, knowing the man would catch his meaning. "And if you ever call my wife that again, or disrespect her or my mother in any way, you'll find out how much of your son I really am."

Vernon turned on his heels and marched back into the conference room, leaving his father staring after him.

The meeting lasted eight full hours. The longest in the League's history. By the time it ended, there was a new board and new by-laws. Letters had been drafted to all members—new and old and those who were considered in bad standing. And the men had all agreed to let up on Brandi.

Not bad for a single day's work.

CHAPTER *Fifty-Eight*

Brandi walked into The Perfect Match with every intention of shutting the place down. While she appreciated the sacrifices Michael, Renee, and Ella had made, she had to face reality—she had failed. She was so close to the bottom that the house would be in foreclosure in a few months. She had turned down the many offers of financial help from Michael—she didn't want to add that into the dynamics of things. He would have been an easy save. But at what cost? The kind of money he was offering would require more than a thank-you, no matter what he said.

Every loan request she had put in over the last two months was denied because The Perfect Match was a "new business." No one took her time at The Perfect Fit into consideration. Every resource had dried up because each was in some way tied to members of the League—she'd never known how far their reach really was until now. As though setting the stage for a tragic play, a dark cloud had settled over her life, one that had begun to pour rain only where she walked.

Brandi put one foot off the elevator and froze. The doors almost clanged painfully against her ankle.

A bustle of activity from every corner of the floor made her gasp. "What's going on?"

No one answered because no one could hear. The copiers, the computers, the desks—all had someone behind them doing something. But what?

"She's here!"

A sea of faces, all mature women ranging from fifty-five to seventy, looked back at her, freezing in place as they smiled.

As if on cue, they said a warm, but staggering, "Good morning, Mrs. Spencer," almost loud enough to make Brandi fall back.

The women were professionally dressed in black suits or dresses, black heels, and pearls.

If they had come for a funeral, The Perfect Match was the right place. Or was it? What the hell was going on here?

Tanya was teaching a class of some sort at a bank of computers near the main conference room. She stopped, looked up, and waved at Brandi.

Stunned, Brandi lifted her hand, but wasn't sure if she actually waved back. Who were these women?

Motown music filtered through the office and a few shoulders and wide hips wiggled gleefully, paperwork in one hand and finger snapping with the other.

Bettye rushed forward, entwining her arm with Brandi's. "Girl, close your mouth. We've got work to do!"

"Work?" she said, gazing out at all the women as Bettye dragged her along.

"You know, that thing that begins with a W and ends with a K."

"These women —"

"Are your new staff!"

Brandi gasped, stopping their march forward. "Have you lost your mind? I can't pay all these people! I came here to shut the place down today."

"I know that, but we're not going to let you go down without a fair fight. You don't have to pay us right now, but some of the women would like part-time jobs when you're on your feet."

Brandi took a minute to absorb that piece of information. "Who are they?"

Bettye stood next to Brandi looking out at the people in front of them. "The ex-wives of some of the current League members."

"*All* of them?"

"Every last one," she said with a bright smile. "Well, except the two little ones in the communications center over there."

Brandi almost didn't recognize her own daughters. They, too, were dressed like everyone else. Which meant the little heifers had known and hadn't said a word.

"Tanya also brought in some of her family from Social Circle." Bettye leaned into Brandi, whispering, "You never told me she was Black."

"She isn't—" Brandi clamped down. To tell the truth she didn't know what the hell Tanya was—vanilla coating on the outside, chocolate on the inside—oh, the contradictions. But the fact that she had stuck with her contract and found a way to help Brandi had said plenty about the woman's character.

Her youngest sprinted across the room. "We're working, Mommy," Sierra said, wrapping her arms around Brandi's waist, eliciting the smiles of nearby women.

"Yes, baby, I can see that," Brandi said, hugging her little girl. "And it looks like you're doing a wonderful job."

Sierra's round face beamed. "I'm sending faxes."

"And I'm filing," Simone chimed in. Looking every bit like her handsome father, and in her suit, she looked almost grown. Time to have that birds and bees talk for the fourth time. "When do we eat around this camp?"

"Soon, baby, soon," Brandi said, still looking at the women in the office. She saw Avie posted up on the phone scribbling on her famous pad. She didn't even look up.

Bettye tweaked her granddaughter's cheek, and was rewarded with a small giggle. "There's pastries in the main conference room."

"Tanya said we can't eat those before lunch," Simone said, rolling her eyes. "She said it might make us wired for sound."

Tears of joy sprang into Brandi's eyes. She wiped them away with the back of her hand. "How did you...?"

"I got together with a few of my friends and told them about The Perfect Match. Though they may have been housewives, they learned enough from their husbands to possibly open their own businesses." She gestured gracefully to the women. "Now that experience will be put to work here—helping you."

Brandi moved forward, trying to keep pace with her mother-in-law.

"Thanks to Tanya, More than Enough is allowing us to use their night-club to sign up people every Friday and Saturday for the next month. Beau

Visage II is also giving us space the next four Saturdays. Tanya and her family helped orchestrate everything for this Friday. The way she figures it, all we need is a hundred and fifty paying members and we're in the game."

Brandi reached out, pulling Bettye in for a warm embrace. "Thank you."

"Don't thank me," Bettye said softly. "Thank Tanya. Thank your husband."

Brandi paused, trying to understand how the man who had caused her business life to dry up faster than an Arizona desert had put these new developments into motion. "Vernon?"

"I'll tell you about it later." Bettye entwined her arm in Brandi's and marched her forward. "Come on, you've got a business to run."

"First I need to thank these women," Brandi said, struggling to keep up with her mother-in-law. Lord, that woman could move!

"Thank them at lunch, don't stop the flow right now. Some of them have never worked a day in their lives." Then she laughed. "Well, no job outside of their ex-husbands. And that's some serious office time." She pointed to the place where Tanya had set up a makeshift training area. "Some have never touched a computer, but they're willing to learn."

"And whose idea was this?"

Bettye beamed with pleasure. "Your husband's."

"Vernon?" Brandi choked out.

"Did you suddenly become married to someone else?"

"No, but I just—I—I—" she stammered, unable to come up with a single word.

"He loves you, honey," Bettye said with a soft, caressing laugh as Brandi struggled to compose herself. "And this whole thing has given him a chance to grow and learn. Anytime he listens to me because he's concerned about you, it says he's changing."

Brandi thought about that for a moment. "So should I…? You know."

"Honey," she said, with a warm smile. "I don't think you wanted to be away from him in the first place."

"No, I was just so hurt by what he'd done, and felt so…not enough."

Bettye grinned. "Honey, nothing a man does with his dick should make you feel that way."

Brandi opened the door to her office. Bettye sat in one of the guest chairs; Brandi sat in the other, next to her. "Then why did you divorce William?"

"If I had told him the truth he would have fought me for the divorce instead of just fighting about the details. The details kept him running for cover. He was so busy protecting his assets, he didn't realize he'd left his ass hanging out."

Brandi took a moment to mull that over. "If you don't mind, may I ask what the real reason was."

Bettye's gloss-covered lips twitched before saying, "I loved him, I just didn't like him as a person anymore. At first I stayed because of Vernon, 'cause Lord knows, if I wasn't around, no telling what would've become of that young man."

"I'd hate to picture it." Brandi grimaced at the thought. "But just because I value Vernon for all the things he does right, doesn't mean I'm supposed to expect less of him in other areas."

"No one's saying you should." Bettye crossed one leg over the other, looking every bit as regal as the first day Brandi met her.

"I can't just turn the other cheek," Brandi said after shifting through the memories of the last time they made love. Her body quivered in response. Reason swept in quickly. "I've only got four and he's smacked each one of them. He has to know I won't tolerate this lying down or standing up straight. When he comes to the house to pick up the girls and sees that blonde Amazon serving dinner to me and his children, it brings the point home a hell of a lot faster than a divorce ever could. I love him, but I love me, too."

Bettye reached out to touch Brandi's hand. "Then hold on to the lesson you're trying to teach him and still love him. There's nothing wrong with that."

"I lost my mother over this." Brandi suddenly felt the overwhelming loss of her mother's voice and her guidance. But the woman had held true to her word. She wouldn't take Brandi's calls and she didn't open the door whenever she showed up. She did let the kids in, but slammed the door in Brandi's face right after.

"Honey, you didn't lose her. Jean's just a stubborn old biddy." Then Bettye gave her hand a gentle squeeze. "Actually, she'll be here first thing in the morning to help out. You'll have your chance to lay a bridge between you."

"Bettye," Brandi said, settling back in the leather chair, hoping her mother would be receptive. "All those women out there are college-educated?"

"That's right, dear."

"Then why did they settle for just being housewives?"

Bettye blinked and took a long breath. "In our day, we had only a few choices: teacher, nurse, stewardess, secretary, or housewife. The world was male-dominated. Women doctors and business women were practically unheard of—especially Black women doctors and Black Businesswomen. You wouldn't find a female construction worker to save your soul. Then the Sixties happened—flower children, and the marches for civil and equal rights and all that, and doors that had once been closed to us were suddenly flung wide open. But *we* were already housewives, *we* were already raising children and had also made a commitment to support our husbands. And that's exactly what we did," she said, looking Brandi square in the eye.

"And if you were married back then to our type of husbands—who were all about status—they became our jobs." Bettye sighed softly. "And with the egos and everything else it was sometimes harder than just having a nine-to-five. No one knows the sacrifices I've had to make. But it was my choice and I stuck with it until I figured out that I didn't have to put my needs on hold to satisfy anyone. I was almost sixty before I understood that. You've picked that up a whole lot faster."

Brandi nodded, absorbing that bit of knowledge. "How did you convince all of these women to work for free?"

"They've wanted to do something for a while, but they don't need the money, their husbands are still chucking out top dollars in alimony—none of them have remarried."

"So they stay celibate!" Brandi shrieked, picturing years of keeping the delta on hold. It wasn't gonna happen.

"Oh, hell no, honey," she said with a little sway of her hips. "We need to get our stroke on just like everybody else. We just do it in a way that doesn't compromise our…investment plan. Our time was money." Then Bettye took Brandi's hand. "And what better women to help counsel new couples or single women in relationships than women who've been part of society's changes? We've been Coloreds, Negroes, Blacks, and now we're African-American."

"Great point. So what's the plan?"

Brandi felt a renewed sense of purpose as her mother-in-law recounted recent developments. After Bettye left the office, Brandi had even more mixed feelings about Vernon. Why would he help her when he'd been so dead set against her working in the first place? Was he changing? And where did that leave their marriage? Still on the path of ending or on the path to true reconciliation?

Sierra poked her head into the office. "Mommy, you have anything I can fax?"

"Not right now," Brandi replied absently.

"Okay." She turned and went out the door.

"No, wait a minute."

Sierra strolled in as Brandi scribbled a short note on The Perfect Match letterhead:

I can't thank you enough. Dinner's on me.
You name the time and place.
Your loving wife.

She resisted the urge to write. "Bring your condom," because they needed to have a serious talk. No judges, no lawyers, nothing between them but air and opportunity. She passed it to her youngest daughter.

"Fax this to Daddy?" Sierra asked with a wide grin.

Brandi nodded. "Right away, little Miss Spencer, Vice President of Communications."

"I don't want to be *vice president,*" the little girl said with a proud lift of her chin. "I want to be *president* of faxing!"

Laughing as she held her daughter close, Brandi said, "That's my girl!"

CHAPTER *Fifty-Nine*

Steppers music blared from every corner of the second level of More than Enough. The place now had four levels, each catering to a different type of music and dances. Latin/Salsa on the first floor, Steppers music on the second, Jazz and New Age on three, and World Music/Reggae on four.

The Perfect Match team wore black and pearls once again—soon to become a standard. Those old women were giving the young men in the place a run for their money on the dance floor. They could step their asses off—smooth turns, two short moves forward, then two long strides, the cradle and matador turns—almost like ballroom dancing with a bit of R&B style. Tanya's relatives were right by her side. Brandi and Michelle could have been twins! And Mama Diane and Grandma Belle were absolute delights. They'd planned and coordinated the menu for the evening. Brandi was too nervous to eat, but she had threatened everyone that if she didn't end up with a plate to take home, someone was gonna catch the wrath.

The music scratched to a halt as Vernon took the cordless mic and strolled across the room to Brandi. They had seen each other in passing, but never made mention of that rainy night of passion. And when he woke up that next morning and she wasn't next to him, an emptiness filled him that he hadn't been able to shake. He knew exactly what he needed to do.

He dropped to one knee and looked up at her. "For better or worse? I've done the worst thing a man could possibly do to his wife. I committed my one and only unforgivable lifetime infraction." Then he took her hand.

"But if you find it in your heart to forgive me, I would be eternally grateful and forever in your debt for redeeming my lonely heart and healing our marriage."

Murmurs erupted around them as people came closer and stared at the couple.

"I am not the same man you married fresh out of college; that man is long gone. So divorce him. Let's bury him. And will you please marry the new and improved me?

Brandi paused, feeling an overwhelming sense of happiness engulf her.

Disappointment flashed into his eyes. "If you can't answer now, that's all right. Here are the divorce papers," he said, passing the court documents to her. "Sign them and let's put that time behind us and start from here. I'll even..." He swallowed hard. "You know...um—wash dishes and stuff."

Brandi laughed through her tears.

"It's against my religion to cook and all that, but I can take a stab at it once a week, but it's gonna be take-out the other two days. I don't want you to lose a pound."

She chuckled.

"I'll even do—" he placed a single hand over his chest and choked—"laundry."

This time Brandi roared with laughter. "Okay, okay, okaaay!"

"Is that close to yes or just a maybe?" he asked with a wide grin.

She waited, searching her heart and knew without a doubt. "It's a yes!"

"Whooo hooo, hoooo!" He picked her up and hugged her to him.

The entire nightclub applauded and cheered for the: divorced? soon-to-be remarried? never-got-divorced? couple. Who knew what to call them these days?

"On one condition," Brandi said into the mic and the cheers halted.

Vernon didn't lose his smile as he looked up at her.

"We renew our vows. This time I want you to repeat them three times so you don't forget."

Laughter and applause filled the room.

"Done," he said quickly, "as long as Avie's not springing for the food."

They both looked over to the lawyer. "I am not having the Corner Bakery for my reception."

Avie's middle finger popped up on its journey to brush over her eyebrow. Carlton popped her on the rear and she turned and kissed his cheek.

"Hey, if the results are that good, sign me up right away!" said a tall, leggy woman with long black hair.

William Spencer stood near the doorway and lifted his glass in the direction of the reunited couple. Vernon nodded once before turning to kiss Brandi with a passion that made their night together a few days ago seem like foreplay.

A stampede followed as a crowd formed in front of the registration tables.

In a matter of an hour, they signed up more people for TPM than they expected—even women who were already married wanted to check out their current husbands. Hmph!

❤❤❤

Michael waited for the crowd to die down some before approaching Brandi. "You're going back to him?"

She turned to face him. "Michael, I've never left him." Wearing a black suit with a red, white, and black print tie, he looked more like a man who had stepped out of the pages of *GQ* than a man holding out for the woman who got away. She waited a few seconds, but he didn't respond.

"He's learned his lesson."

"But he could do it again. And now this Tanya person's vice president of The Perfect Match. That's just like dangling the mouse in front of the cat. He could cheat on you again," Michael pointed out.

"And so could you. Can you promise me that you'd never, never, never do what he did? Some men are better at hiding their indiscretions than others. As secretive as you are, you could pull it off. And there's no guarantee, no matter how many vows are said and promises are made. You don't think I see how you watch Tanya?"

Michael lowered his gaze a little. "That's just appreciation for the female form. Hell, I'm amazed that a white woman has a shape that I've only seen on Black women."

Brandi laughed. "Yeah, kind of shocked me, too." She looked across the room to Tanya who stood next to Michelle. "With that much backfield, I still swear up and down, she's got a drop of Black blood in her family."

"She's a good person," Brandi said softly, elbowing him in the ribs. "And she's single and she likes good men."

Michael linked Brandi's hand in his. "No you're not trying to pimp me off."

"Only if she pays me. I think you're quality stock." Then she turned to him so their eyes locked. "Since we're not going to be together, I'd like to at least make sure you're in good hands and where I can keep an eye on you."

Michael's eyes held a glint of sadness. He stroked a thumb across her open palm.

"Plus as my friend she'll drop all the juicy details so I'll know exactly how jealous I should be."

He grinned at the thought. "Are you sure you won't reconsider?"

Brandi cast a glance at her husband, who waved to her from across the room, then strolled confidently in her direction. She looked up at Michael, kissed his cheek, and said, "Not ever."

Chapter Sixty

Brandi cuddled next to her husband on the sofa, watching *The Long Kiss Goodnight*, one of their favorite movies. That Geena Davis could really kick some serious bad boy butt!

"Are you sure about me moving back in this weekend?" Vernon asked, tearing his eyes away from the screen.

"I told you, I've never had a problem with you being right where you belong—with me."

"And we'll share the same bed?"

Her lips twitched in an effort not to smile. "I think first we'll have a probation period..."

"Very funny," he said dryly. "You know that judge sent us an Anniversary card?"

"That's sweet."

"With his crazy ass."

Brandi roared with laughter. "But if he hadn't cared enough to send us to counseling, you wouldn't be here right now."

"True, true," he said, kissing her fingertips. "I still think we need to commit him to the Rubber Room Hilton."

"Get over it, Vernon. You were wrong and he helped bring that point home. End of discussion."

Vernon sighed wearily, conceding her point. "I'm glad the new buyers closed yesterday. It'll take a week for me to wrap things up. Mama wanted to make sure I was on the right track, so she took my key and I had to move everything into storage. I can't wait to move back home."

"Sounds like a plan."

Snuggling up to his wife, he said, "I've missed you, woman."

"I've missed you...sometimes," she replied with a sly grin.

Her peered at her. "That's cold."

"That's the truth." She lifted her glass, taking a long sip. "Thank God for Doc Johnson."

Vernon stiffened as he looked over to her. "You slept with someone named Doc?"

She laughed so hard a single tear streamed down. "I've been sleeping with him off and on since last year."

"What—what! Woman, I—what!"

"And he's actually here right now."

Vernon paused to take that in, and sighed wearily. "That damn vibrator?"

"A dildo," she corrected with a wide grin.

"I'm getting rid of that thing the moment I—"

"You do and I *will* divorce you. No if, ands, or buts about it. Just like Tanya, he's part of the family now."

Somehow that statement didn't sound too good. "Well, Doc or Johnson or whoever the hell he is better recognize authority," he said, guiding her hands to his erection.

She laughed. "That might be tough, he's been sleeping on your side of the bed since you've been gone." Brandi stroked his face. "It took being away from you to discover how much I like myself. I think we did get married too soon."

"*You* think we got married too soon. I've always wanted the stability of marriage." He kissed her gently, exploring the moist depths of her mouth with an expert tongue. "I'm going to make it up to you."

She smiled, her sexy lips parting in a wide smile. "You damn sure will. I'll take mine in ass coupon."

Vernon laughed as he curled his wife into his arms, relishing the soft, lush feel of her. "Are you sure you've forgiven me?"

"Of course I forgive you, honey," she said, kissing him softly. "I still love you."

"And there'll be no hard feelings when I come back home?"

"Absolutely, it'll be business as usual." She kissed him again. "Personally, I think you should've taken my advice and kept the house on Wabash. We could just date."

Grimacing at the thought of being separated from his wife any more than he had to, Vernon looked down at her and said, "That defeats the purpose of being married."

"Okay," she said after a moment. "I guess I can see the logic in that."

"And I—"

Tanya strolled in, wearing a bright blue miniskirt and white halter top. She had pulled her hair back into a youthful ponytail; her face glowed with a healthy tan. Vernon watched as she exchanged Brandi's glass of Spumanti for another.

"Anything I can get for you, Mr. Spencer?" she asked, looking Vernon square in the eyes.

"Uhhhh, Martell would be nice," he answered, and realized she had changed…a lot. Had being around Brandi rubbed off on her?

Vernon looked from Tanya to Brandi and back to Tanya. Had the women actually…No! Never! Shifting his attention to something more certain he wondered why Tanya was still in the house. Didn't she just get a large inheritance? Hadn't the Pitchford family practically ordered her to come home?

Vernon looked his wife square in the eye. "Um, when are you going to tell Tanya?"

"Right away," she said sweetly. "We don't have secrets."

Realization slowly dawned on Vernon. "When will she be leaving?"

Brandi's lips lengthened into a small smile. "There's still one year left on our contract. Who said I was giving up my wife?"

AUTHOR'S NOTE

This story started as a late-night conversation with my best friend, Yosha. When comparing notes on what women bring into a marriage and how after sacrificing so much, sometimes it's *still* not enough, we came to the conclusion that: Every woman needs a wife. We're doing our part and then some.

That conversation turned into a seven-page short story. The title alone resonated with so many women—women of varied ethnic backgrounds as they responded with: "I've always said that," "My mother told me that one time," "You're right about that!" and "I was just discussing that with my friends last week."

In 2005, I decided to turn the seven pages into a full novel. The two-month undertaking was a labor of love and one of the most humorous, heart-wrenching, and fantastic experiences I've had in a while. Healing, forgiveness, humor, and tolerance are main themes woven into the literary fabric of this novel. It is my hope that while women read the story they may, in fact, see themselves in one or more of their characters. Maybe some will also come to the realization that we have more in common than previously believed.

It is also my hope that men who read this (if they're brave enough), will gain an understanding that there has to be balance in relationships—women should not have to do it all. Bringing home the bacon, frying it, cleaning up after it, keeping the keep AND working a 9-to-5 and paying the bills, too? Help us out, men.

Our mothers, sisters, aunts, cousins, and grandmothers were superwomen of noteworthy accomplishment, but some worked themselves into poor health and possibly an early grave trying to pull it off. They gave up their hopes and dreams and put themselves on the backburner so often that they forgot the "pot of dreams and desires" still existed. Do women of today have to do it quite the same way? No, that's where balance comes in. Stop holding us up to standards that may have worked centuries and decades ago. Respect us for the superwomen we are, and we'll love you for the wonderfully intelligent, purpose-driven and sexy supermen we've always desired.

Naleighna Kai

AUTHOR BIO

Naleighna Kai, a Chicago native, is the coauthor of *Speak it into Existence* and *How to Win the Publishing Game* and now writes fiction, romance, erotica, new age, and science fiction. Her next novel, *She Touched My Soul*, will be released in January. She works for a major law firm in Chicago and is currently working on her next projects: *Open Door Marriage*, *Was It Good for You, Too?* and *Right Place, Right Time*. She also is marketing director for the Jones Dishman Foundation, a privately held family foundation which raises funds for college scholarships and literary endeavors. Please be sure to visit www.naleighnakai.com.

Available from
Strebor Books International

Baptiste, Michael
Cracked Dreams 1-59309-035-8
Godchild 1-59309-044-7

Bernard, D.V.
The Last Dream Before Dawn
0-9711953-2-3
God in the Image of Woman
1-59309-019-6
How to Kill Your Boyfriend (in Ten Easy Steps) 1-59309-066-8

Billingsley, ReShonda Tate
Help! I've Turned Into My Mother
1-59309-050-1

Brown, Laurinda D.
Fire & Brimstone 1-59309-015-3
UnderCover 1-59309-030-7
The Highest Price for Passion
1-59309-053-6

Cheekes, Shonda
Another Man's Wife 1-59309-008-0
Blackgentlemen.com 0-9711953-8-2
In the Midst of it All 1-59309-038-2

Cooper, William Fredrick
Six Days in January 1-59309-017-X
Sistergirls.com 1-59309-004-8

Crockett, Mark
Turkeystuffer 0-9711953-3-1

Daniels, J and Bacon, Shonell
Luvalwayz: The Opposite Sex and Relationships 0-9711953-1-5
Draw Me With Your Love
1-59309-000-5

Darden, J. Marie
Enemy Fields 1-59309-023-4
Finding Dignity 1-59309-051-X

De Leon, Michelle
Missed Conceptions 1-59309-010-2
Love to the Third 1-59309-016-1
Once Upon a Family Tree
1-59309-028-5

Faye, Cheryl
Be Careful What You Wish For
1-59309-034-X

Halima, Shelley
Azucar Moreno 1-59309-032-3
Los Morenos 1-59309-049-8

Handfield, Laurel
My Diet Starts Tomorrow
1-59309-005-6
Mirror Mirror 1-59309-014-5

Hayes, Lee
Passion Marks 1-59309-006-4
A Deeper Blue: Passion Marks II
1-59309-047-1

Hobbs, Allison
Pandora's Box 1-59309-011-0
Insatiable 1-59309-031-5
Dangerously in Love 1-59309-048-X
Double Dippin' 1-59309-065-X

Hurd, Jimmy
Turnaround 1-59309-045-5
Ice Dancer 1-59309-062-5

Jenkins, Nikki
Playing with the Hand I Was Dealt
1-59309-046-3

Johnson, Keith Lee
Sugar & Spice 1-59309-013-7
Pretenses 1-59309-018-8
Fate's Redemption 1-59309-039-0

Johnson, Rique
Love & Justice 1-59309-002-1
Whispers from a Troubled Heart
1-59309-020-X
Every Woman's Man 1-59309-036-6
Sistergirls.com 1-59309-004-8
A Dangerous Return 1-59309-043-9
Another Time, Another Place
1-59309-058-7

Kai, Naleighna
Every Woman Needs a Wife
1-59309-060-9
She Touched My Soul
1-59309-104-4

Kinyua, Kimani
The Brotherhood of Man
1-59309-064-1

Lee, Darrien
All That and a Bag of Chips
0-9711953-0-7
Been There, Done That
1-59309-001-3
What Goes Around Comes Around
1-59309-024-2
When Hell Freezes Over
1-59309-042-0
Brotherly Love 1-59309-061-7

Luckett, Jonathan
Jasminium 1-59309-007-2
How Ya Livin' 1-59309-025-0
Dissolve 1-59309-041-2
Another Time, Another Place
1-59309-058-7

McKinney, Tina Brooks
All That Drama 1-59309-033-1
Lawd, Mo' Drama 1-59309-052-8

Perkins, Suzetta L.
Behind the Veil 1-59309-063-3

Pinnock, Janice
The Last Good Kiss 1-59309-055-2

Quartay, Nane
Feenin 0-9711953-7-4
The Badness 1-59309-037-4

Rivera, Jr., David
Harlem's Dragon 1-59309-056-0

Rivers, V. Anthony
Daughter by Spirit 0-9674601-4-X
Everybody Got Issues 1-59309-003-X
Sistergirls.com 1-59309-004-8
My Life is All I Have 1-59309-057-9

Roberts, J. Deotis
Roots of a Black Future
0-9674601-6-6
Christian Beliefs 0-9674601-5-8

Stephens, Sylvester
Our Time Has Come 1-59309-026-9

Turley II, Harold L.
Love's Game 1-59309-029-3
Confessions of a Lonely Soul
1-59309-054-4

Valentine, Michelle
Nyagra's Falls 0-9711953-4-X

White, A.J.
Ballad of a Ghetto Poet
1-59309-009-9

White, Franklin
Money for Good 1-59309-012-9
1-59309-040-4 (trade)
Potentially Yours 1-59309-027-7

Woodson, J.L.
Superwoman's Child 1-59309-059-5

Zane (Editor)
Breaking the Cycle 1-59309-021-8
Another Time, Another Place
1-59309-058-7